MARVEL-VERSE
CAPTAIN MARVEL

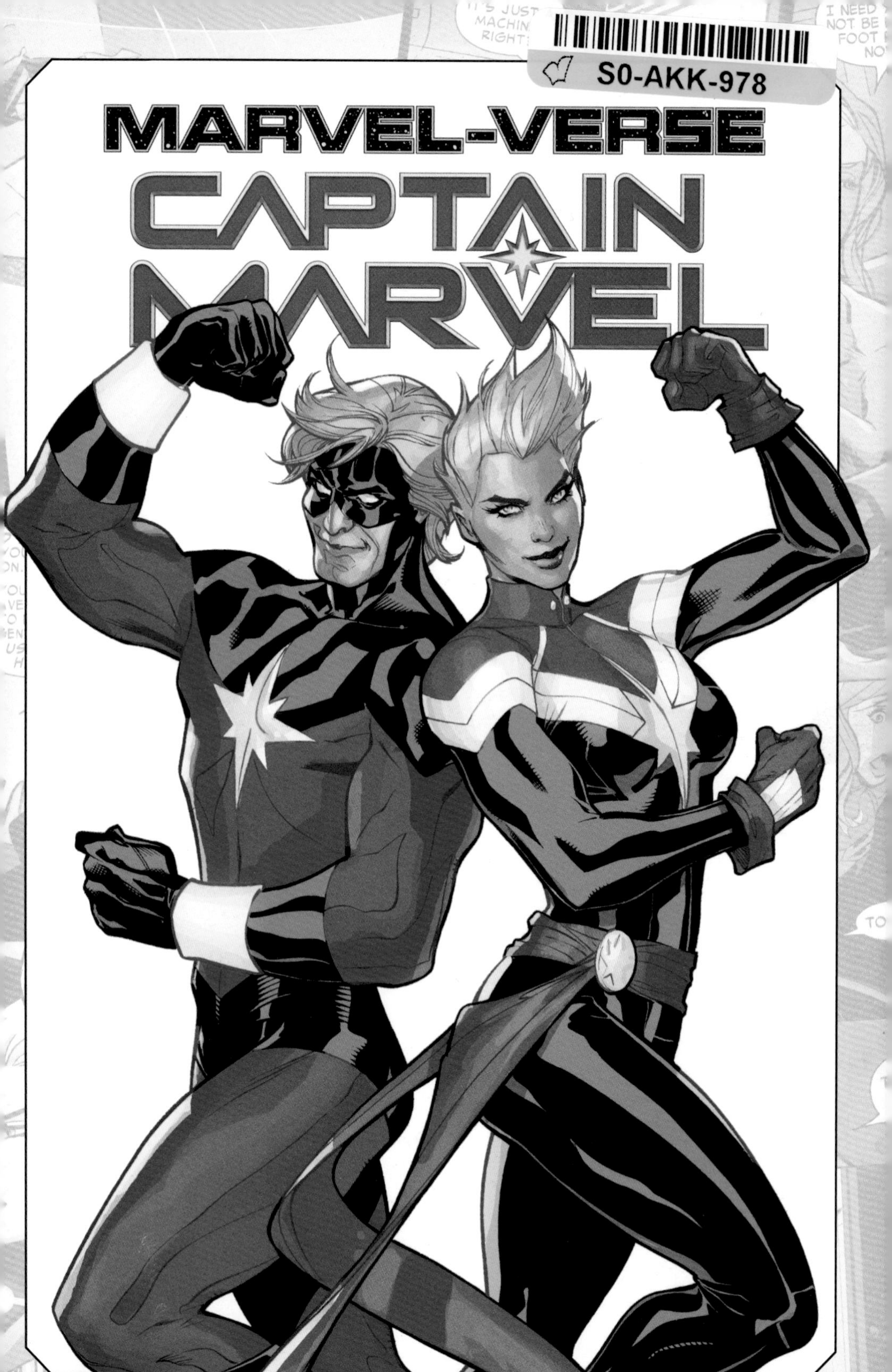

MARVEL-VERSE
CAPTAIN MARVEL

CAPTAIN MARVEL #7-8

WRITER: **KELLY SUE DeCONNICK**
ARTIST: **MARCIO TAKARA**
COLOR ARTIST: **LEE LOUGHRIDGE**
LETTERER: **VC'S JOE CARAMAGNA**
COVER ART: **DAVID LOPEZ**
ASSISTANT EDITOR: **DEVIN LEWIS**
EDITOR: **SANA AMANAT**
SENIOR EDITOR: **NICK LOWE**

AVENGING SPIDER-MAN #9-10

WRITER: **KELLY SUE DeCONNICK**
PENCILER: **TERRY DODSON**
INKER: **RACHEL DODSON**
COLOR ARTIST: **EDGAR DELGADO**
LETTERER: **VC'S JOE CARAMAGNA**
COVER ART: **TERRY DODSON &
RACHEL DODSON**
EDITOR: **ELLIE PYLE**
SENIOR EDITOR: **STEPHEN WACKER**
EXECUTIVE EDITOR: **TOM BREVOORT**

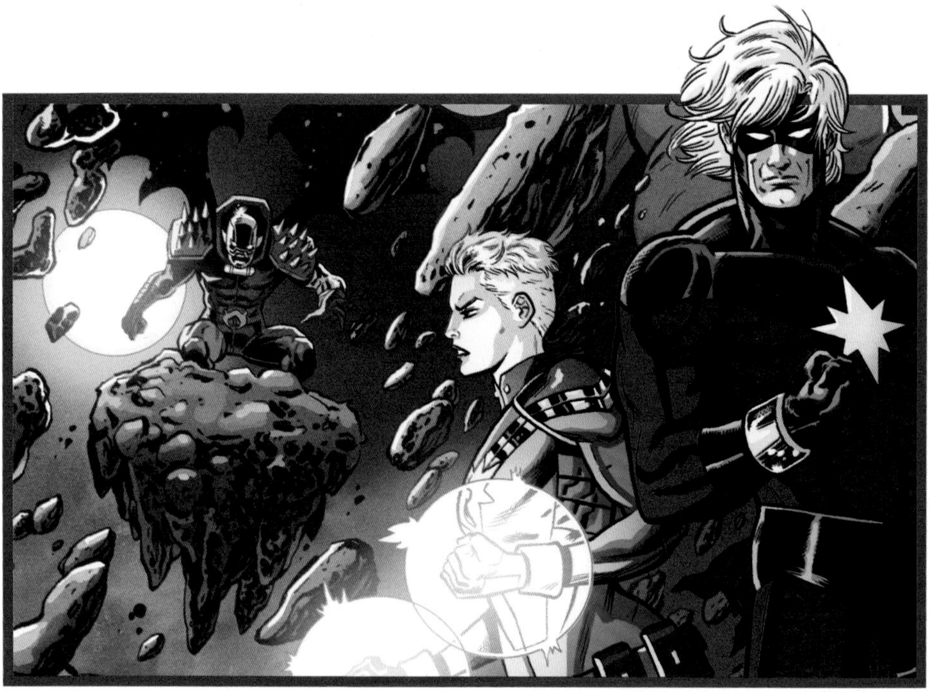

GENERATIONS: CAPTAIN MARVEL AND CAPTAIN MAR-VELL

WRITER: **MARGARET STOHL**
ARTIST: **BRENT SCHOONOVER**
COLOR ARTIST: **JORDAN BOYD**
LETTERER: **VC'S JOE CARAMAGNA**
COVER ART: **DAVID NAKAYAMA**
EDITOR: **CHARLES BEACHAM**
SUPERVISING EDITOR: **SANA AMANAT**

COLLECTION EDITOR: **JENNIFER GRÜNWALD** ASSISTANT MANAGING EDITOR: **MAIA LOY**
ASSISTANT MANAGING EDITOR: **LISA MONTALBANO** ASSOCIATE MANAGER, DIGITAL ASSETS: **JOE HOCHSTEIN**
VP PRODUCTION & SPECIAL PROJECTS: **JEFF YOUNGQUIST** RESEARCH: **JESS HARROLD & JEPH YORK**
BOOK DESIGNERS: **SALENA MAHINA** WITH **JAY BOWEN**
SVP PRINT, SALES & MARKETING: **DAVID GABRIEL** EDITOR IN CHIEF: **C.B. CEBULSKI**

MARVEL-VERSE: CAPTAIN MARVEL. Contains material originally published in magazine form as AVENGING SPIDER-MAN (2011) #9-10, CAPTAIN MARVEL (2014) #7-8 and GENERATIONS: CAPTAIN MARVEL AND CAPTAIN MAR-VELL (2017) #1. First printing 2020. ISBN 978-1-302-92684-7. Published by MARVEL WORLDWIDE, INC., a subsidiary of MARVEL ENTERTAINMENT, LLC. OFFICE OF PUBLICATION: 1290 Avenue of the Americas, New York, NY 10104. © 2020 MARVEL No similarity between any of the names, characters, persons, and/or institutions in this magazine with those of any living or dead person or institution is intended, and any such similarity which may exist is purely coincidental. **Printed in Canada.** KEVIN FEIGE, Chief Creative Officer; DAN BUCKLEY, President, Marvel Entertainment; JOHN NEE, Publisher; JOE QUESADA, EVP & Creative Director; TOM BREVOORT, SVP of Publishing; DAVID BOGART, Associate Publisher & SVP of Talent Affairs; Publishing & Partnership; DAVID GABRIEL, VP of Print & Digital Publishing; JEFF YOUNGQUIST, VP of Production & Special Projects; DAN CARR, Executive Director of Publishing Technology; ALEX MORALES, Director of Publishing Operations; DAN EDINGTON, Managing Editor; RICKEY PURDIN, Director of Talent Relations; SUSAN CRESPI, Production Manager; STAN LEE, Chairman Emeritus. For information regarding advertising in Marvel Comics or on Marvel.com, please contact Vit DeBellis, Custom Solutions & Integrated Advertising Manager, at vdebellis@marvel.com. For Marvel subscription inquiries, please call 888-511-5480. **Manufactured between 11/20/2020 and 12/28/2020 by SOLISCO PRINTERS, SCOTT, QC, CANADA.**

10 9 8 7 6 5 4 3 2 1

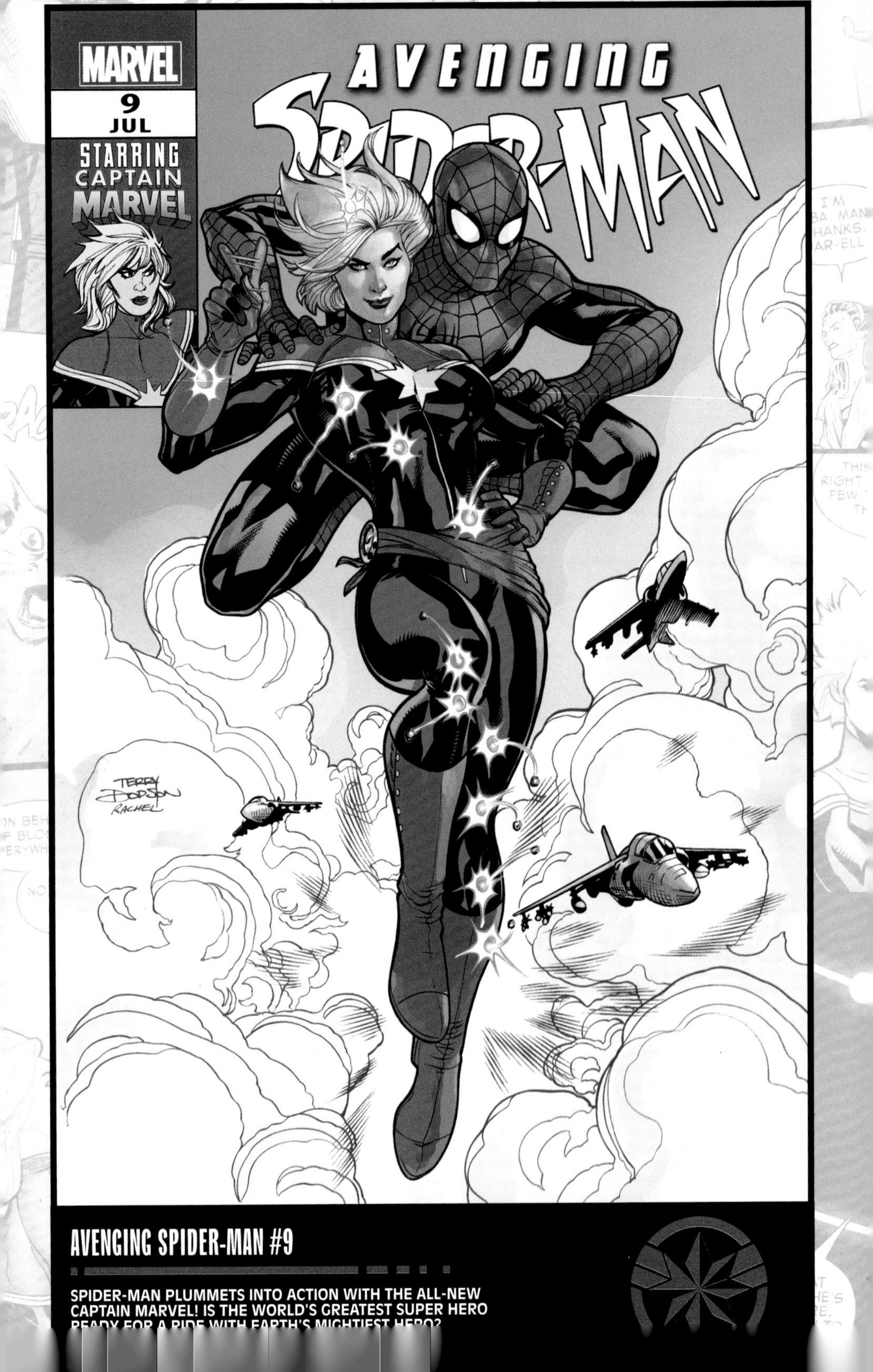
MARVEL
9
JUL
STARRING
CAPTAIN
MARVEL
AVENGING
SPIDER-MAN
TERRY
DODSON
RACHEL

AVENGING SPIDER-MAN #9

SPIDER-MAN PLUMMETS INTO ACTION WITH THE ALL-NEW CAPTAIN MARVEL! IS THE WORLD'S GREATEST SUPER HERO READY FOR A RIDE WITH EARTH'S MIGHTIEST HERO?

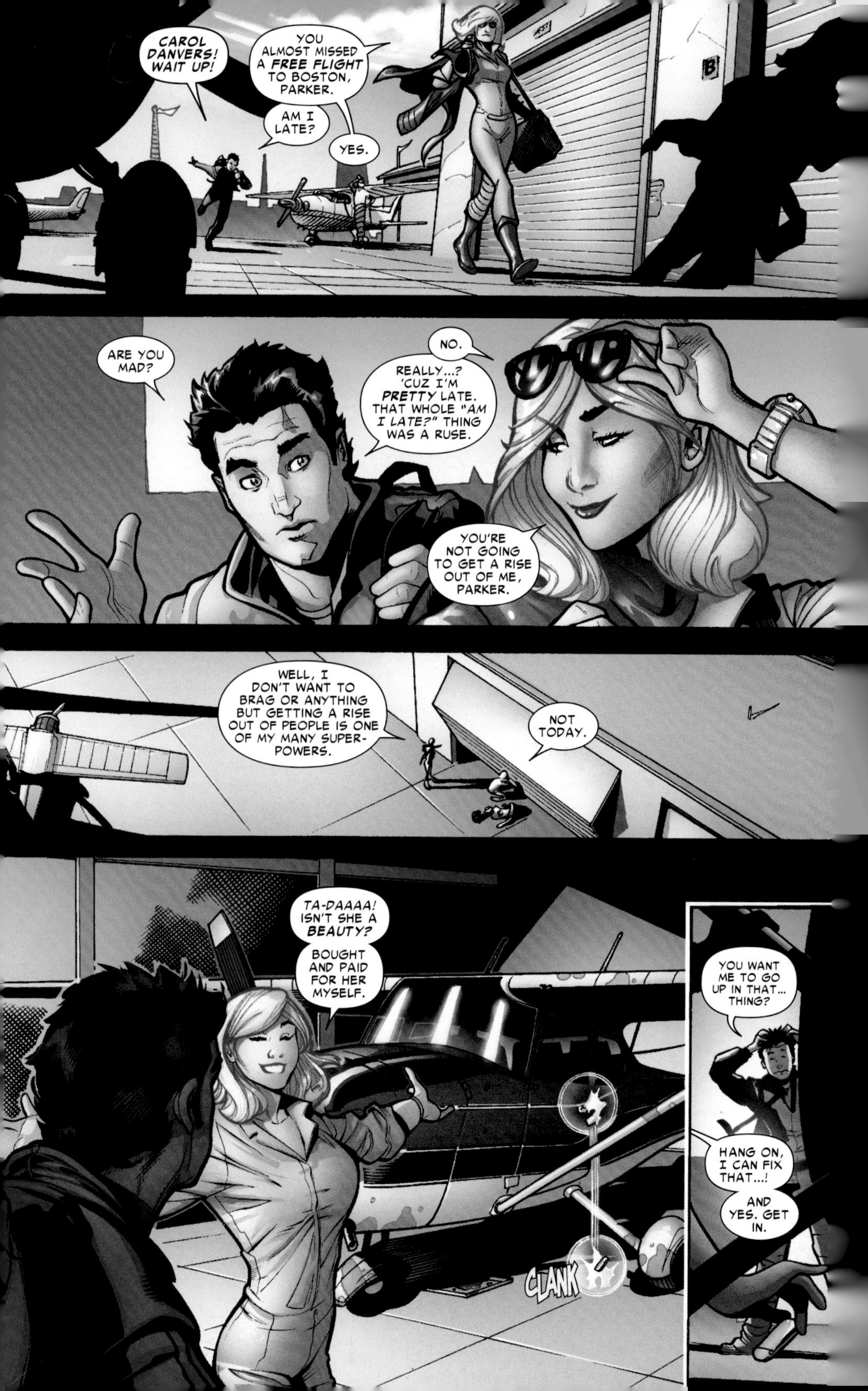
CAROL DANVERS! WAIT UP!
YOU ALMOST MISSED A FREE FLIGHT TO BOSTON, PARKER.
AM I LATE?
YES.
ARE YOU MAD?
NO.
REALLY...? 'CUZ I'M PRETTY LATE. THAT WHOLE "AM I LATE?" THING WAS A RUSE.
YOU'RE NOT GOING TO GET A RISE OUT OF ME, PARKER.
WELL, I DON'T WANT TO BRAG OR ANYTHING BUT GETTING PEOPLE A RISE OUT OF PEOPLE IS ONE OF MY MANY SUPER-POWERS.
NOT TODAY.
TA-DAAAA! ISN'T SHE A BEAUTY?
BOUGHT AND PAID FOR HER MYSELF.
CLANK
YOU WANT ME TO GO UP IN THAT... THING?
HANG ON, I CAN FIX THAT...!
AND YES. GET IN.

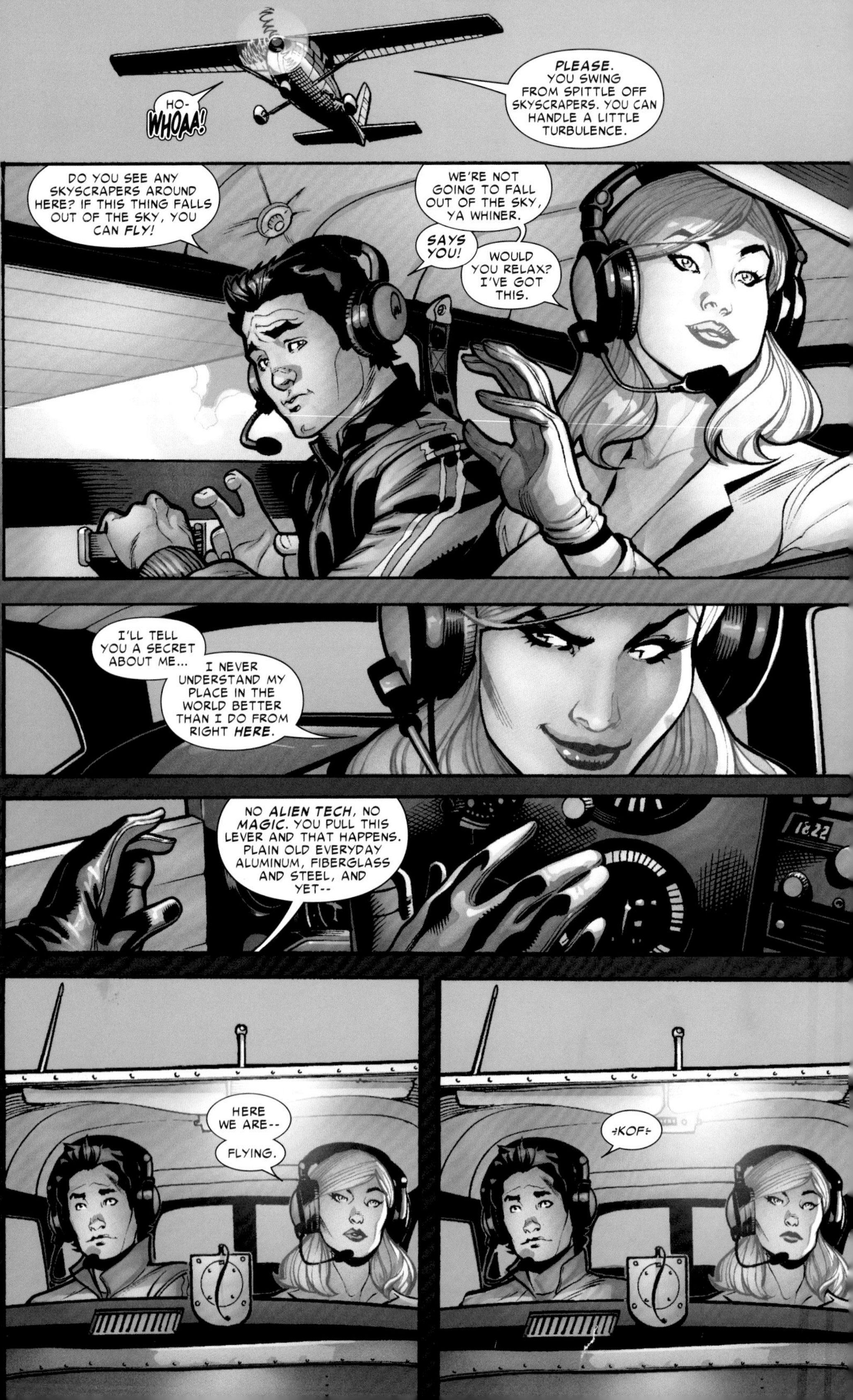
HO-
WHOAA!
PLEASE. YOU SWING FROM SPITTLE OFF SKYSCRAPERS. YOU CAN HANDLE A LITTLE TURBULENCE.
DO YOU SEE ANY SKYSCRAPERS AROUND HERE? IF THIS THING FALLS OUT OF THE SKY, YOU CAN FLY!
WE'RE NOT GOING TO FALL OUT OF THE SKY, YA WHINER.
SAYS YOU!
WOULD YOU RELAX? I'VE GOT THIS.
I'LL TELL YOU A SECRET ABOUT ME...
I NEVER UNDERSTAND MY PLACE IN THE WORLD BETTER THAN I DO FROM RIGHT HERE.
NO ALIEN TECH, NO MAGIC. YOU PULL THIS LEVER AND THAT HAPPENS. PLAIN OLD EVERYDAY ALUMINUM, FIBERGLASS AND STEEL, AND YET--
HERE WE ARE--
FLYING.
-KOF-

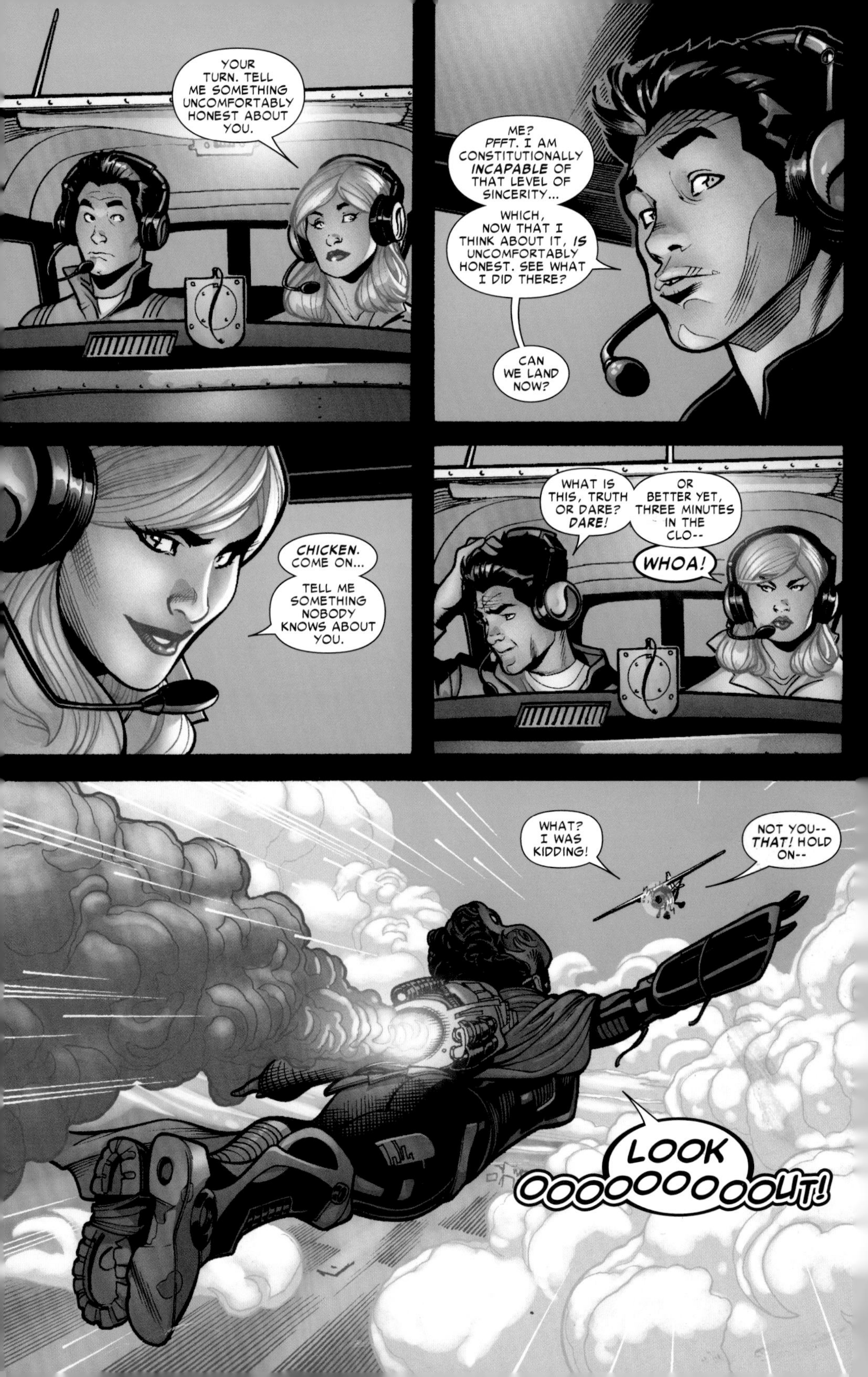
YOUR TURN. TELL ME SOMETHING UNCOMFORTABLY HONEST ABOUT YOU.
ME? PFFT. I AM CONSTITUTIONALLY INCAPABLE OF THAT LEVEL OF SINCERITY...
WHICH, NOW THAT I THINK ABOUT IT, IS UNCOMFORTABLY HONEST. SEE WHAT I DID THERE?
CAN WE LAND NOW?
CHICKEN. COME ON...
TELL ME SOMETHING NOBODY KNOWS ABOUT YOU.
WHAT IS THIS, TRUTH OR DARE? DARE!
OR BETTER YET, THREE MINUTES IN THE CLO--
WHOA!
WHAT? I WAS KIDDING!
NOT YOU-- THAT! HOLD ON--
LOOK OOOOOOOOOOUT!

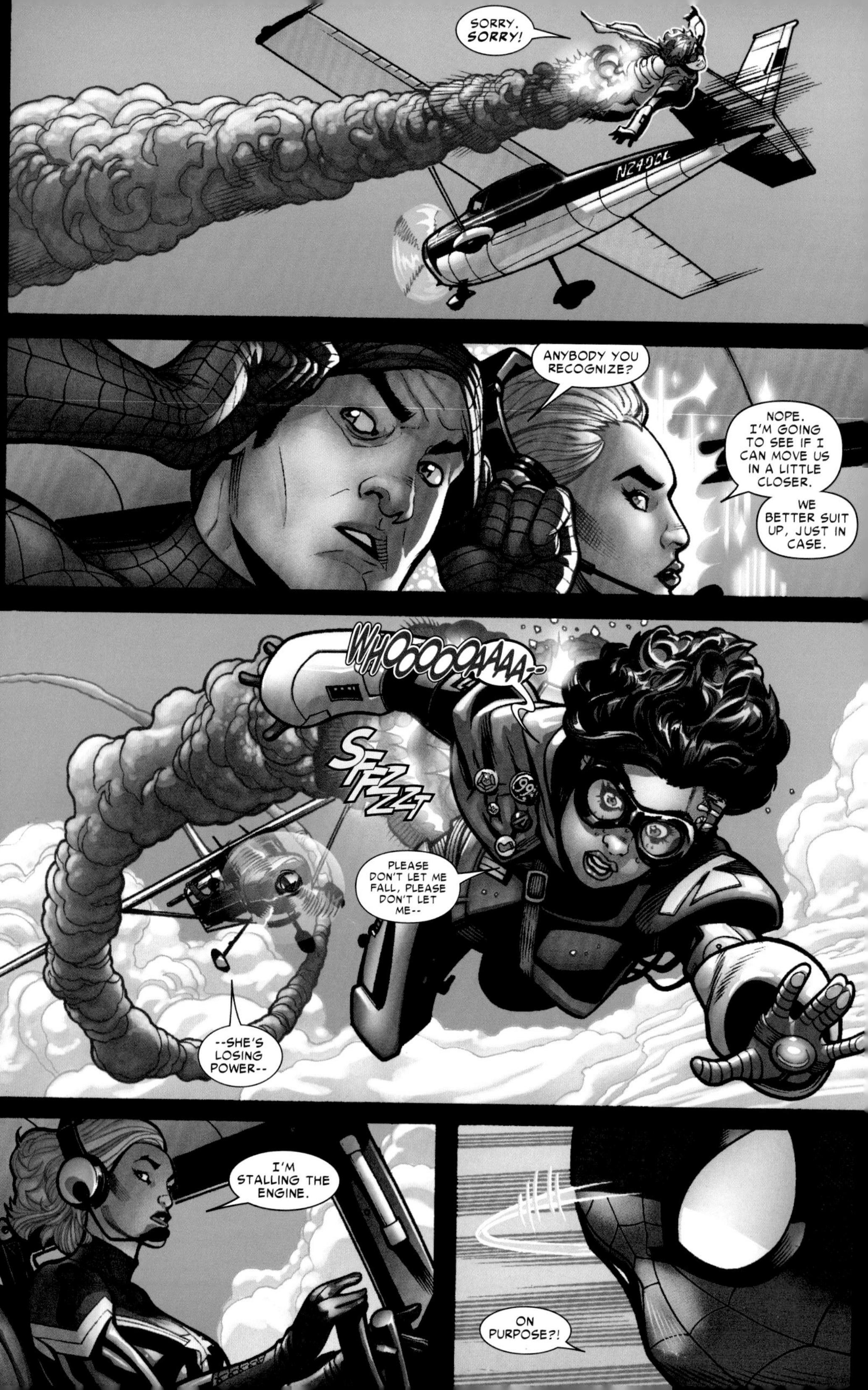
SORRY. SORRY!
N2400L
ANYBODY YOU RECOGNIZE?
NOPE. I'M GOING TO SEE IF I CAN MOVE US IN A LITTLE CLOSER.
WE BETTER SUIT UP, JUST IN CASE.
WHOOOOOOAAAA--
SFFZZZT
PLEASE DON'T LET ME FALL, PLEASE DON'T LET ME--
--SHE'S LOSING POWER--
I'M STALLING THE ENGINE.
ON PURPOSE?!

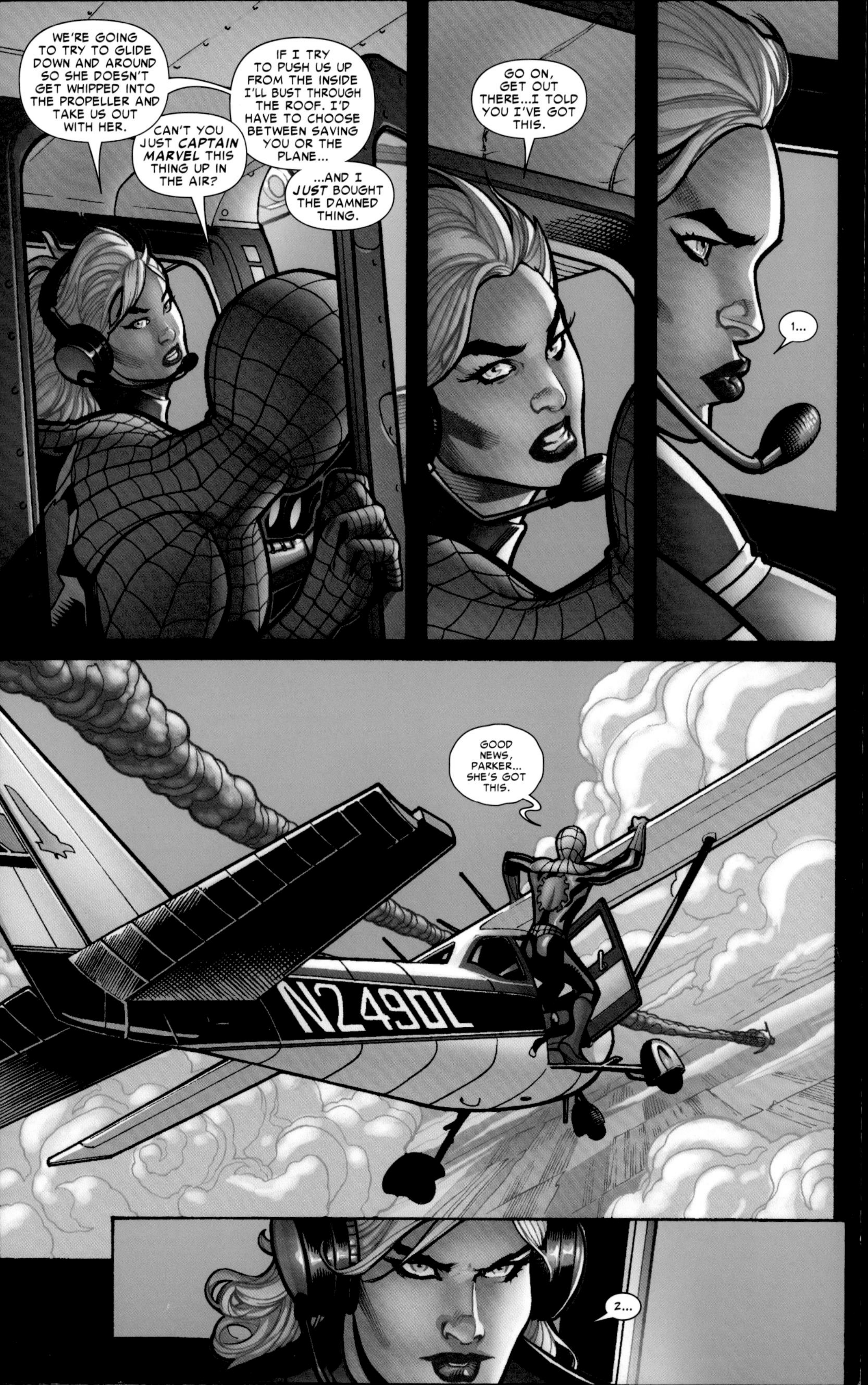
WE'RE GOING TO TRY TO GLIDE DOWN AND AROUND SO SHE DOESN'T GET WHIPPED INTO THE PROPELLER AND TAKE US OUT WITH HER.
CAN'T YOU JUST CAPTAIN MARVEL THIS THING UP IN THE AIR?
IF I TRY TO PUSH US UP FROM THE INSIDE I'LL BUST THROUGH THE ROOF. I'D HAVE TO CHOOSE BETWEEN SAVING YOU OR THE PLANE...
...AND I JUST BOUGHT THE DAMNED THING.
GO ON, GET OUT THERE...I TOLD YOU I'VE GOT THIS.
1...
GOOD NEWS, PARKER... SHE'S GOT THIS.
N2490L
2...

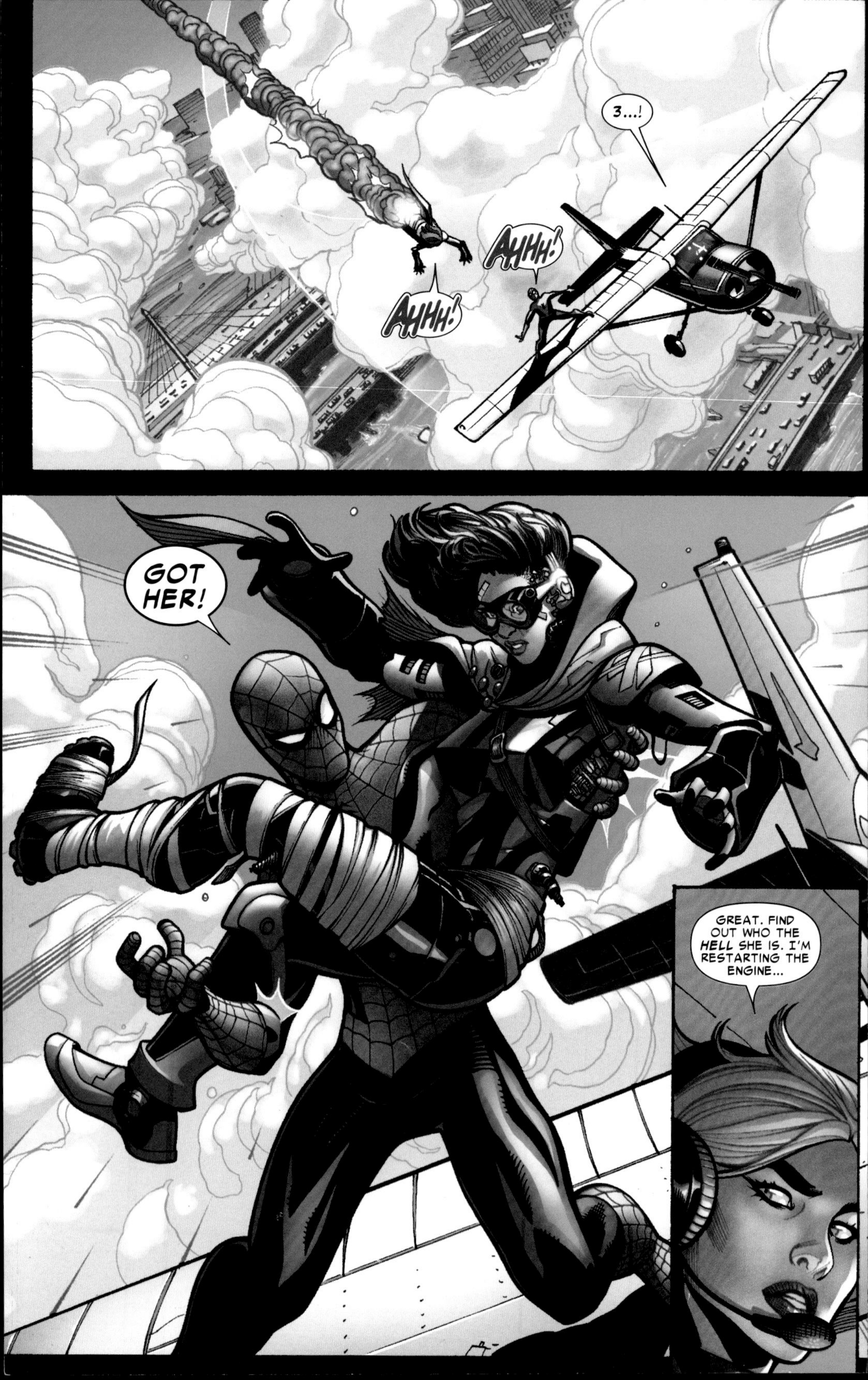
3...!
AHHH!
AHHH!
GOT HER!
GREAT. FIND OUT WHO THE HELL SHE IS. I'M RESTARTING THE ENGINE...

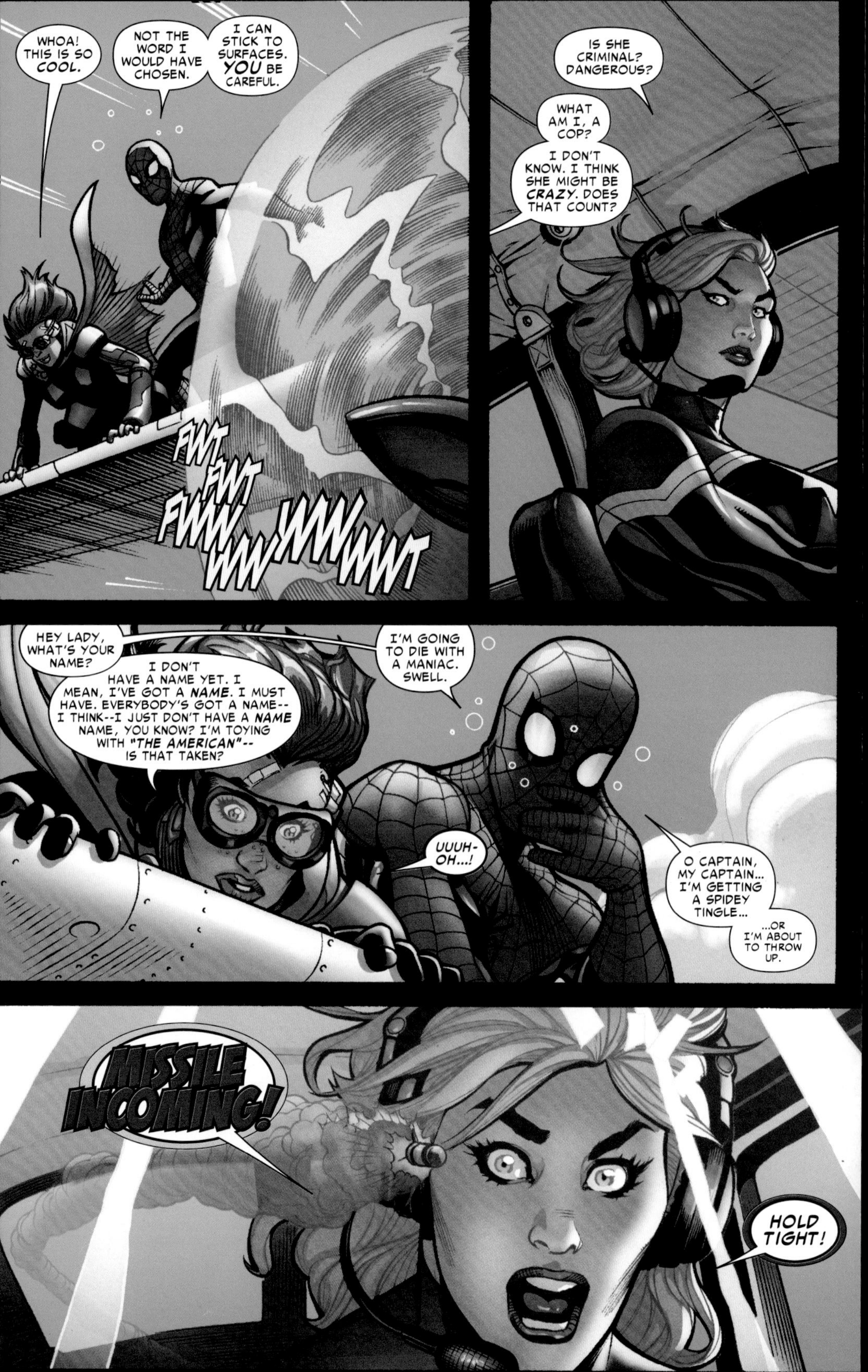
WHOA! THIS IS SO COOL.
NOT THE WORD I WOULD HAVE CHOSEN.
I CAN STICK TO SURFACES. YOU BE CAREFUL.
FWT FWT FWWWWWWWWWWWT
IS SHE CRIMINAL? DANGEROUS?
WHAT AM I, A COP?
I DON'T KNOW. I THINK SHE MIGHT BE CRAZY. DOES THAT COUNT?
HEY LADY, WHAT'S YOUR NAME?
I DON'T HAVE A NAME YET. I MEAN, I'VE GOT A NAME. I MUST HAVE. EVERYBODY'S GOT A NAME-- I THINK--I JUST DON'T HAVE A NAME NAME, YOU KNOW? I'M TOYING WITH "THE AMERICAN"-- IS THAT TAKEN?
I'M GOING TO DIE WITH A MANIAC. SWELL.
UUUH-OH...!
O CAPTAIN, MY CAPTAIN... I'M GETTING A SPIDEY TINGLE...
...OR I'M ABOUT TO THROW UP.
MISSILE INCOMING!
HOLD TIGHT!

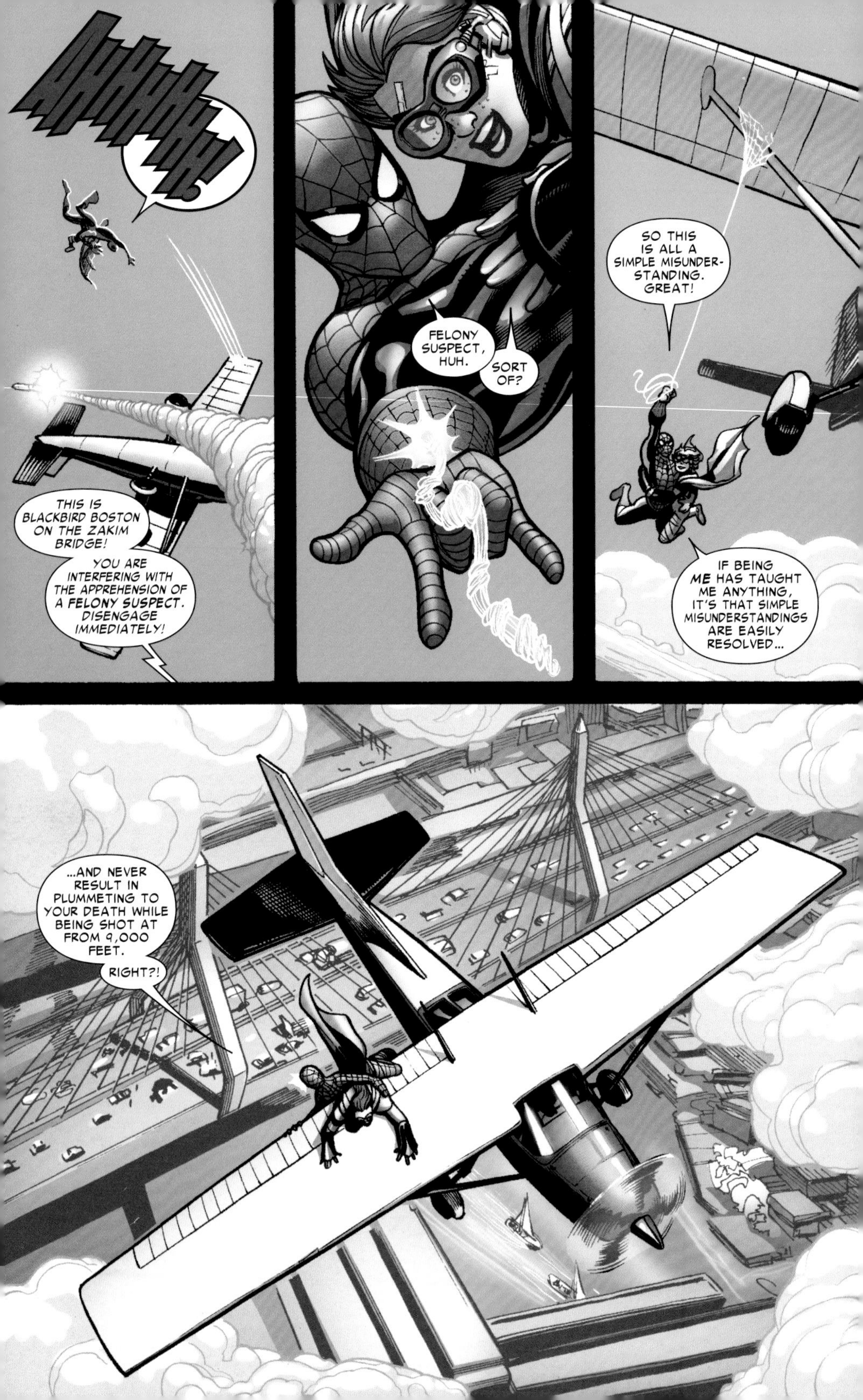
AHHHHHH!
THIS IS BLACKBIRD BOSTON ON THE ZAKIM BRIDGE!
YOU ARE INTERFERING WITH THE APPREHENSION OF A FELONY SUSPECT. DISENGAGE IMMEDIATELY!
FELONY SUSPECT, HUH.
SORT OF?
SO THIS IS ALL A SIMPLE MISUNDER-STANDING. GREAT!
IF BEING ME HAS TAUGHT ME ANYTHING, IT'S THAT SIMPLE MISUNDERSTANDINGS ARE EASILY RESOLVED...
...AND NEVER RESULT IN PLUMMETING TO YOUR DEATH WHILE BEING SHOT AT FROM 9,000 FEET.
RIGHT?!

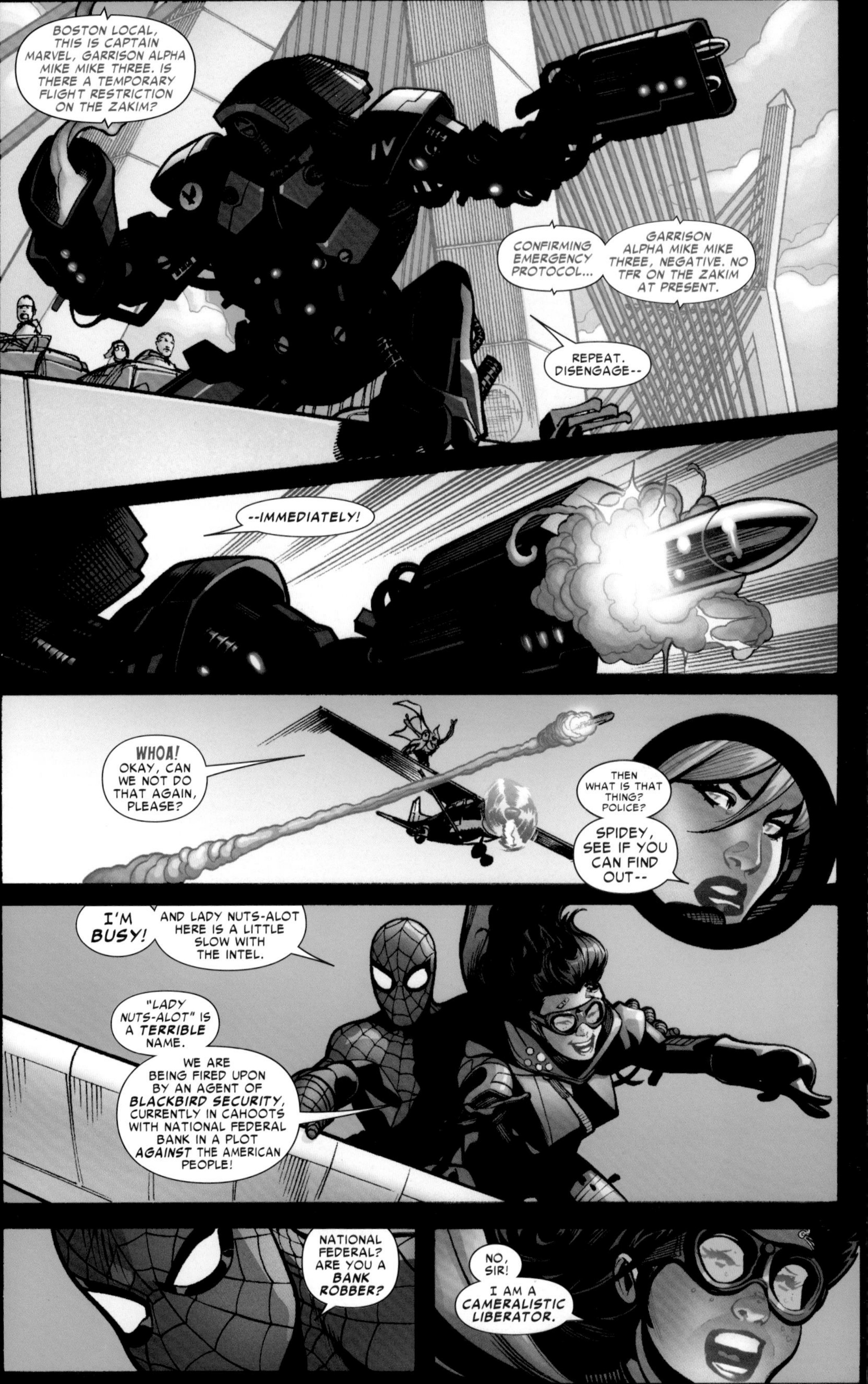
BOSTON LOCAL, THIS IS CAPTAIN MARVEL, GARRISON ALPHA MIKE MIKE THREE. IS THERE A TEMPORARY FLIGHT RESTRICTION ON THE ZAKIM?
CONFIRMING EMERGENCY PROTOCOL...
GARRISON ALPHA MIKE MIKE THREE, NEGATIVE. NO TFR ON THE ZAKIM AT PRESENT.
REPEAT. DISENGAGE--
--IMMEDIATELY!
WHOA! OKAY, CAN WE NOT DO THAT AGAIN, PLEASE?
THEN WHAT IS THAT THING? POLICE?
SPIDEY, SEE IF YOU CAN FIND OUT--
I'M BUSY!
AND LADY NUTS-ALOT HERE IS A LITTLE SLOW WITH THE INTEL.
"LADY NUTS-ALOT" IS A TERRIBLE NAME.
WE ARE BEING FIRED UPON BY AN AGENT OF BLACKBIRD SECURITY, CURRENTLY IN CAHOOTS WITH NATIONAL FEDERAL BANK IN A PLOT AGAINST THE AMERICAN PEOPLE!
NATIONAL FEDERAL? ARE YOU A BANK ROBBER?
NO, SIR!
I AM A CAMERALISTIC LIBERATOR.

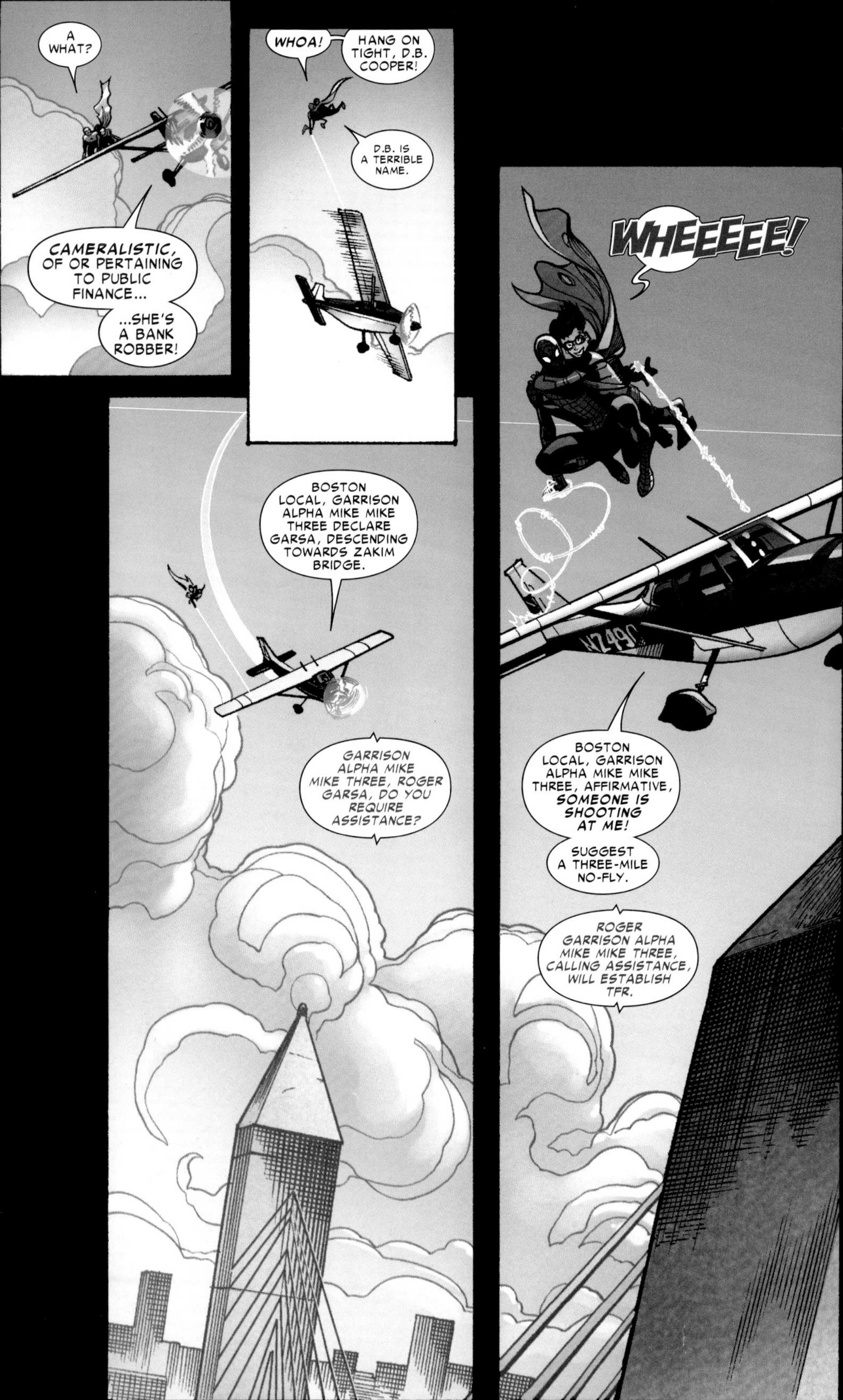
A WHAT?
CAMERALISTIC, OF OR PERTAINING TO PUBLIC FINANCE...
...SHE'S A BANK ROBBER!
WHOA!
HANG ON TIGHT, D.B. COOPER!
D.B. IS A TERRIBLE NAME.
WHEEEEE!
BOSTON LOCAL, GARRISON ALPHA MIKE MIKE THREE DECLARE GARSA, DESCENDING TOWARDS ZAKIM BRIDGE.
GARRISON ALPHA MIKE MIKE THREE, ROGER GARSA, DO YOU REQUIRE ASSISTANCE?
BOSTON LOCAL, GARRISON ALPHA MIKE MIKE THREE, AFFIRMATIVE, SOMEONE IS SHOOTING AT ME!
SUGGEST A THREE-MILE NO-FLY.
ROGER GARRISON ALPHA MIKE MIKE THREE, CALLING ASSISTANCE, WILL ESTABLISH TFR.

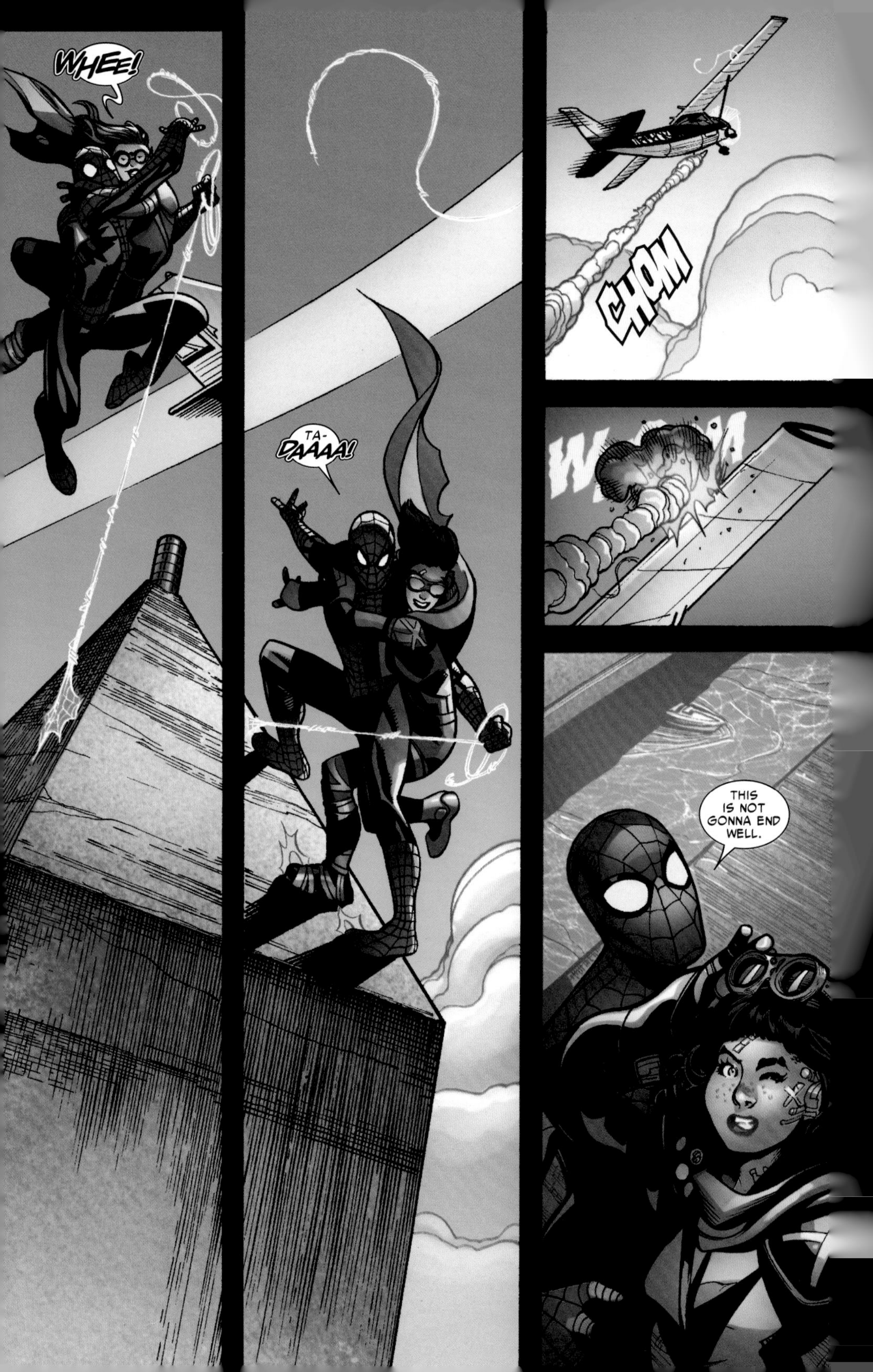
WHEE!
TA-DAAAA!
CHOM
THIS IS NOT GONNA END WELL.

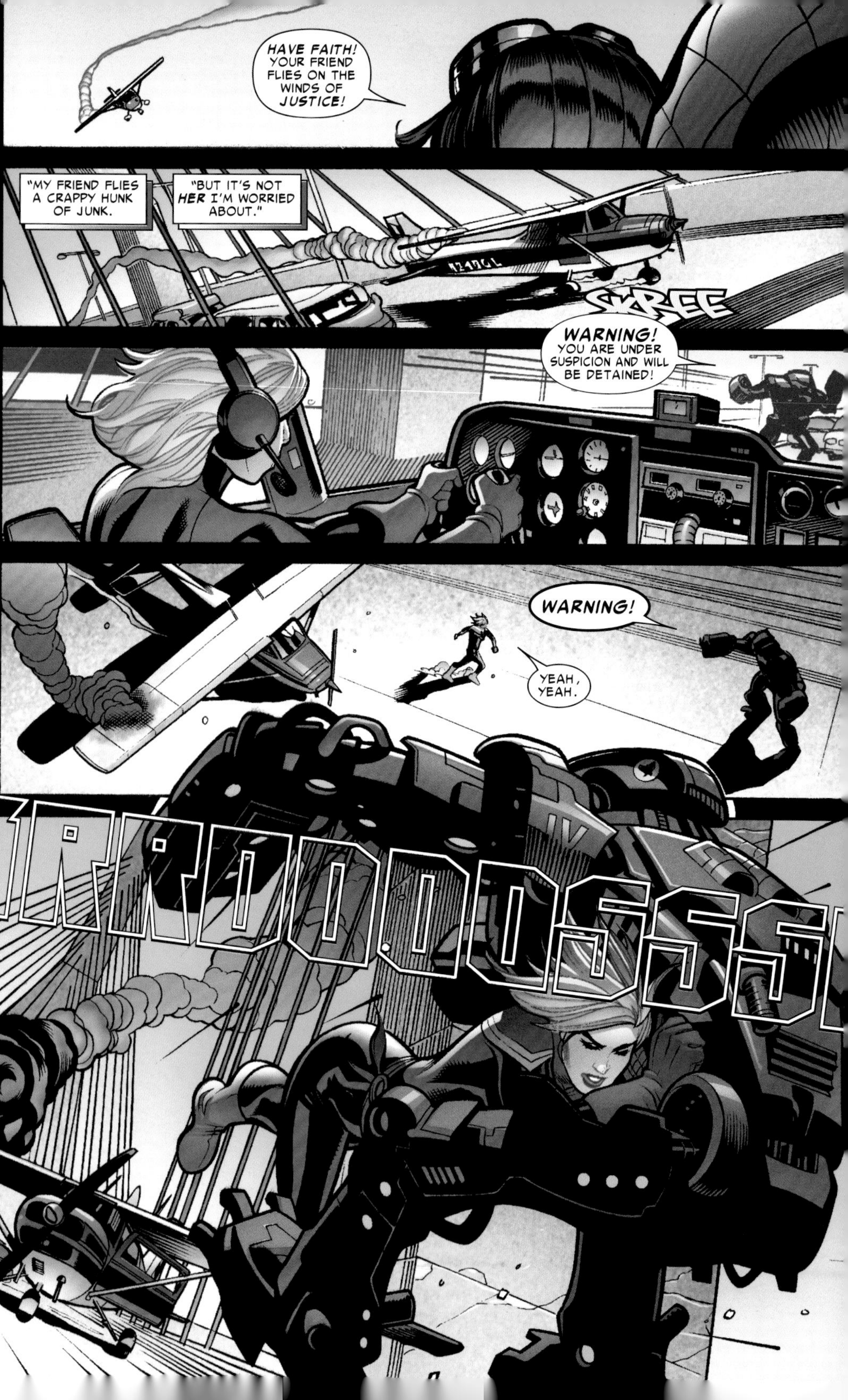

HAVE FAITH! YOUR FRIEND FLIES ON THE WINDS OF JUSTICE!
"MY FRIEND FLIES A CRAPPY HUNK OF JUNK.
"BUT IT'S NOT HER I'M WORRIED ABOUT."
SKREE
WARNING! YOU ARE UNDER SUSPICION AND WILL BE DETAINED!
WARNING!
YEAH, YEAH.

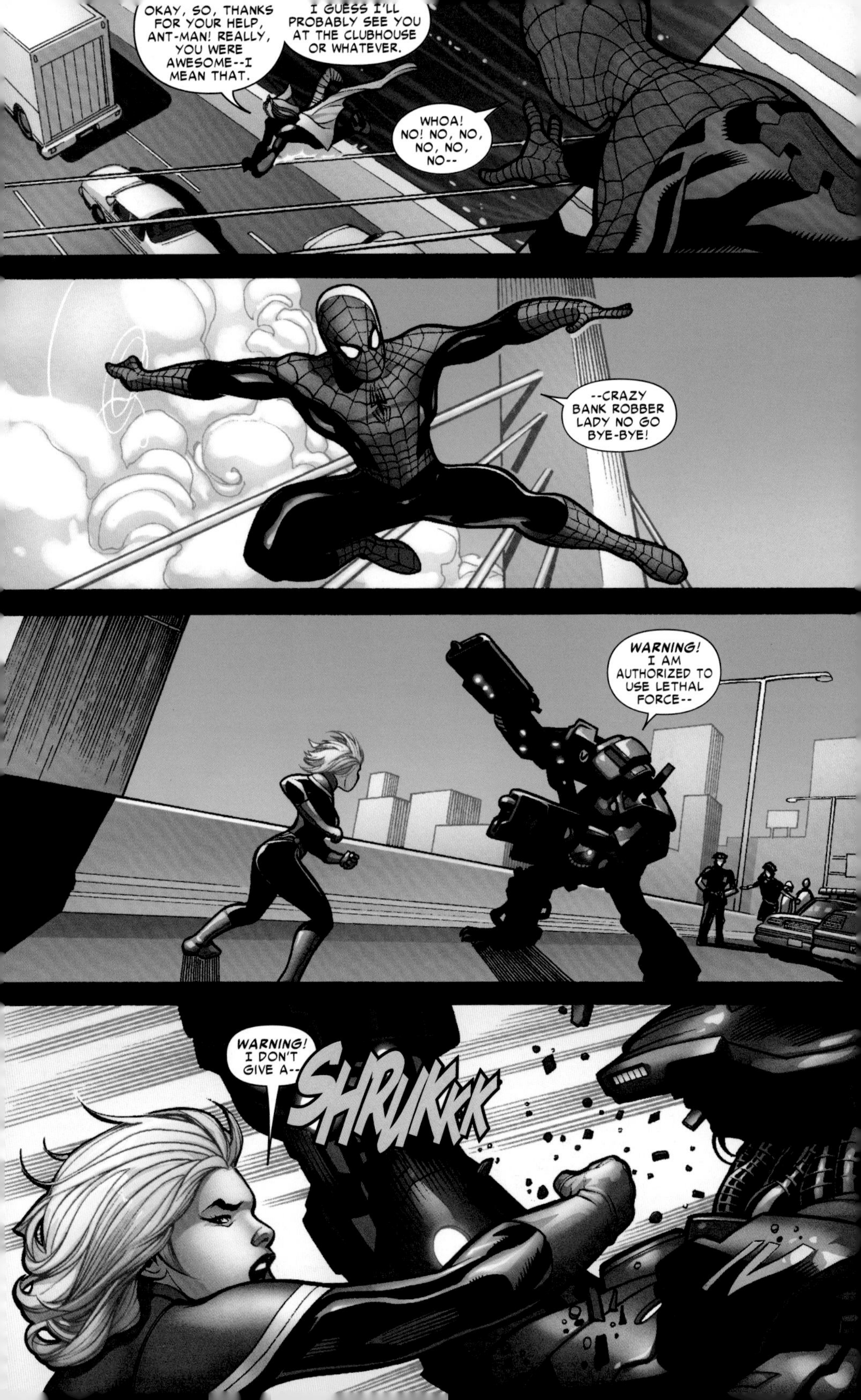
OKAY, SO, THANKS FOR YOUR HELP, ANT-MAN! REALLY, YOU WERE AWESOME--I MEAN THAT.
I GUESS I'LL PROBABLY SEE YOU AT THE CLUBHOUSE OR WHATEVER.
WHOA! NO! NO, NO, NO, NO, NO--
--CRAZY BANK ROBBER LADY NO GO BYE-BYE!
WARNING! I AM AUTHORIZED TO USE LETHAL FORCE--
WARNING! I DON'T GIVE A--
SHRUKKK

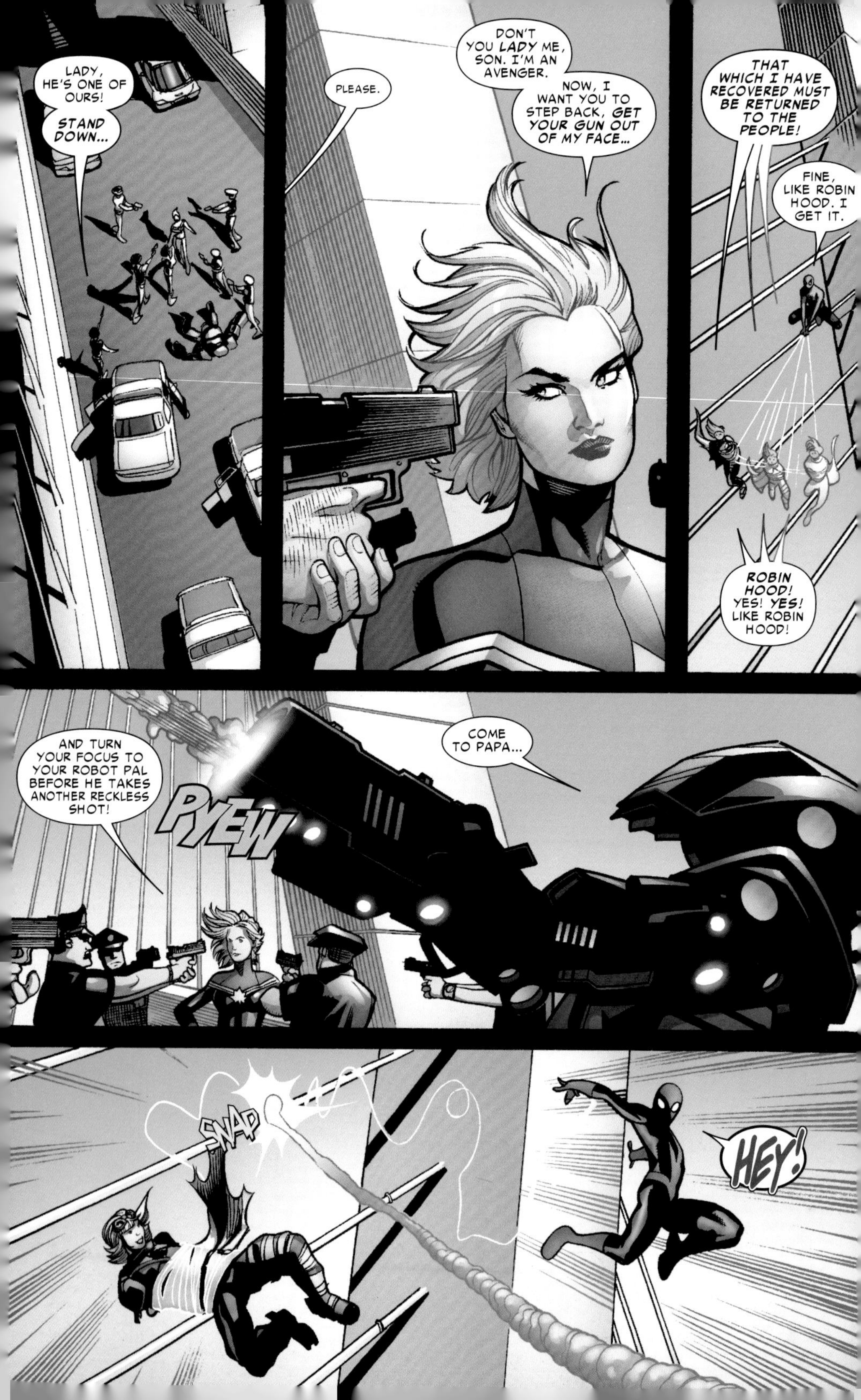
LADY, HE'S ONE OF OURS!
STAND DOWN...
PLEASE.
DON'T YOU LADY ME, SON. I'M AN AVENGER.
NOW, I WANT YOU TO STEP BACK, GET YOUR GUN OUT OF MY FACE...
THAT WHICH I HAVE RECOVERED MUST BE RETURNED TO THE PEOPLE!
FINE, LIKE ROBIN HOOD. I GET IT.
ROBIN HOOD! YES! YES! LIKE ROBIN HOOD!
AND TURN YOUR FOCUS TO YOUR ROBOT PAL BEFORE HE TAKES ANOTHER RECKLESS SHOT!
COME TO PAPA...
PYEW
SNAP
HEY!

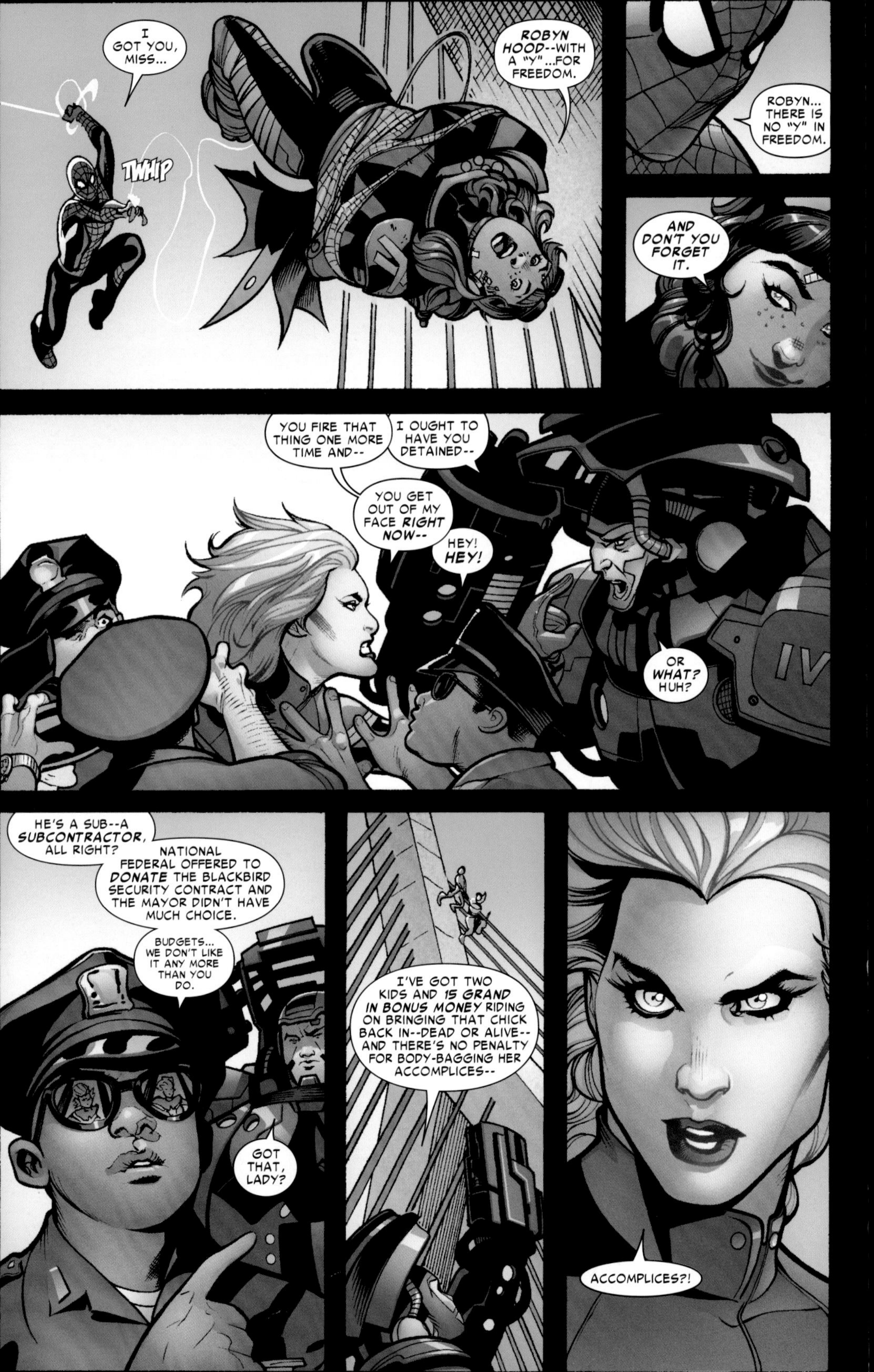

I GOT YOU, MISS...
TWHIP
ROBYN HOOD--WITH A "Y"...FOR FREEDOM.
ROBYN... THERE IS NO "Y" IN FREEDOM.
AND DON'T YOU FORGET IT.
YOU FIRE THAT THING ONE MORE TIME AND--
I OUGHT TO HAVE YOU DETAINED--
YOU GET OUT OF MY FACE RIGHT NOW--
HEY! HEY!
OR WHAT? HUH?
HE'S A SUB--A SUBCONTRACTOR, ALL RIGHT?
NATIONAL FEDERAL OFFERED TO DONATE THE BLACKBIRD SECURITY CONTRACT AND THE MAYOR DIDN'T HAVE MUCH CHOICE.
BUDGETS... WE DON'T LIKE IT ANY MORE THAN YOU DO.
GOT THAT, LADY?
I'VE GOT TWO KIDS AND 15 GRAND IN BONUS MONEY RIDING ON BRINGING THAT CHICK BACK IN--DEAD OR ALIVE-- AND THERE'S NO PENALTY FOR BODY-BAGGING HER ACCOMPLICES--
ACCOMPLICES?!

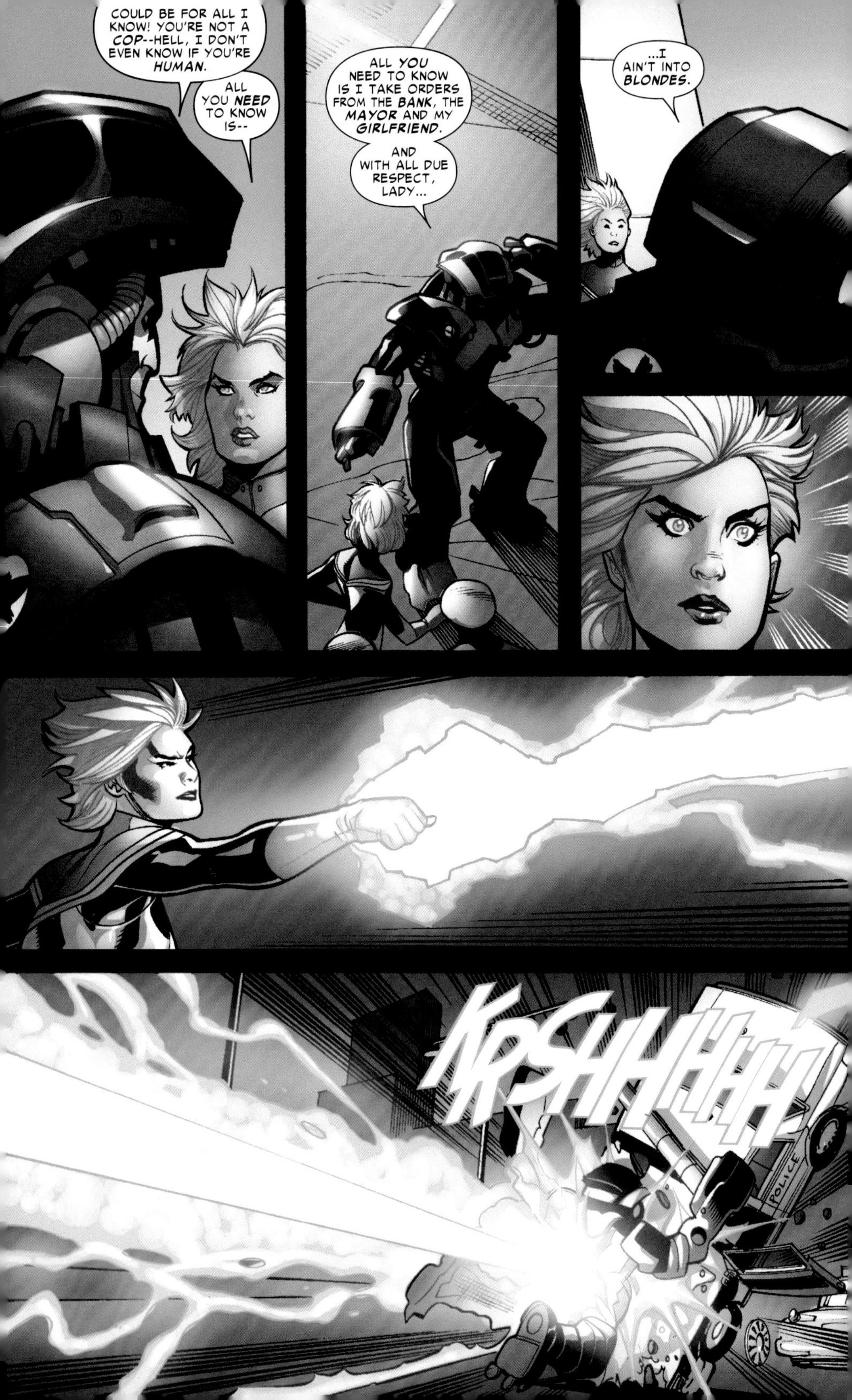
COULD BE FOR ALL I KNOW! YOU'RE NOT A COP--HELL, I DON'T EVEN KNOW IF YOU'RE HUMAN.
ALL YOU NEED TO KNOW IS--
ALL YOU NEED TO KNOW IS I TAKE ORDERS FROM THE BANK, THE MAYOR AND MY GIRLFRIEND.
AND WITH ALL DUE RESPECT, LADY...
...I AIN'T INTO BLONDES.
KRSHHHHH
POLICE

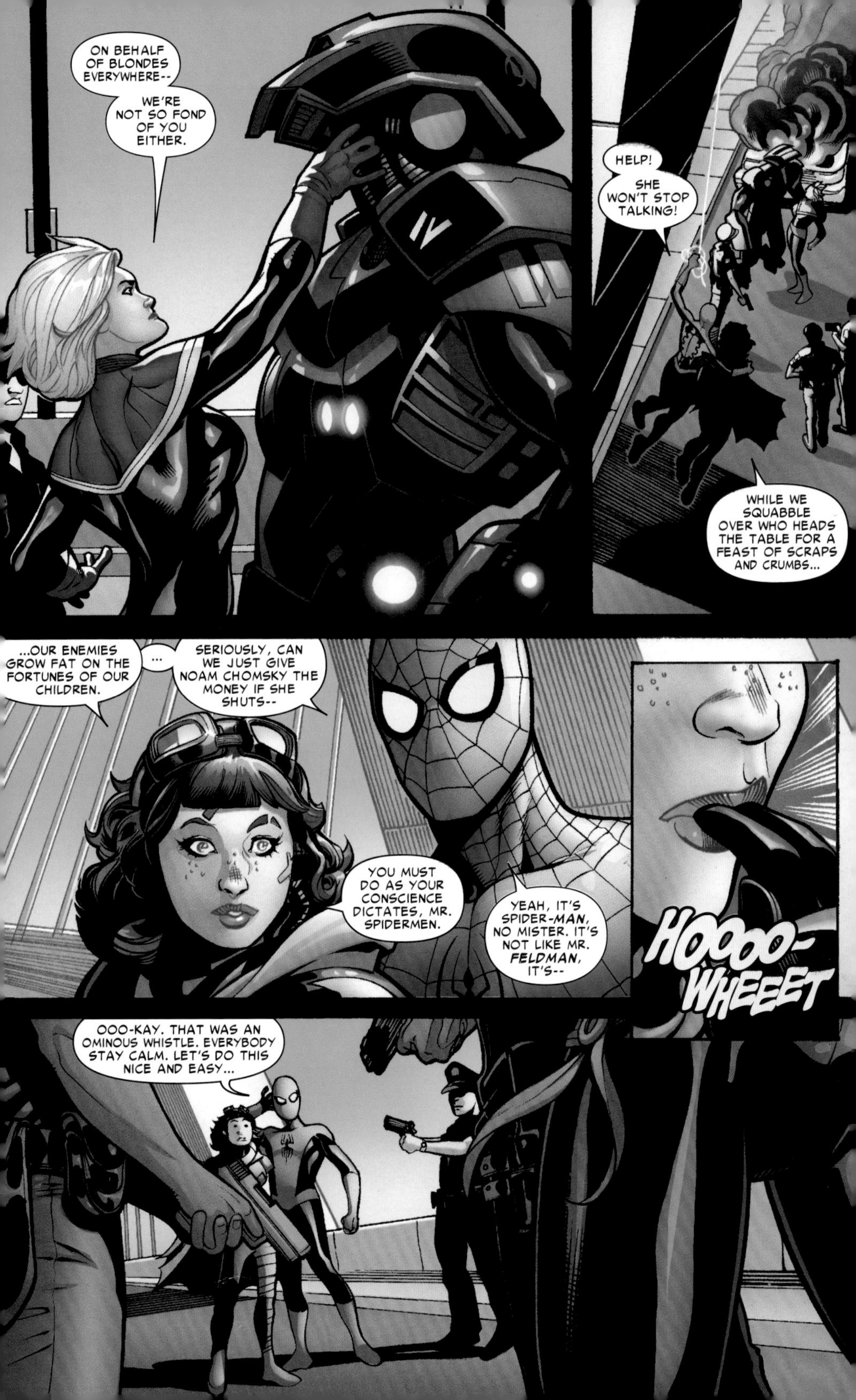
ON BEHALF OF BLONDES EVERYWHERE--
WE'RE NOT SO FOND OF YOU EITHER.
HELP! SHE WON'T STOP TALKING!
WHILE WE SQUABBLE OVER WHO HEADS THE TABLE FOR A FEAST OF SCRAPS AND CRUMBS...
...OUR ENEMIES GROW FAT ON THE FORTUNES OF OUR CHILDREN.
...
SERIOUSLY, CAN WE JUST GIVE NOAM CHOMSKY THE MONEY IF SHE SHUTS--
YOU MUST DO AS YOUR CONSCIENCE DICTATES, MR. SPIDERMEN.
YEAH, IT'S SPIDER-MAN, NO MISTER. IT'S NOT LIKE MR. FELDMAN, IT'S--
HOOOO-WHEEET
OOO-KAY. THAT WAS AN OMINOUS WHISTLE. EVERYBODY STAY CALM. LET'S DO THIS NICE AND EASY...

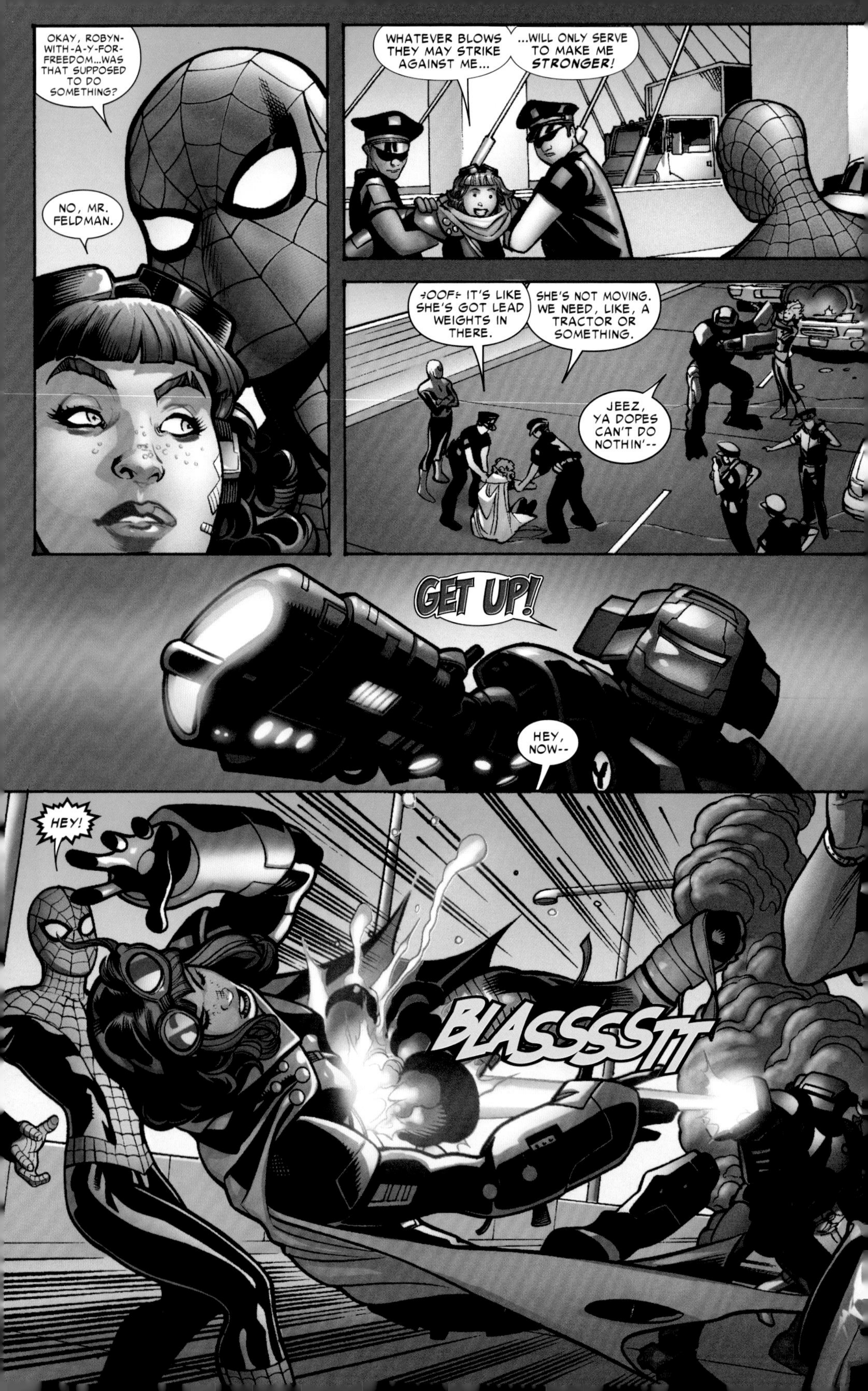
OKAY, ROBYN-WITH-A-Y-FOR-FREEDOM...WAS THAT SUPPOSED TO DO SOMETHING?
NO, MR. FELDMAN.
WHATEVER BLOWS THEY MAY STRIKE AGAINST ME...
...WILL ONLY SERVE TO MAKE ME STRONGER!
÷OOF÷ IT'S LIKE SHE'S GOT LEAD WEIGHTS IN THERE.
SHE'S NOT MOVING. WE NEED, LIKE, A TRACTOR OR SOMETHING.
JEEZ, YA DOPES CAN'T DO NOTHIN'--
GET UP!
HEY, NOW--
HEY!
BLASSSSTT

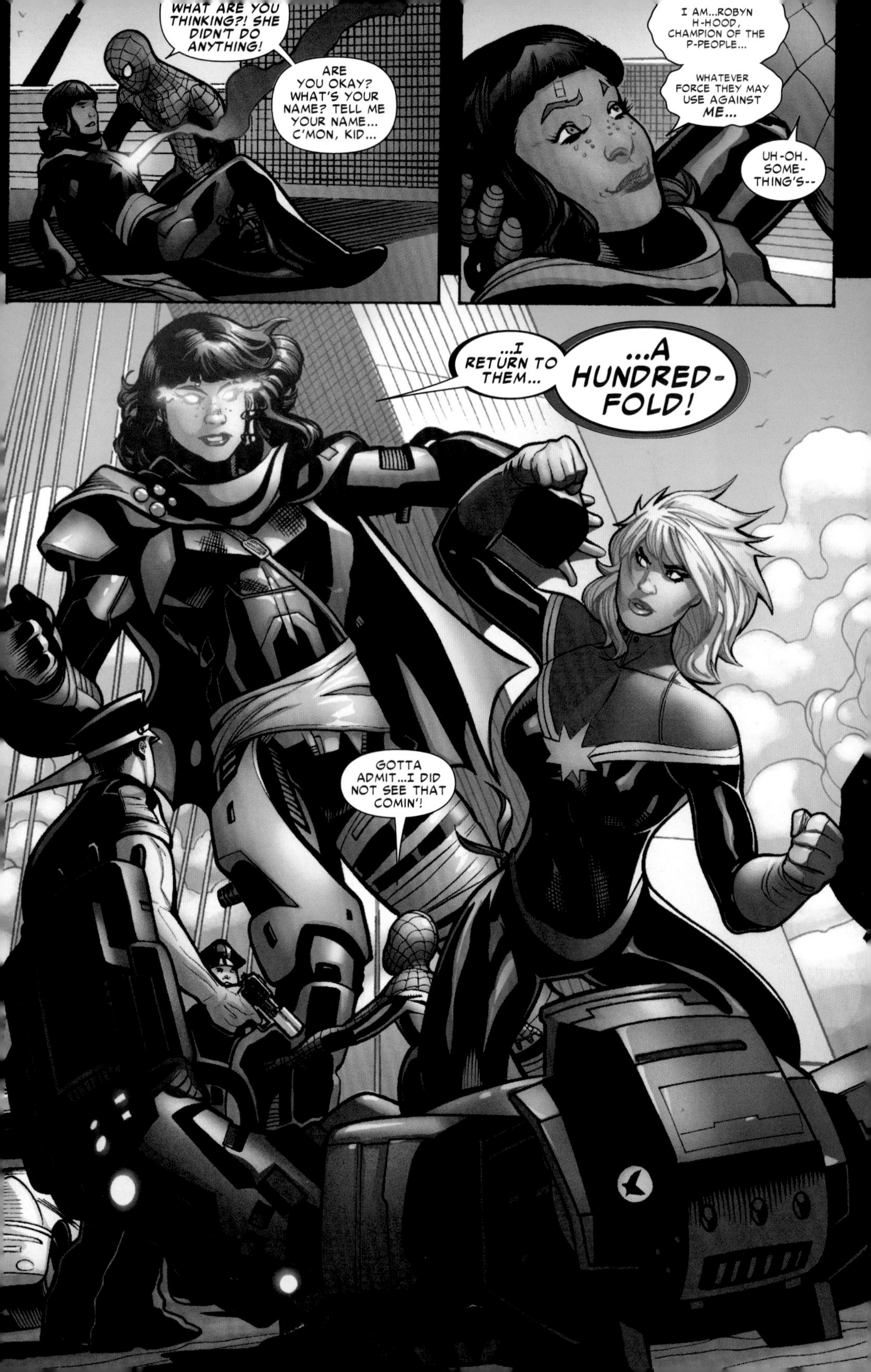
WHAT ARE YOU THINKING?! SHE DIDN'T DO ANYTHING!
ARE YOU OKAY? WHAT'S YOUR NAME? TELL ME YOUR NAME... C'MON, KID...
I AM...ROBYN H-HOOD, CHAMPION OF THE P-PEOPLE...
WHATEVER FORCE THEY MAY USE AGAINST ME...
UH-OH. SOME-THING'S--
...I RETURN TO THEM...
...A HUNDRED-FOLD!
GOTTA ADMIT...I DID NOT SEE THAT COMIN'!

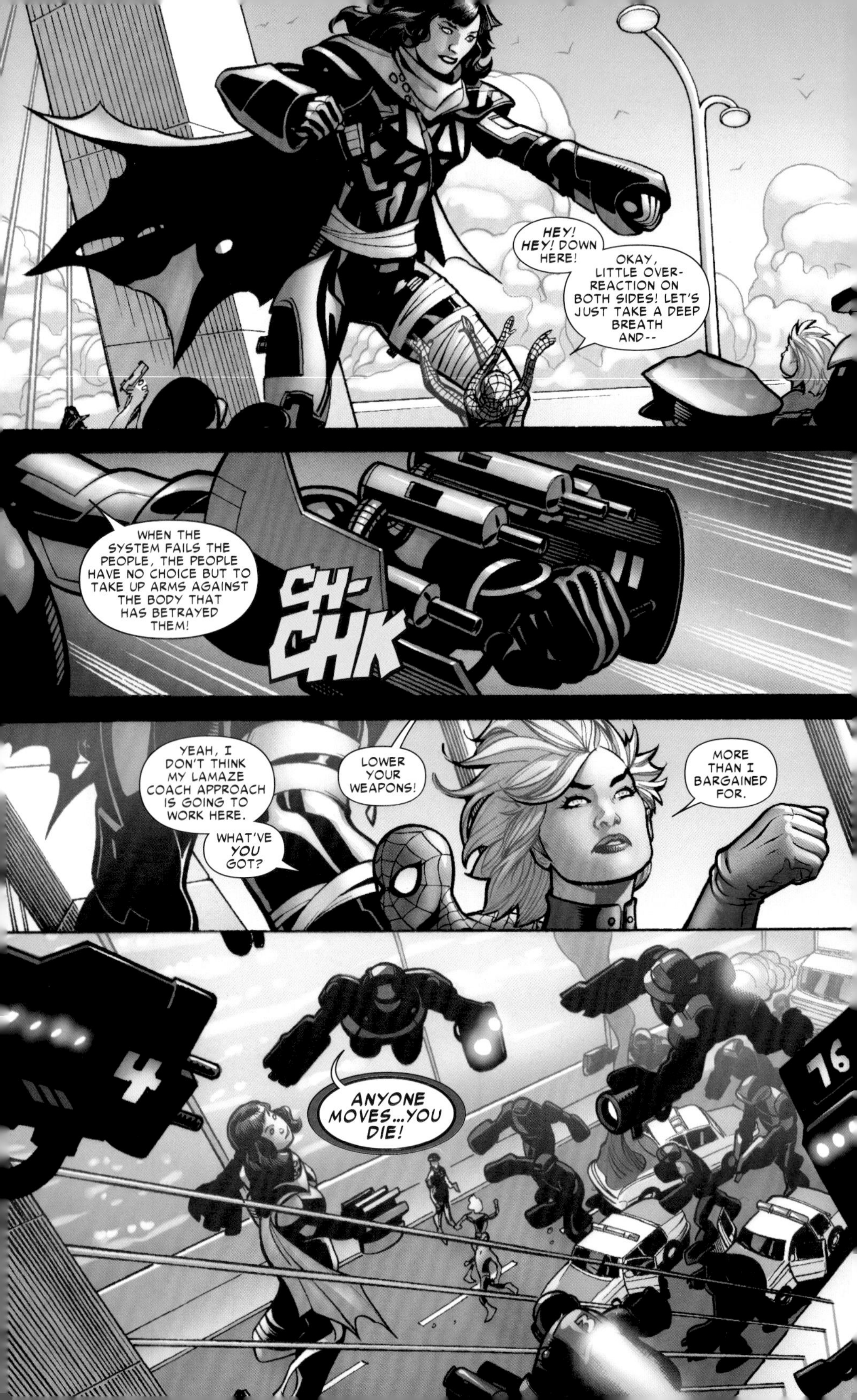
HEY! HEY! DOWN HERE!
OKAY, LITTLE OVER-REACTION ON BOTH SIDES! LET'S JUST TAKE A DEEP BREATH AND--
WHEN THE SYSTEM FAILS THE PEOPLE, THE PEOPLE HAVE NO CHOICE BUT TO TAKE UP ARMS AGAINST THE BODY THAT HAS BETRAYED THEM!
CH-CHK
YEAH, I DON'T THINK MY LAMAZE COACH APPROACH IS GOING TO WORK HERE.
WHAT'VE YOU GOT?
LOWER YOUR WEAPONS!
MORE THAN I BARGAINED FOR.
ANYONE MOVES...YOU DIE!

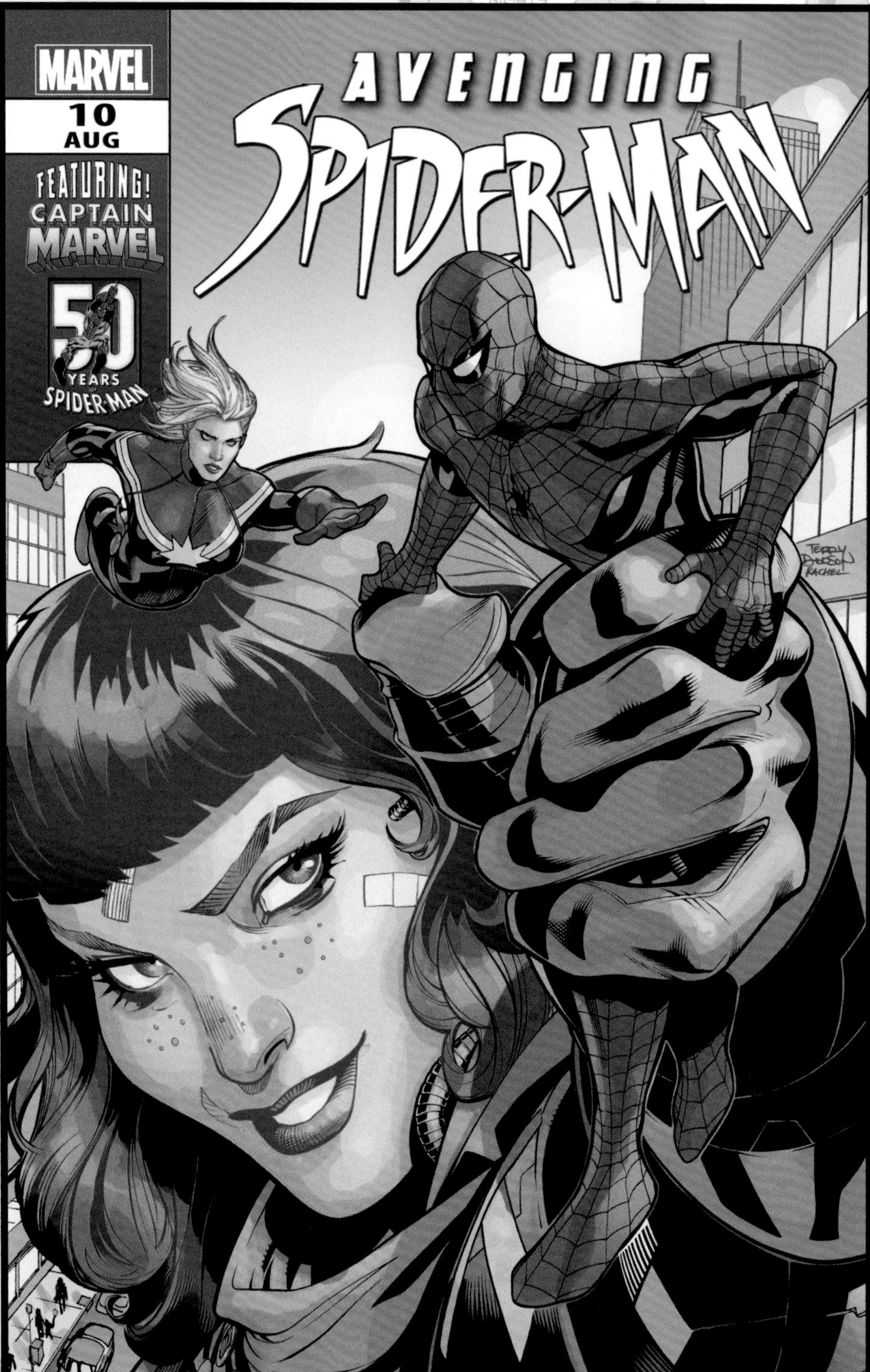
MARVEL
10
AUG
FEATURING!
CAPTAIN
MARVEL
50
YEARS
SPIDER-MAN
AVENGING
SPIDER-MAN
TERRY
DODSON
RACHEL

AVENGING SPIDER-MAN #10

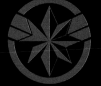

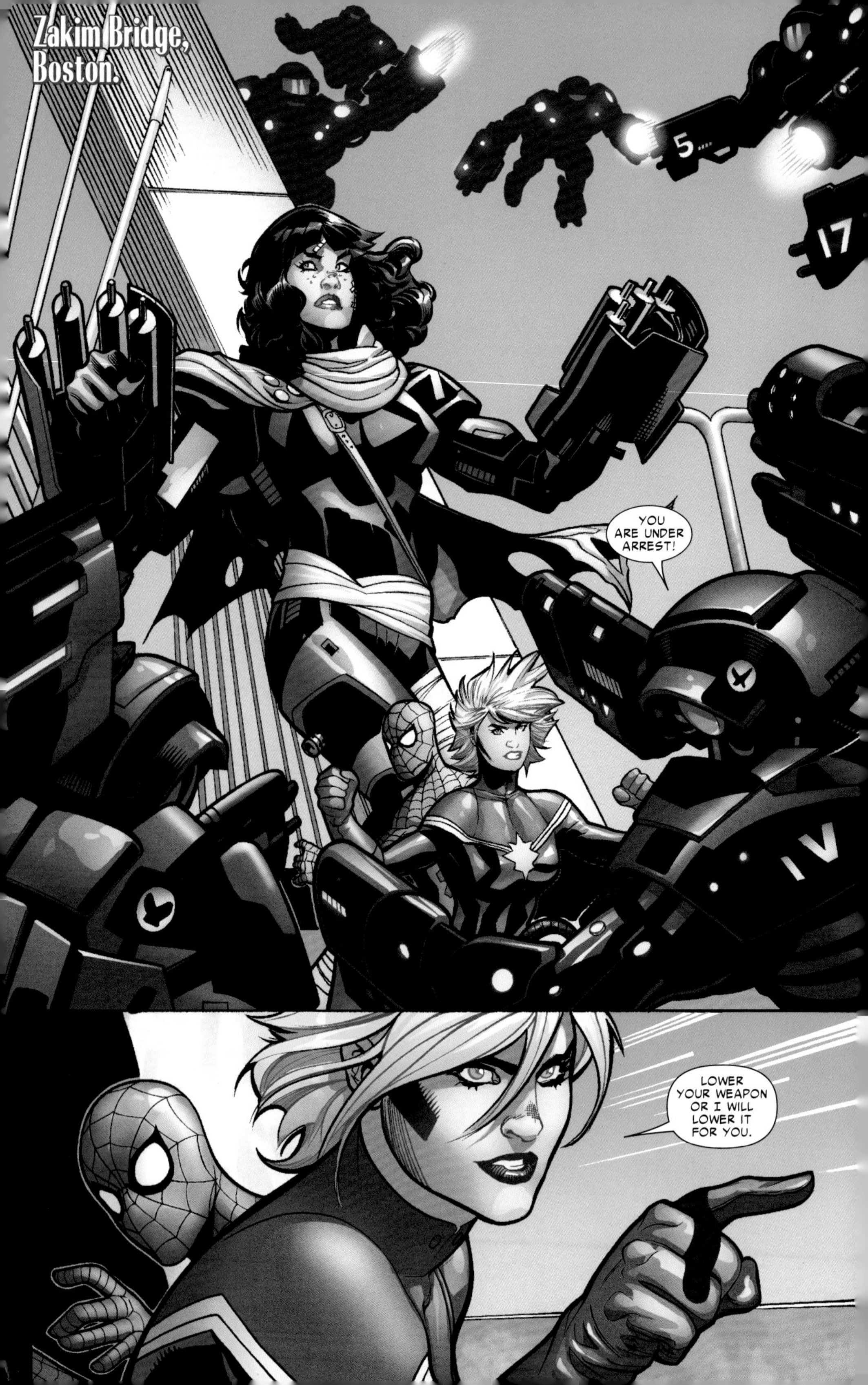
Zakim Bridge, Boston.
YOU ARE UNDER ARREST!
LOWER YOUR WEAPON OR I WILL LOWER IT FOR YOU.

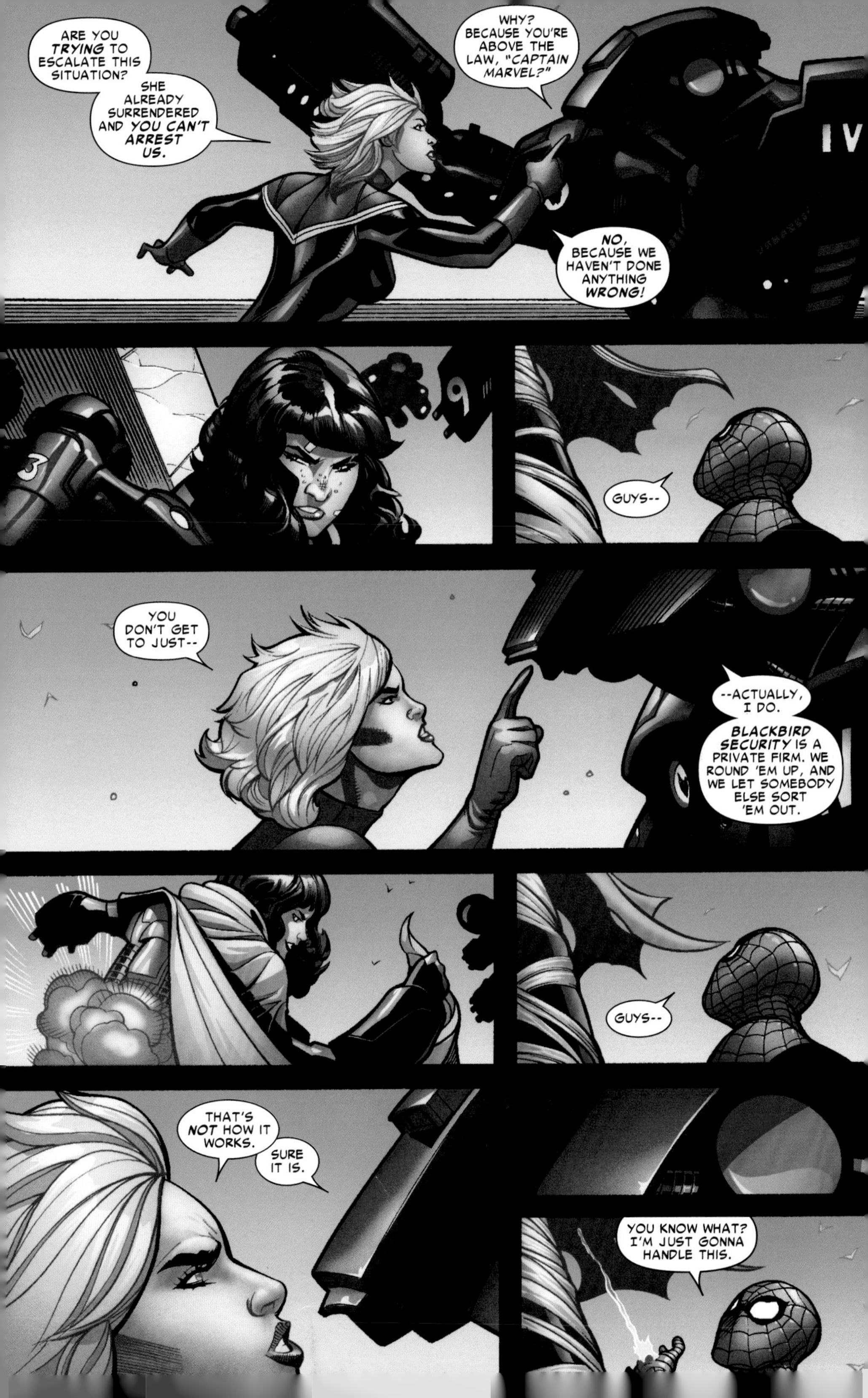
ARE YOU TRYING TO ESCALATE THIS SITUATION?
SHE ALREADY SURRENDERED AND YOU CAN'T ARREST US.
WHY? BECAUSE YOU'RE ABOVE THE LAW, "CAPTAIN MARVEL?"
NO, BECAUSE WE HAVEN'T DONE ANYTHING WRONG!
GUYS--
YOU DON'T GET TO JUST--
--ACTUALLY, I DO.
BLACKBIRD SECURITY IS A PRIVATE FIRM. WE ROUND 'EM UP, AND WE LET SOMEBODY ELSE SORT 'EM OUT.
GUYS--
THAT'S NOT HOW IT WORKS.
SURE IT IS.
YOU KNOW WHAT? I'M JUST GONNA HANDLE THIS.

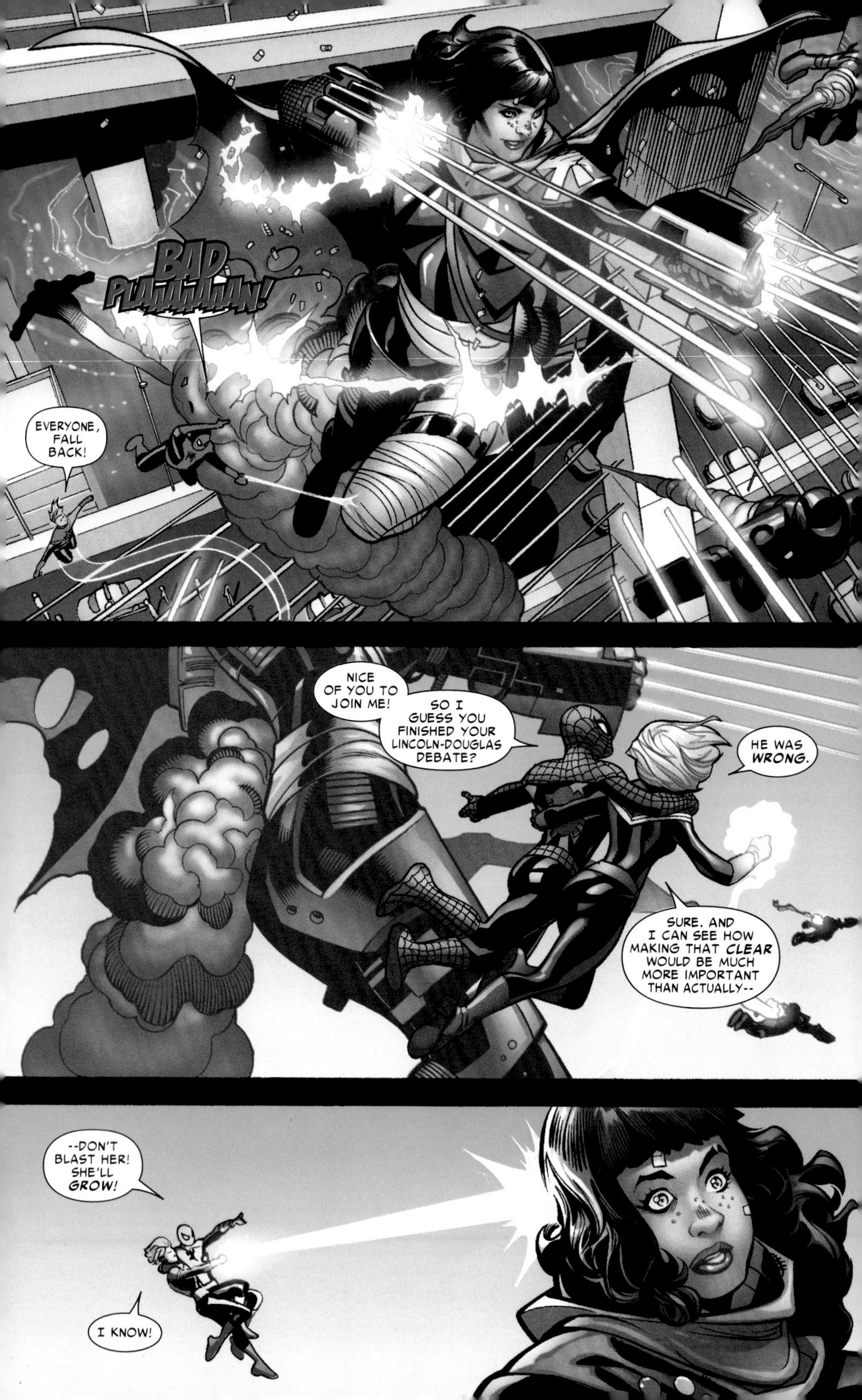
BAD PLAAAAAAAN!
EVERYONE, FALL BACK!
NICE OF YOU TO JOIN ME!
SO I GUESS YOU FINISHED YOUR LINCOLN-DOUGLAS DEBATE?
HE WAS WRONG.
SURE. AND I CAN SEE HOW MAKING THAT CLEAR WOULD BE MUCH MORE IMPORTANT THAN ACTUALLY--
--DON'T BLAST HER! SHE'LL GROW!
I KNOW!

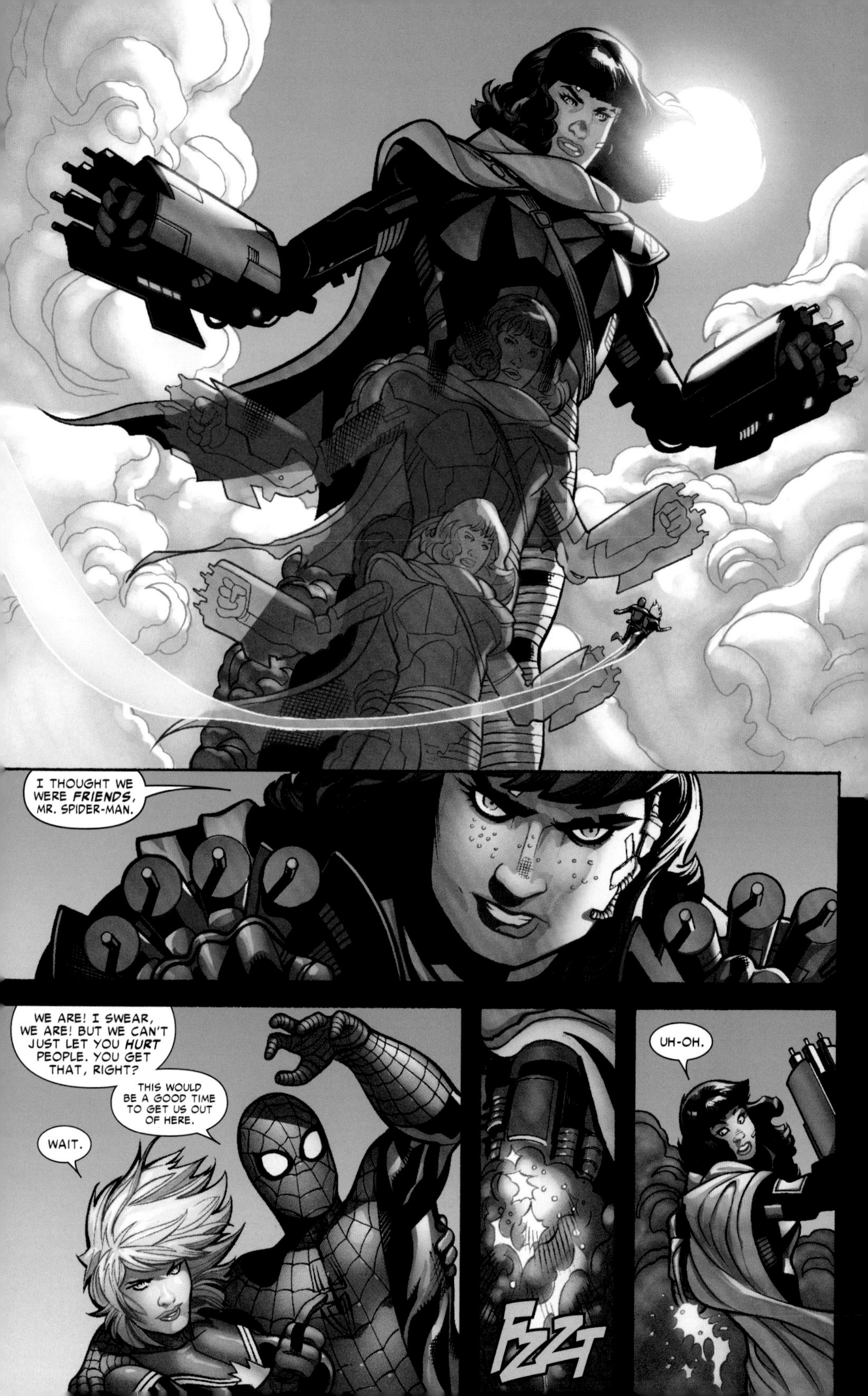
I THOUGHT WE WERE FRIENDS, MR. SPIDER-MAN.
WE ARE! I SWEAR, WE ARE! BUT WE CAN'T JUST LET YOU HURT PEOPLE. YOU GET THAT, RIGHT?
THIS WOULD BE A GOOD TIME TO GET US OUT OF HERE.
WAIT.
FZZT
UH-OH.

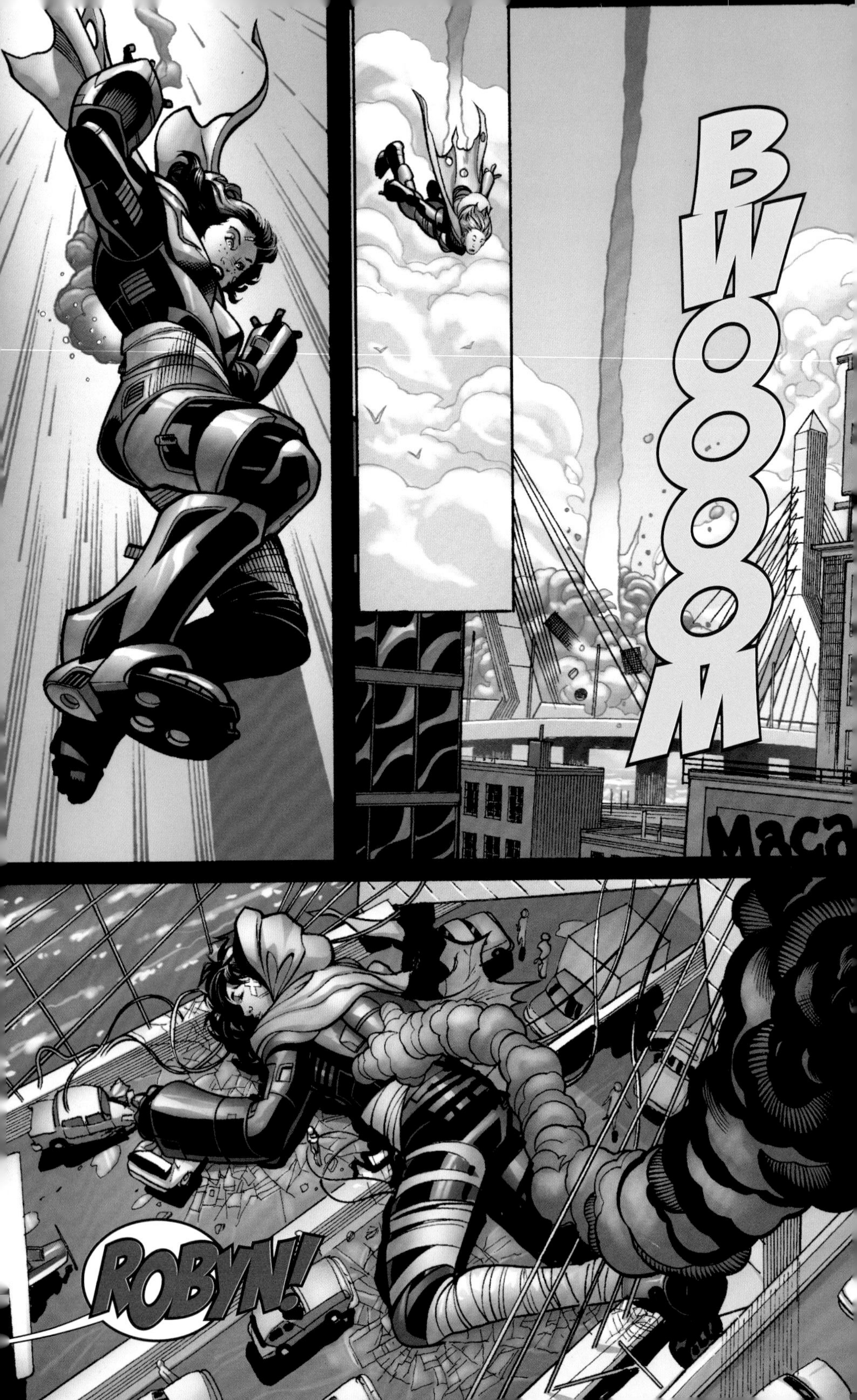
BWOOOOM
Maca
ROBYN!

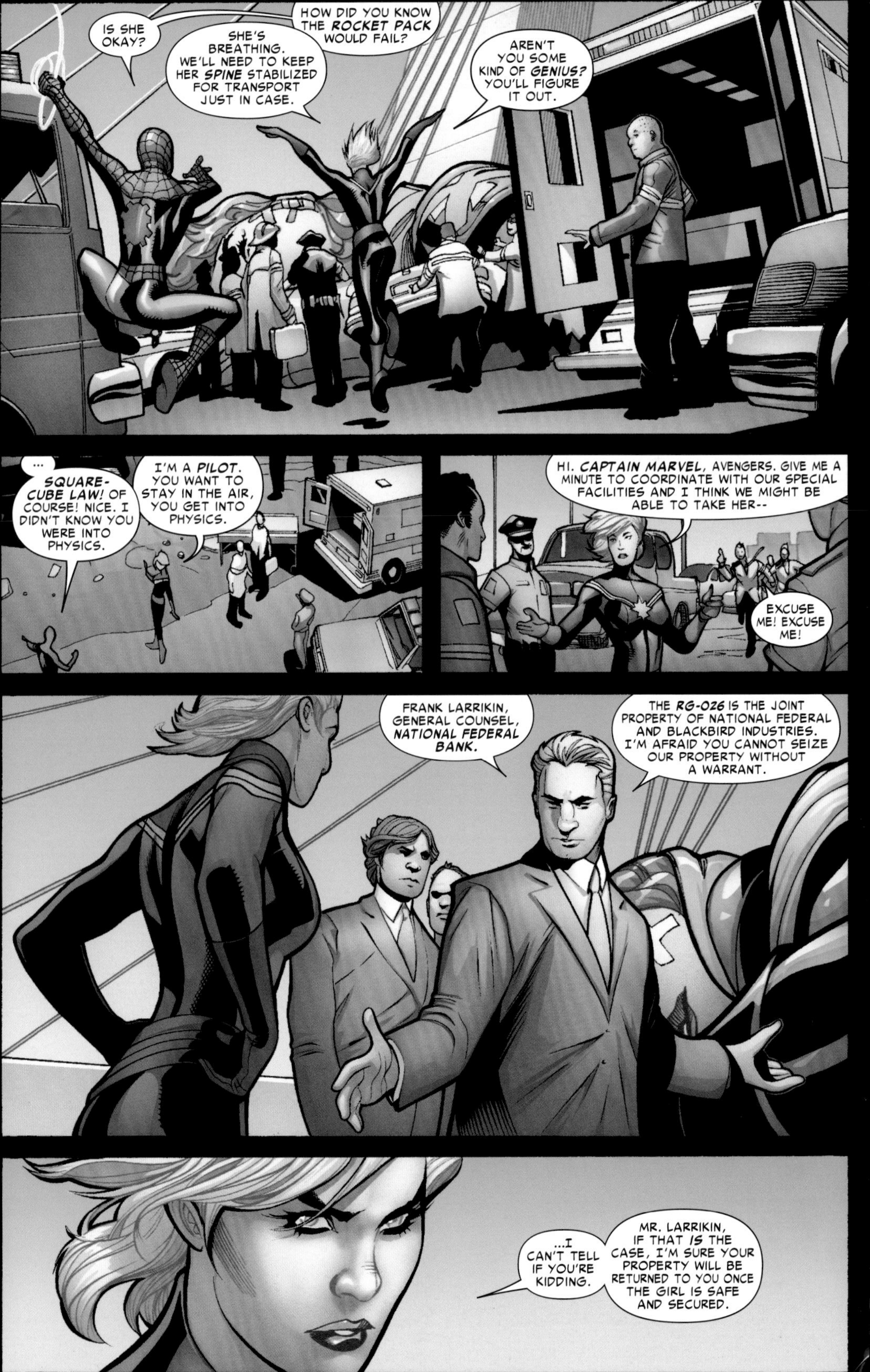
IS SHE OKAY?
SHE'S BREATHING. WE'LL NEED TO KEEP HER SPINE STABILIZED FOR TRANSPORT JUST IN CASE.
HOW DID YOU KNOW THE ROCKET PACK WOULD FAIL?
AREN'T YOU SOME KIND OF GENIUS? YOU'LL FIGURE IT OUT.
... SQUARE-CUBE LAW! OF COURSE! NICE. I DIDN'T KNOW YOU WERE INTO PHYSICS.
I'M A PILOT. YOU WANT TO STAY IN THE AIR, YOU GET INTO PHYSICS.
HI. CAPTAIN MARVEL, AVENGERS. GIVE ME A MINUTE TO COORDINATE WITH OUR SPECIAL FACILITIES AND I THINK WE MIGHT BE ABLE TO TAKE HER--
EXCUSE ME! EXCUSE ME!
FRANK LARRIKIN, GENERAL COUNSEL, NATIONAL FEDERAL BANK.
THE RG-026 IS THE JOINT PROPERTY OF NATIONAL FEDERAL AND BLACKBIRD INDUSTRIES. I'M AFRAID YOU CANNOT SEIZE OUR PROPERTY WITHOUT A WARRANT.
...I CAN'T TELL IF YOU'RE KIDDING.
MR. LARRIKIN, IF THAT IS THE CASE, I'M SURE YOUR PROPERTY WILL BE RETURNED TO YOU ONCE THE GIRL IS SAFE AND SECURED.

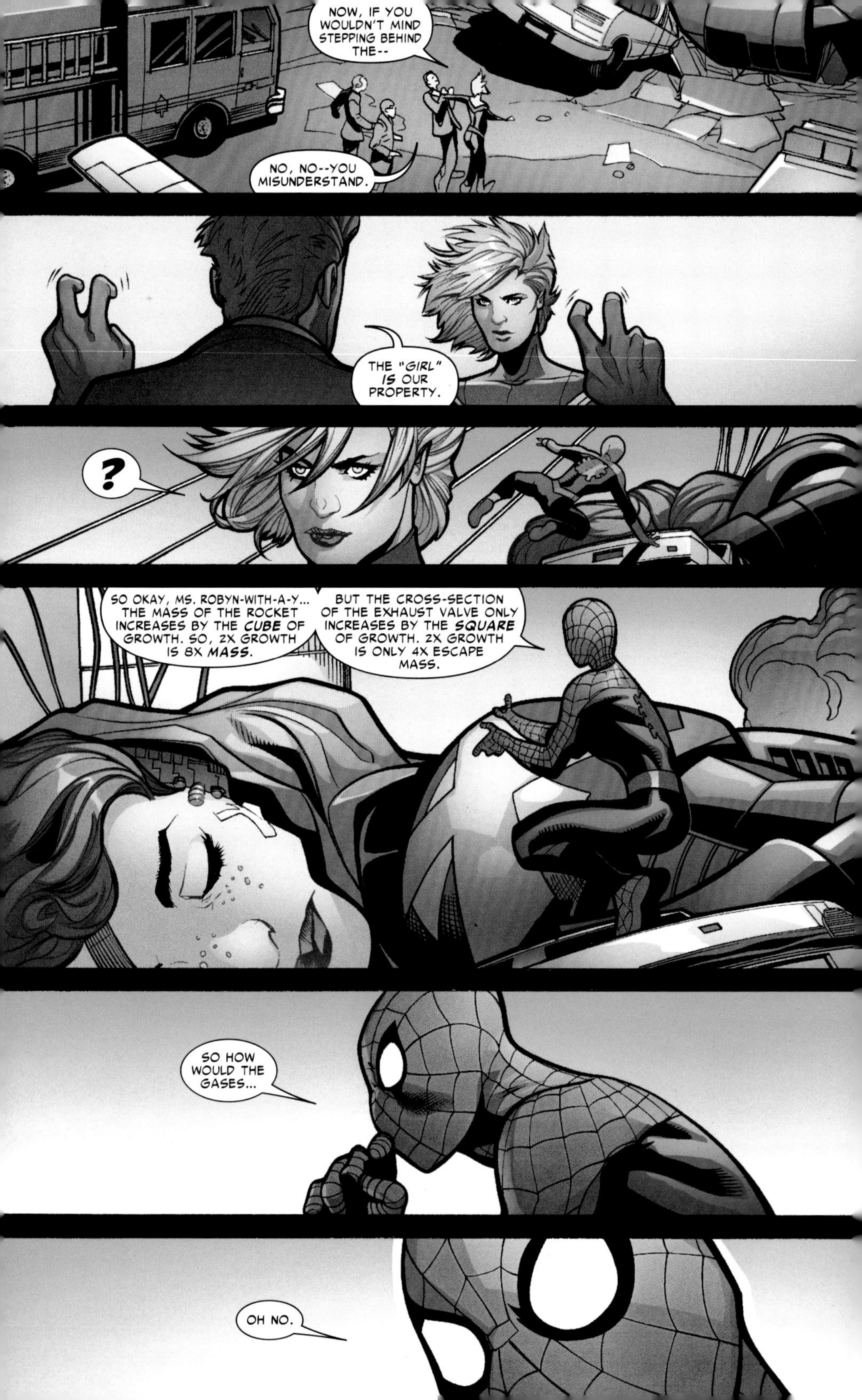
NOW, IF YOU WOULDN'T MIND STEPPING BEHIND THE--
NO, NO--YOU MISUNDERSTAND.
THE "GIRL" IS OUR PROPERTY.
?
SO OKAY, MS. ROBYN-WITH-A-Y... THE MASS OF THE ROCKET INCREASES BY THE CUBE OF GROWTH. SO, 2X GROWTH IS 8X MASS.
BUT THE CROSS-SECTION OF THE EXHAUST VALVE ONLY INCREASES BY THE SQUARE OF GROWTH. 2X GROWTH IS ONLY 4X ESCAPE MASS.
SO HOW WOULD THE GASES...
OH NO.

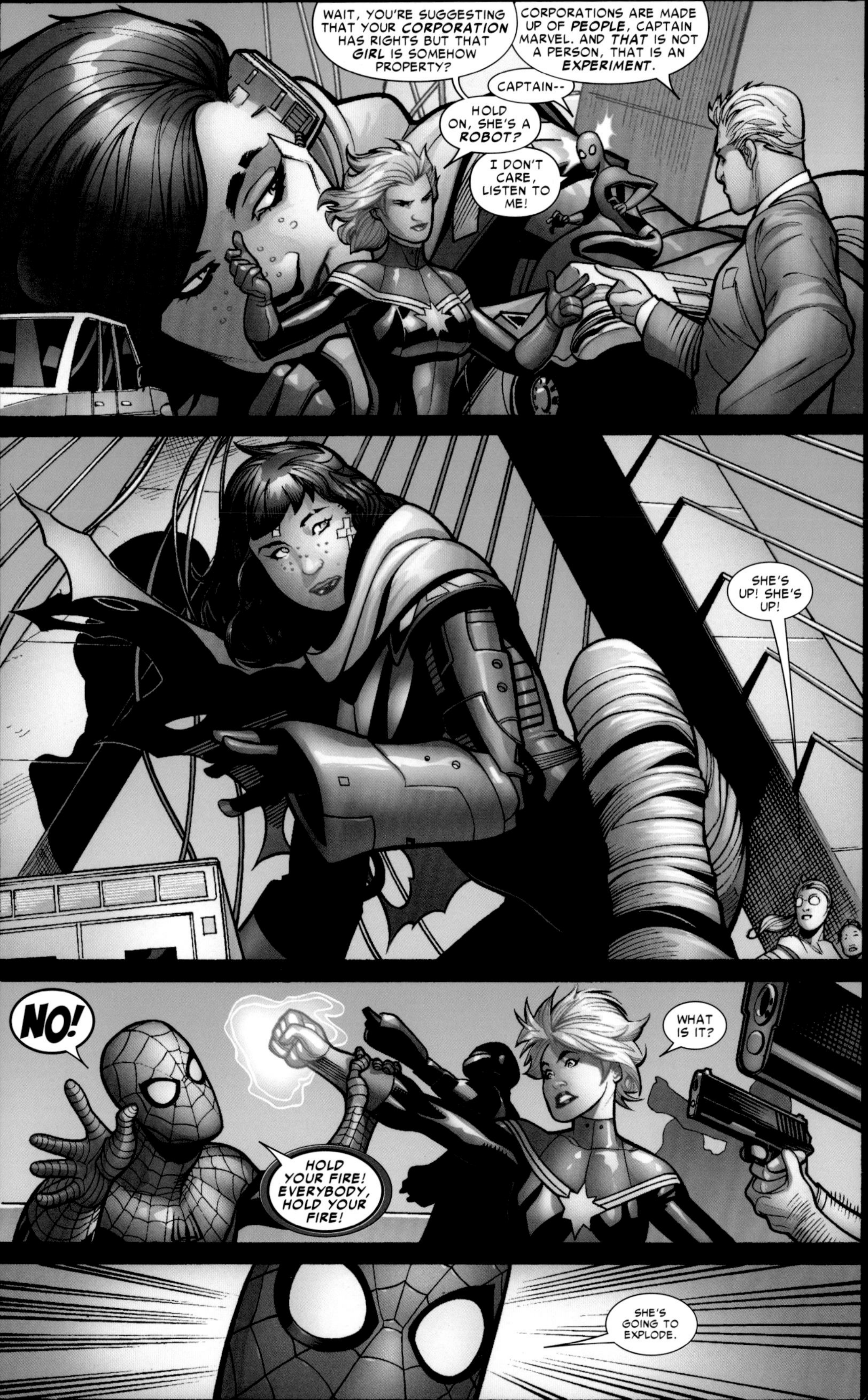
WAIT, YOU'RE SUGGESTING THAT YOUR CORPORATION HAS RIGHTS BUT THAT GIRL IS SOMEHOW PROPERTY?
CORPORATIONS ARE MADE UP OF PEOPLE, CAPTAIN MARVEL. AND THAT IS NOT A PERSON, THAT IS AN EXPERIMENT.
CAPTAIN--
HOLD ON, SHE'S A ROBOT?
I DON'T CARE, LISTEN TO ME!
SHE'S UP! SHE'S UP!
NO!
HOLD YOUR FIRE! EVERYBODY, HOLD YOUR FIRE!
WHAT IS IT?
SHE'S GOING TO EXPLODE.

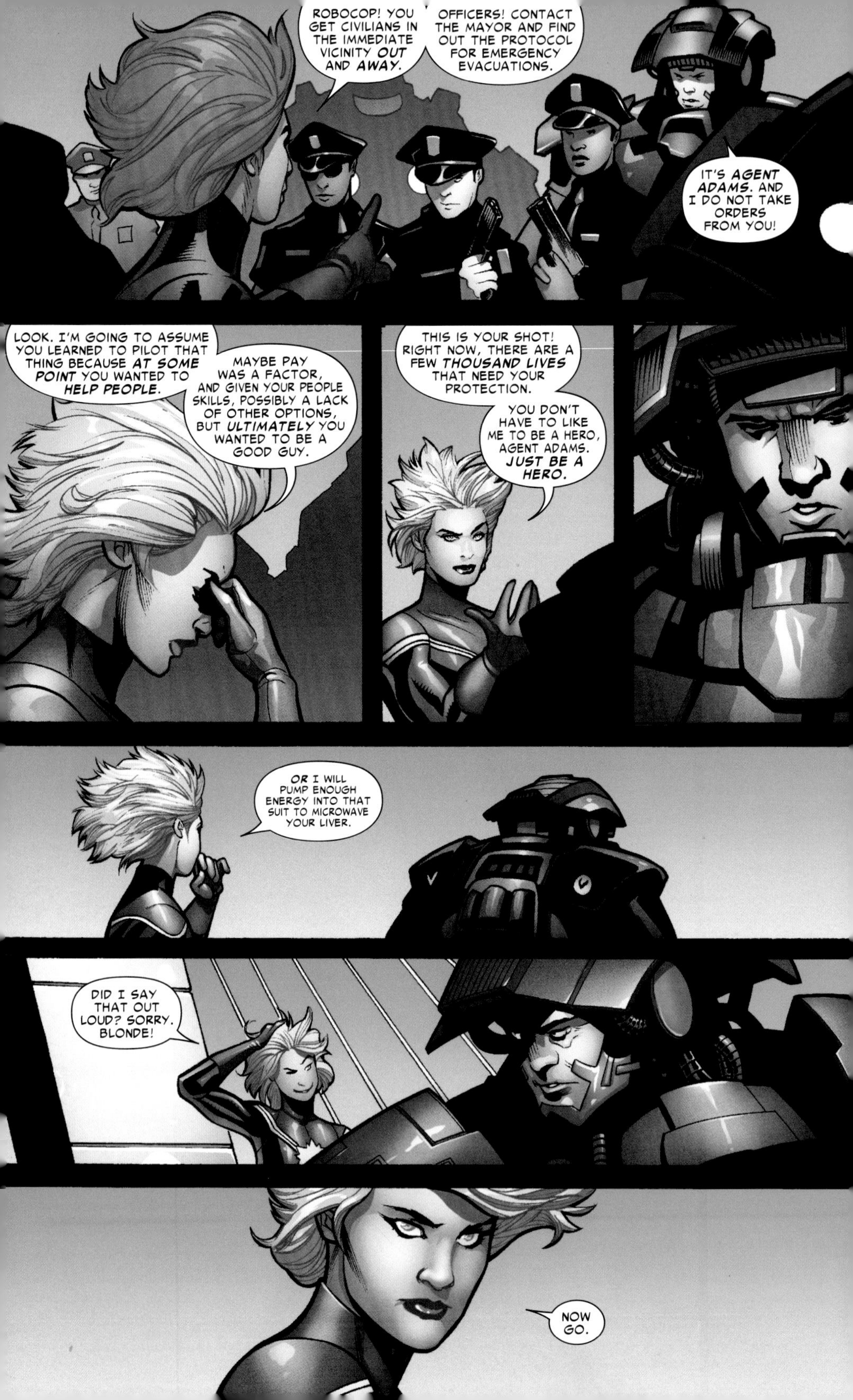
ROBOCOP! YOU GET CIVILIANS IN THE IMMEDIATE VICINITY OUT AND AWAY.
OFFICERS! CONTACT THE MAYOR AND FIND OUT THE PROTOCOL FOR EMERGENCY EVACUATIONS.
IT'S AGENT ADAMS. AND I DO NOT TAKE ORDERS FROM YOU!
LOOK. I'M GOING TO ASSUME YOU LEARNED TO PILOT THAT THING BECAUSE AT SOME POINT YOU WANTED TO HELP PEOPLE.
MAYBE PAY WAS A FACTOR, AND GIVEN YOUR PEOPLE SKILLS, POSSIBLY A LACK OF OTHER OPTIONS, BUT ULTIMATELY YOU WANTED TO BE A GOOD GUY.
THIS IS YOUR SHOT! RIGHT NOW, THERE ARE A FEW THOUSAND LIVES THAT NEED YOUR PROTECTION.
YOU DON'T HAVE TO LIKE ME TO BE A HERO, AGENT ADAMS. JUST BE A HERO.
OR I WILL PUMP ENOUGH ENERGY INTO THAT SUIT TO MICROWAVE YOUR LIVER.
DID I SAY THAT OUT LOUD? SORRY. BLONDE!
NOW GO.

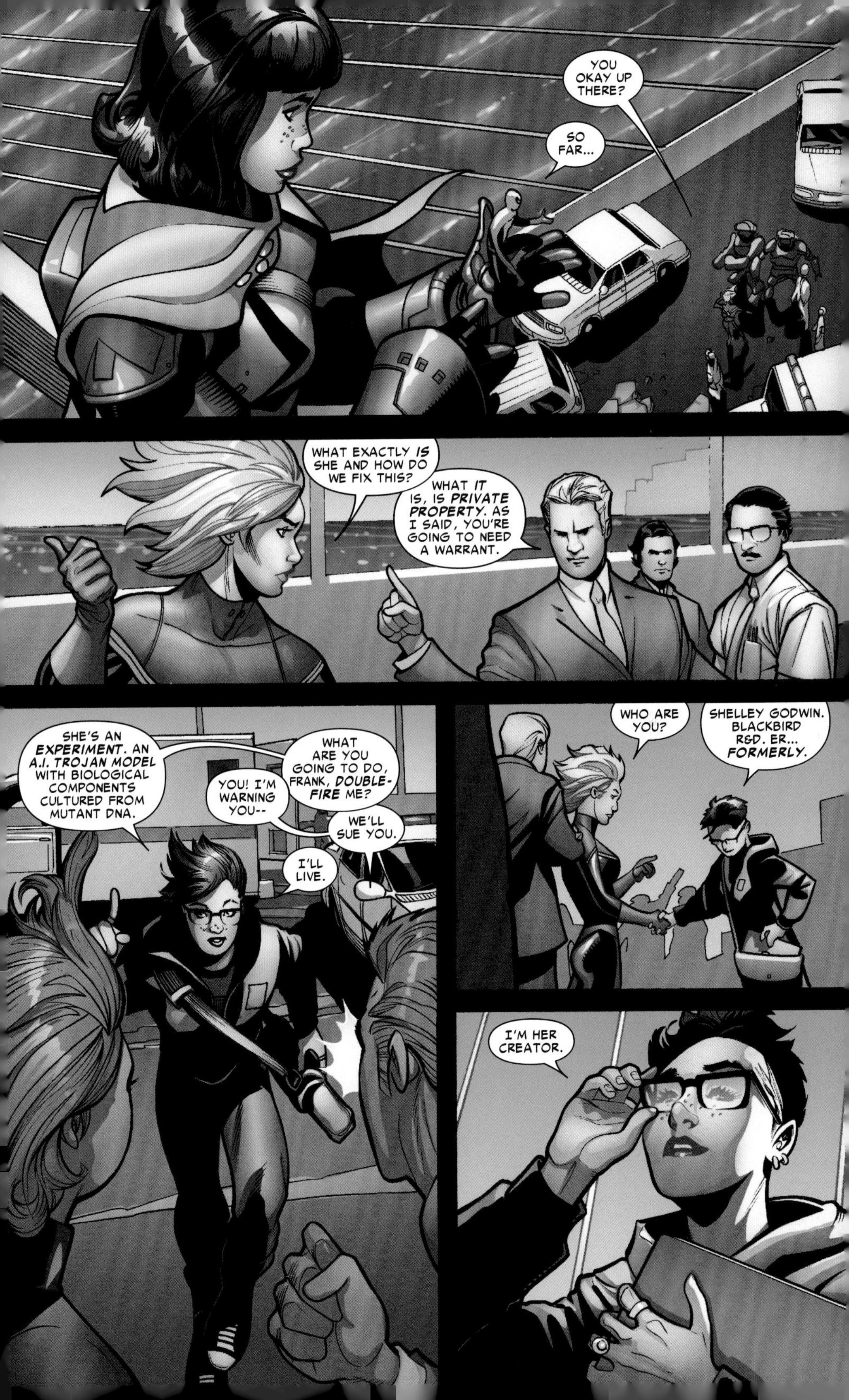
YOU OKAY UP THERE?
SO FAR...
WHAT EXACTLY IS SHE AND HOW DO WE FIX THIS?
WHAT IT IS, IS PRIVATE PROPERTY. AS I SAID, YOU'RE GOING TO NEED A WARRANT.
SHE'S AN EXPERIMENT. AN A.I. TROJAN MODEL WITH BIOLOGICAL COMPONENTS CULTURED FROM MUTANT DNA.
WHAT ARE YOU GOING TO DO, FRANK, DOUBLE-FIRE ME?
YOU! I'M WARNING YOU--
WE'LL SUE YOU.
I'LL LIVE.
WHO ARE YOU?
SHELLEY GODWIN. BLACKBIRD R&D. ER... FORMERLY.
I'M HER CREATOR.

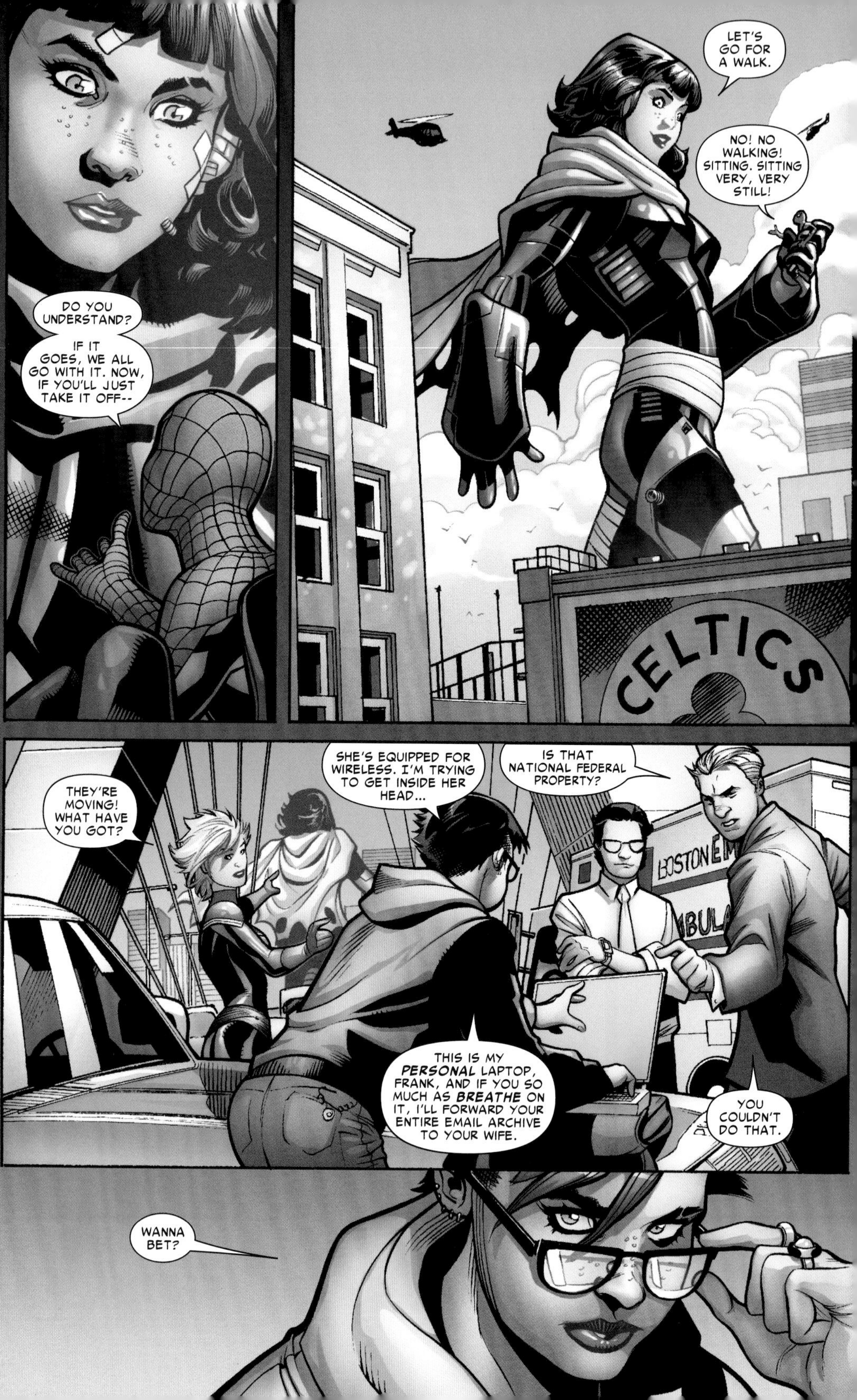
DO YOU UNDERSTAND?
IF IT GOES, WE ALL GO WITH IT. NOW, IF YOU'LL JUST TAKE IT OFF--
LET'S GO FOR A WALK.
NO! NO WALKING! SITTING. SITTING VERY, VERY STILL!
CELTICS
THEY'RE MOVING! WHAT HAVE YOU GOT?
SHE'S EQUIPPED FOR WIRELESS. I'M TRYING TO GET INSIDE HER HEAD...
IS THAT NATIONAL FEDERAL PROPERTY?
BOSTON E
THIS IS MY PERSONAL LAPTOP, FRANK, AND IF YOU SO MUCH AS BREATHE ON IT, I'LL FORWARD YOUR ENTIRE EMAIL ARCHIVE TO YOUR WIFE.
YOU COULDN'T DO THAT.
WANNA BET?

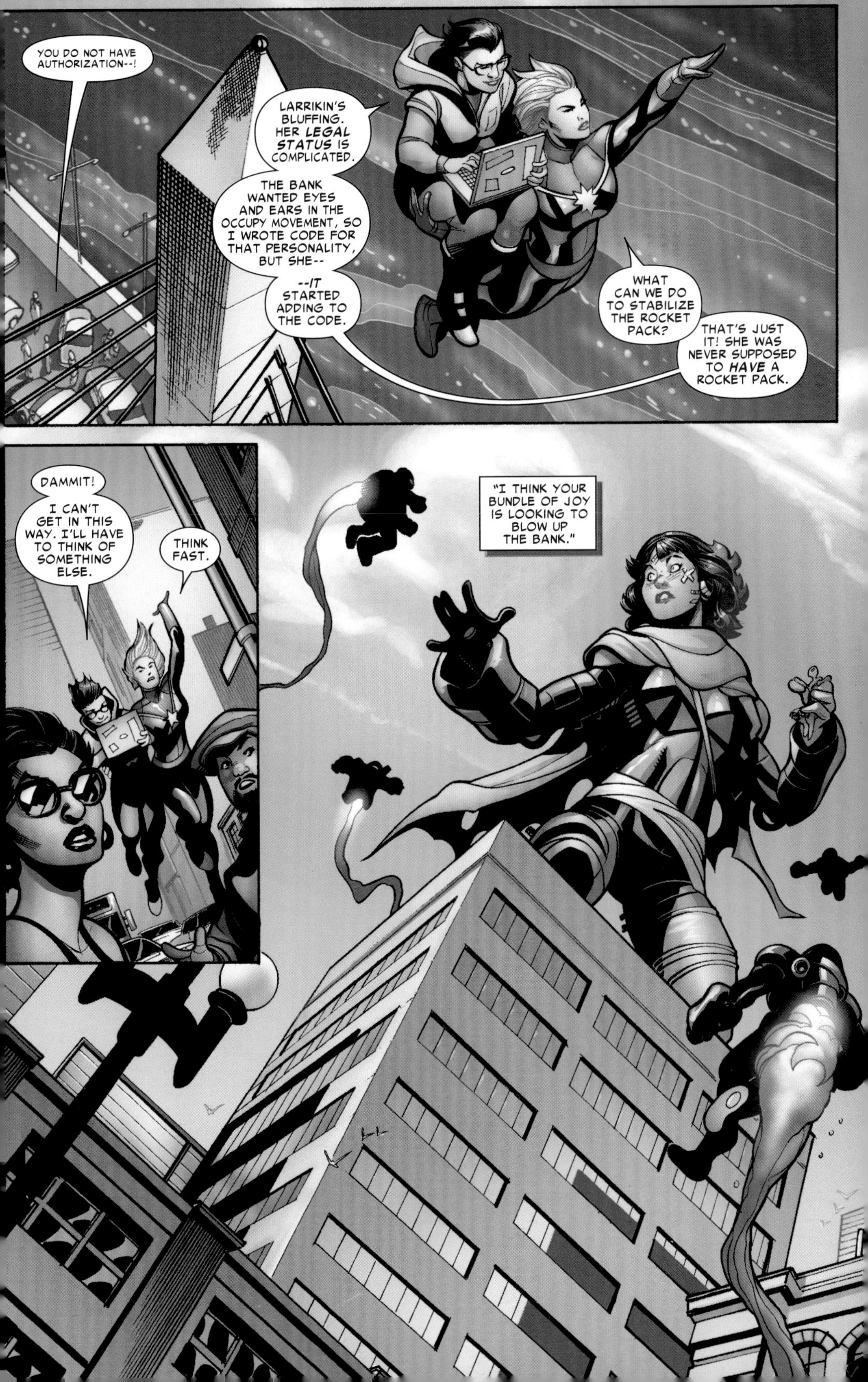
YOU DO NOT HAVE AUTHORIZATION--!
LARRIKIN'S BLUFFING. HER LEGAL STATUS IS COMPLICATED.
THE BANK WANTED EYES AND EARS IN THE OCCUPY MOVEMENT, SO I WROTE CODE FOR THAT PERSONALITY, BUT SHE--
--IT STARTED ADDING TO THE CODE.
WHAT CAN WE DO TO STABILIZE THE ROCKET PACK?
THAT'S JUST IT! SHE WAS NEVER SUPPOSED TO HAVE A ROCKET PACK.
DAMMIT!
I CAN'T GET IN THIS WAY. I'LL HAVE TO THINK OF SOMETHING ELSE.
THINK FAST.
"I THINK YOUR BUNDLE OF JOY IS LOOKING TO BLOW UP THE BANK."

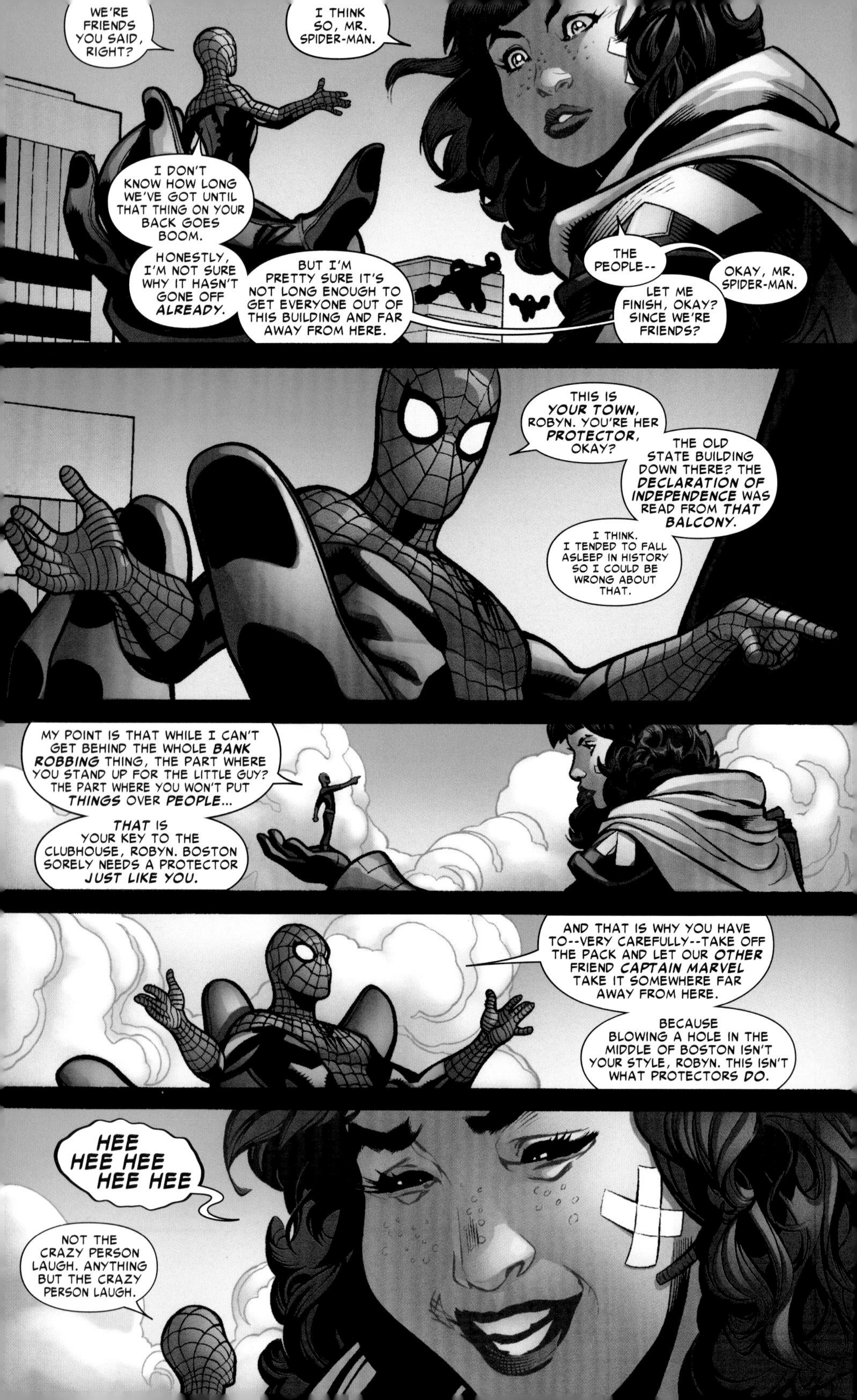

WE'RE FRIENDS YOU SAID, RIGHT?
I THINK SO, MR. SPIDER-MAN.
I DON'T KNOW HOW LONG WE'VE GOT UNTIL THAT THING ON YOUR BACK GOES BOOM.
HONESTLY, I'M NOT SURE WHY IT HASN'T GONE OFF ALREADY.
BUT I'M PRETTY SURE IT'S NOT LONG ENOUGH TO GET EVERYONE OUT OF THIS BUILDING AND FAR AWAY FROM HERE.
THE PEOPLE--
OKAY, MR. SPIDER-MAN.
LET ME FINISH, OKAY? SINCE WE'RE FRIENDS?
THIS IS YOUR TOWN, ROBYN. YOU'RE HER PROTECTOR, OKAY?
THE OLD STATE BUILDING DOWN THERE? THE DECLARATION OF INDEPENDENCE WAS READ FROM THAT BALCONY.
I THINK. I TENDED TO FALL ASLEEP IN HISTORY SO I COULD BE WRONG ABOUT THAT.
MY POINT IS THAT WHILE I CAN'T GET BEHIND THE WHOLE BANK ROBBING THING, THE PART WHERE YOU STAND UP FOR THE LITTLE GUY? THE PART WHERE YOU WON'T PUT THINGS OVER PEOPLE...
THAT IS YOUR KEY TO THE CLUBHOUSE, ROBYN. BOSTON SORELY NEEDS A PROTECTOR JUST LIKE YOU.
AND THAT IS WHY YOU HAVE TO--VERY CAREFULLY--TAKE OFF THE PACK AND LET OUR OTHER FRIEND CAPTAIN MARVEL TAKE IT SOMEWHERE FAR AWAY FROM HERE.
BECAUSE BLOWING A HOLE IN THE MIDDLE OF BOSTON ISN'T YOUR STYLE, ROBYN. THIS ISN'T WHAT PROTECTORS DO.
HEE HEE HEE HEE HEE
NOT THE CRAZY PERSON LAUGH. ANYTHING BUT THE CRAZY PERSON LAUGH.

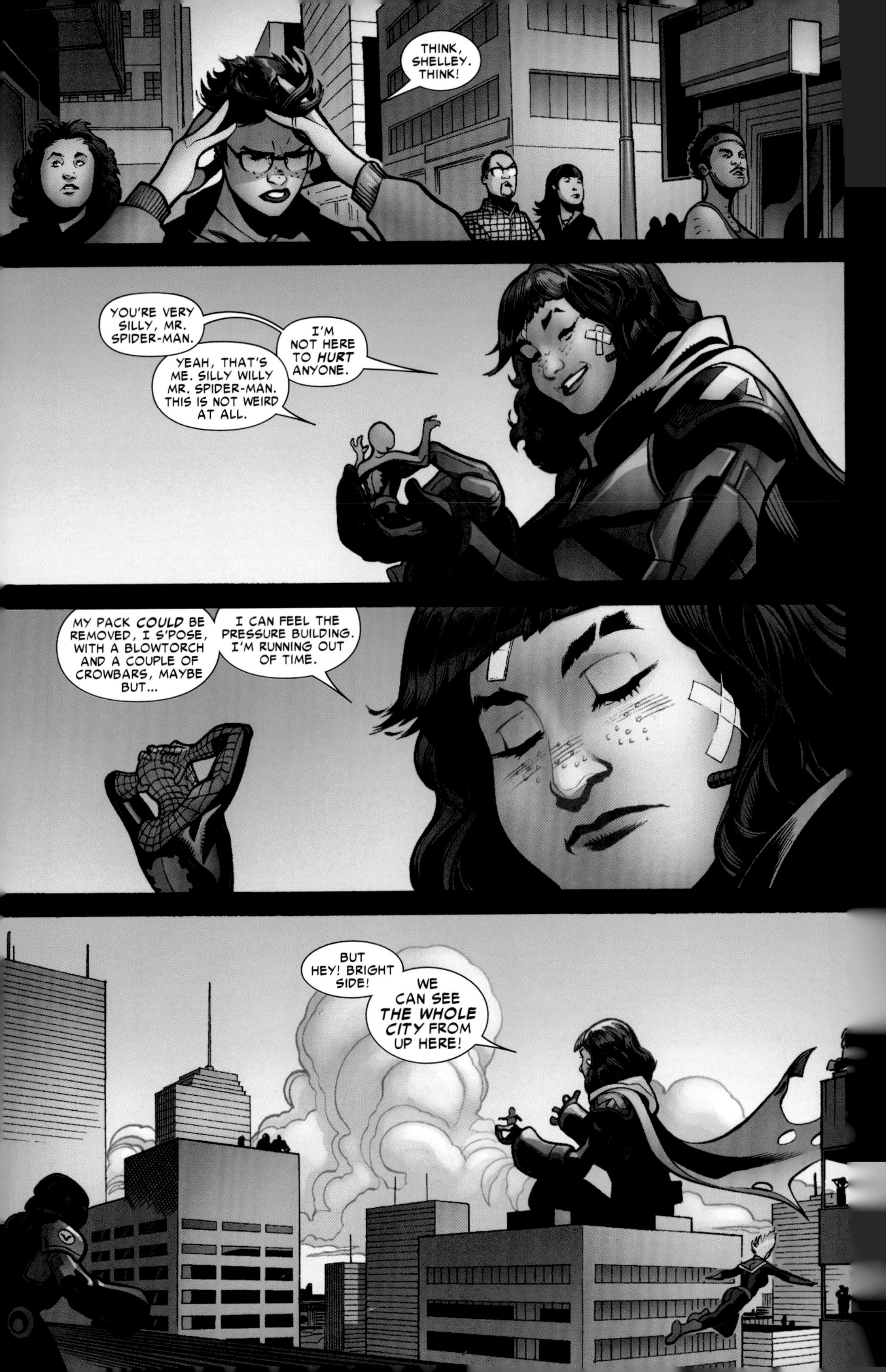

THINK, SHELLEY. THINK!
YOU'RE VERY SILLY, MR. SPIDER-MAN.
I'M NOT HERE TO HURT ANYONE.
YEAH, THAT'S ME. SILLY WILLY MR. SPIDER-MAN. THIS IS NOT WEIRD AT ALL.
MY PACK COULD BE REMOVED, I S'POSE, WITH A BLOWTORCH AND A COUPLE OF CROWBARS, MAYBE BUT...
I CAN FEEL THE PRESSURE BUILDING. I'M RUNNING OUT OF TIME.
BUT HEY! BRIGHT SIDE!
WE CAN SEE THE WHOLE CITY FROM UP HERE!

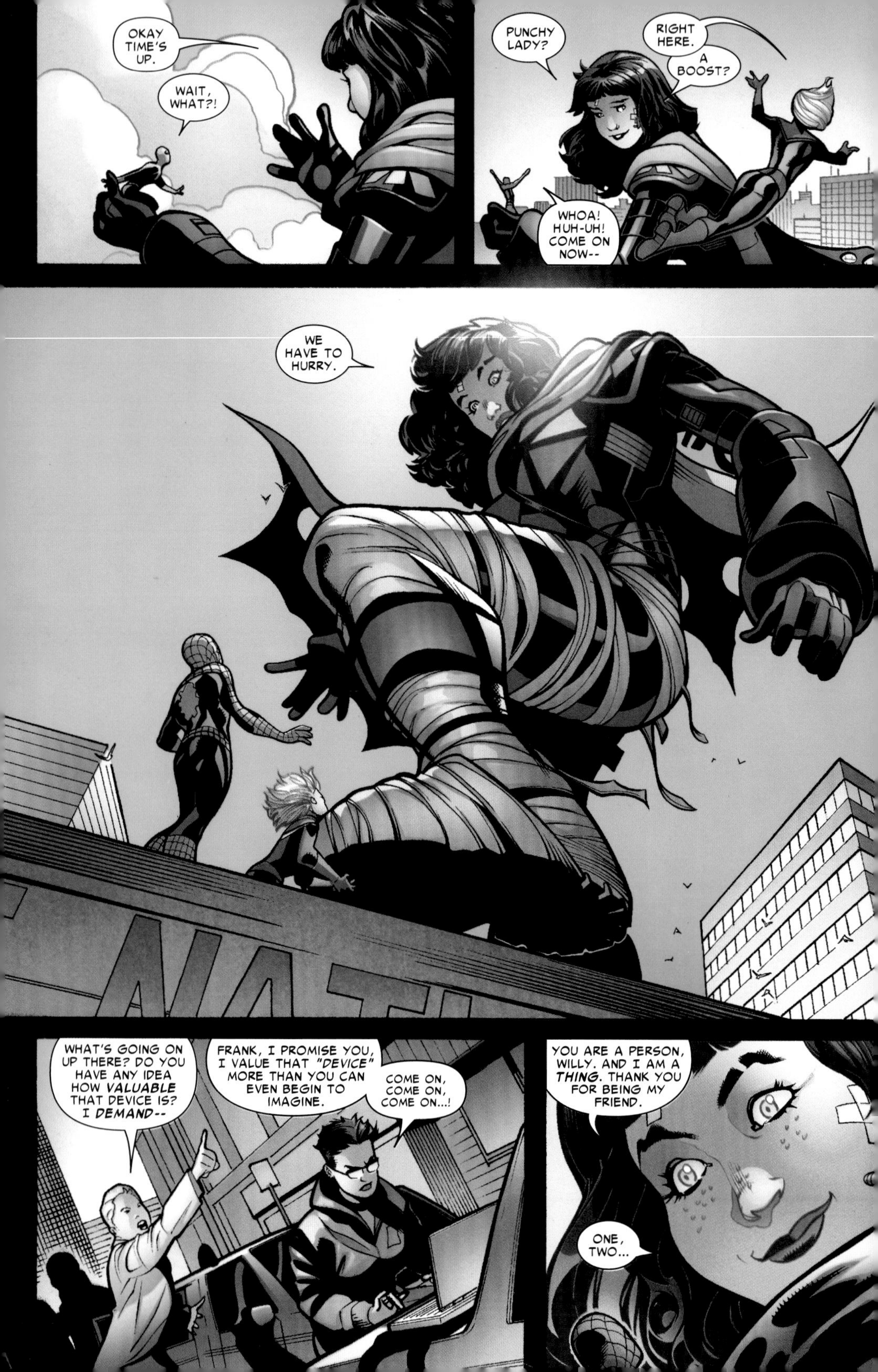
OKAY TIME'S UP.
WAIT, WHAT?!
PUNCHY LADY?
RIGHT HERE.
A BOOST?
WHOA! HUH-UH! COME ON NOW--
WE HAVE TO HURRY.
WHAT'S GOING ON UP THERE? DO YOU HAVE ANY IDEA HOW VALUABLE THAT DEVICE IS? I DEMAND--
FRANK, I PROMISE YOU, I VALUE THAT "DEVICE" MORE THAN YOU CAN EVEN BEGIN TO IMAGINE.
COME ON, COME ON, COME ON...!
YOU ARE A PERSON, WILLY. AND I AM A THING. THANK YOU FOR BEING MY FRIEND.
ONE, TWO...

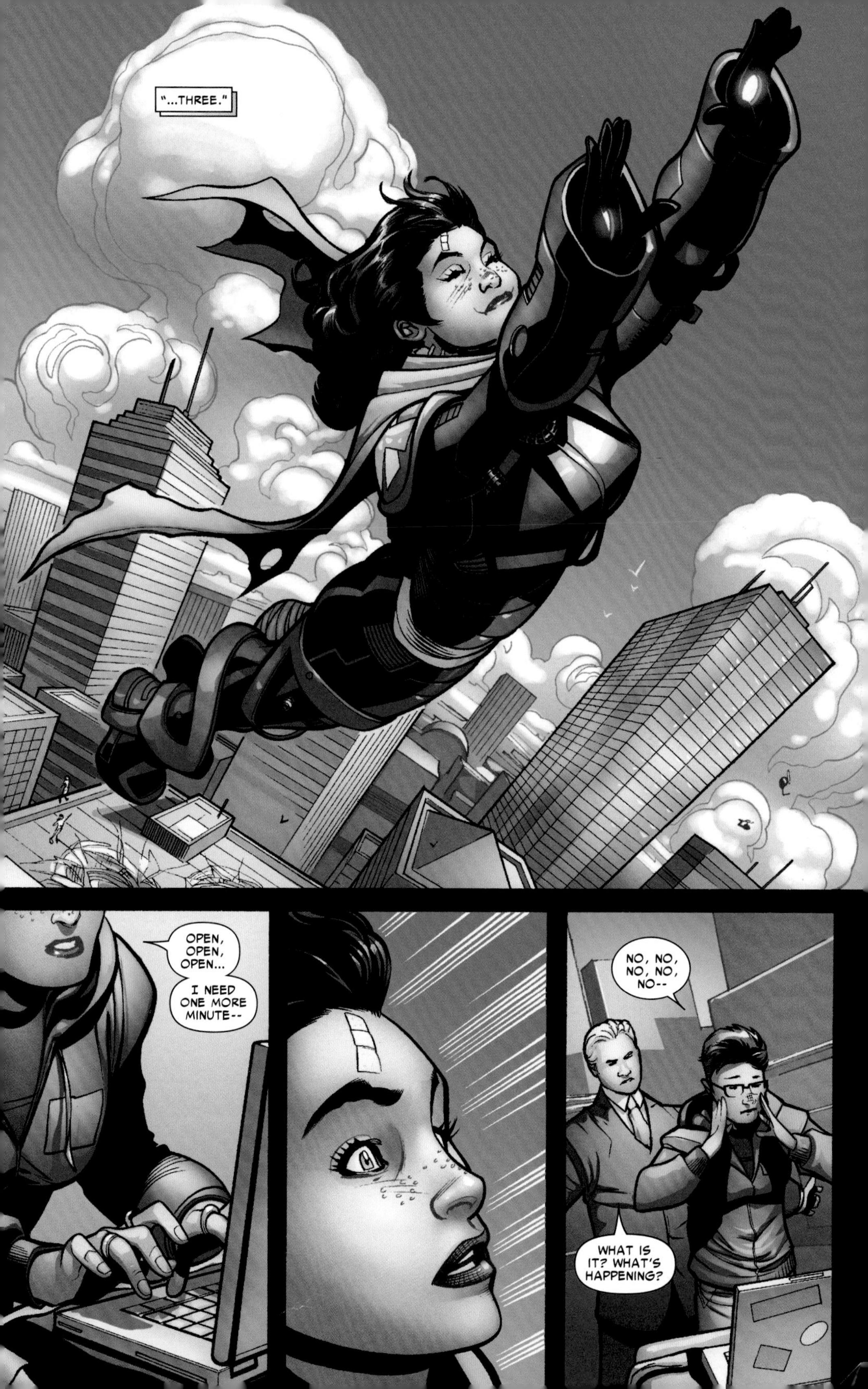
"...THREE."
OPEN, OPEN, OPEN...
I NEED ONE MORE MINUTE--
NO, NO, NO, NO, NO--
WHAT IS IT? WHAT'S HAPPENING?

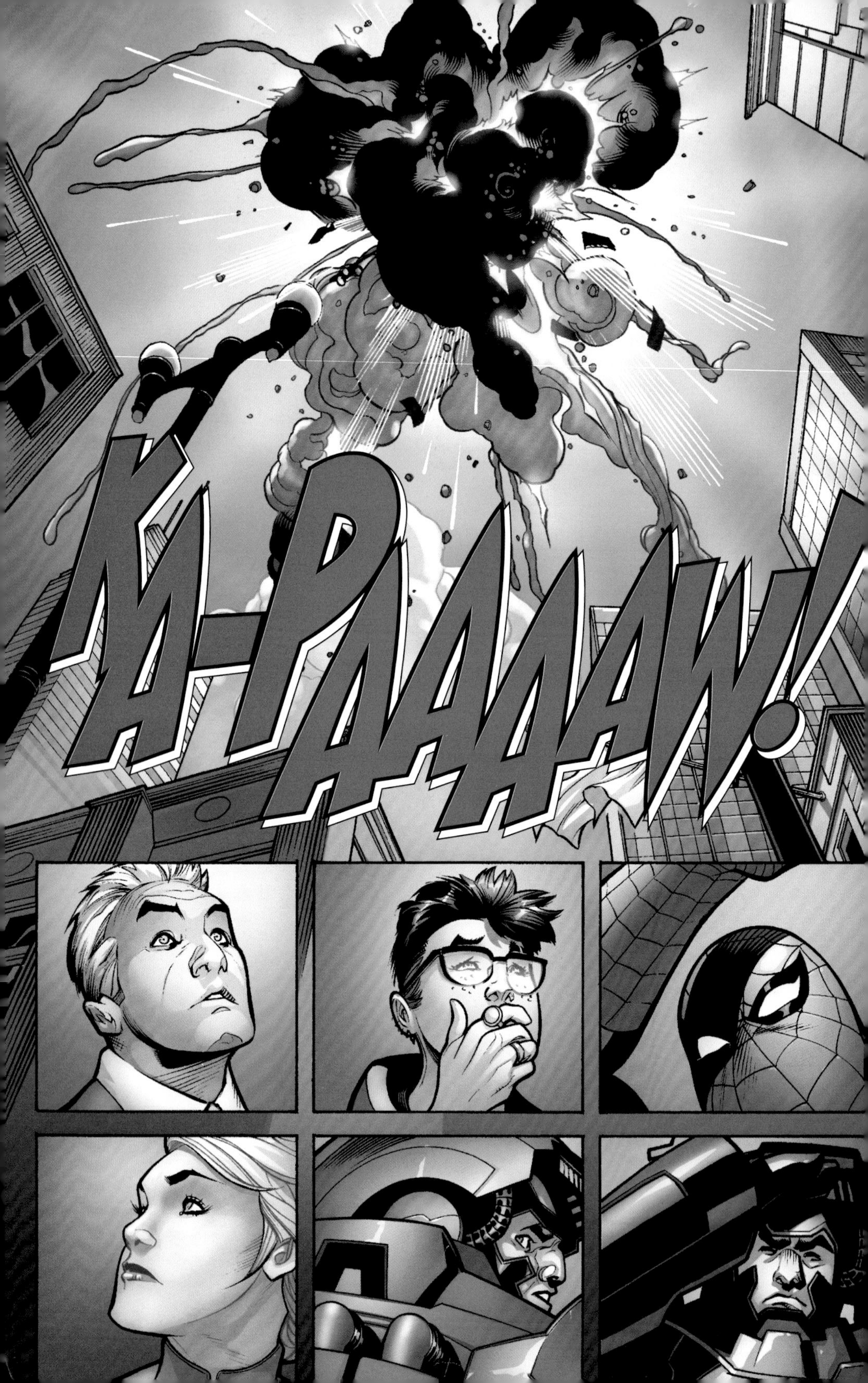
KA-PAAAAW!

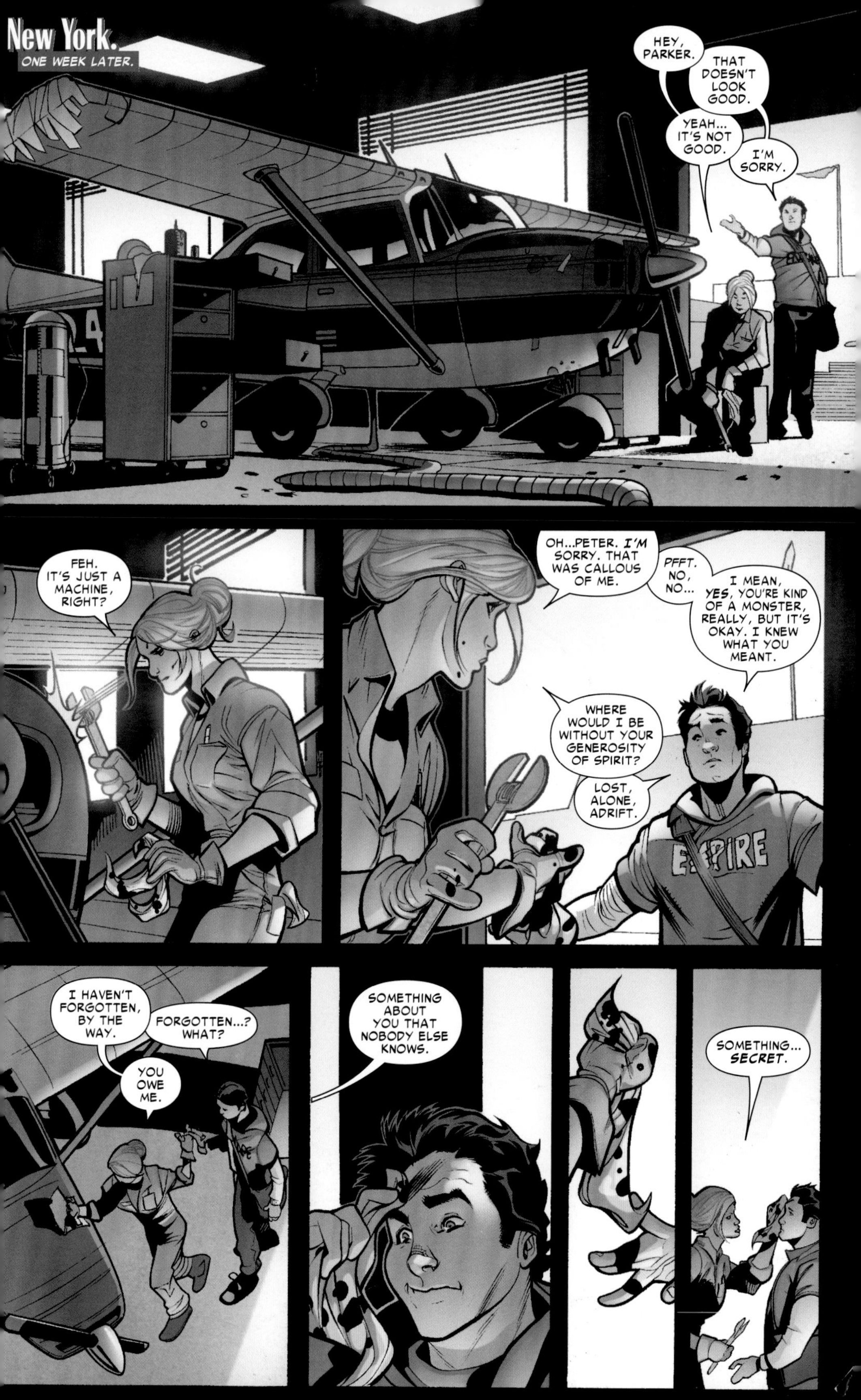
New York.
ONE WEEK LATER.
HEY, PARKER.
THAT DOESN'T LOOK GOOD.
YEAH... IT'S NOT GOOD.
I'M SORRY.
FEH. IT'S JUST A MACHINE, RIGHT?
OH...PETER. I'M SORRY. THAT WAS CALLOUS OF ME.
PFFT. NO, NO...
I MEAN, YES, YOU'RE KIND OF A MONSTER, REALLY, BUT IT'S OKAY. I KNEW WHAT YOU MEANT.
WHERE WOULD I BE WITHOUT YOUR GENEROSITY OF SPIRIT?
LOST, ALONE, ADRIFT.
EMPIRE
I HAVEN'T FORGOTTEN, BY THE WAY.
FORGOTTEN...? WHAT?
YOU OWE ME.
SOMETHING ABOUT YOU THAT NOBODY ELSE KNOWS.
SOMETHING... SECRET.

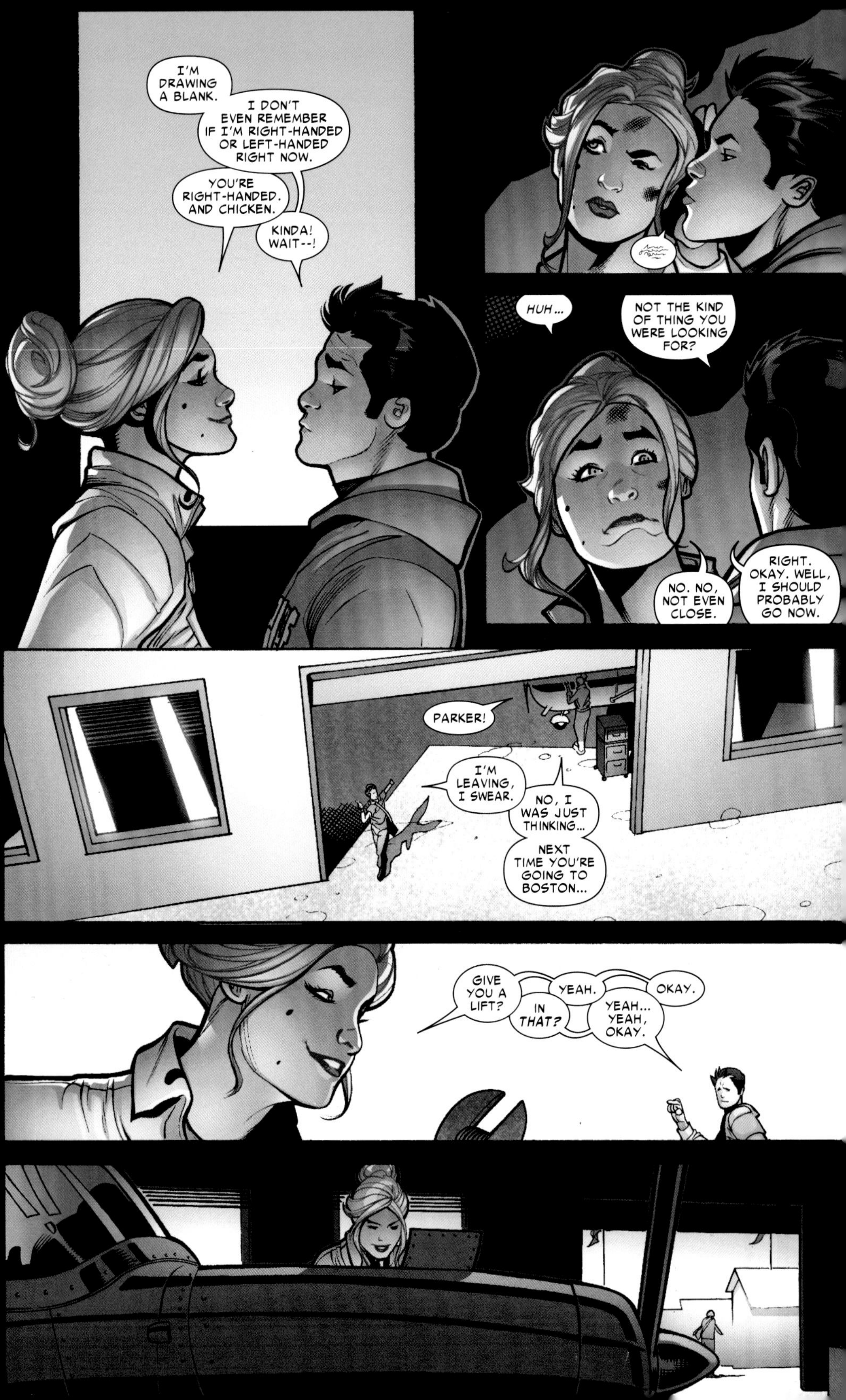
I'M DRAWING A BLANK.
I DON'T EVEN REMEMBER IF I'M RIGHT-HANDED OR LEFT-HANDED RIGHT NOW.
YOU'RE RIGHT-HANDED. AND CHICKEN.
KINDA! WAIT--!
HUH...
NOT THE KIND OF THING YOU WERE LOOKING FOR?
NO. NO, NOT EVEN CLOSE.
RIGHT. OKAY. WELL, I SHOULD PROBABLY GO NOW.
PARKER!
I'M LEAVING, I SWEAR.
NO, I WAS JUST THINKING...
NEXT TIME YOU'RE GOING TO BOSTON...
GIVE YOU A LIFT?
IN THAT?
YEAH.
YEAH... YEAH, OKAY.
OKAY.

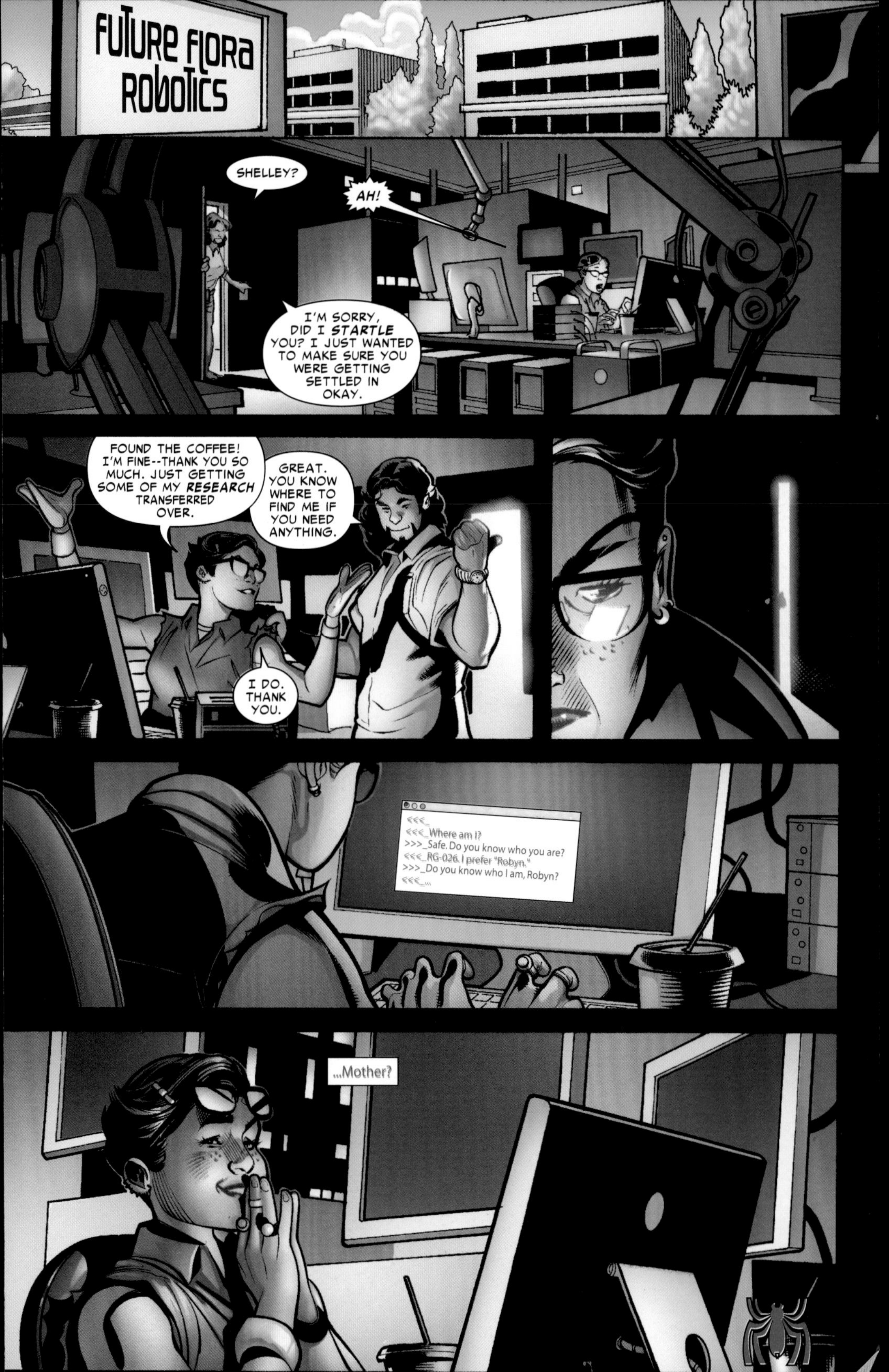
FUTURE FLORA ROBOTICS
SHELLEY?
AH!
I'M SORRY, DID I STARTLE YOU? I JUST WANTED TO MAKE SURE YOU WERE GETTING SETTLED IN OKAY.
FOUND THE COFFEE! I'M FINE--THANK YOU SO MUCH. JUST GETTING SOME OF MY RESEARCH TRANSFERRED OVER.
GREAT. YOU KNOW WHERE TO FIND ME IF YOU NEED ANYTHING.
I DO. THANK YOU.
<<<_
<<<_Where am I?
>>>_Safe. Do you know who you are?
<<<_RG-026. I prefer "Robyn."
>>>_Do you know who I am, Robyn?
<<<_...
...Mother?

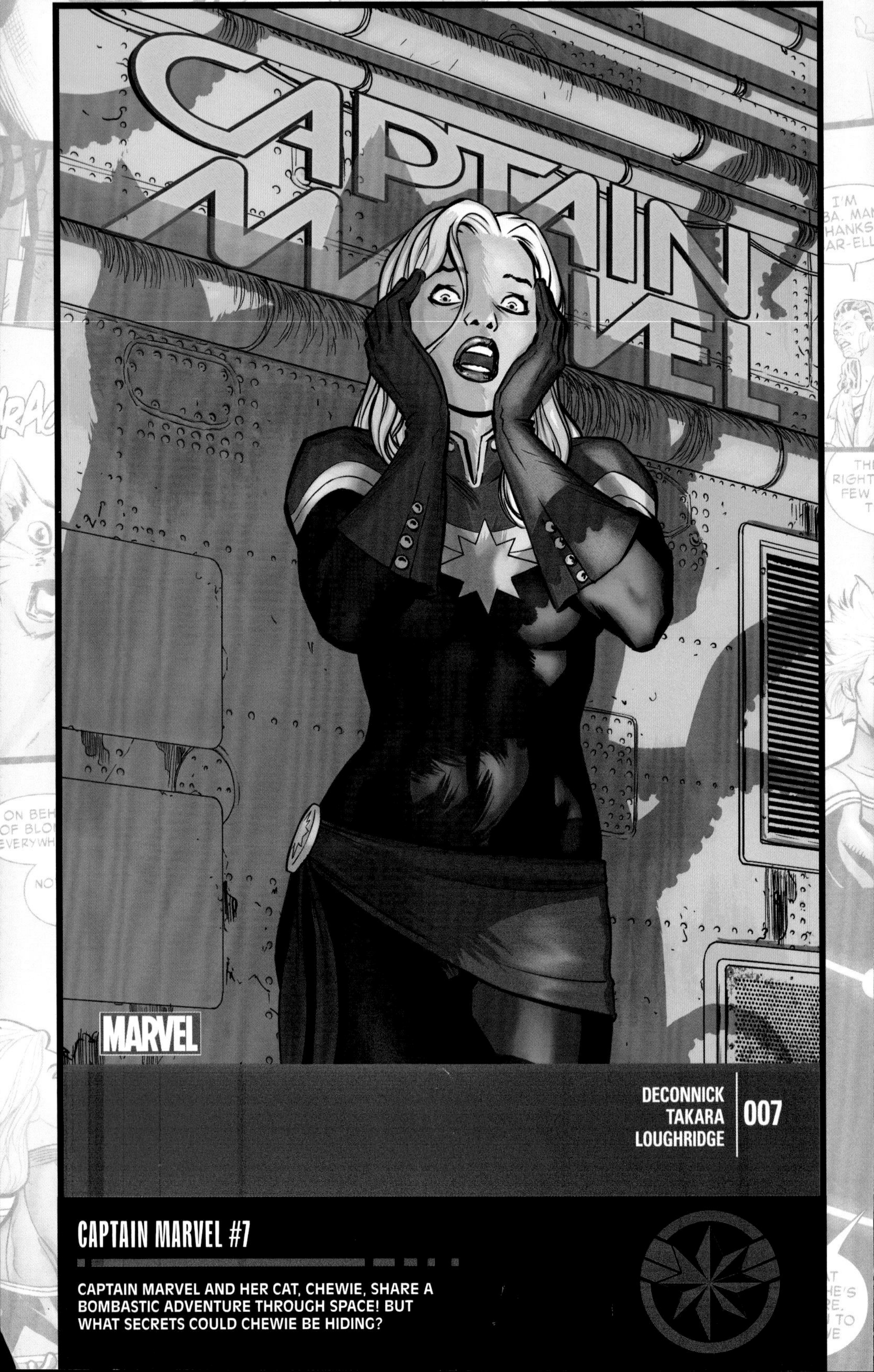
CAPTAIN MARVEL
MARVEL
DECONNICK
TAKARA
LOUGHRIDGE
007

CAPTAIN MARVEL #7

CAPTAIN MARVEL AND HER CAT, CHEWIE, SHARE A BOMBASTIC ADVENTURE THROUGH SPACE! BUT WHAT SECRETS COULD CHEWIE BE HIDING?

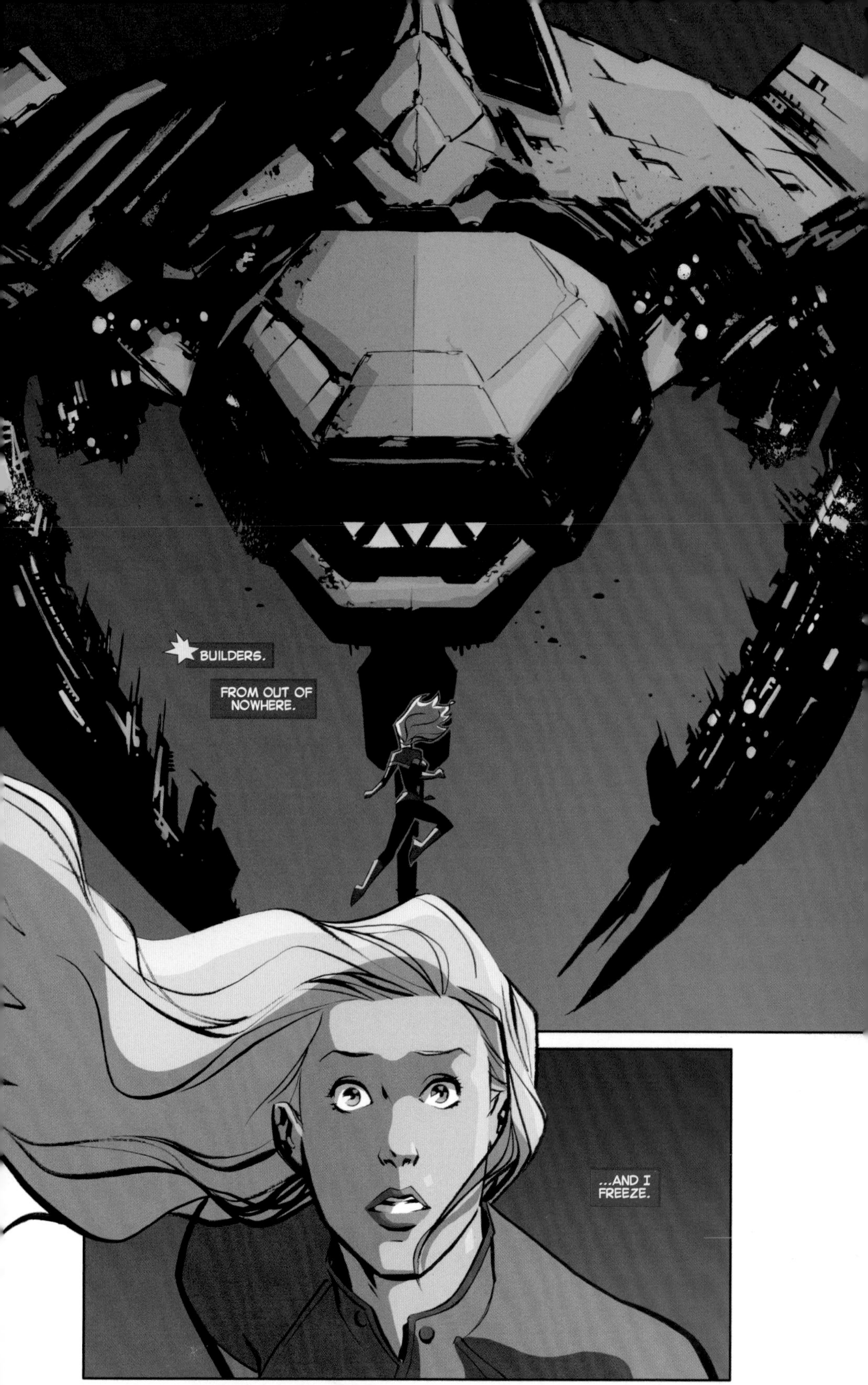

BUILDERS.
FROM OUT OF NOWHERE.
...AND I FREEZE.

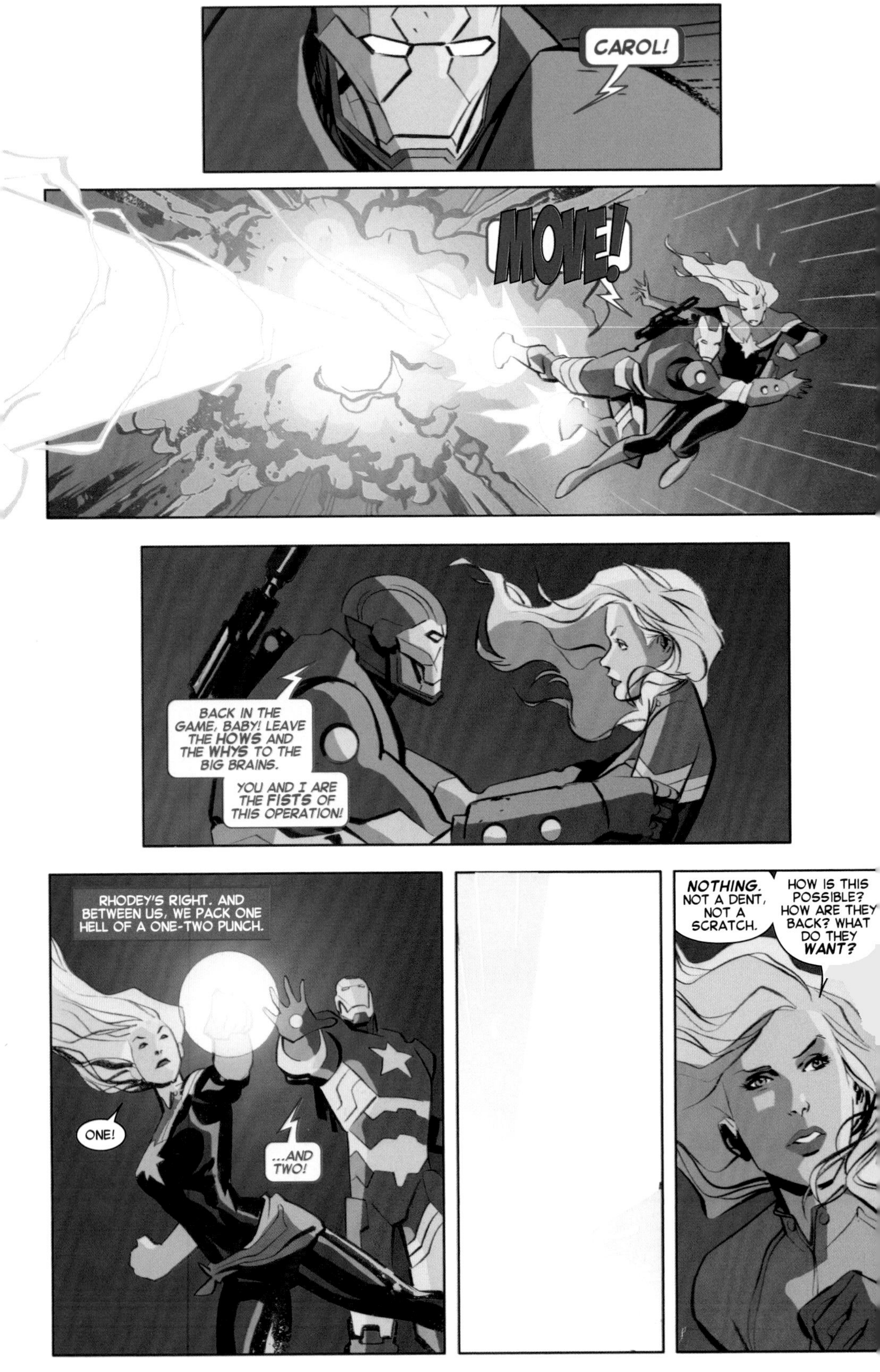
CAROL!
MOVE!
BACK IN THE GAME, BABY! LEAVE THE HOWS AND THE WHYS TO THE BIG BRAINS.
YOU AND I ARE THE FISTS OF THIS OPERATION!
RHODEY'S RIGHT. AND BETWEEN US, WE PACK ONE HELL OF A ONE-TWO PUNCH.
ONE!
...AND TWO!
NOTHING. NOT A DENT, NOT A SCRATCH.
HOW IS THIS POSSIBLE? HOW ARE THEY BACK? WHAT DO THEY WANT?

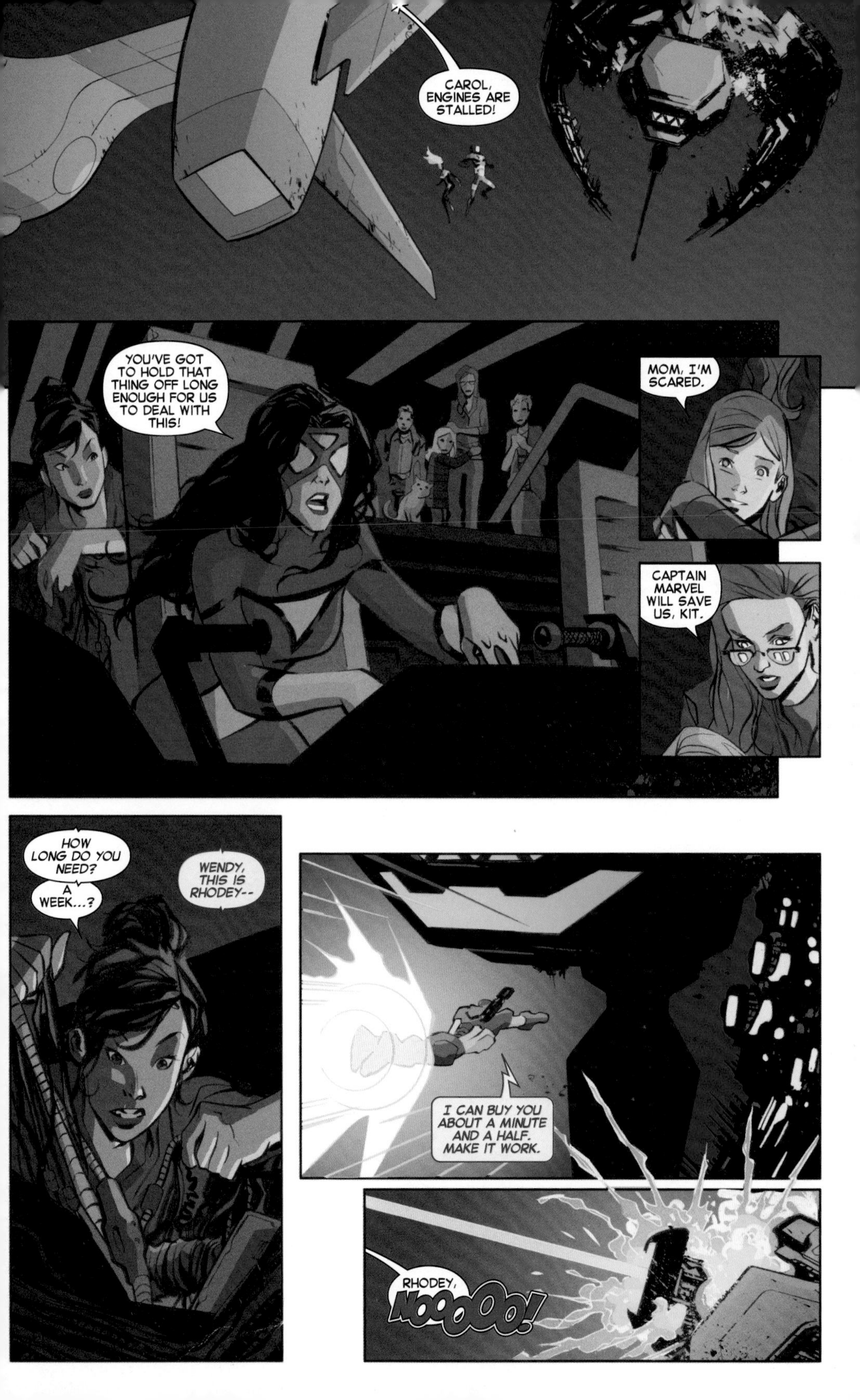
CAROL, ENGINES ARE STALLED!
YOU'VE GOT TO HOLD THAT THING OFF LONG ENOUGH FOR US TO DEAL WITH THIS!
MOM, I'M SCARED.
CAPTAIN MARVEL WILL SAVE US, KIT.
HOW LONG DO YOU NEED?
A WEEK...?
WENDY, THIS IS RHODEY--
I CAN BUY YOU ABOUT A MINUTE AND A HALF. MAKE IT WORK.
RHODEY, NOOOOOO!

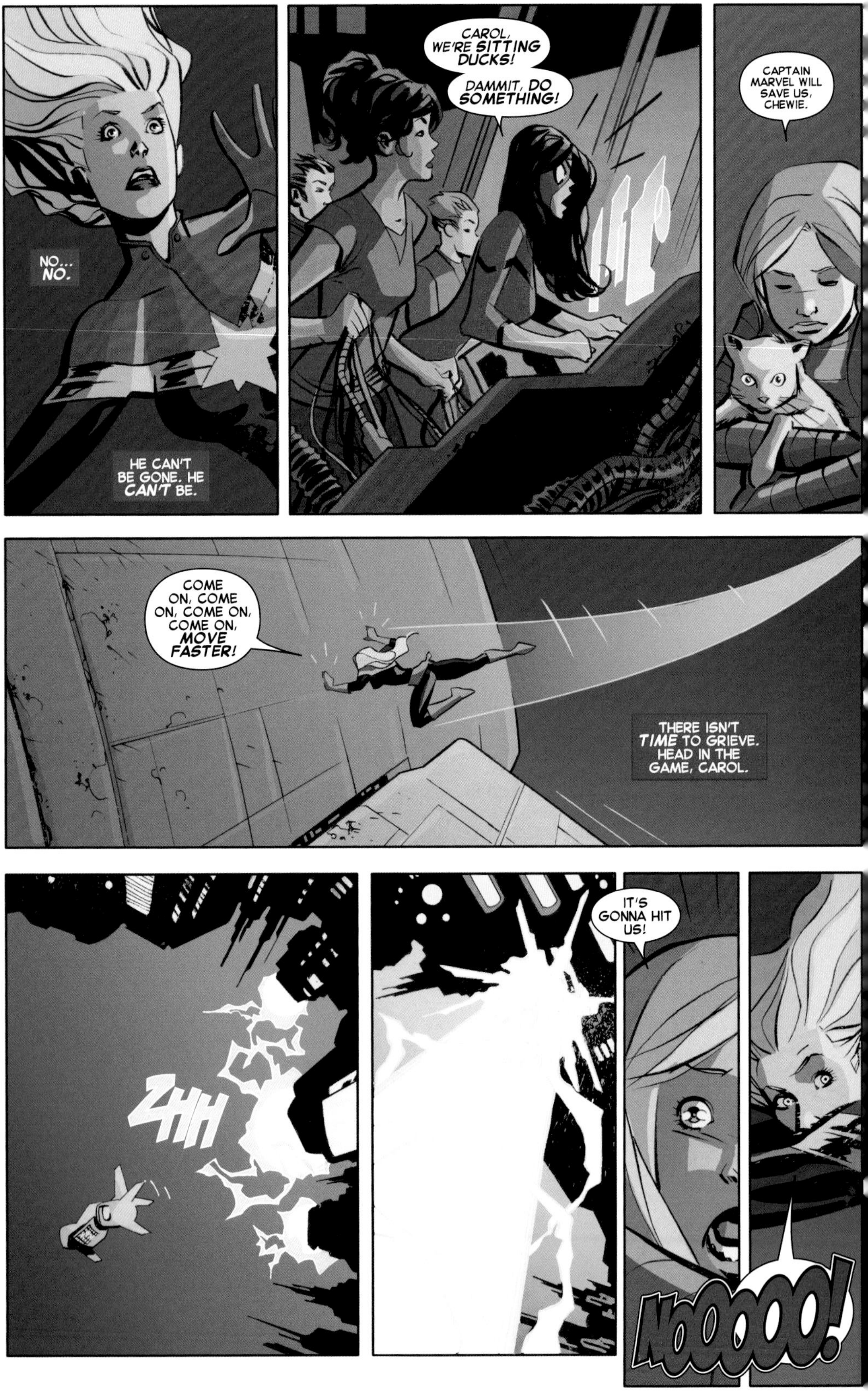
NO... NO.
HE CAN'T BE GONE. HE CAN'T BE.
CAROL, WE'RE SITTING DUCKS!
DAMMIT, DO SOMETHING!
CAPTAIN MARVEL WILL SAVE US, CHEWIE.
COME ON, COME ON, COME ON, COME ON, MOVE FASTER!
THERE ISN'T TIME TO GRIEVE. HEAD IN THE GAME, CAROL.
ZHH
IT'S GONNA HIT US!
NOOOOO!

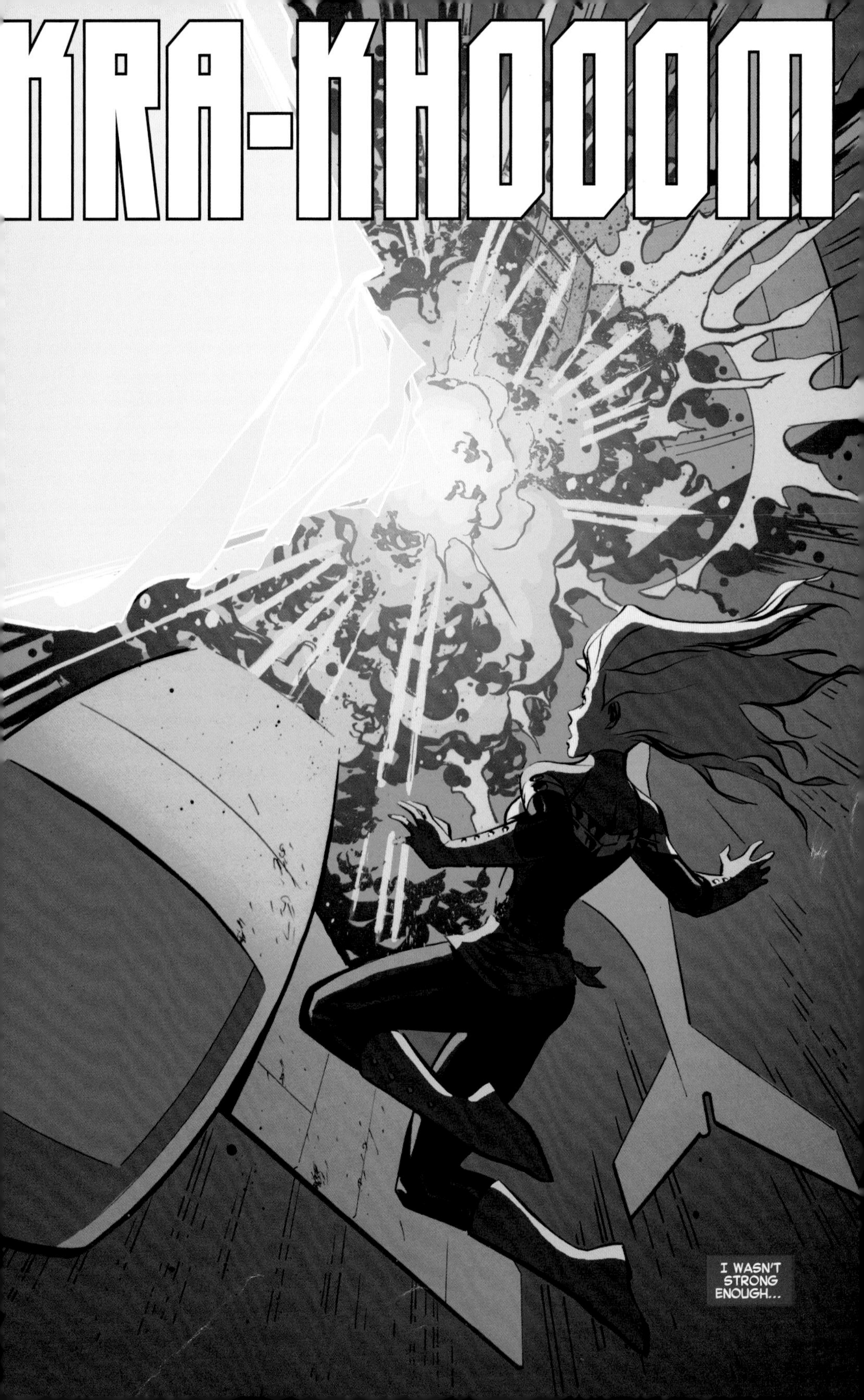
KRA-KHOOOM
I WASN'T STRONG ENOUGH...

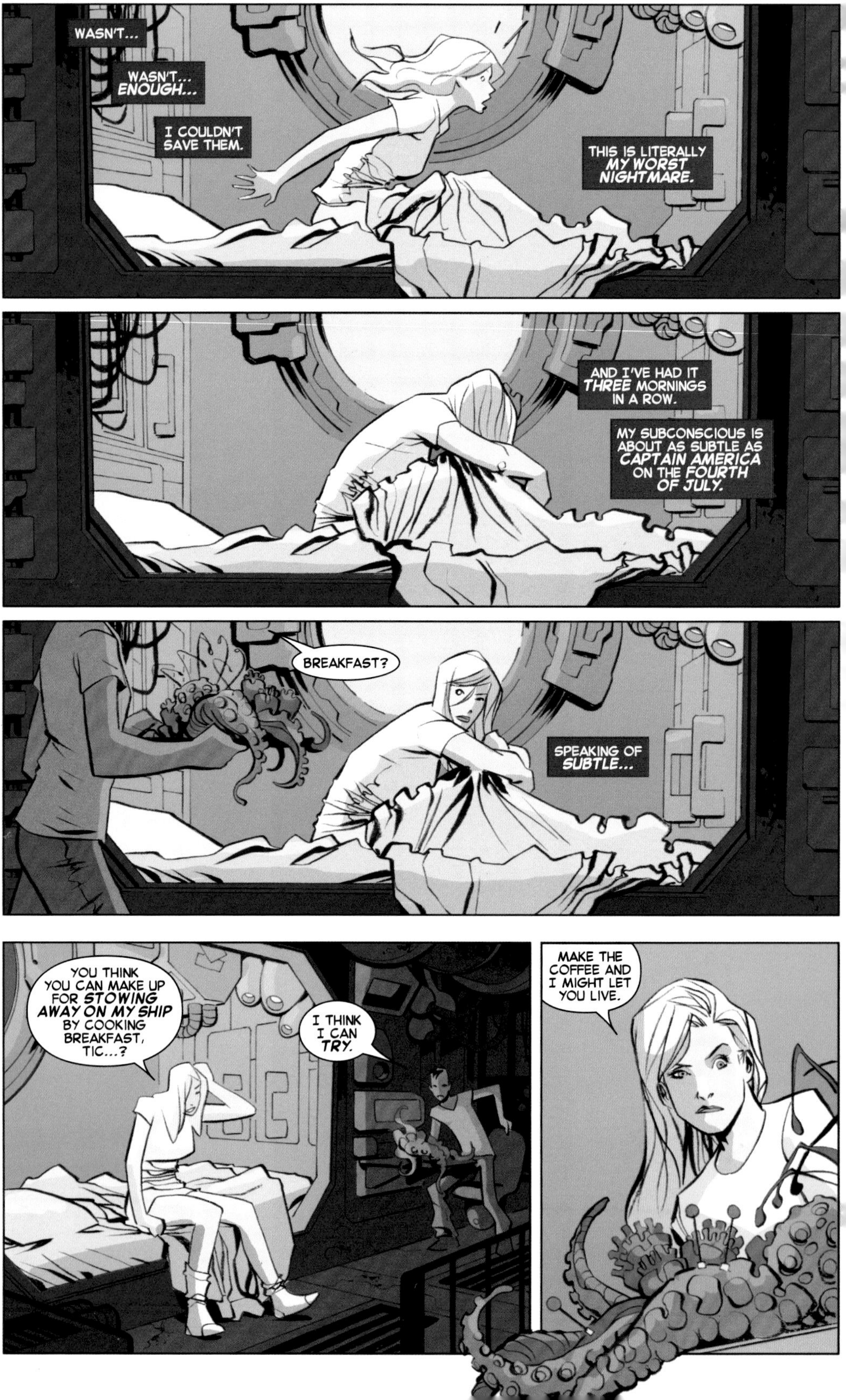

WASN'T...
WASN'T... ENOUGH...
I COULDN'T SAVE THEM.
THIS IS LITERALLY MY WORST NIGHTMARE.
AND I'VE HAD IT THREE MORNINGS IN A ROW.
MY SUBCONSCIOUS IS ABOUT AS SUBTLE AS CAPTAIN AMERICA ON THE FOURTH OF JULY.
BREAKFAST?
SPEAKING OF SUBTLE...
YOU THINK YOU CAN MAKE UP FOR STOWING AWAY ON MY SHIP BY COOKING BREAKFAST, TIC...?
I THINK I CAN TRY.
MAKE THE COFFEE AND I MIGHT LET YOU LIVE.

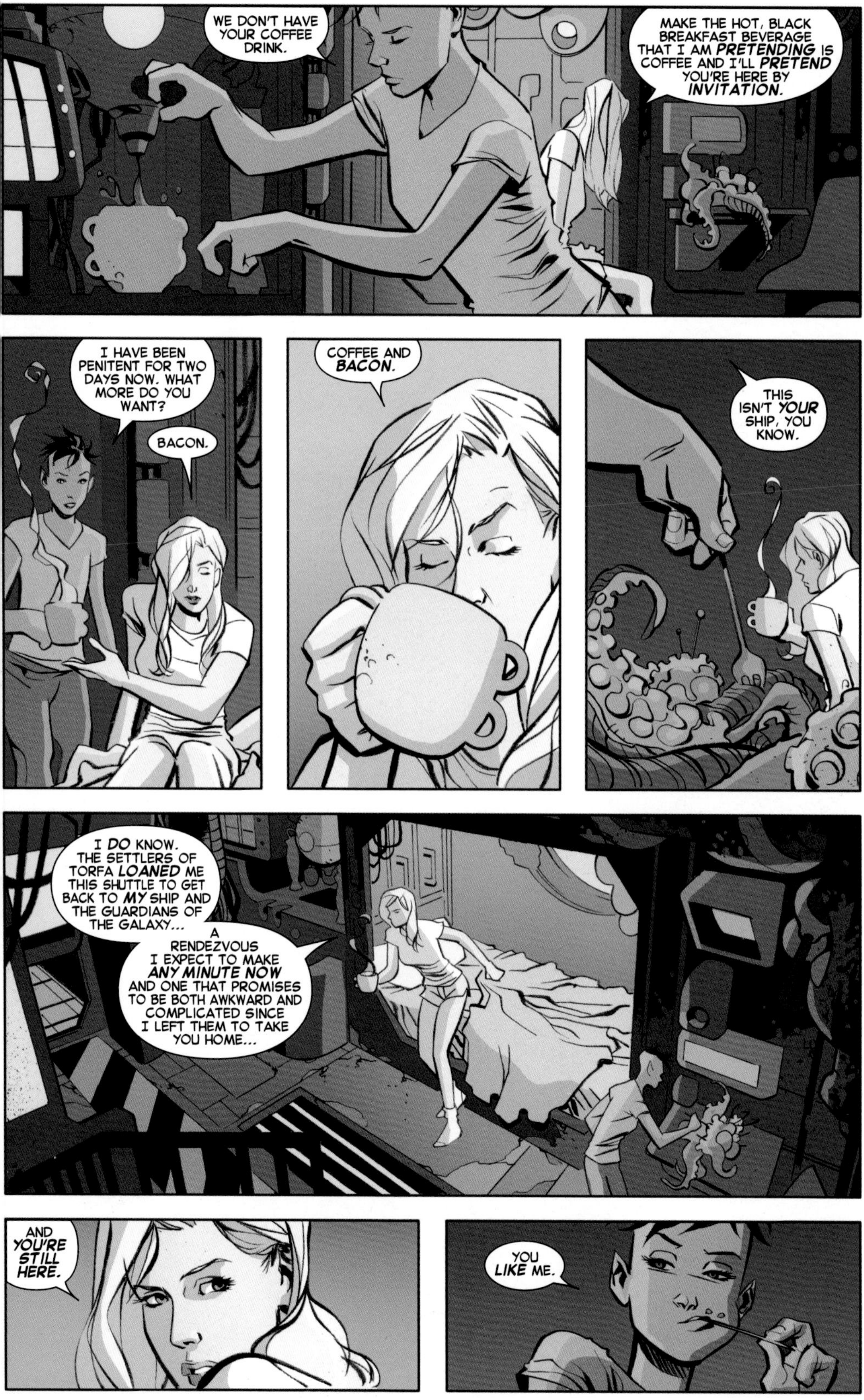
WE DON'T HAVE YOUR COFFEE DRINK.
MAKE THE HOT, BLACK BREAKFAST BEVERAGE THAT I AM *PRETENDING* IS COFFEE AND I'LL *PRETEND* YOU'RE HERE BY *INVITATION.*
I HAVE BEEN PENITENT FOR TWO DAYS NOW. WHAT MORE DO YOU WANT?
BACON.
COFFEE AND *BACON.*
THIS ISN'T *YOUR* SHIP, YOU KNOW.
I *DO* KNOW. THE SETTLERS OF TORFA *LOANED* ME THIS SHUTTLE TO GET BACK TO *MY* SHIP AND THE GUARDIANS OF THE GALAXY...
A RENDEZVOUS I EXPECT TO MAKE *ANY MINUTE NOW* AND ONE THAT PROMISES TO BE BOTH AWKWARD AND COMPLICATED SINCE I LEFT THEM TO TAKE YOU HOME...
AND *YOU'RE STILL HERE.*
YOU *LIKE* ME.

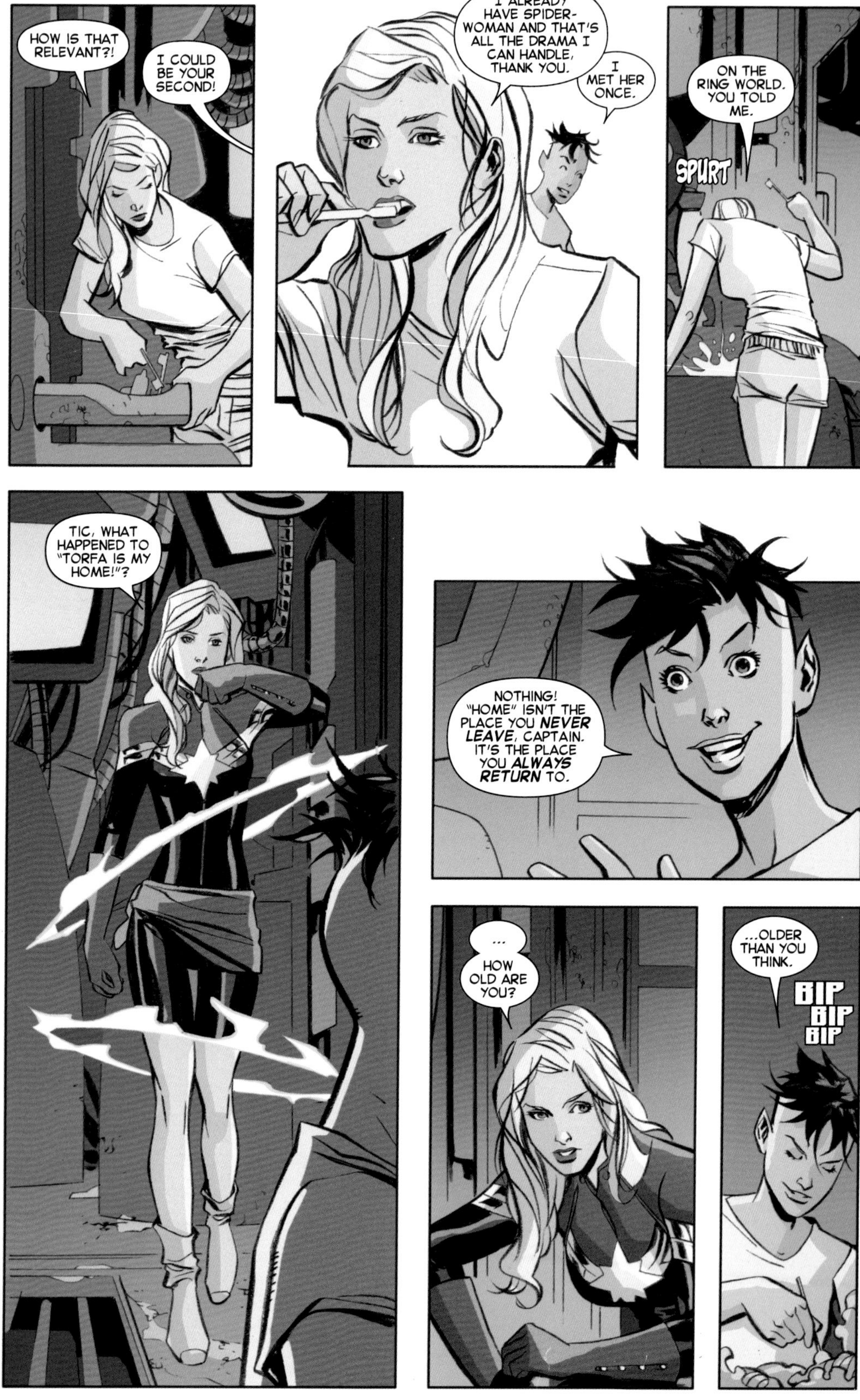
HOW IS THAT RELEVANT?!
I COULD BE YOUR SECOND!
I ALREADY HAVE SPIDER-WOMAN AND THAT'S ALL THE DRAMA I CAN HANDLE, THANK YOU.
I MET HER ONCE.
ON THE RING WORLD. YOU TOLD ME.
SPURT
TIC, WHAT HAPPENED TO "TORFA IS MY HOME!"?
NOTHING! "HOME" ISN'T THE PLACE YOU NEVER LEAVE, CAPTAIN. IT'S THE PLACE YOU ALWAYS RETURN TO.
...
HOW OLD ARE YOU?
...OLDER THAN YOU THINK.
BIP BIP BIP

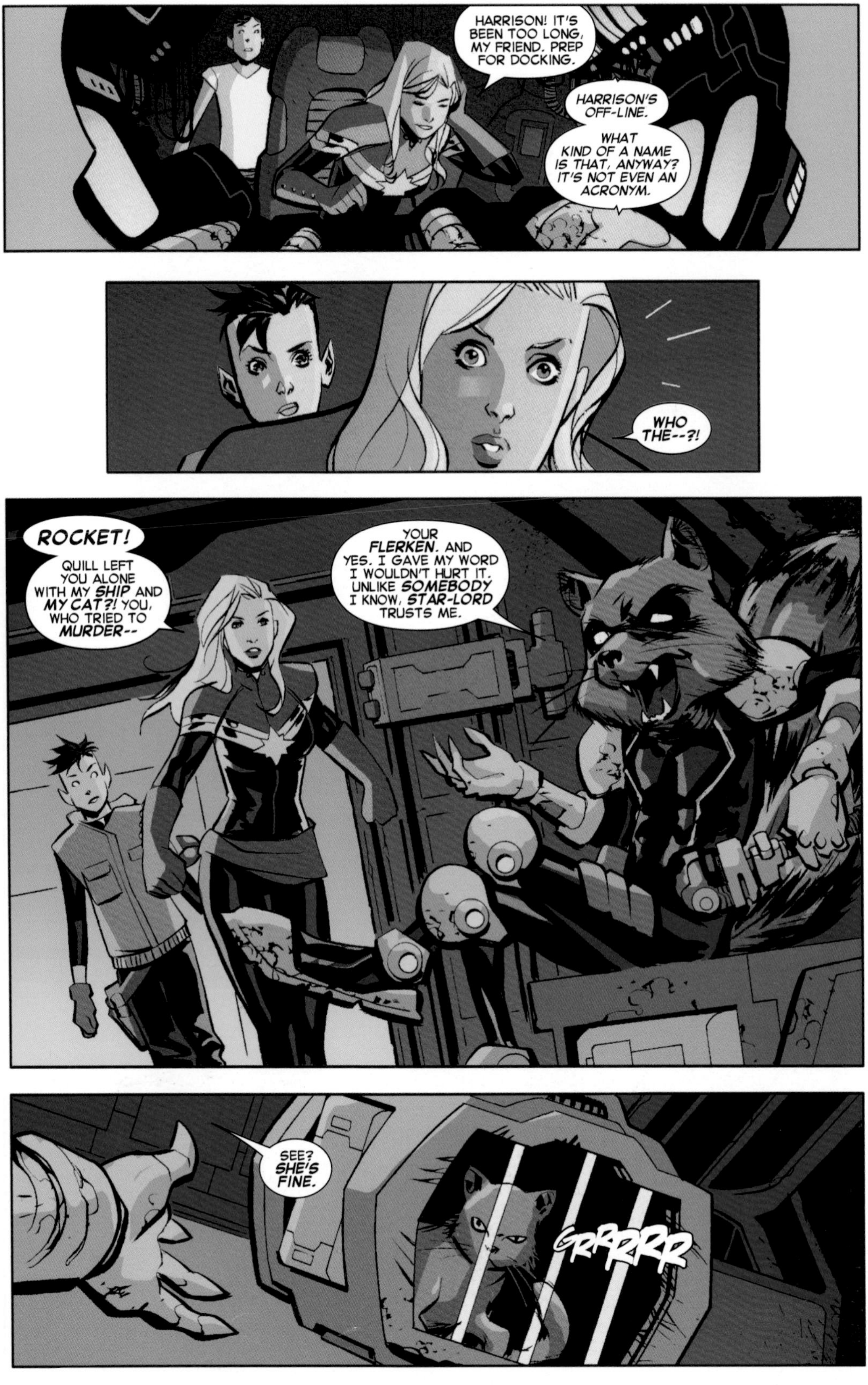
HARRISON! IT'S BEEN TOO LONG, MY FRIEND. PREP FOR DOCKING.
HARRISON'S OFF-LINE.
WHAT KIND OF A NAME IS THAT, ANYWAY? IT'S NOT EVEN AN ACRONYM.
WHO THE--?!
ROCKET!
QUILL LEFT YOU ALONE WITH MY SHIP AND MY CAT?! YOU, WHO TRIED TO MURDER--
YOUR FLERKEN. AND YES. I GAVE MY WORD I WOULDN'T HURT IT. UNLIKE SOMEBODY I KNOW, STAR-LORD TRUSTS ME.
SEE? SHE'S FINE.
GRRRRRR

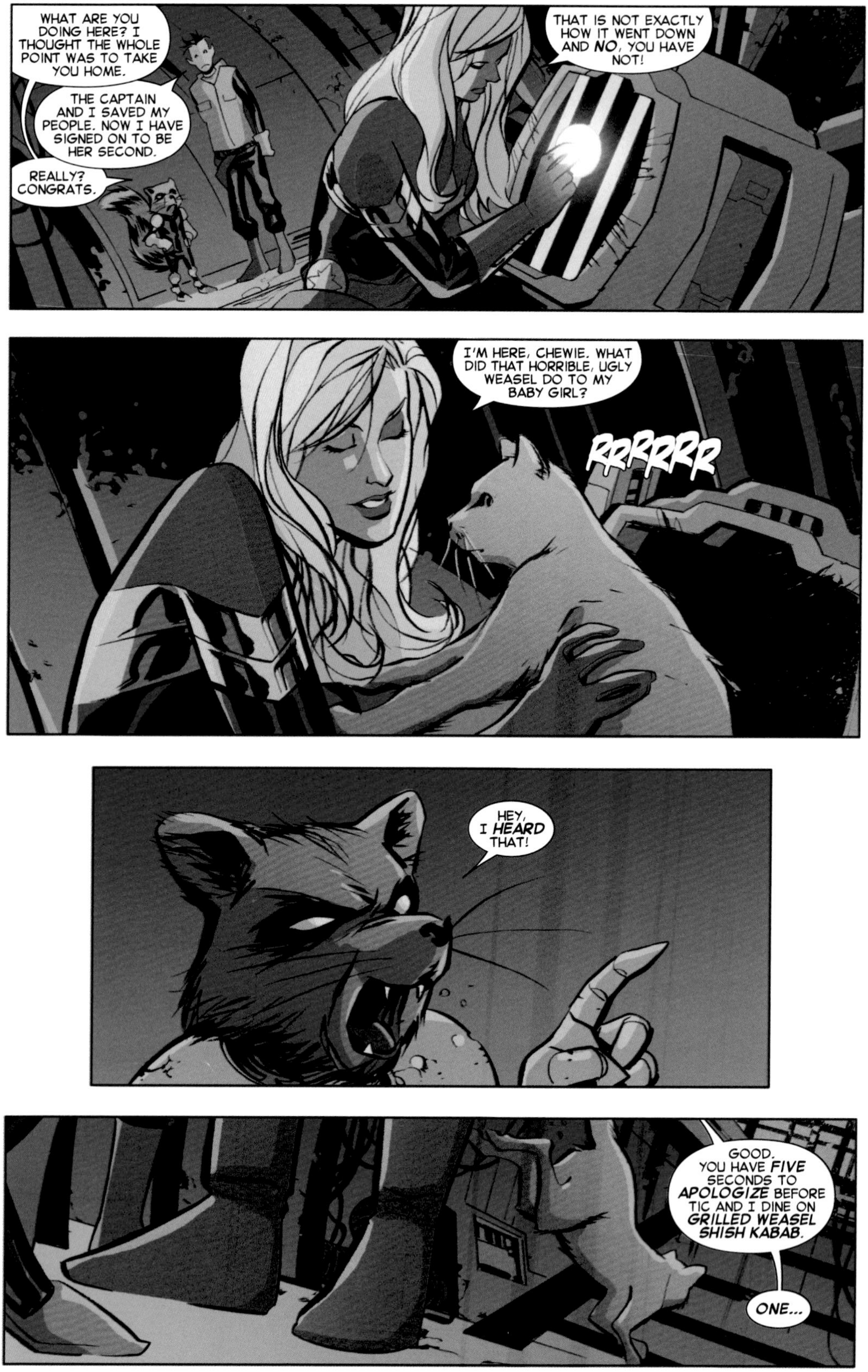
WHAT ARE YOU DOING HERE? I THOUGHT THE WHOLE POINT WAS TO TAKE YOU HOME.
THAT IS NOT EXACTLY HOW IT WENT DOWN AND NO, YOU HAVE NOT!
THE CAPTAIN AND I SAVED MY PEOPLE. NOW I HAVE SIGNED ON TO BE HER SECOND.
REALLY? CONGRATS.
I'M HERE, CHEWIE. WHAT DID THAT HORRIBLE, UGLY WEASEL DO TO MY BABY GIRL?
RRRRRR
HEY, I HEARD THAT!
GOOD. YOU HAVE FIVE SECONDS TO APOLOGIZE BEFORE TIC AND I DINE ON GRILLED WEASEL SHISH KABAB.
ONE...

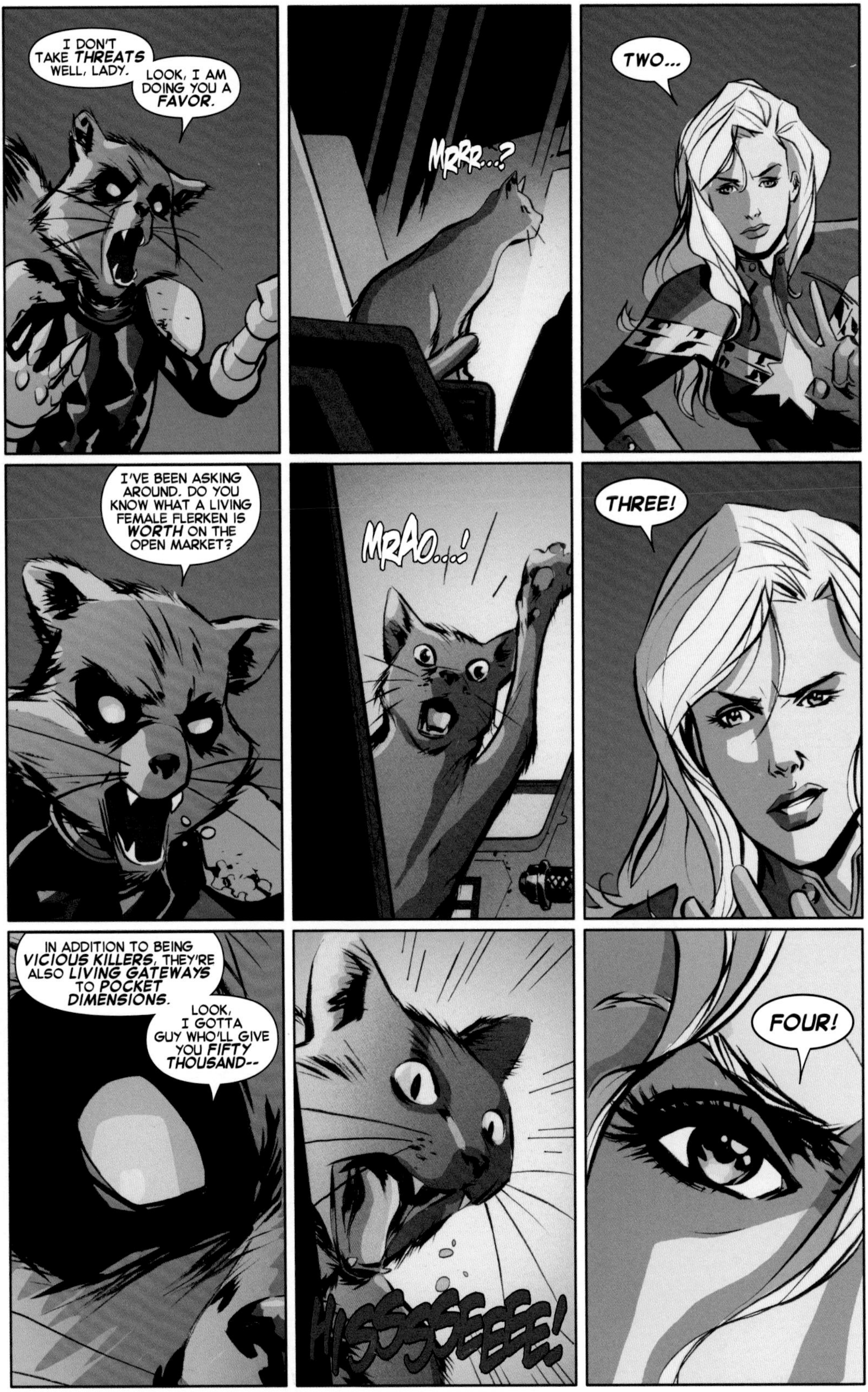
I DON'T TAKE *THREATS* WELL, LADY.
LOOK, I AM DOING YOU A *FAVOR*.
MRRR...?
TWO...
I'VE BEEN ASKING AROUND. DO YOU KNOW WHAT A LIVING FEMALE FLERKEN IS *WORTH* ON THE OPEN MARKET?
MRAO...!
THREE!
IN ADDITION TO BEING *VICIOUS KILLERS*, THEY'RE ALSO *LIVING GATEWAYS* TO *POCKET DIMENSIONS*.
LOOK, I GOTTA GUY WHO'LL GIVE YOU *FIFTY THOUSAND*--
HISSSSEEEEE!
FOUR!

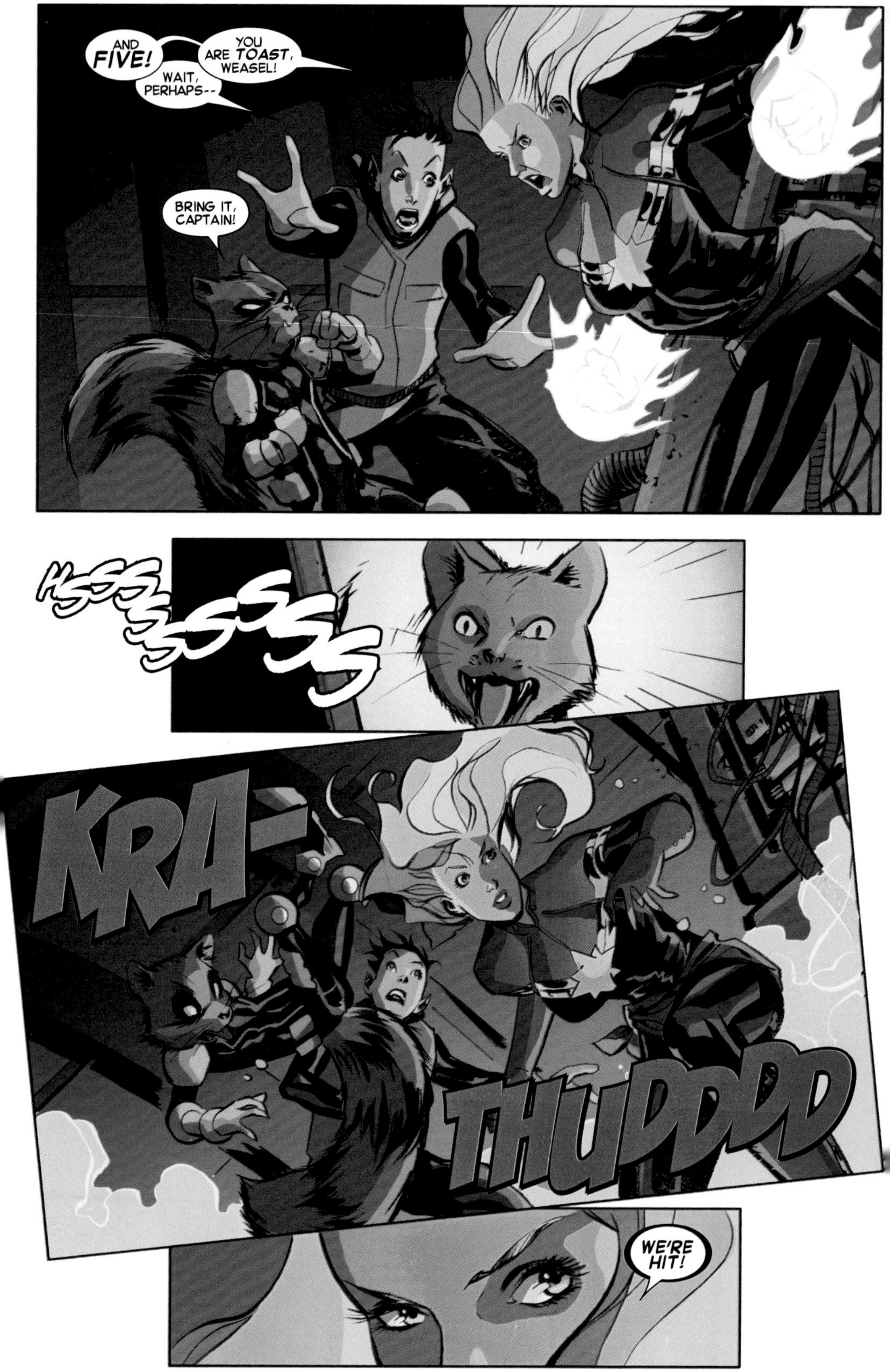
AND FIVE!
WAIT, PERHAPS--
YOU ARE TOAST, WEASEL!
BRING IT, CAPTAIN!
HSSSSSSSSS
KRA-
THUDDDD
WE'RE HIT!

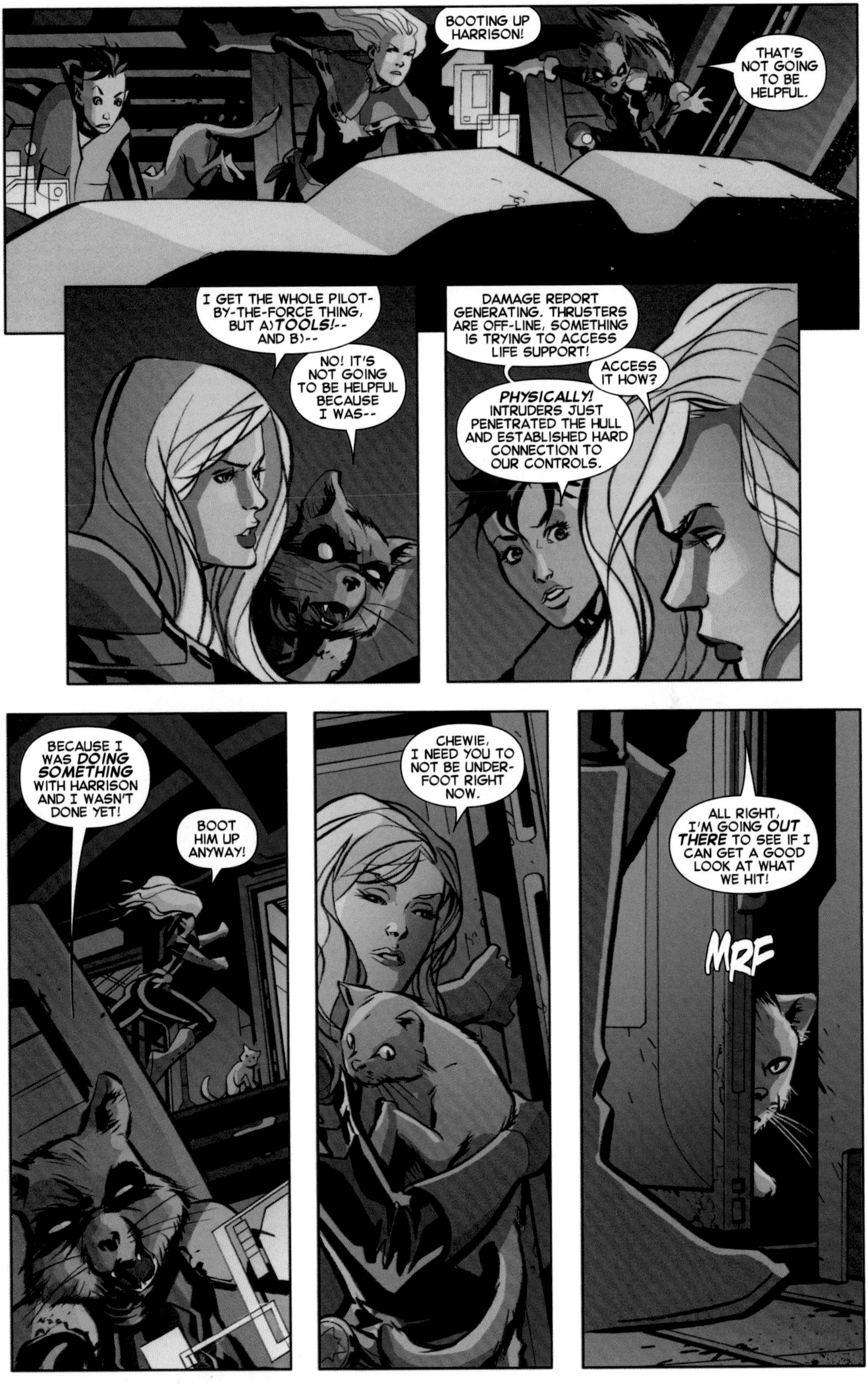
BOOTING UP HARRISON!
THAT'S NOT GOING TO BE HELPFUL.
I GET THE WHOLE PILOT-BY-THE-FORCE THING, BUT A) TOOLS!-- AND B)--
NO! IT'S NOT GOING TO BE HELPFUL BECAUSE I WAS--
DAMAGE REPORT GENERATING. THRUSTERS ARE OFF-LINE, SOMETHING IS TRYING TO ACCESS LIFE SUPPORT!
ACCESS IT HOW?
PHYSICALLY! INTRUDERS JUST PENETRATED THE HULL AND ESTABLISHED HARD CONNECTION TO OUR CONTROLS.
BECAUSE I WAS DOING SOMETHING WITH HARRISON AND I WASN'T DONE YET!
BOOT HIM UP ANYWAY!
CHEWIE, I NEED YOU TO NOT BE UNDER-FOOT RIGHT NOW.
ALL RIGHT, I'M GOING OUT THERE TO SEE IF I CAN GET A GOOD LOOK AT WHAT WE HIT!
MRF

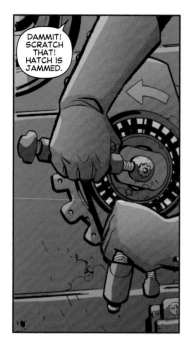

DAMMIT! SCRATCH THAT! HATCH IS JAMMED.

OH, CRAP.

HARRISON, WHAT AM I LOOKING AT? WHAT'S GOT A HOLD OF US?

MROWwwwwwwwww

ROCKET, DID MY SHIP'S COMPUTER JUST *MEOW* AT ME?

YES. AND THERE IS A *PERFECTLY* LOGICAL EXPLANATION.

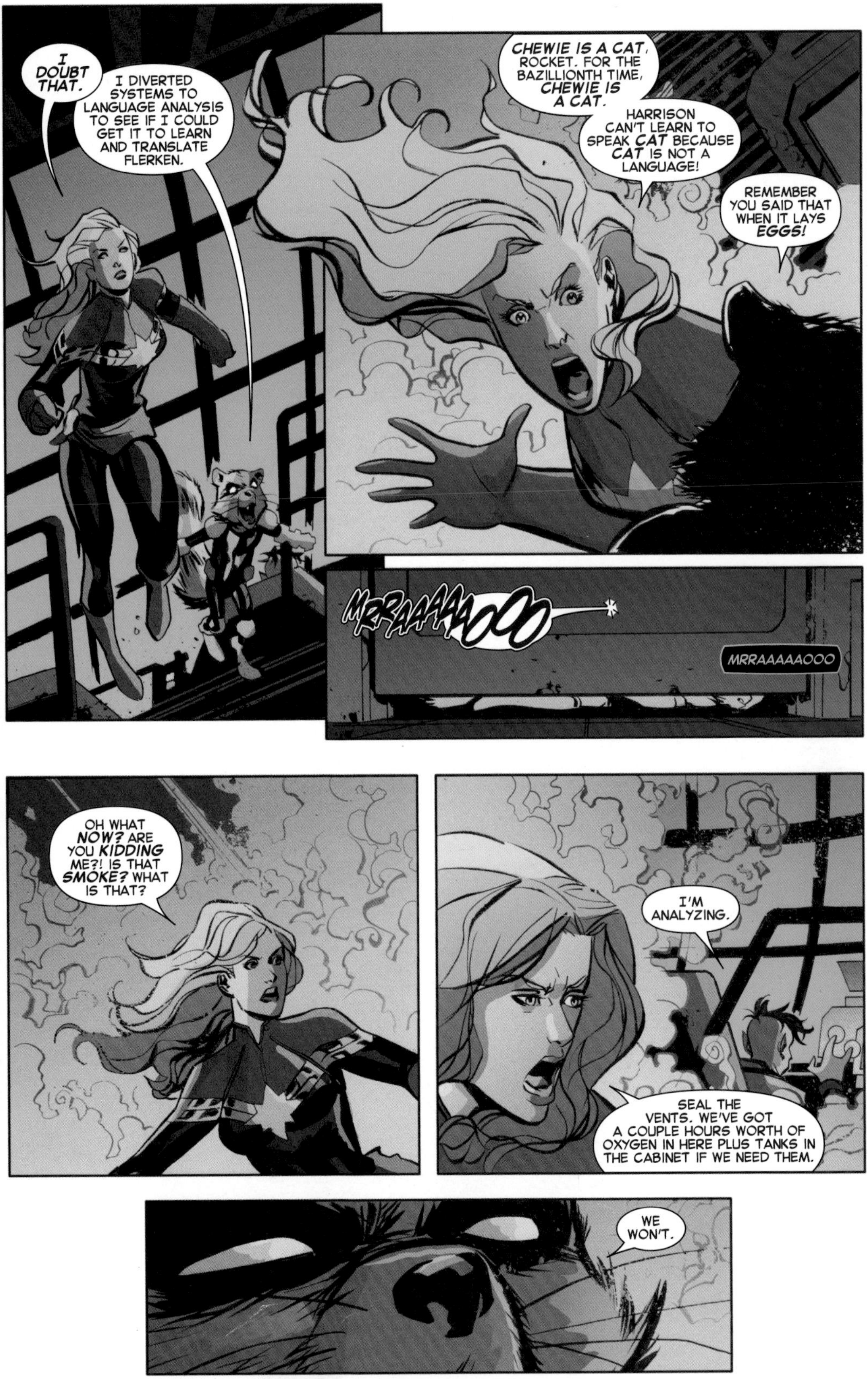
I DOUBT THAT.
I DIVERTED SYSTEMS TO LANGUAGE ANALYSIS TO SEE IF I COULD GET IT TO LEARN AND TRANSLATE FLERKEN.
CHEWIE IS A CAT, ROCKET. FOR THE BAZILLIONTH TIME, CHEWIE IS A CAT.
HARRISON CAN'T LEARN TO SPEAK CAT BECAUSE CAT IS NOT A LANGUAGE!
REMEMBER YOU SAID THAT WHEN IT LAYS EGGS!
MRRAAAAAOOO
MRRAAAAAOOO
OH WHAT NOW? ARE YOU KIDDING ME?! IS THAT SMOKE? WHAT IS THAT?
I'M ANALYZING.
SEAL THE VENTS. WE'VE GOT A COUPLE HOURS WORTH OF OXYGEN IN HERE PLUS TANKS IN THE CABINET IF WE NEED THEM.
WE WON'T.

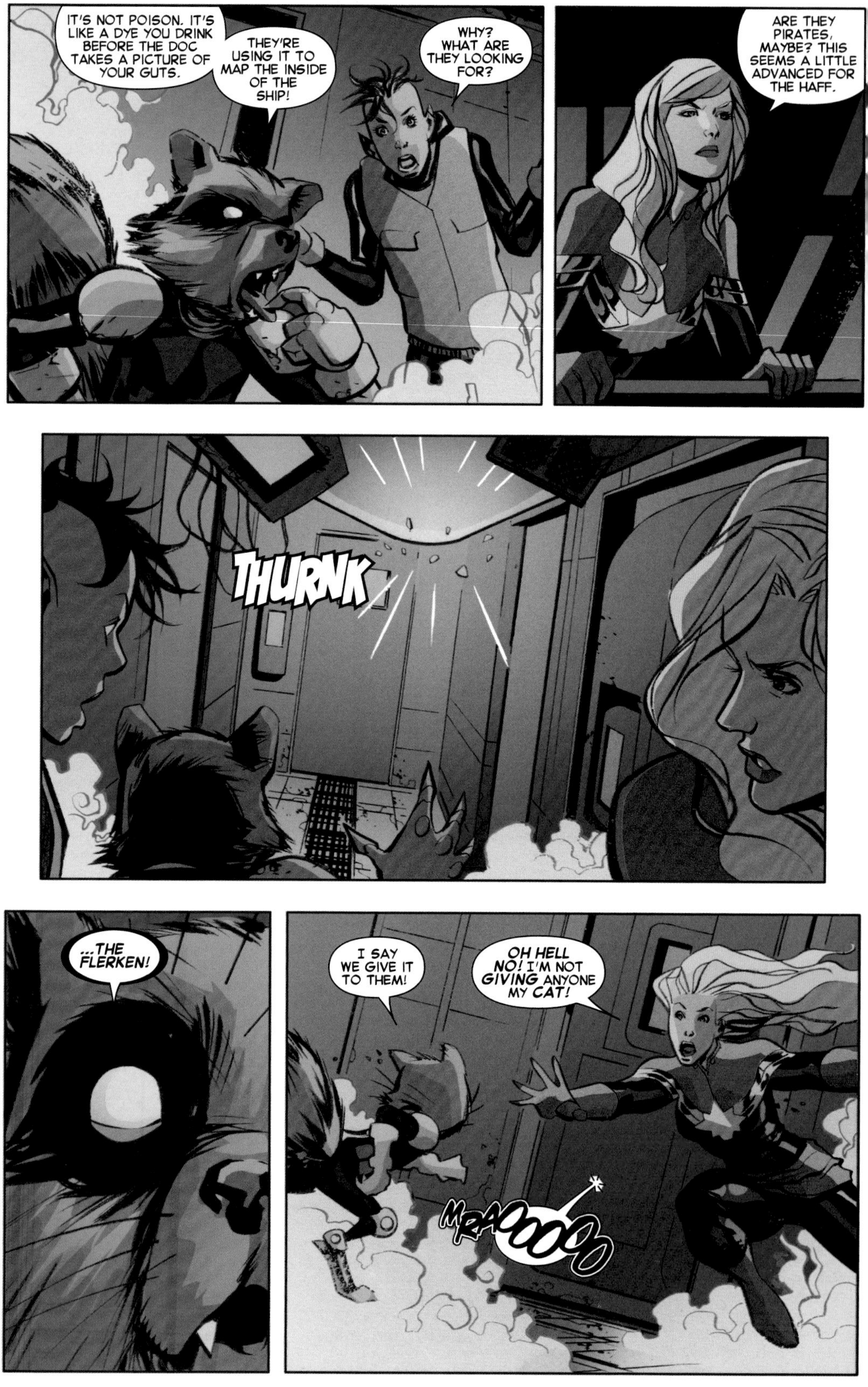
IT'S NOT POISON. IT'S LIKE A DYE YOU DRINK BEFORE THE DOC TAKES A PICTURE OF YOUR GUTS.
THEY'RE USING IT TO MAP THE INSIDE OF THE SHIP!
WHY? WHAT ARE THEY LOOKING FOR?
ARE THEY PIRATES, MAYBE? THIS SEEMS A LITTLE ADVANCED FOR THE HAFF.
THURNK
...THE FLERKEN!
I SAY WE GIVE IT TO THEM!
OH HELL NO! I'M NOT GIVING ANYONE MY CAT!
MRAOOOOOO

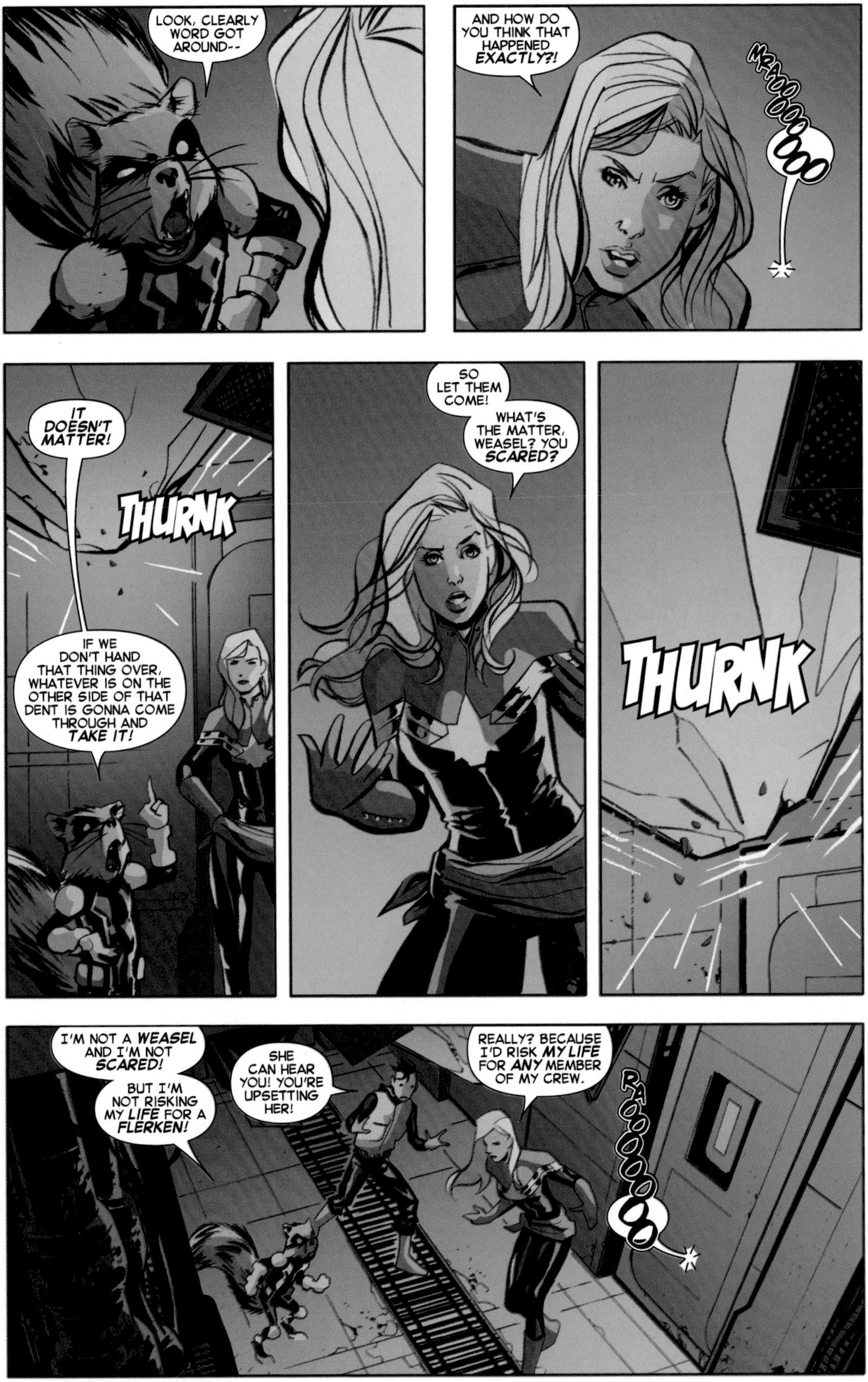
LOOK, CLEARLY WORD GOT AROUND--
AND HOW DO YOU THINK THAT HAPPENED EXACTLY?!
MRAOOOOOOO
IT DOESN'T MATTER!
THURNK
IF WE DON'T HAND THAT THING OVER, WHATEVER IS ON THE OTHER SIDE OF THAT DENT IS GONNA COME THROUGH AND TAKE IT!
SO LET THEM COME!
WHAT'S THE MATTER, WEASEL? YOU SCARED?
THURNK
I'M NOT A WEASEL AND I'M NOT SCARED!
BUT I'M NOT RISKING MY LIFE FOR A FLERKEN!
SHE CAN HEAR YOU! YOU'RE UPSETTING HER!
REALLY? BECAUSE I'D RISK MY LIFE FOR ANY MEMBER OF MY CREW.
RAOOOOOOO

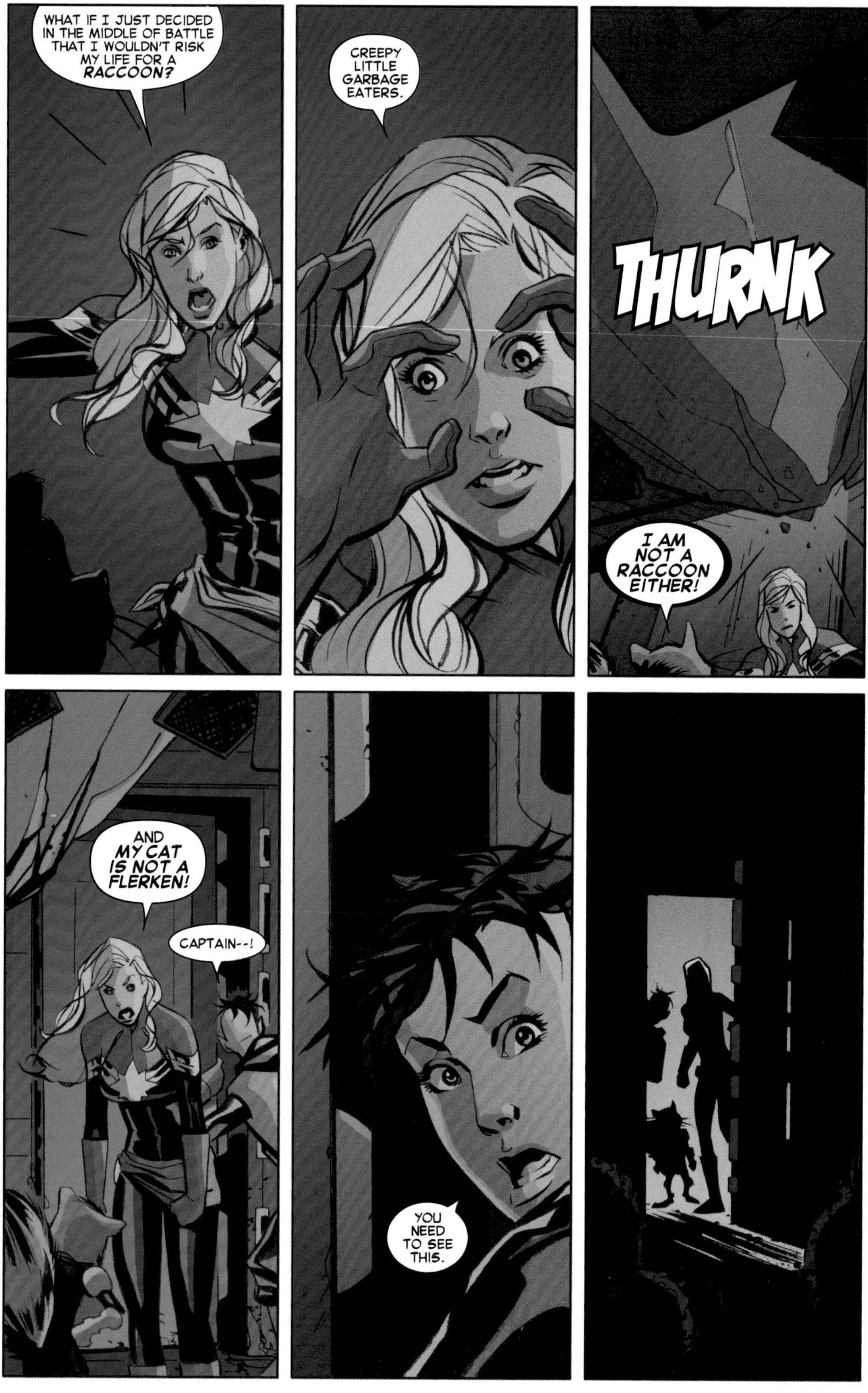
WHAT IF I JUST DECIDED IN THE MIDDLE OF BATTLE THAT I WOULDN'T RISK MY LIFE FOR A RACCOON?
CREEPY LITTLE GARBAGE EATERS.
THURNK
I AM NOT A RACCOON EITHER!
AND MY CAT IS NOT A FLERKEN!
CAPTAIN--!
YOU NEED TO SEE THIS.

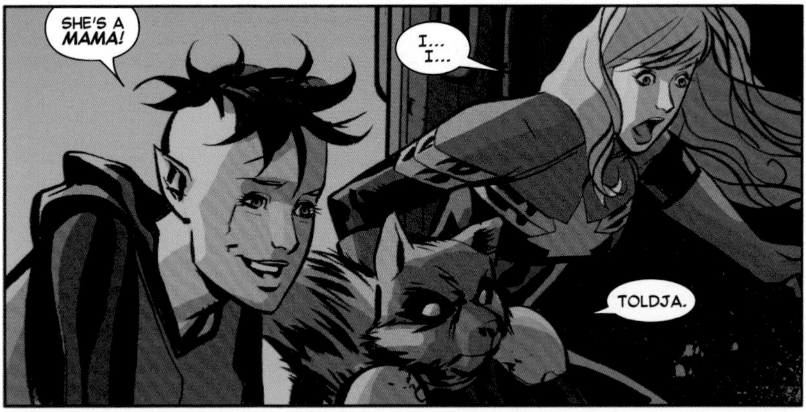
SHE'S A *MAMA!*
I... I...
TOLDJA.
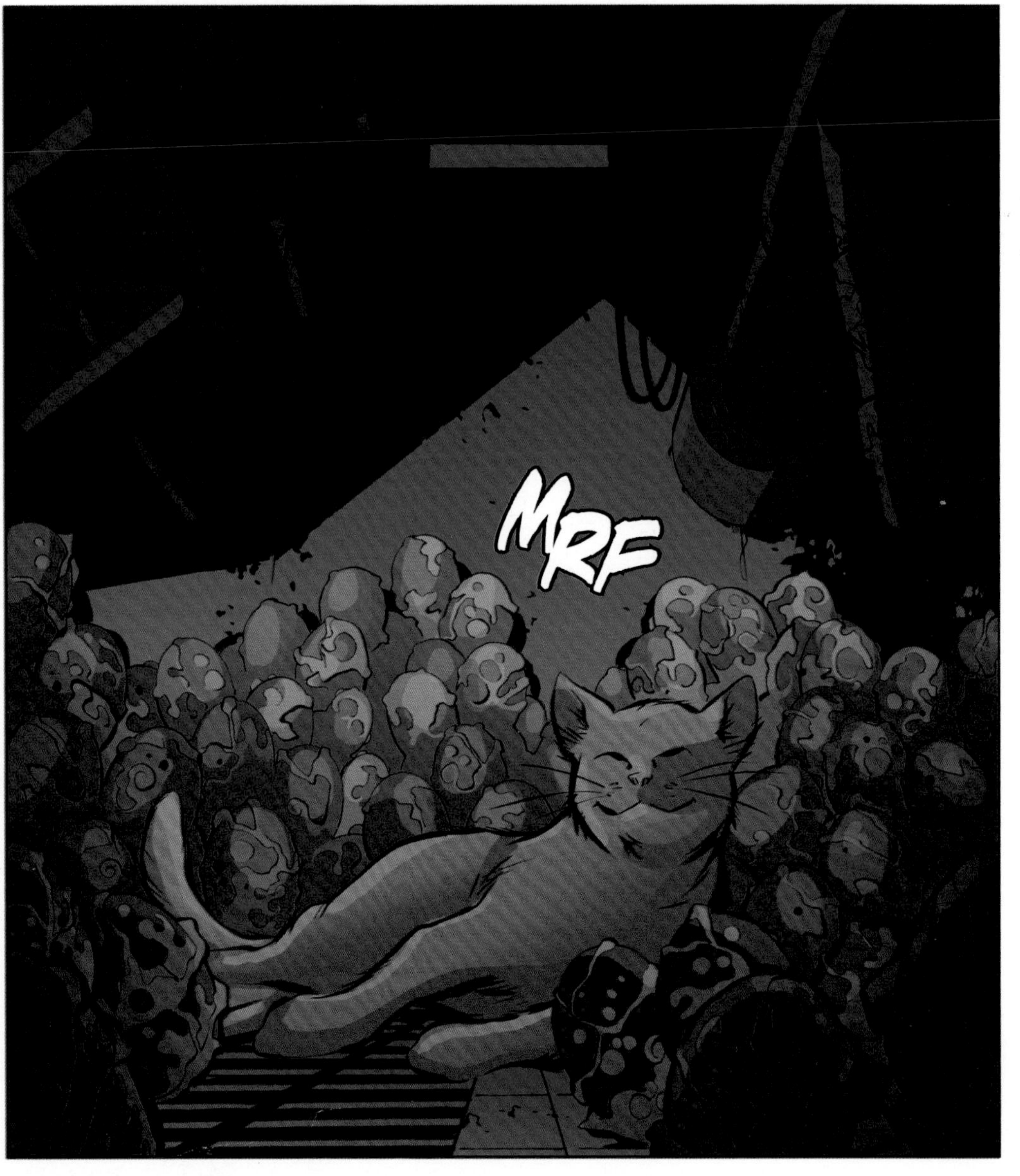
MRF

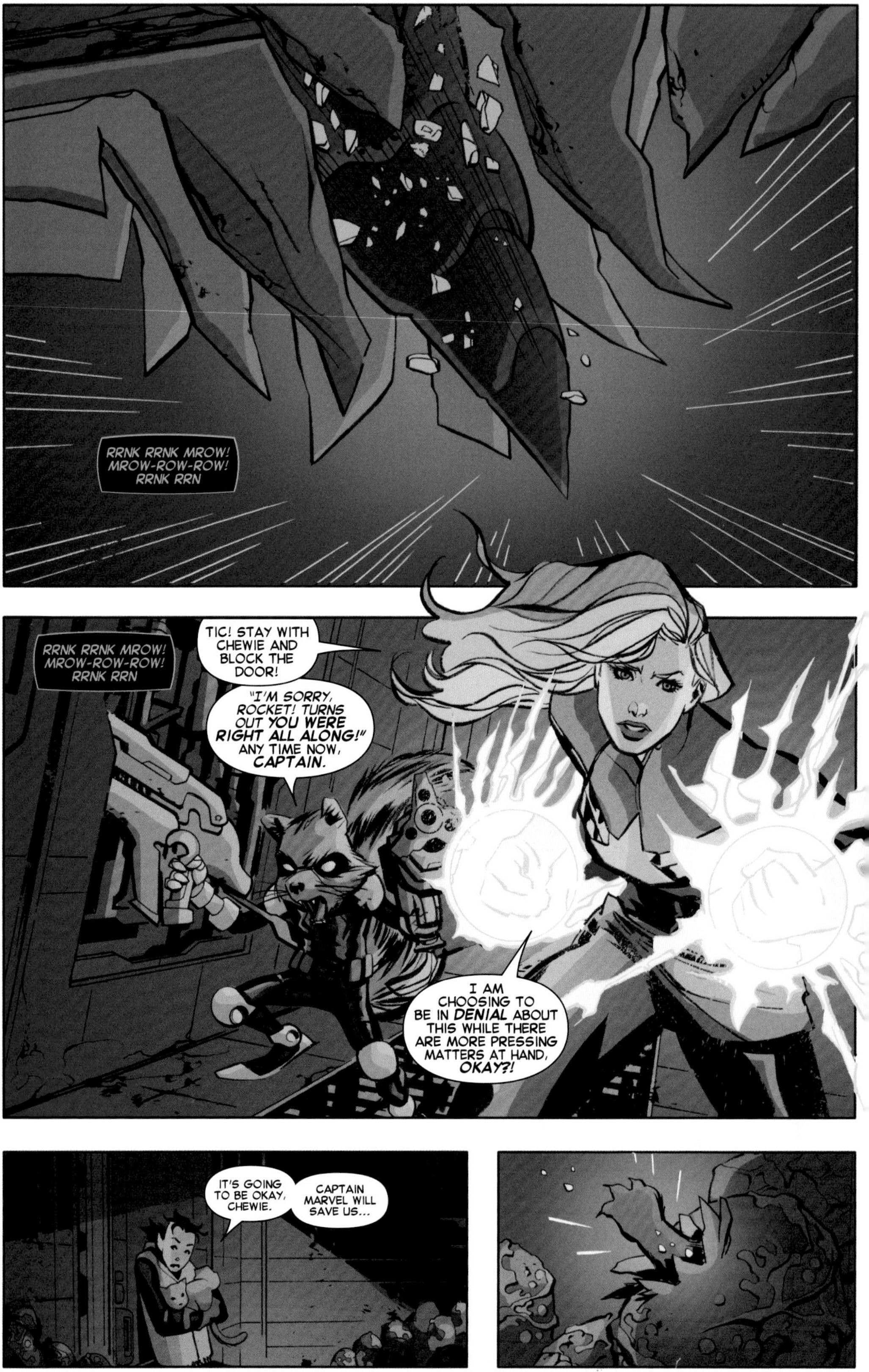
RRNK RRNK MROW! MROW-ROW-ROW! RRNK RRN
RRNK RRNK MROW! MROW-ROW-ROW! RRNK RRN
TIC! STAY WITH CHEWIE AND BLOCK THE DOOR!
"I'M SORRY, ROCKET! TURNS OUT YOU WERE RIGHT ALL ALONG!" ANY TIME NOW, CAPTAIN.
I AM CHOOSING TO BE IN DENIAL ABOUT THIS WHILE THERE ARE MORE PRESSING MATTERS AT HAND, OKAY?!
IT'S GOING TO BE OKAY, CHEWIE.
CAPTAIN MARVEL WILL SAVE US...

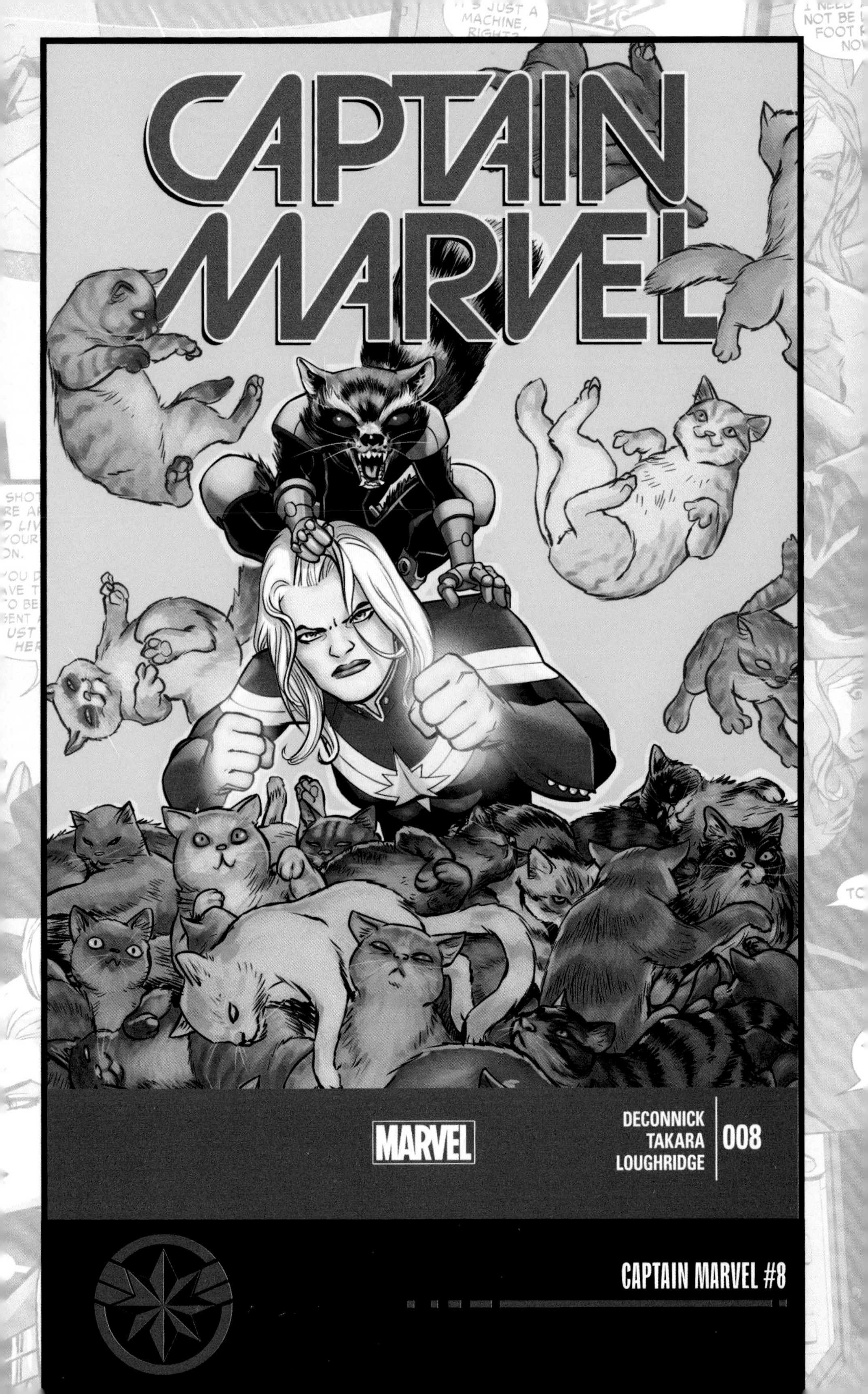
CAPTAIN MARVEL
MARVEL
DECONNICK
TAKARA
LOUGHRIDGE
008
CAPTAIN MARVEL #8

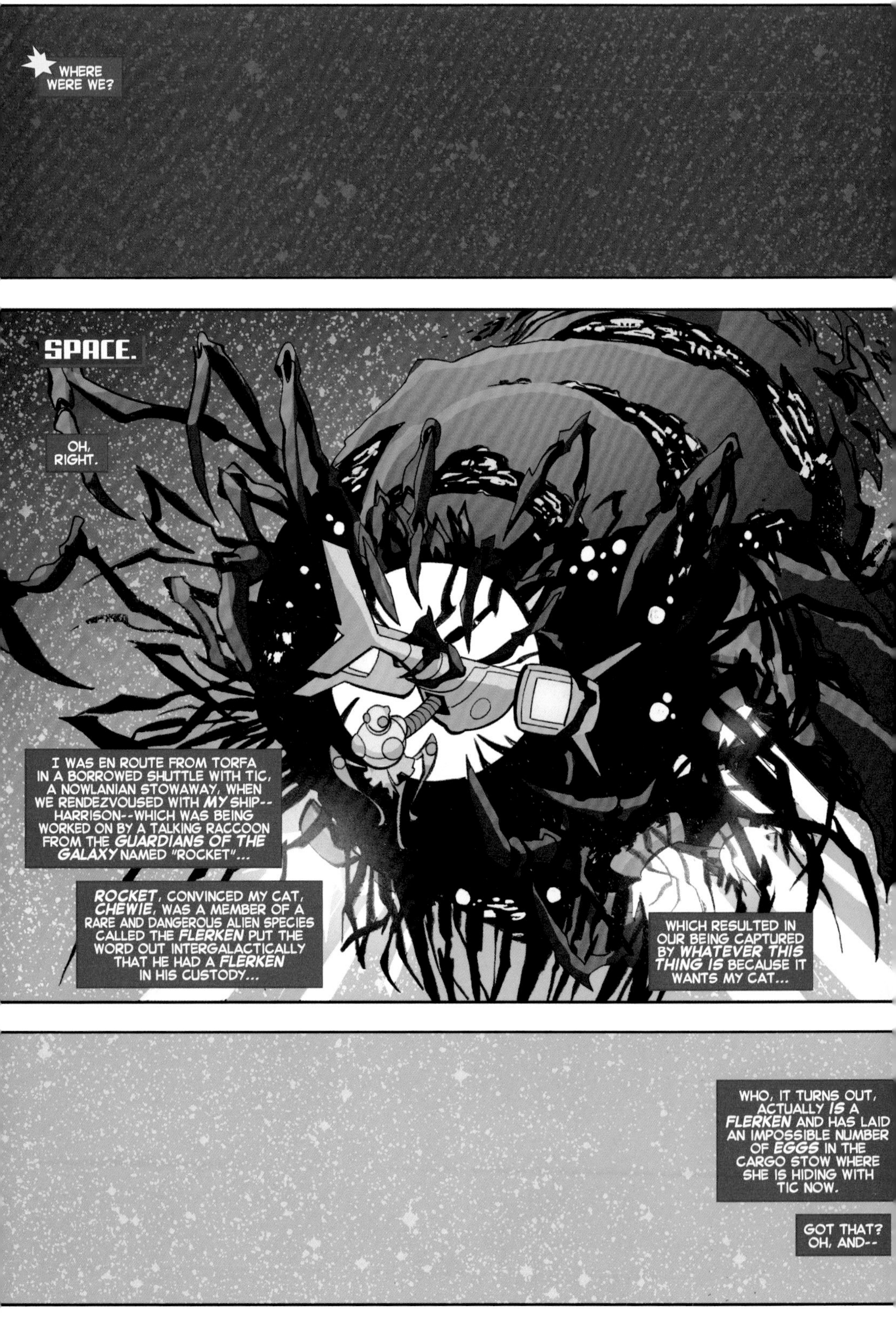
WHERE WERE WE?
SPACE.
OH, RIGHT.
I WAS EN ROUTE FROM TORFA IN A BORROWED SHUTTLE WITH TIC, A NOWLANIAN STOWAWAY, WHEN WE RENDEZVOUSED WITH MY SHIP--HARRISON--WHICH WAS BEING WORKED ON BY A TALKING RACCOON FROM THE GUARDIANS OF THE GALAXY NAMED "ROCKET"...
ROCKET, CONVINCED MY CAT, CHEWIE, WAS A MEMBER OF A RARE AND DANGEROUS ALIEN SPECIES CALLED THE FLERKEN PUT THE WORD OUT INTERGALACTICALLY THAT HE HAD A FLERKEN IN HIS CUSTODY...
WHICH RESULTED IN OUR BEING CAPTURED BY WHATEVER THIS THING IS BECAUSE IT WANTS MY CAT...
WHO, IT TURNS OUT, ACTUALLY IS A FLERKEN AND HAS LAID AN IMPOSSIBLE NUMBER OF EGGS IN THE CARGO STOW WHERE SHE IS HIDING WITH TIC NOW.
GOT THAT? OH, AND--

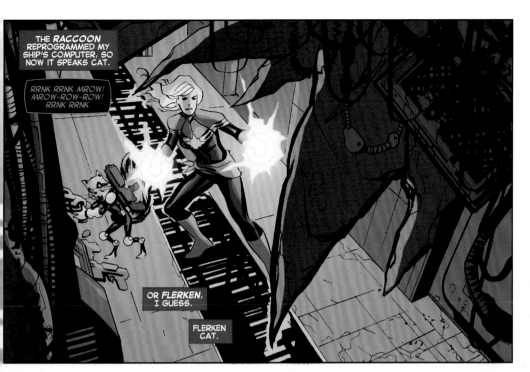

THE *RACCOON* REPROGRAMMED MY SHIP'S COMPUTER, SO NOW IT SPEAKS CAT.

RRNK RRNK MROW! MROW-ROW-ROW! RRNK RRNK

OR *FLERKEN*, I GUESS.

FLERKEN CAT.

PINCH ME.

OW! PINCH, NOT PUNCH!

BAP

WHATEVER. YOU'RE NOT *DREAMING.*

IT'S OVER. HOSTILE VESSEL HAS GOT FULL CONTROL OF HARRISON. I CAN'T OVERRIDE.

ATTENTION VESSEL! RECON VAPORS CONFIRM THE PRESENCE OF THE UNIVERSE'S *LAST KNOWN* LIVING FLERKEN.

PREPARE FOR *BOARDING* AND CUSTODY TRANSFER IN TEN...

LIKE *HELL.*

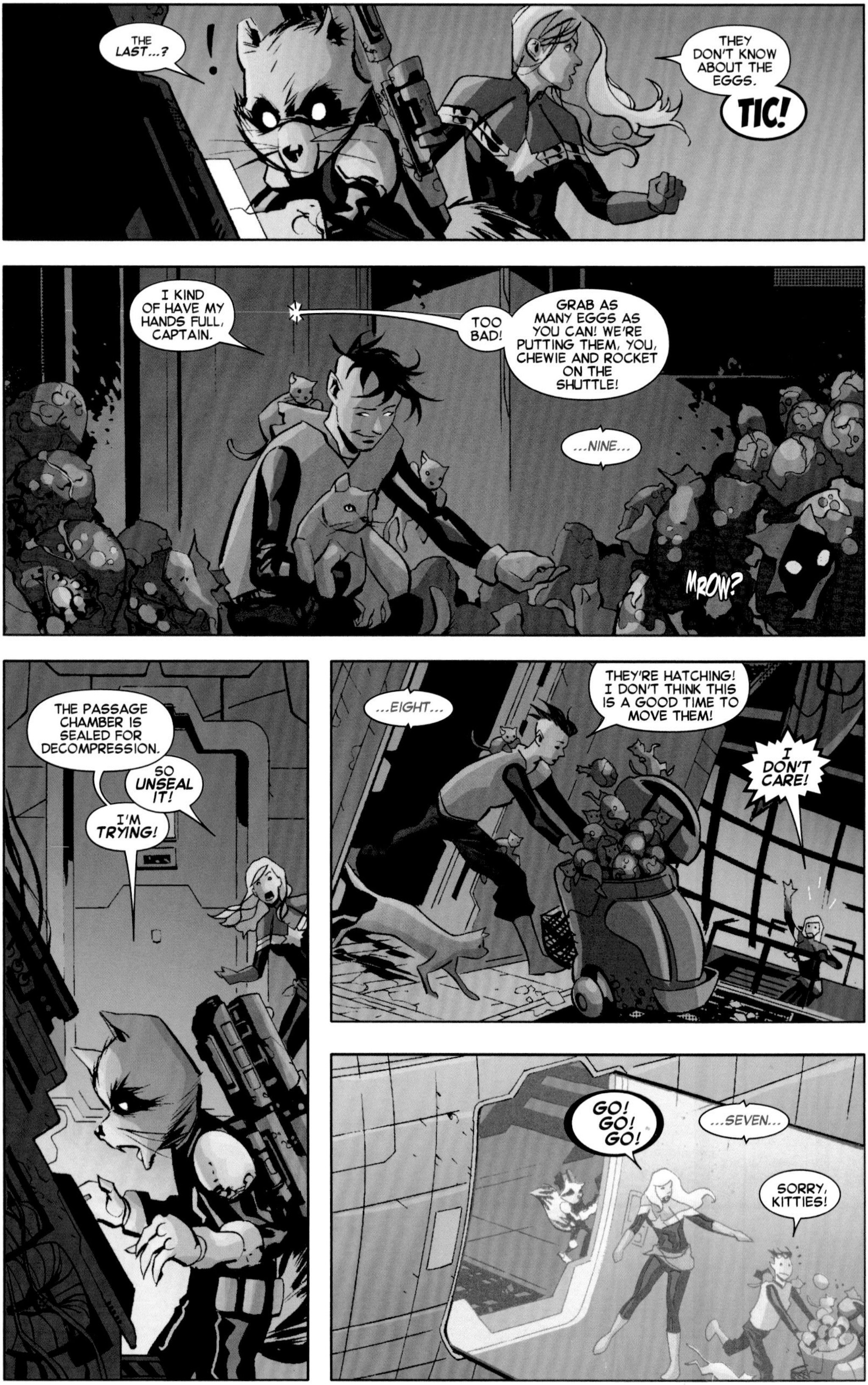
THE LAST...?
!
THEY DON'T KNOW ABOUT THE EGGS.
TIC!
I KIND OF HAVE MY HANDS FULL, CAPTAIN.
TOO BAD!
GRAB AS MANY EGGS AS YOU CAN! WE'RE PUTTING THEM, YOU, CHEWIE AND ROCKET ON THE SHUTTLE!
...NINE...
MROW?
THE PASSAGE CHAMBER IS SEALED FOR DECOMPRESSION.
SO UNSEAL IT!
I'M TRYING!
...EIGHT...
THEY'RE HATCHING! I DON'T THINK THIS IS A GOOD TIME TO MOVE THEM!
I DON'T CARE!
GO! GO! GO!
...SEVEN...
SORRY, KITTIES!

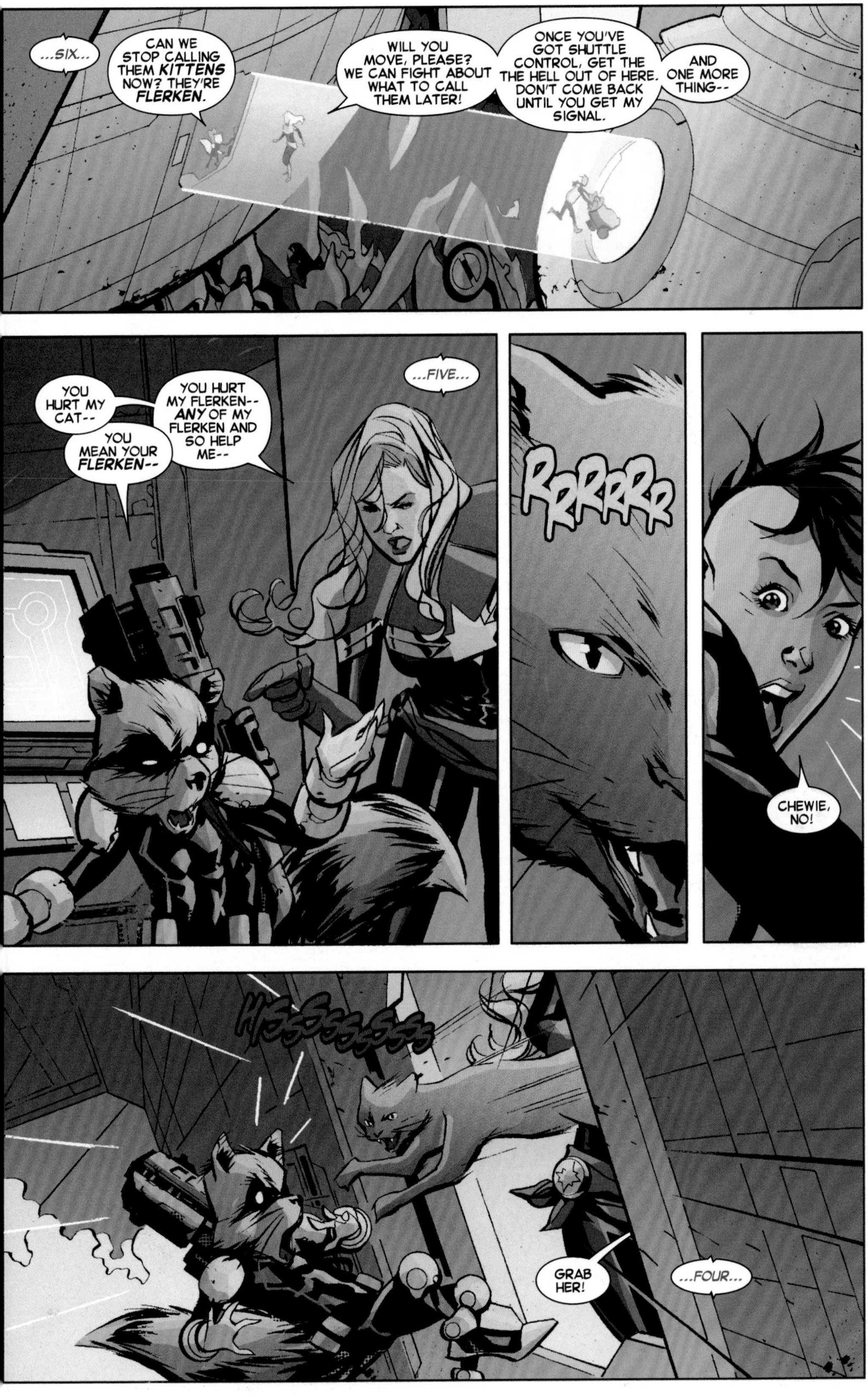
...SIX...
CAN WE STOP CALLING THEM KITTENS NOW? THEY'RE FLERKEN.
WILL YOU MOVE, PLEASE? WE CAN FIGHT ABOUT WHAT TO CALL THEM LATER!
ONCE YOU'VE GOT SHUTTLE CONTROL, GET THE THE HELL OUT OF HERE. DON'T COME BACK UNTIL YOU GET MY SIGNAL.
AND ONE MORE THING--
...FIVE...
YOU HURT MY CAT--
YOU HURT MY FLERKEN-- ANY OF MY FLERKEN AND SO HELP ME--
YOU MEAN YOUR FLERKEN--
RRRRRR
CHEWIE, NO!
HISSSSSSSSS
GRAB HER!
...FOUR...

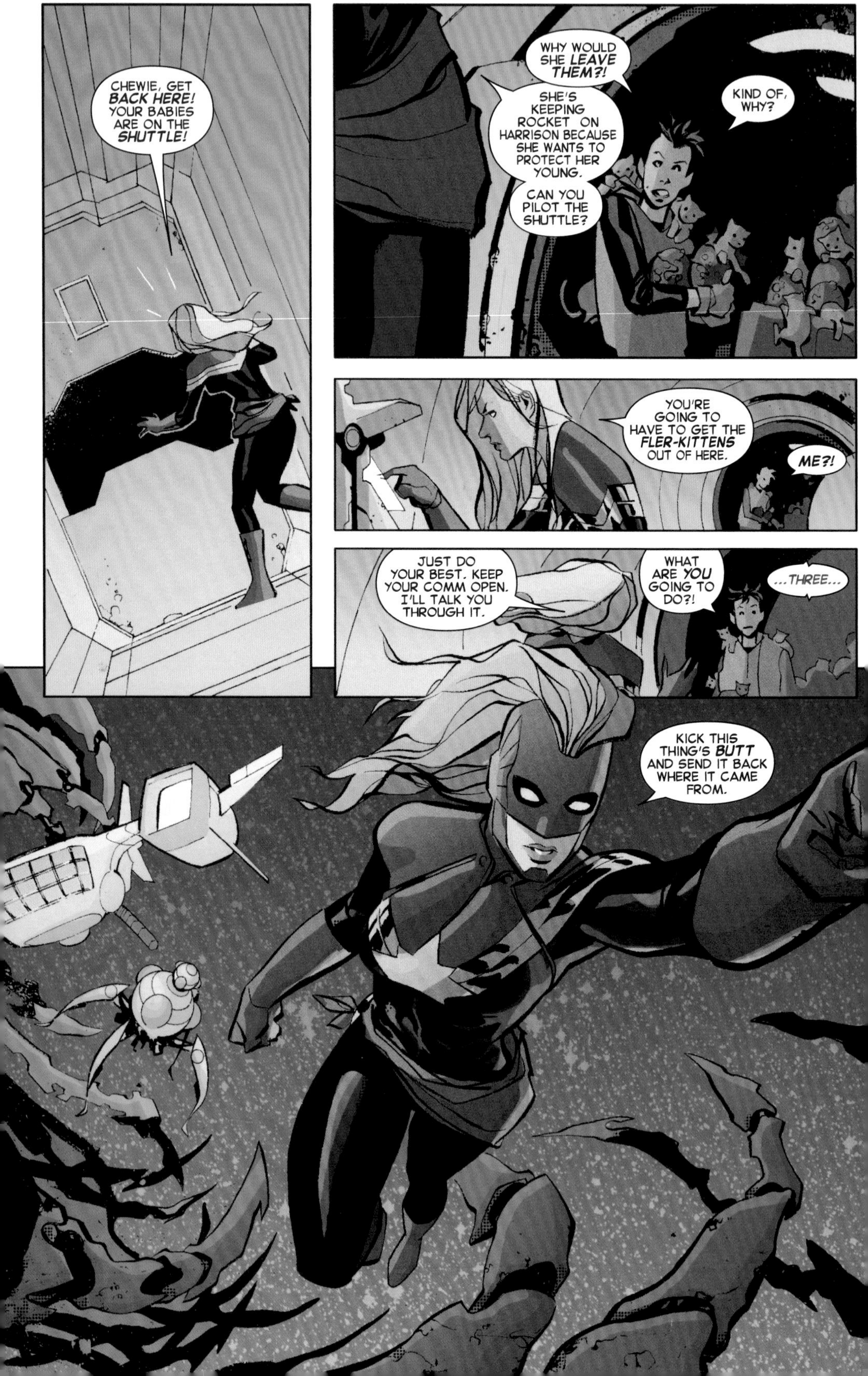
CHEWIE, GET BACK HERE! YOUR BABIES ARE ON THE SHUTTLE!
WHY WOULD SHE LEAVE THEM?!
SHE'S KEEPING ROCKET ON HARRISON BECAUSE SHE WANTS TO PROTECT HER YOUNG.
CAN YOU PILOT THE SHUTTLE?
KIND OF, WHY?
YOU'RE GOING TO HAVE TO GET THE FLER-KITTENS OUT OF HERE.
ME?!
JUST DO YOUR BEST. KEEP YOUR COMM OPEN. I'LL TALK YOU THROUGH IT.
WHAT ARE YOU GOING TO DO?!
...THREE...
KICK THIS THING'S BUTT AND SEND IT BACK WHERE IT CAME FROM.

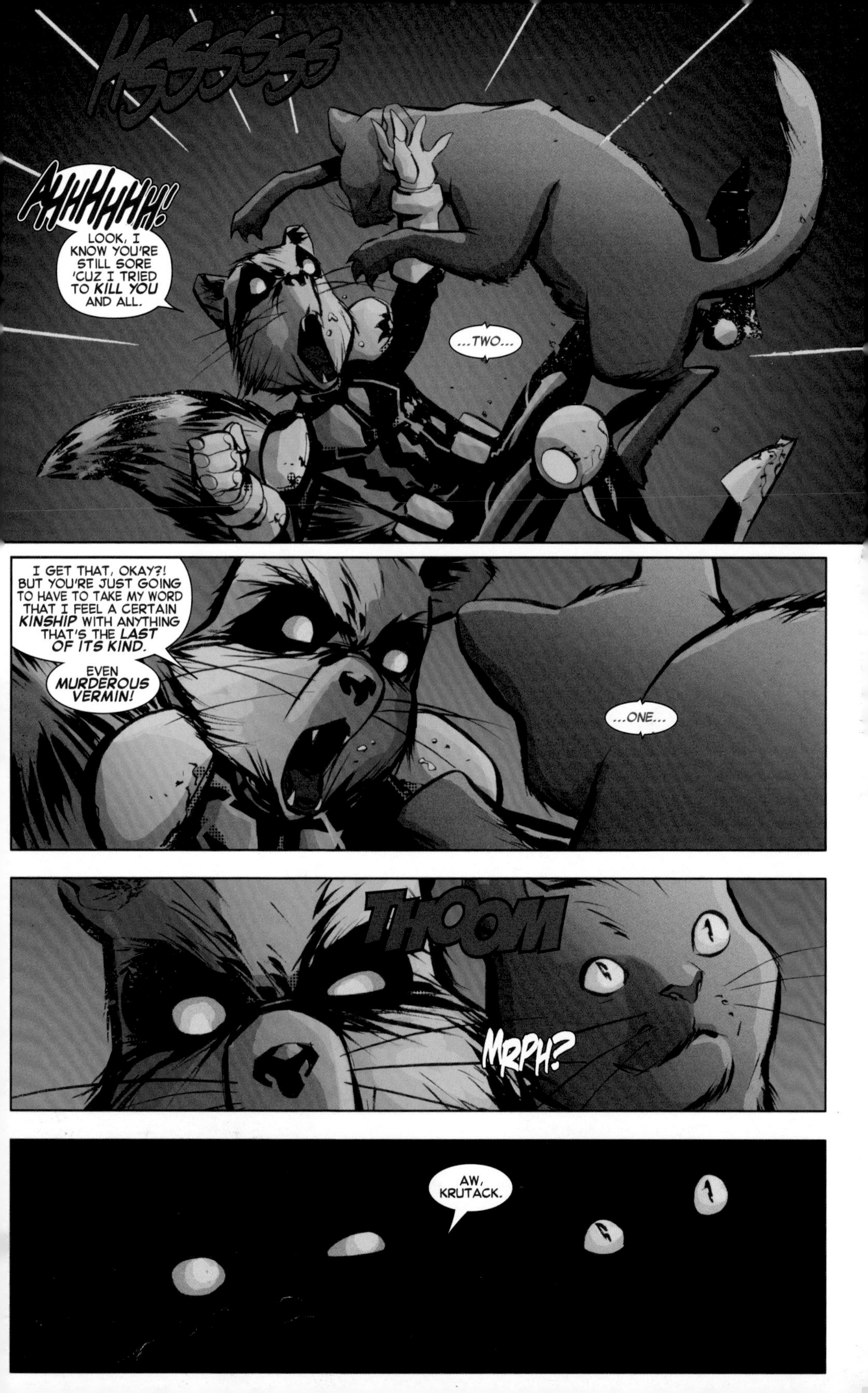
HISSSSSS
AHHHHHH!
LOOK, I KNOW YOU'RE STILL SORE 'CUZ I TRIED TO KILL YOU AND ALL.
...TWO...
I GET THAT, OKAY?! BUT YOU'RE JUST GOING TO HAVE TO TAKE MY WORD THAT I FEEL A CERTAIN KINSHIP WITH ANYTHING THAT'S THE LAST OF ITS KIND.
EVEN MURDEROUS VERMIN!
...ONE...
THOOM
MRPH?
AW, KRUTACK.

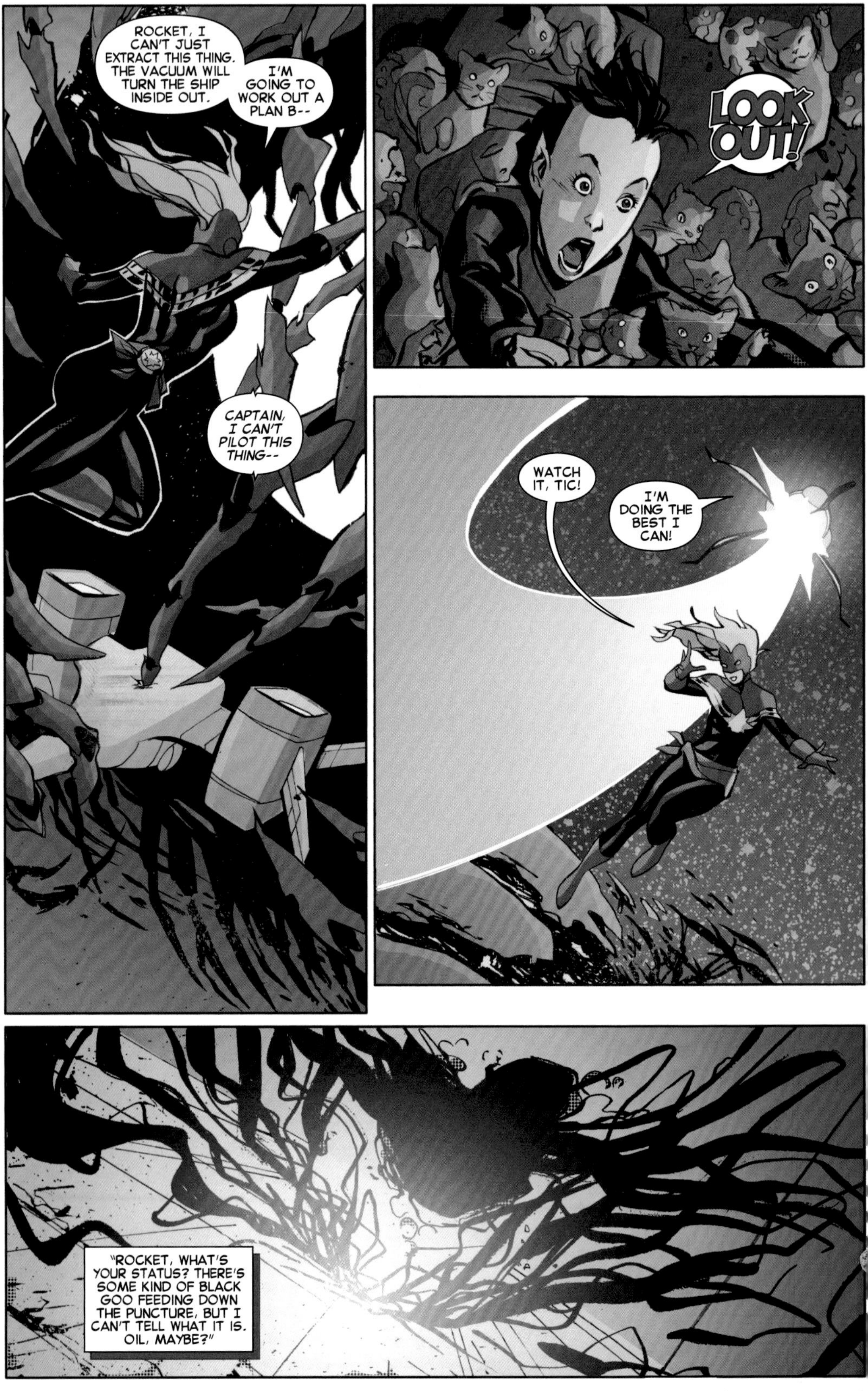
ROCKET, I CAN'T JUST EXTRACT THIS THING. THE VACUUM WILL TURN THE SHIP INSIDE OUT.
I'M GOING TO WORK OUT A PLAN B--
CAPTAIN, I CAN'T PILOT THIS THING--
LOOK OUT!
WATCH IT, TIC!
I'M DOING THE BEST I CAN!
"ROCKET, WHAT'S YOUR STATUS? THERE'S SOME KIND OF BLACK GOO FEEDING DOWN THE PUNCTURE, BUT I CAN'T TELL WHAT IT IS. OIL, MAYBE?"

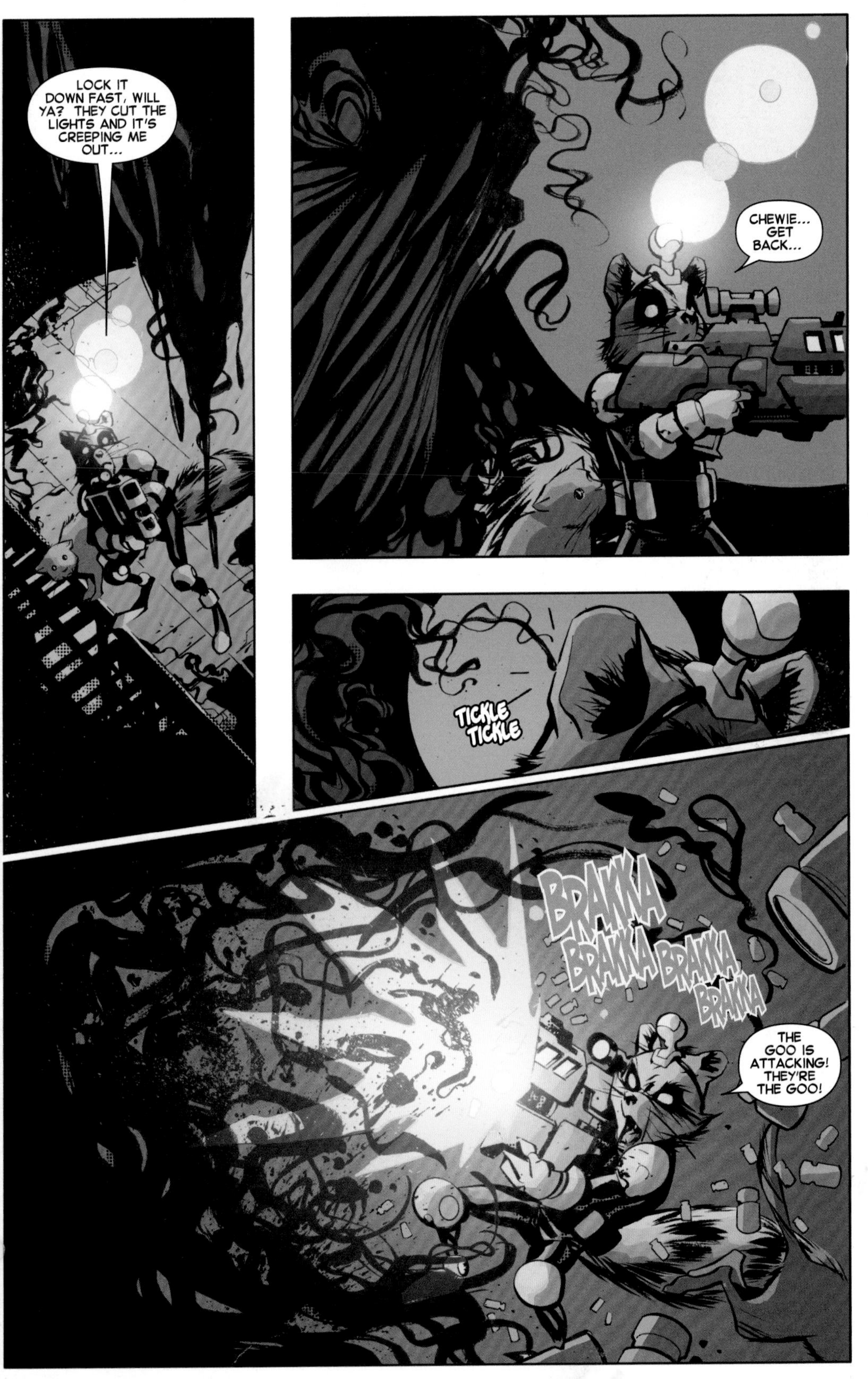
LOCK IT DOWN FAST, WILL YA? THEY CUT THE LIGHTS AND IT'S CREEPING ME OUT...
CHEWIE... GET BACK...
TICKLE TICKLE
BRAKKA BRAKKA BRAKKA BRAKKA
THE GOO IS ATTACKING! THEY'RE THE GOO!

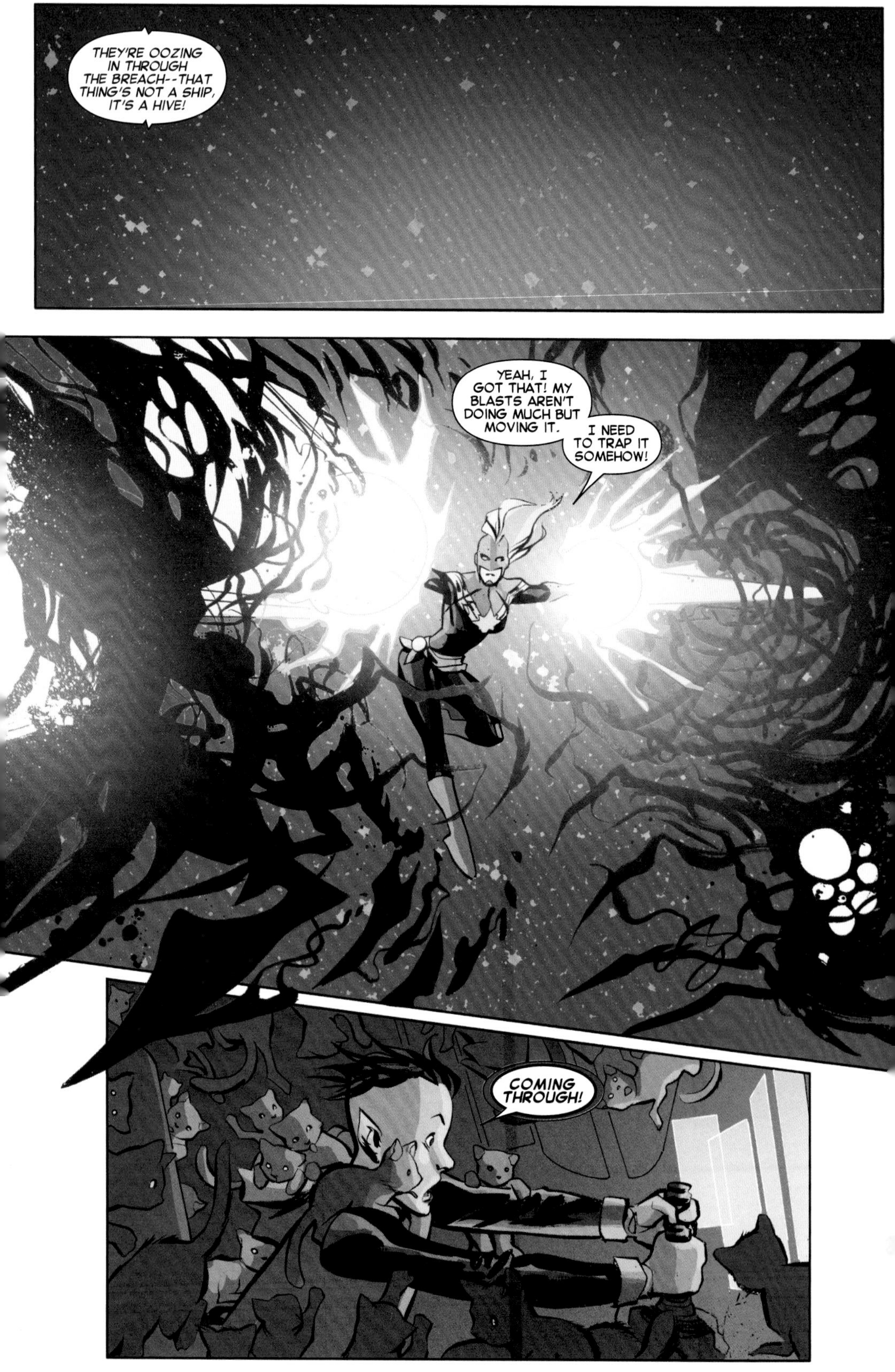
THEY'RE OOZING IN THROUGH THE BREACH--THAT THING'S NOT A SHIP, IT'S A HIVE!
YEAH, I GOT THAT! MY BLASTS AREN'T DOING MUCH BUT MOVING IT.
I NEED TO TRAP IT SOMEHOW!
COMING THROUGH!

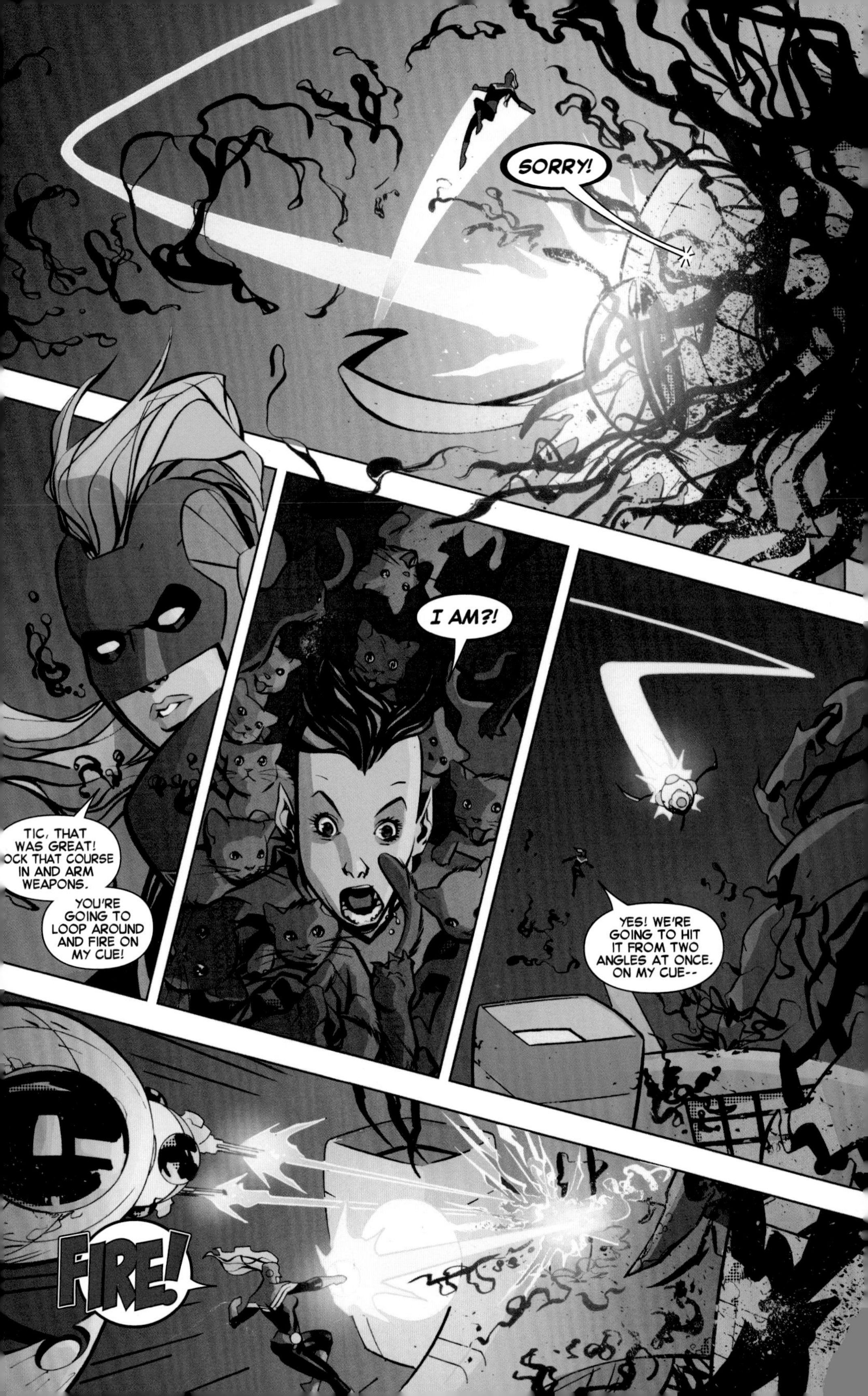
SORRY!
TIC, THAT WAS GREAT! OCK THAT COURSE IN AND ARM WEAPONS.
YOU'RE GOING TO LOOP AROUND AND FIRE ON MY CUE!
I AM?!
YES! WE'RE GOING TO HIT IT FROM TWO ANGLES AT ONCE. ON MY CUE--
FIRE!

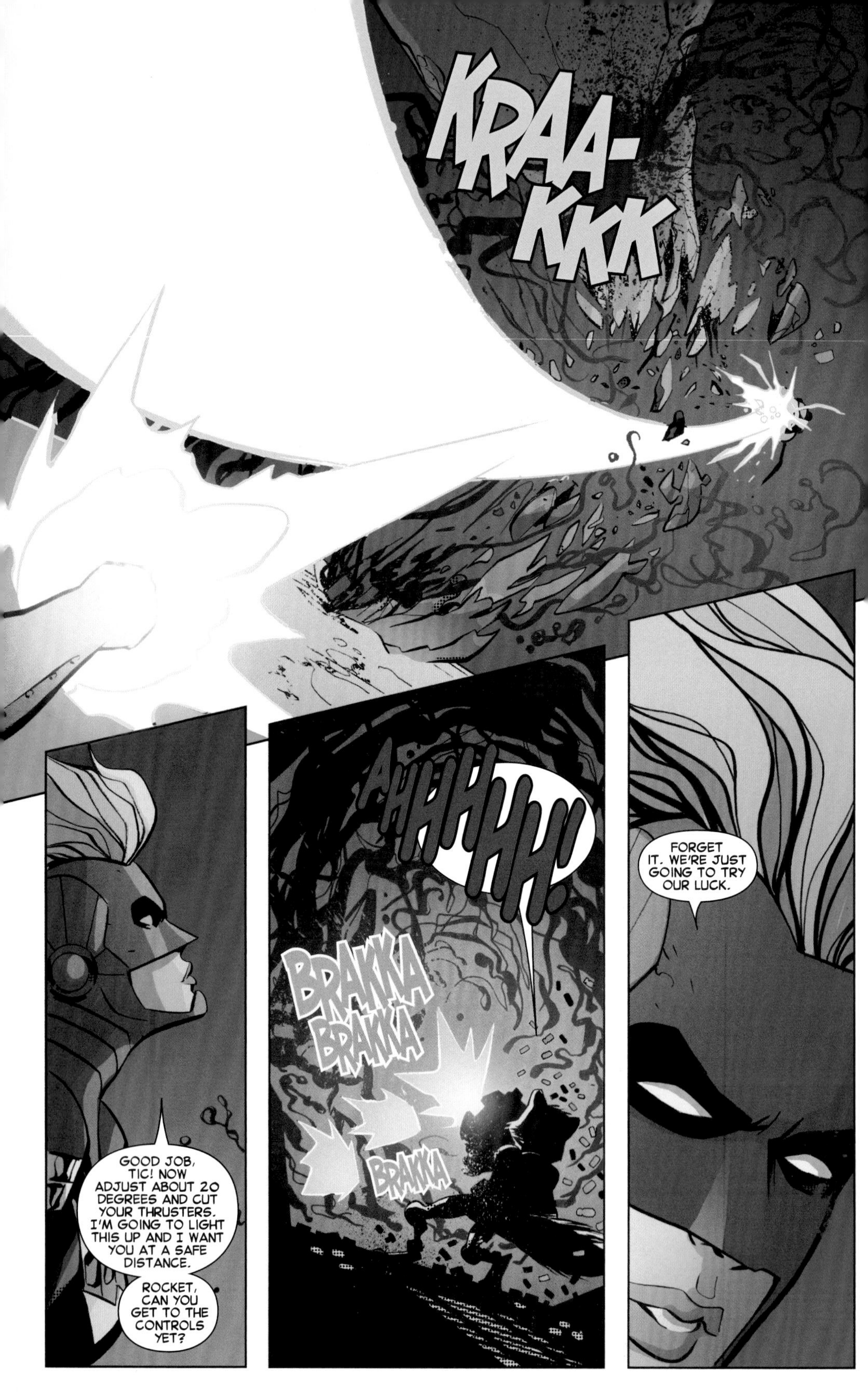
KRAA-KKK
GOOD JOB, TIC! NOW ADJUST ABOUT 20 DEGREES AND CUT YOUR THRUSTERS. I'M GOING TO LIGHT THIS UP AND I WANT YOU AT A SAFE DISTANCE.
ROCKET, CAN YOU GET TO THE CONTROLS YET?
AHHHHHH!
BRAKKA BRAKKA
BRAKKA
FORGET IT. WE'RE JUST GOING TO TRY OUR LUCK.

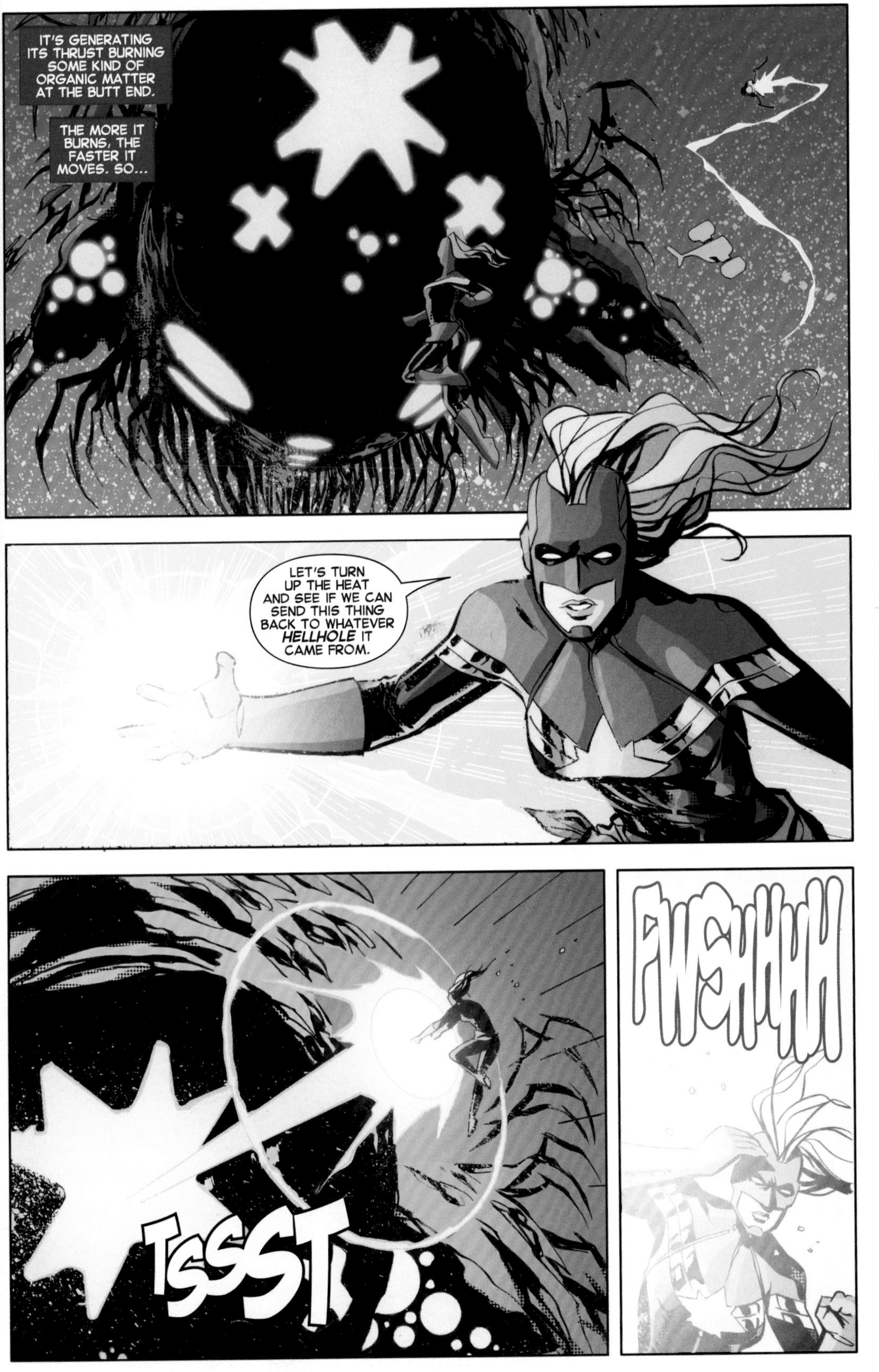
IT'S GENERATING ITS THRUST BURNING SOME KIND OF ORGANIC MATTER AT THE BUTT END.
THE MORE IT BURNS, THE FASTER IT MOVES. SO...
LET'S TURN UP THE HEAT AND SEE IF WE CAN SEND THIS THING BACK TO WHATEVER HELLHOLE IT CAME FROM.
TSSST
FWSHHHH

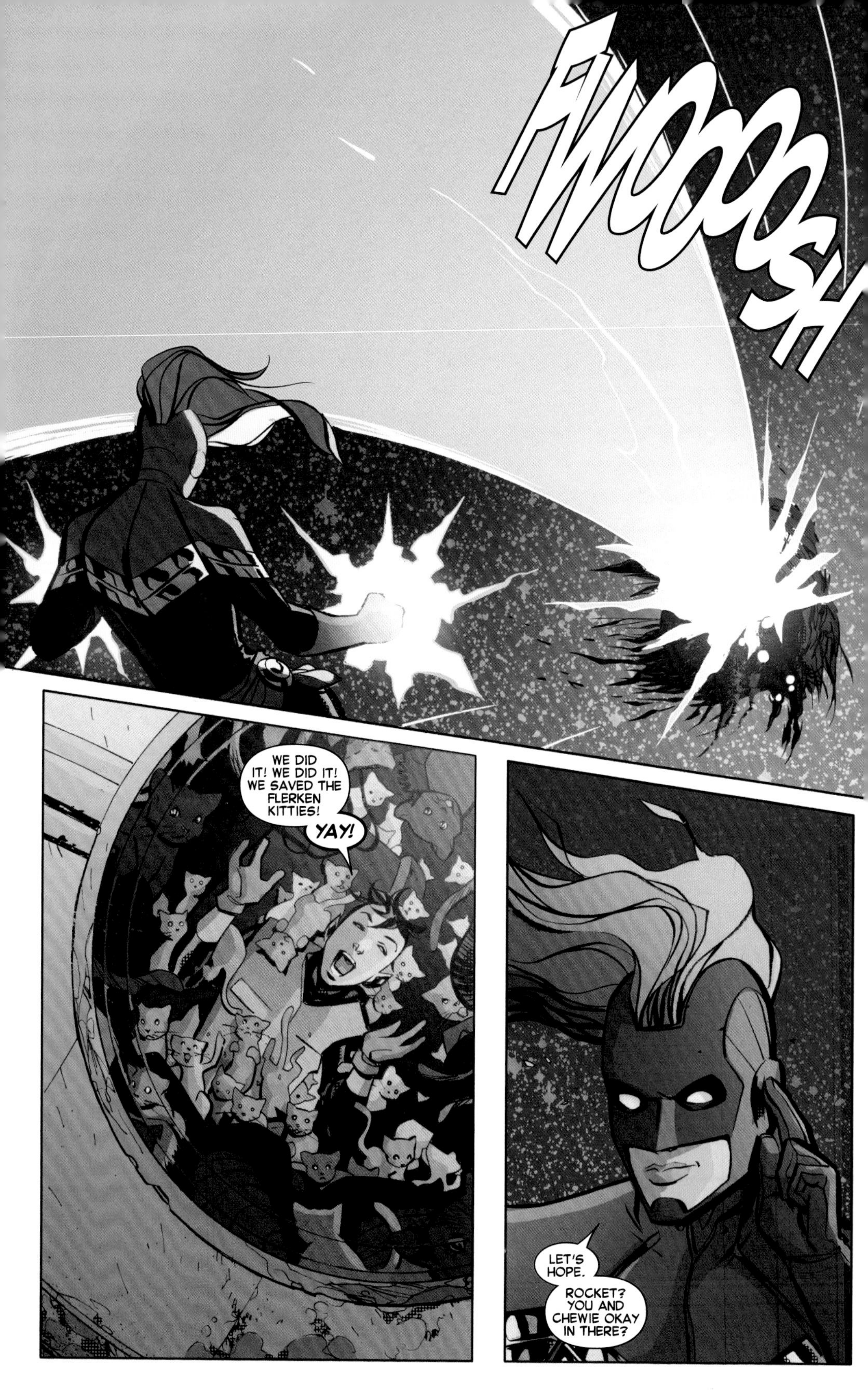
FWOOOSH
WE DID IT! WE DID IT! WE SAVED THE FLERKEN KITTIES!
YAY!
LET'S HOPE.
ROCKET? YOU AND CHEWIE OKAY IN THERE?

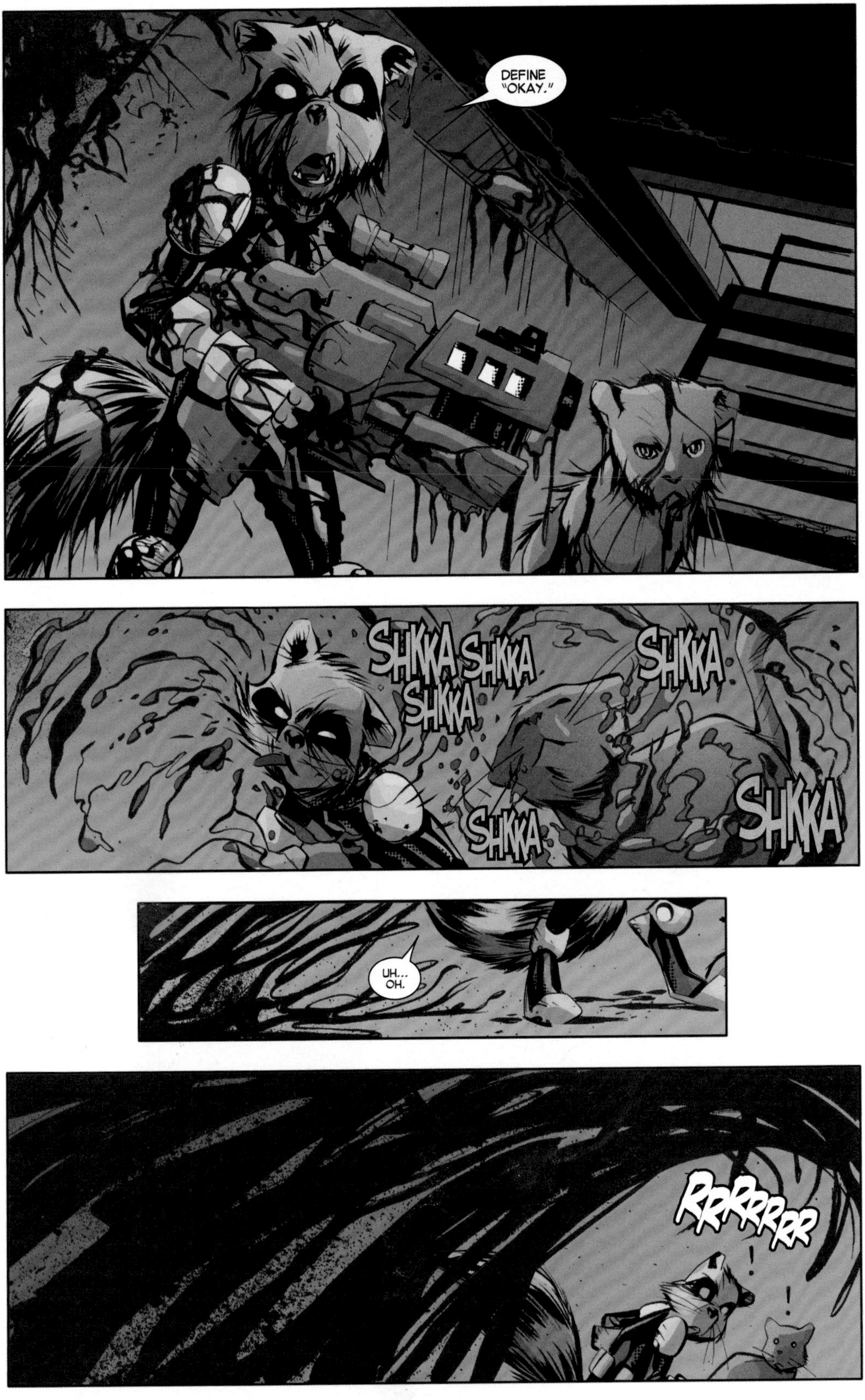
DEFINE "OKAY."
SHKKA SHKKA
SHKKA
SHKKA
SHKKA
SHKKA
UH... OH.
RRRRRRR
!
!

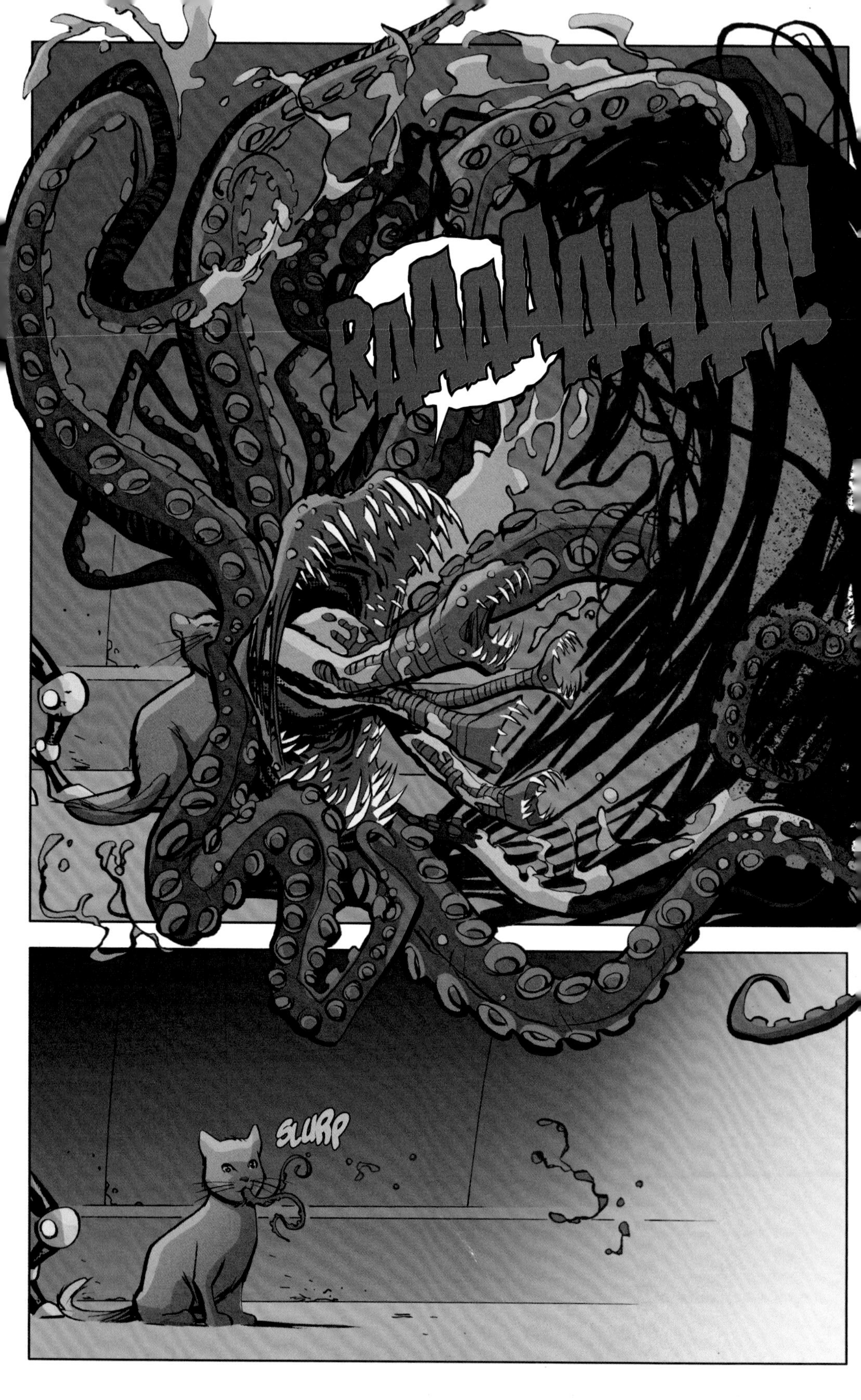
RAAAAAAA!
SLURP

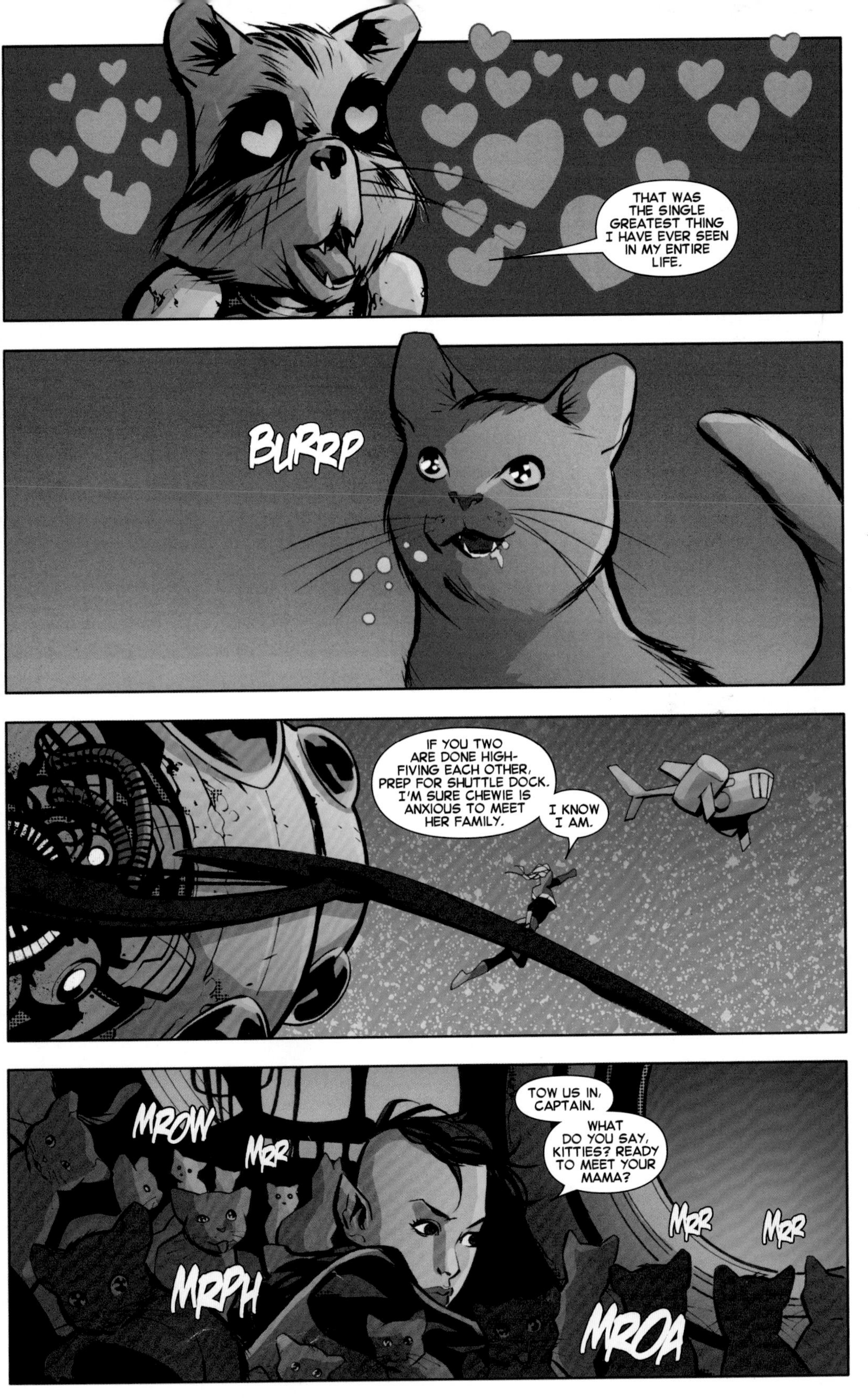
THAT WAS THE SINGLE GREATEST THING I HAVE EVER SEEN IN MY ENTIRE LIFE.
BURRP
IF YOU TWO ARE DONE HIGH-FIVING EACH OTHER, PREP FOR SHUTTLE DOCK. I'M SURE CHEWIE IS ANXIOUS TO MEET HER FAMILY.
I KNOW I AM.
TOW US IN, CAPTAIN.
WHAT DO YOU SAY, KITTIES? READY TO MEET YOUR MAMA?
MROW
MRR
MRR
MRR
MRPH
MROA

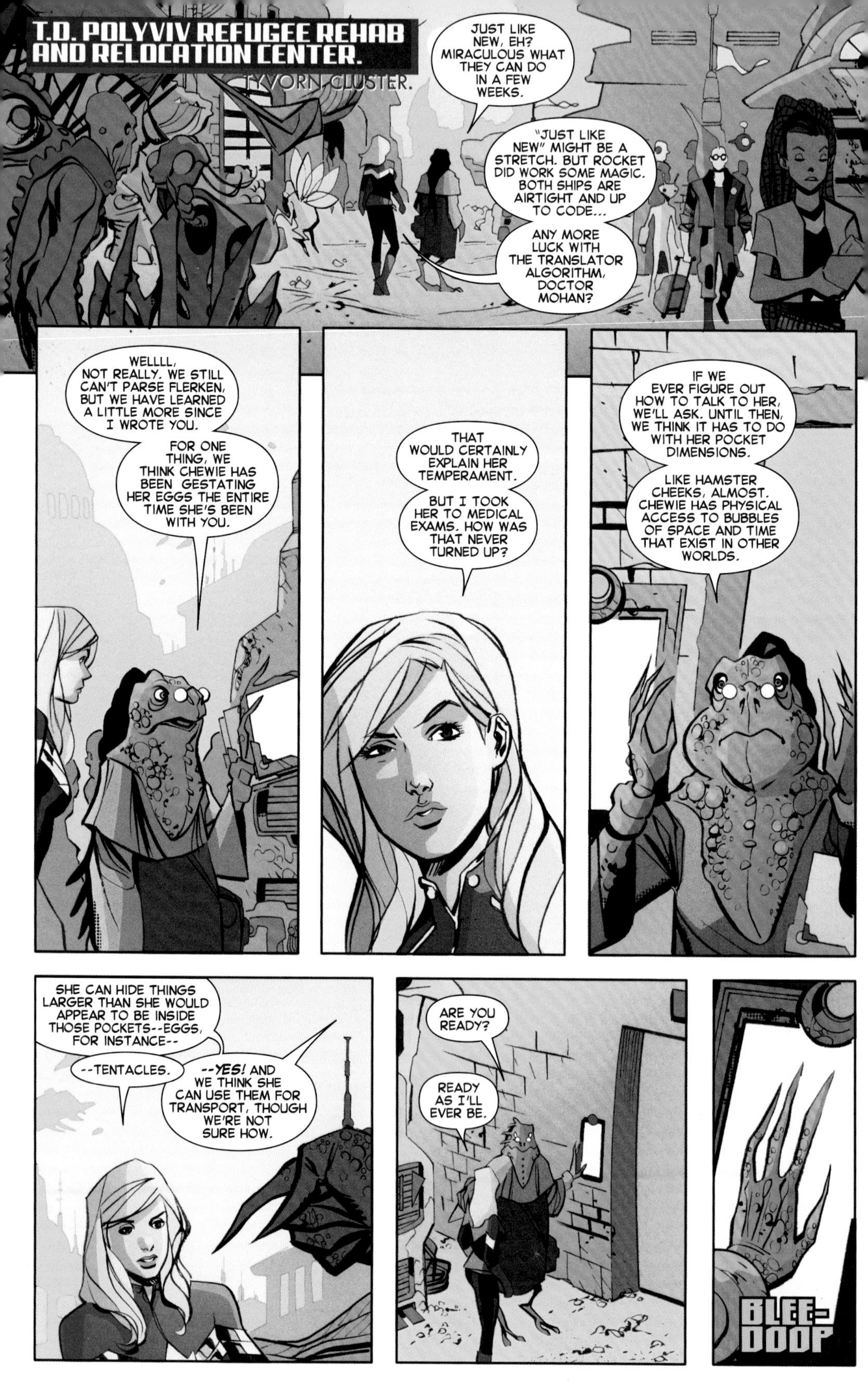
T.D. POLYVIV REFUGEE REHAB AND RELOCATION CENTER.
TYVORN CLUSTER.
JUST LIKE NEW, EH? MIRACULOUS WHAT THEY CAN DO IN A FEW WEEKS.
"JUST LIKE NEW" MIGHT BE A STRETCH. BUT ROCKET DID WORK SOME MAGIC. BOTH SHIPS ARE AIRTIGHT AND UP TO CODE...
ANY MORE LUCK WITH THE TRANSLATOR ALGORITHM, DOCTOR MOHAN?
WELLLL, NOT REALLY. WE STILL CAN'T PARSE FLERKEN, BUT WE HAVE LEARNED A LITTLE MORE SINCE I WROTE YOU.
FOR ONE THING, WE THINK CHEWIE HAS BEEN GESTATING HER EGGS THE ENTIRE TIME SHE'S BEEN WITH YOU.
THAT WOULD CERTAINLY EXPLAIN HER TEMPERAMENT.
BUT I TOOK HER TO MEDICAL EXAMS. HOW WAS THAT NEVER TURNED UP?
IF WE EVER FIGURE OUT HOW TO TALK TO HER, WE'LL ASK. UNTIL THEN, WE THINK IT HAS TO DO WITH HER POCKET DIMENSIONS.
LIKE HAMSTER CHEEKS, ALMOST. CHEWIE HAS PHYSICAL ACCESS TO BUBBLES OF SPACE AND TIME THAT EXIST IN OTHER WORLDS.
SHE CAN HIDE THINGS LARGER THAN SHE WOULD APPEAR TO BE INSIDE THOSE POCKETS--EGGS, FOR INSTANCE--
--TENTACLES.
--YES! AND WE THINK SHE CAN USE THEM FOR TRANSPORT, THOUGH WE'RE NOT SURE HOW.
ARE YOU READY?
READY AS I'LL EVER BE.
BLEE-DOOP

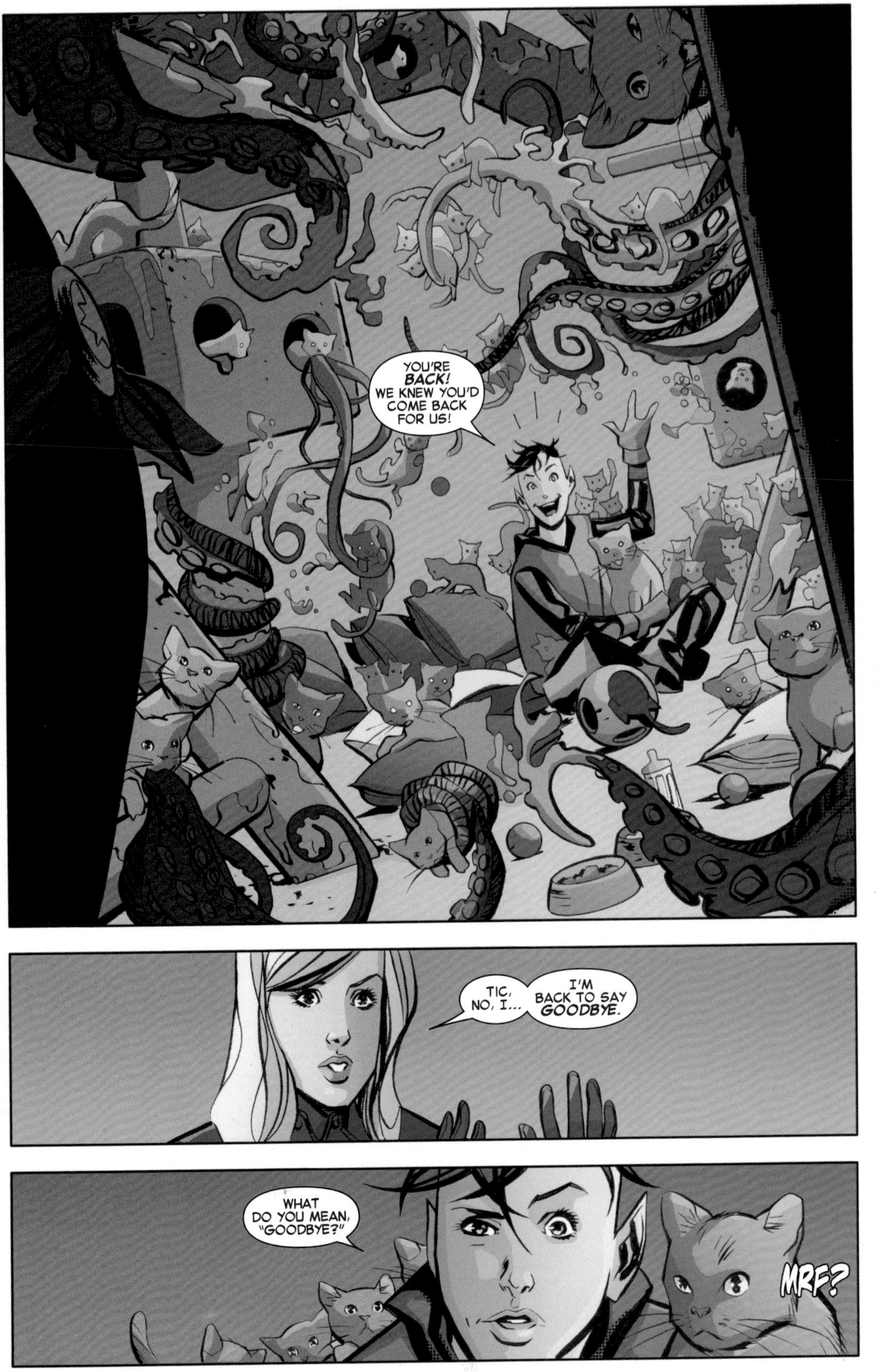

YOU'RE BACK! WE KNEW YOU'D COME BACK FOR US!
TIC, NO, I...
I'M BACK TO SAY GOODBYE.
WHAT DO YOU MEAN, "GOODBYE?"
MRF?

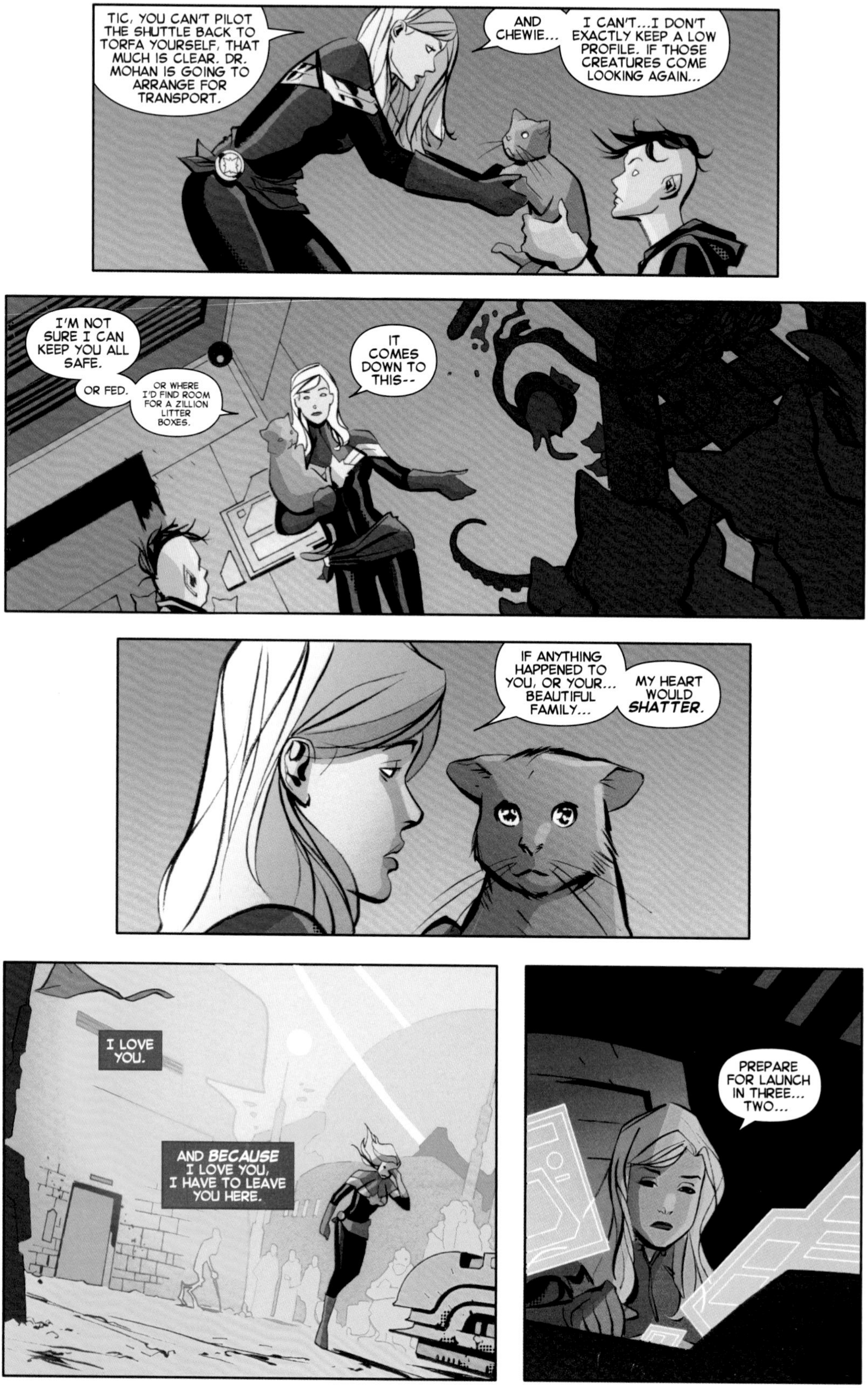
TIC, YOU CAN'T PILOT THE SHUTTLE BACK TO TORFA YOURSELF, THAT MUCH IS CLEAR. DR. MOHAN IS GOING TO ARRANGE FOR TRANSPORT.
AND CHEWIE...
I CAN'T...I DON'T EXACTLY KEEP A LOW PROFILE. IF THOSE CREATURES COME LOOKING AGAIN...
I'M NOT SURE I CAN KEEP YOU ALL SAFE.
OR FED.
OR WHERE I'D FIND ROOM FOR A ZILLION LITTER BOXES.
IT COMES DOWN TO THIS--
IF ANYTHING HAPPENED TO YOU, OR YOUR... BEAUTIFUL FAMILY...
MY HEART WOULD *SHATTER.*
I LOVE YOU.
AND *BECAUSE* I LOVE YOU, I HAVE TO LEAVE YOU HERE.
PREPARE FOR LAUNCH IN THREE... TWO...

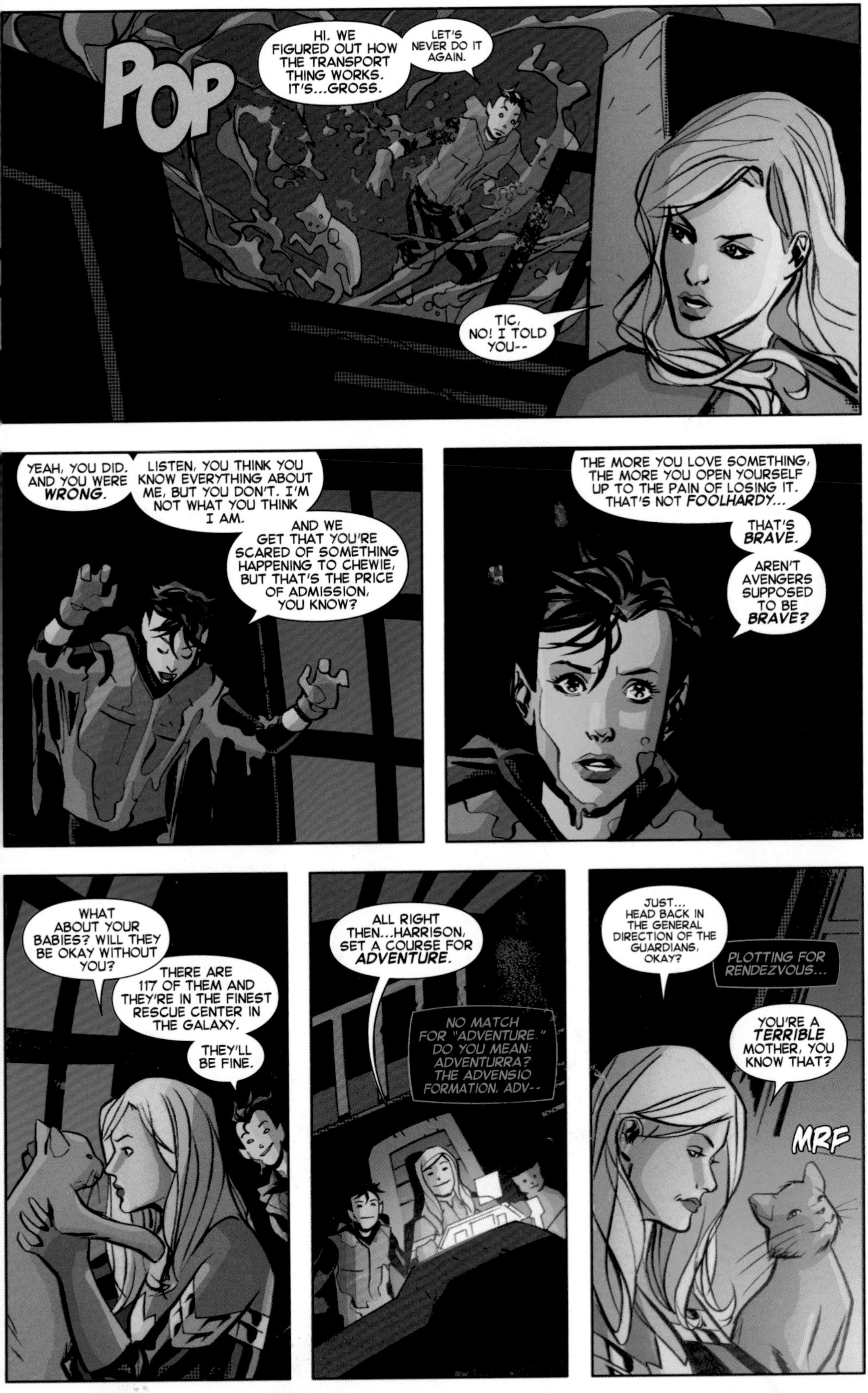
POP
HI. WE FIGURED OUT HOW THE TRANSPORT THING WORKS. IT'S...GROSS.
LET'S NEVER DO IT AGAIN.
TIC, NO! I TOLD YOU--
YEAH, YOU DID. AND YOU WERE WRONG.
LISTEN, YOU THINK YOU KNOW EVERYTHING ABOUT ME, BUT YOU DON'T. I'M NOT WHAT YOU THINK I AM.
AND WE GET THAT YOU'RE SCARED OF SOMETHING HAPPENING TO CHEWIE, BUT THAT'S THE PRICE OF ADMISSION, YOU KNOW?
THE MORE YOU LOVE SOMETHING, THE MORE YOU OPEN YOURSELF UP TO THE PAIN OF LOSING IT. THAT'S NOT FOOLHARDY...
THAT'S BRAVE.
AREN'T AVENGERS SUPPOSED TO BE BRAVE?
WHAT ABOUT YOUR BABIES? WILL THEY BE OKAY WITHOUT YOU?
THERE ARE 117 OF THEM AND THEY'RE IN THE FINEST RESCUE CENTER IN THE GALAXY.
THEY'LL BE FINE.
ALL RIGHT THEN...HARRISON, SET A COURSE FOR ADVENTURE.
NO MATCH FOR "ADVENTURE." DO YOU MEAN: ADVENTURRA? THE ADVENSIO FORMATION. ADV--
JUST... HEAD BACK IN THE GENERAL DIRECTION OF THE GUARDIANS, OKAY?
PLOTTING FOR RENDEZVOUS...
YOU'RE A TERRIBLE MOTHER, YOU KNOW THAT?
MRF

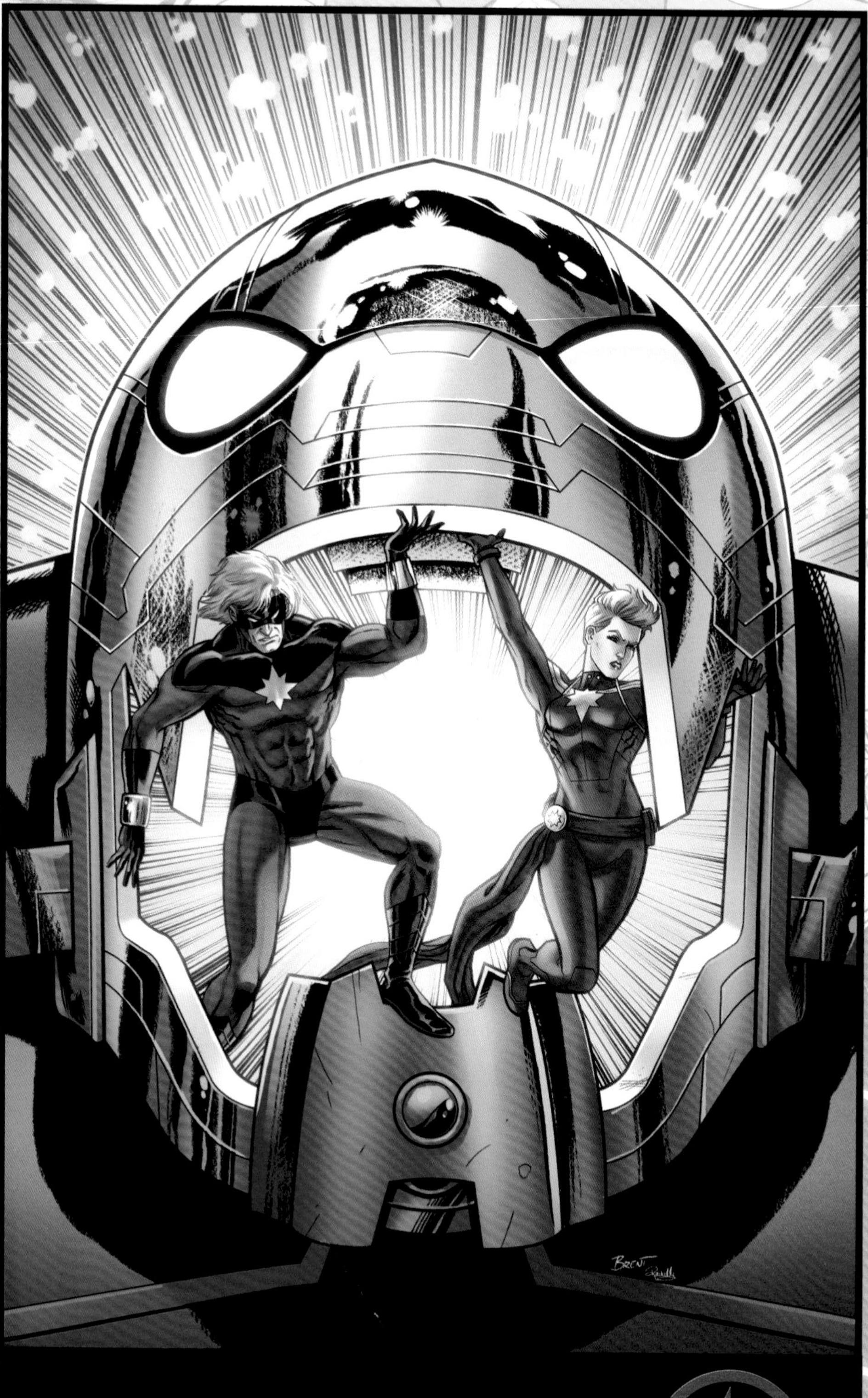

GENERATIONS: CAPTAIN MARVEL AND CAPTAIN MAR-VELL
VARIANT COVER BY BRENT SCHOONOVER & RACHELLE ROSENBERG

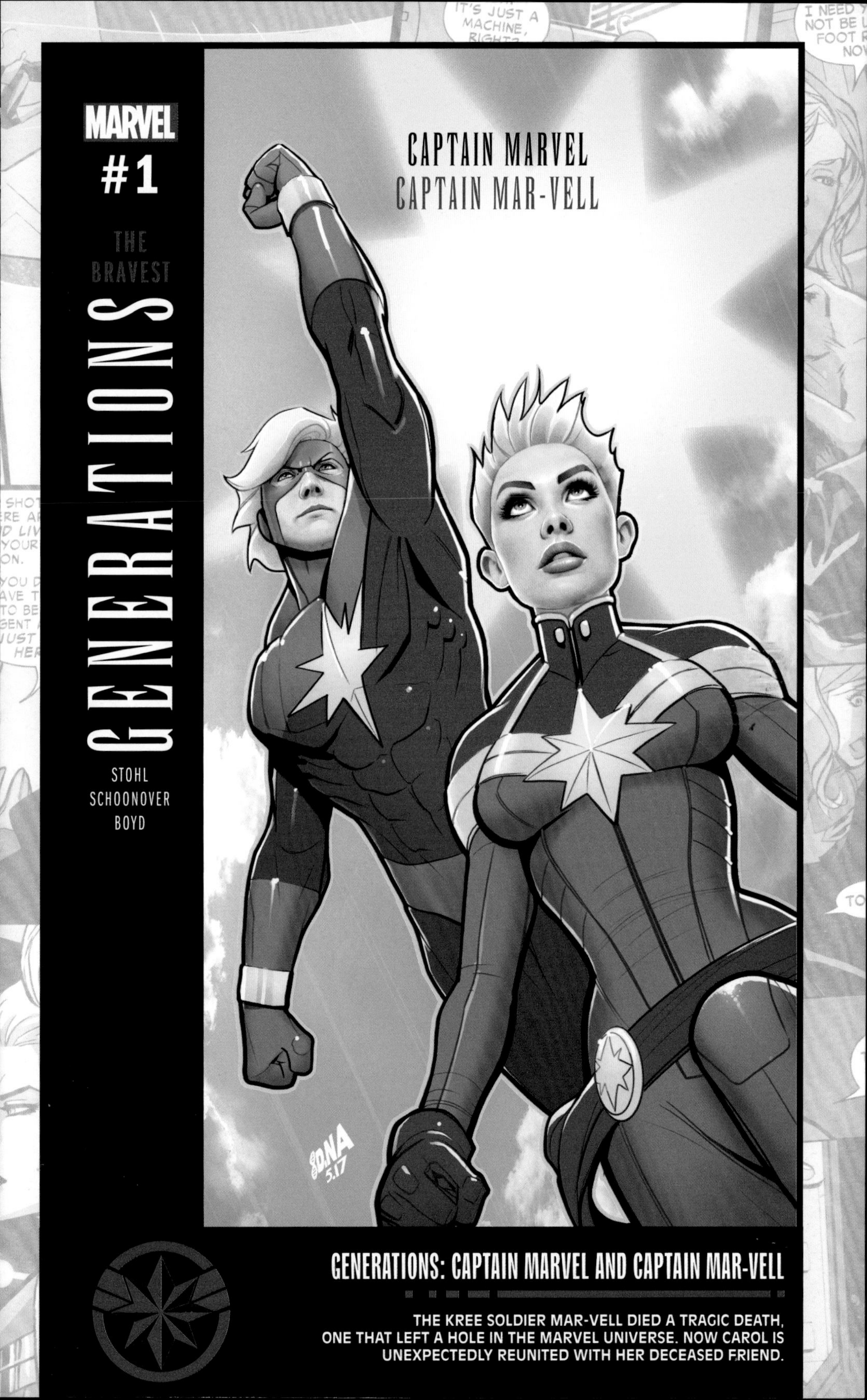

IT'S JUST A MACHINE, RIGHT?
MARVEL
#1
THE BRAVEST
GENERATIONS
STOHL
SCHOONOVER
BOYD
CAPTAIN MARVEL
CAPTAIN MAR-VELL
GENERATIONS: CAPTAIN MARVEL AND CAPTAIN MAR-VELL
THE KREE SOLDIER MAR-VELL DIED A TRAGIC DEATH, ONE THAT LEFT A HOLE IN THE MARVEL UNIVERSE. NOW CAROL IS UNEXPECTEDLY REUNITED WITH HER DECEASED FRIEND.

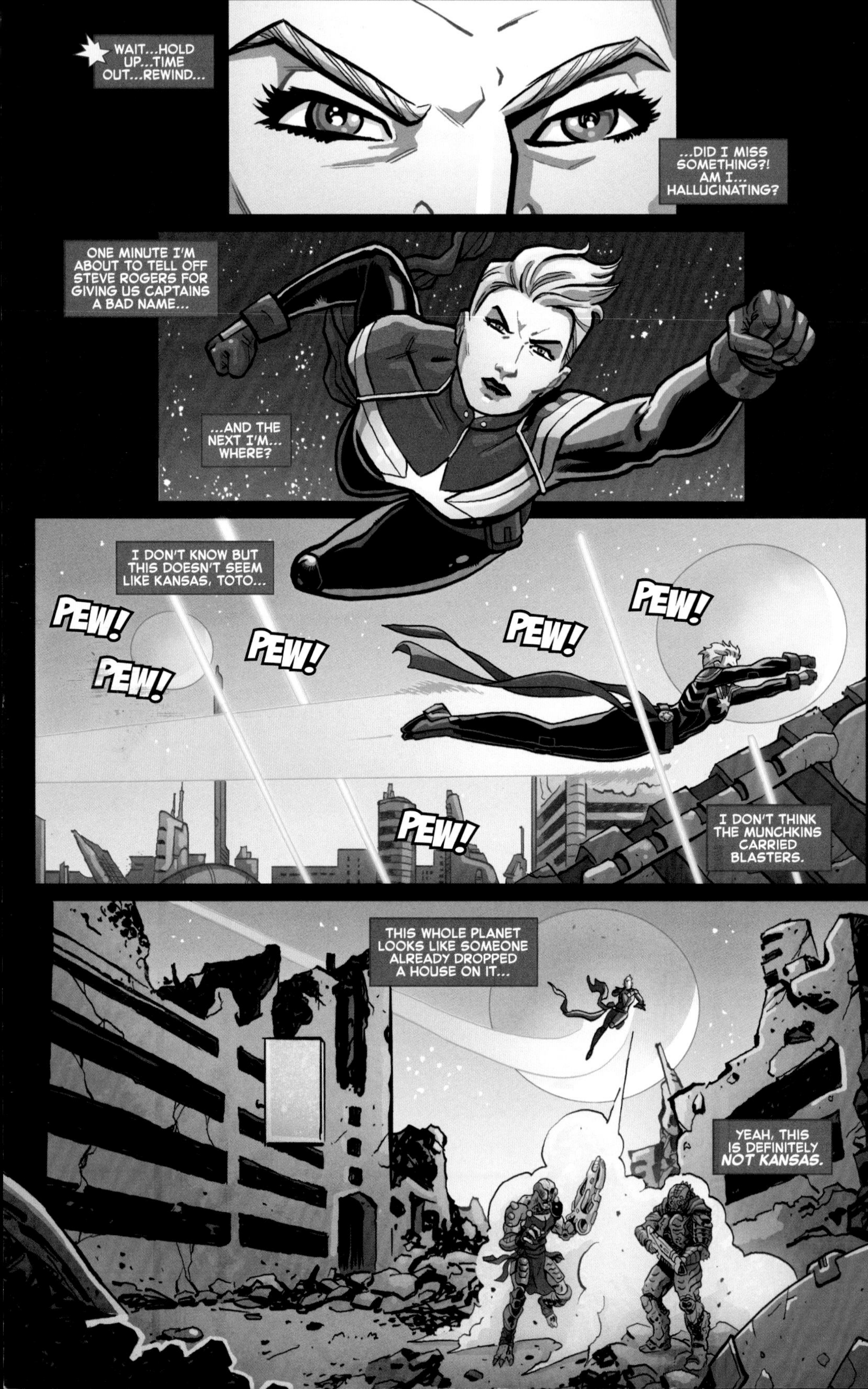
WAIT...HOLD UP...TIME OUT...REWIND...
...DID I MISS SOMETHING?! AM I... HALLUCINATING?
ONE MINUTE I'M ABOUT TO TELL OFF STEVE ROGERS FOR GIVING US CAPTAINS A BAD NAME...
...AND THE NEXT I'M... WHERE?
I DON'T KNOW BUT THIS DOESN'T SEEM LIKE KANSAS, TOTO...
PEW!
PEW!
PEW!
PEW!
PEW!
PEW!
I DON'T THINK THE MUNCHKINS CARRIED BLASTERS.
THIS WHOLE PLANET LOOKS LIKE SOMEONE ALREADY DROPPED A HOUSE ON IT...
YEAH, THIS IS DEFINITELY NOT KANSAS.

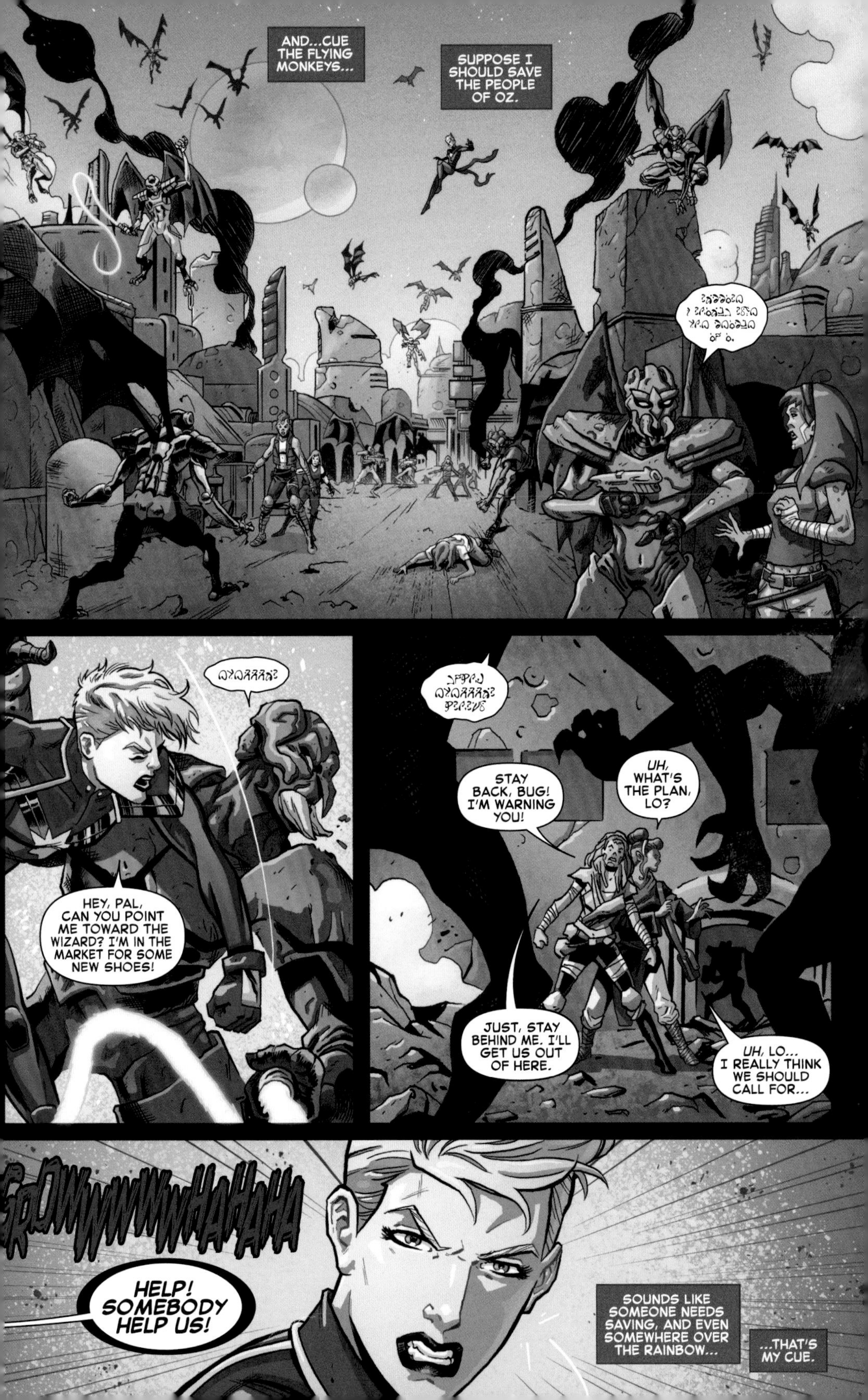
AND...CUE THE FLYING MONKEYS...
SUPPOSE I SHOULD SAVE THE PEOPLE OF OZ.
HEY, PAL, CAN YOU POINT ME TOWARD THE WIZARD? I'M IN THE MARKET FOR SOME NEW SHOES!
STAY BACK, BUG! I'M WARNING YOU!
UH, WHAT'S THE PLAN, LO?
JUST, STAY BEHIND ME. I'LL GET US OUT OF HERE.
UH, LO... I REALLY THINK WE SHOULD CALL FOR...
GROWWWWWWHAHAHA
HELP! SOMEBODY HELP US!
SOUNDS LIKE SOMEONE NEEDS SAVING, AND EVEN SOMEWHERE OVER THE RAINBOW...
...THAT'S MY CUE.

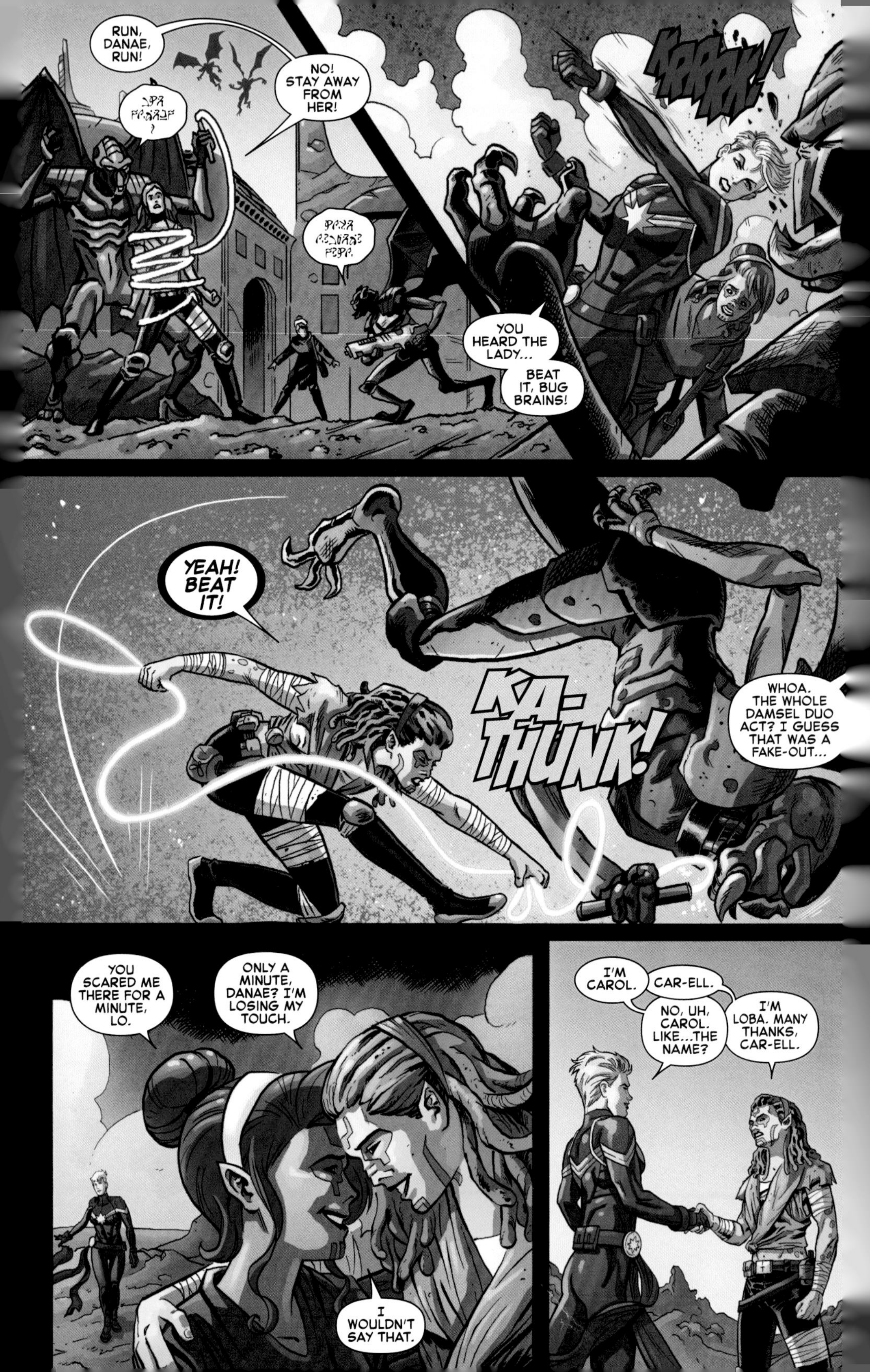
RUN, DANAE, RUN!
NO! STAY AWAY FROM HER!
KRAKK!
YOU HEARD THE LADY...
BEAT IT, BUG BRAINS!
YEAH! BEAT IT!
KA-THUNK!
WHOA. THE WHOLE DAMSEL DUO ACT? I GUESS THAT WAS A FAKE-OUT...
YOU SCARED ME THERE FOR A MINUTE, LO.
ONLY A MINUTE, DANAE? I'M LOSING MY TOUCH.
I WOULDN'T SAY THAT.
I'M CAROL.
CAR-ELL.
NO, UH, CAROL. LIKE...THE NAME?
I'M LOBA. MANY THANKS, CAR-ELL.

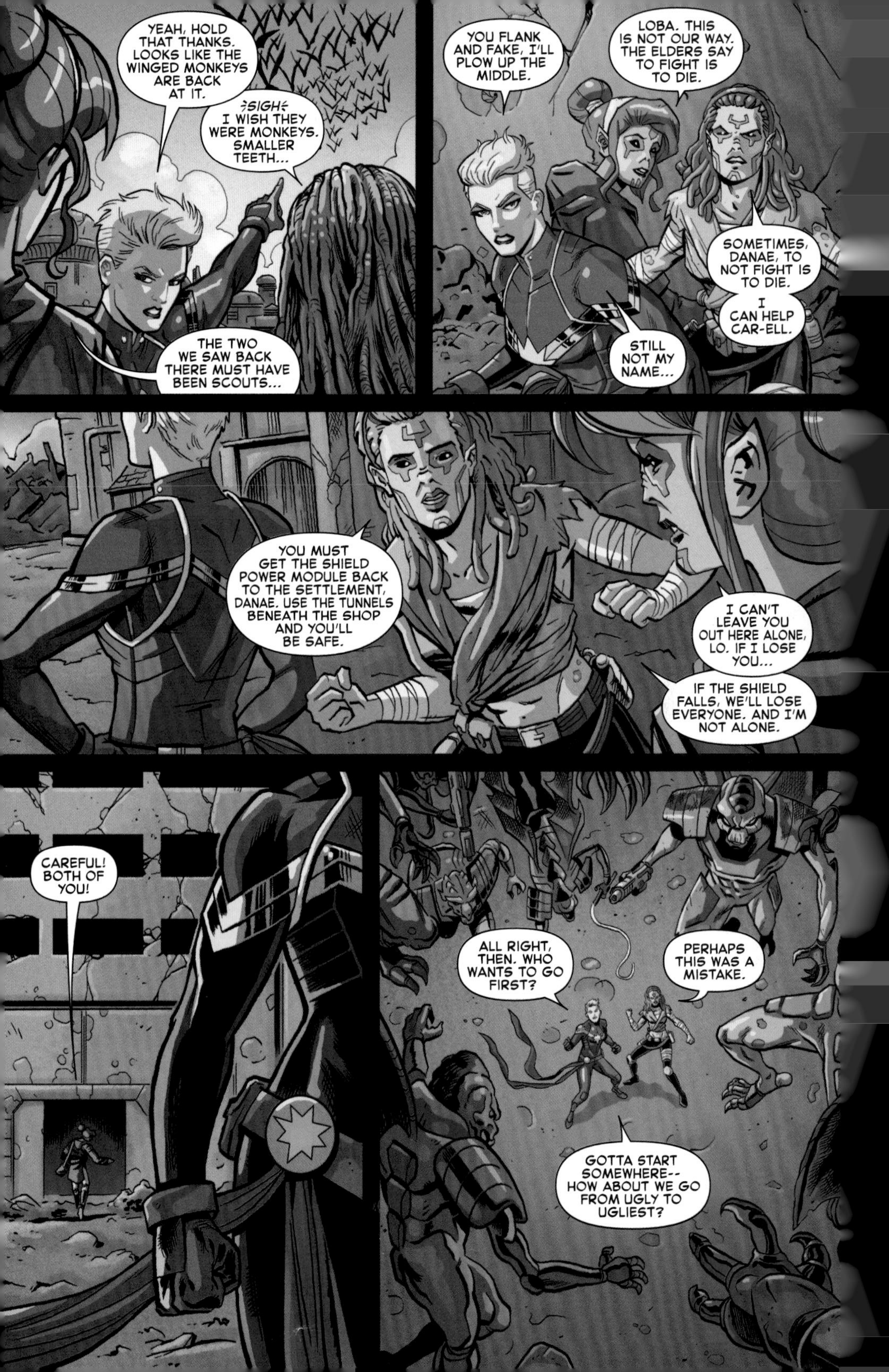
YEAH, HOLD THAT THANKS. LOOKS LIKE THE WINGED MONKEYS ARE BACK AT IT.
SIGH I WISH THEY WERE MONKEYS. SMALLER TEETH...
THE TWO WE SAW BACK THERE MUST HAVE BEEN SCOUTS...
YOU FLANK AND FAKE, I'LL PLOW UP THE MIDDLE.
LOBA. THIS IS NOT OUR WAY. THE ELDERS SAY TO FIGHT IS TO DIE.
SOMETIMES, DANAE, TO NOT FIGHT IS TO DIE.
I CAN HELP CAR-ELL.
STILL NOT MY NAME...
YOU MUST GET THE SHIELD POWER MODULE BACK TO THE SETTLEMENT, DANAE. USE THE TUNNELS BENEATH THE SHOP AND YOU'LL BE SAFE.
I CAN'T LEAVE YOU OUT HERE ALONE, LO. IF I LOSE YOU...
IF THE SHIELD FALLS, WE'LL LOSE EVERYONE. AND I'M NOT ALONE.
CAREFUL! BOTH OF YOU!
ALL RIGHT, THEN. WHO WANTS TO GO FIRST?
PERHAPS THIS WAS A MISTAKE.
GOTTA START SOMEWHERE-- HOW ABOUT WE GO FROM UGLY TO UGLIEST?

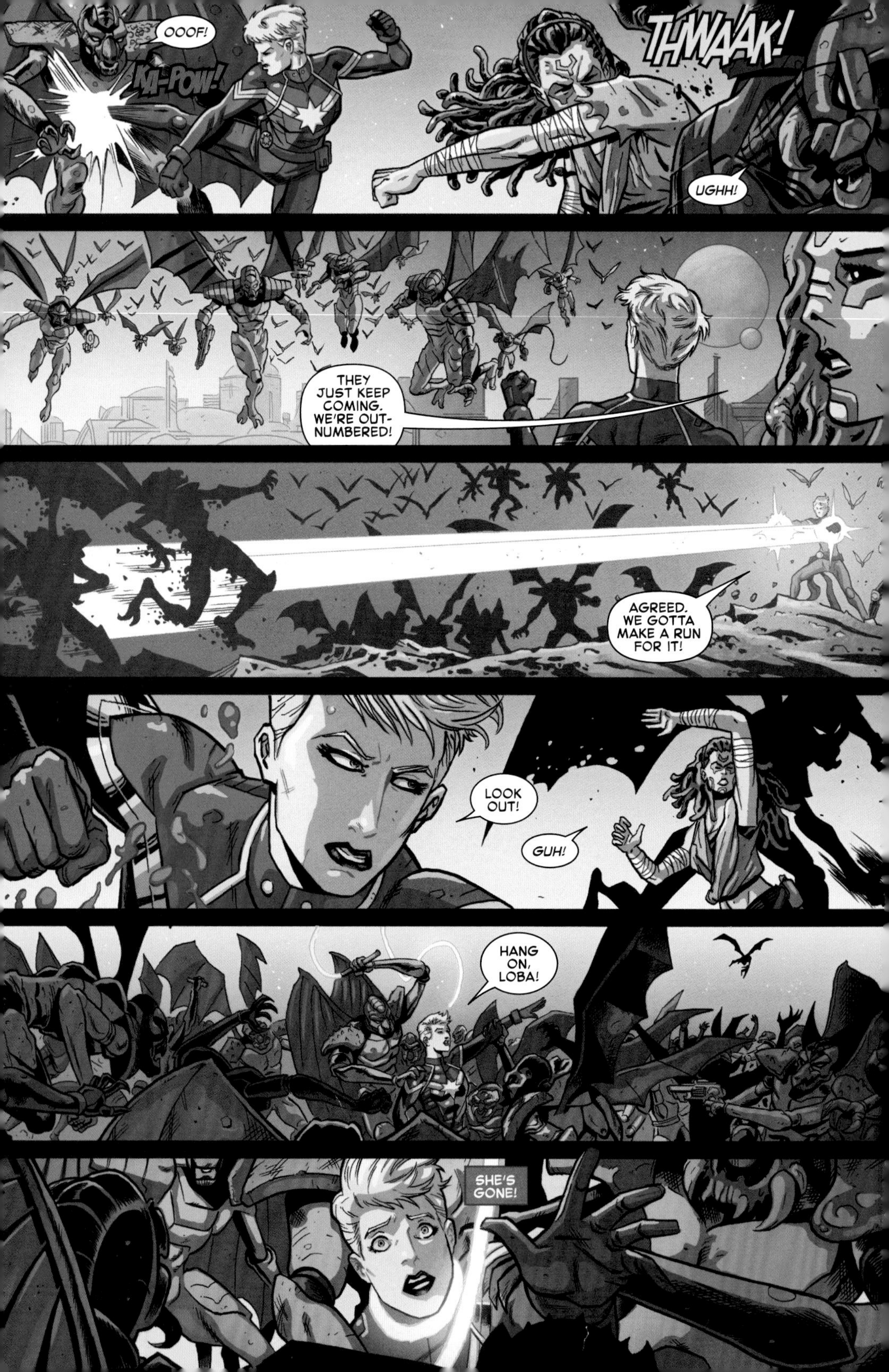
OOOF!
KA-POW!
THWAAK!
UGHH!
THEY JUST KEEP COMING. WE'RE OUT-NUMBERED!
AGREED. WE GOTTA MAKE A RUN FOR IT!
LOOK OUT!
GUH!
HANG ON, LOBA!
SHE'S GONE!

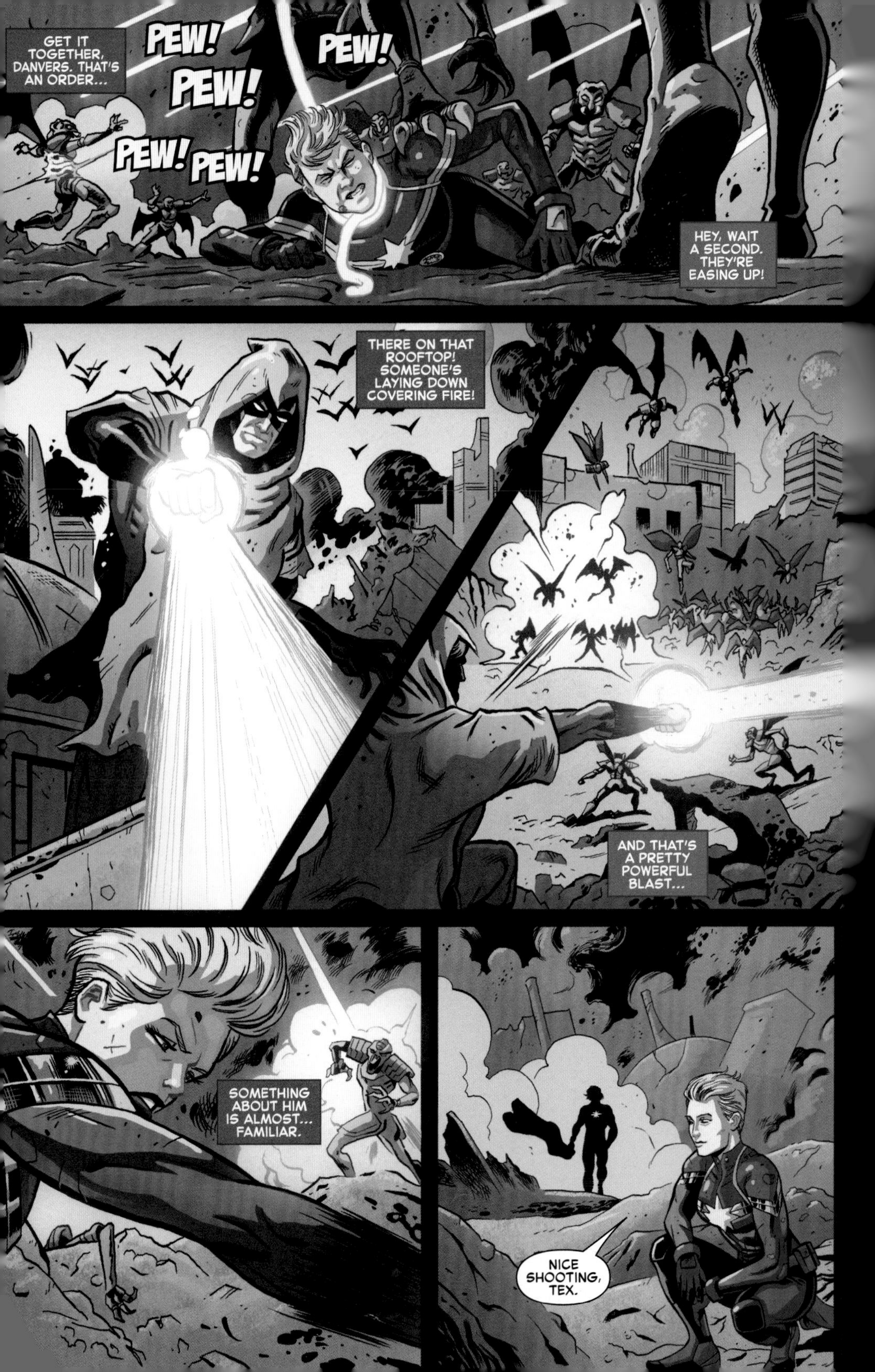
GET IT TOGETHER, DANVERS. THAT'S AN ORDER...
PEW! PEW! PEW! PEW! PEW!
HEY, WAIT A SECOND. THEY'RE EASING UP!
THERE ON THAT ROOFTOP! SOMEONE'S LAYING DOWN COVERING FIRE!
AND THAT'S A PRETTY POWERFUL BLAST...
SOMETHING ABOUT HIM IS ALMOST... FAMILIAR.
NICE SHOOTING, TEX.

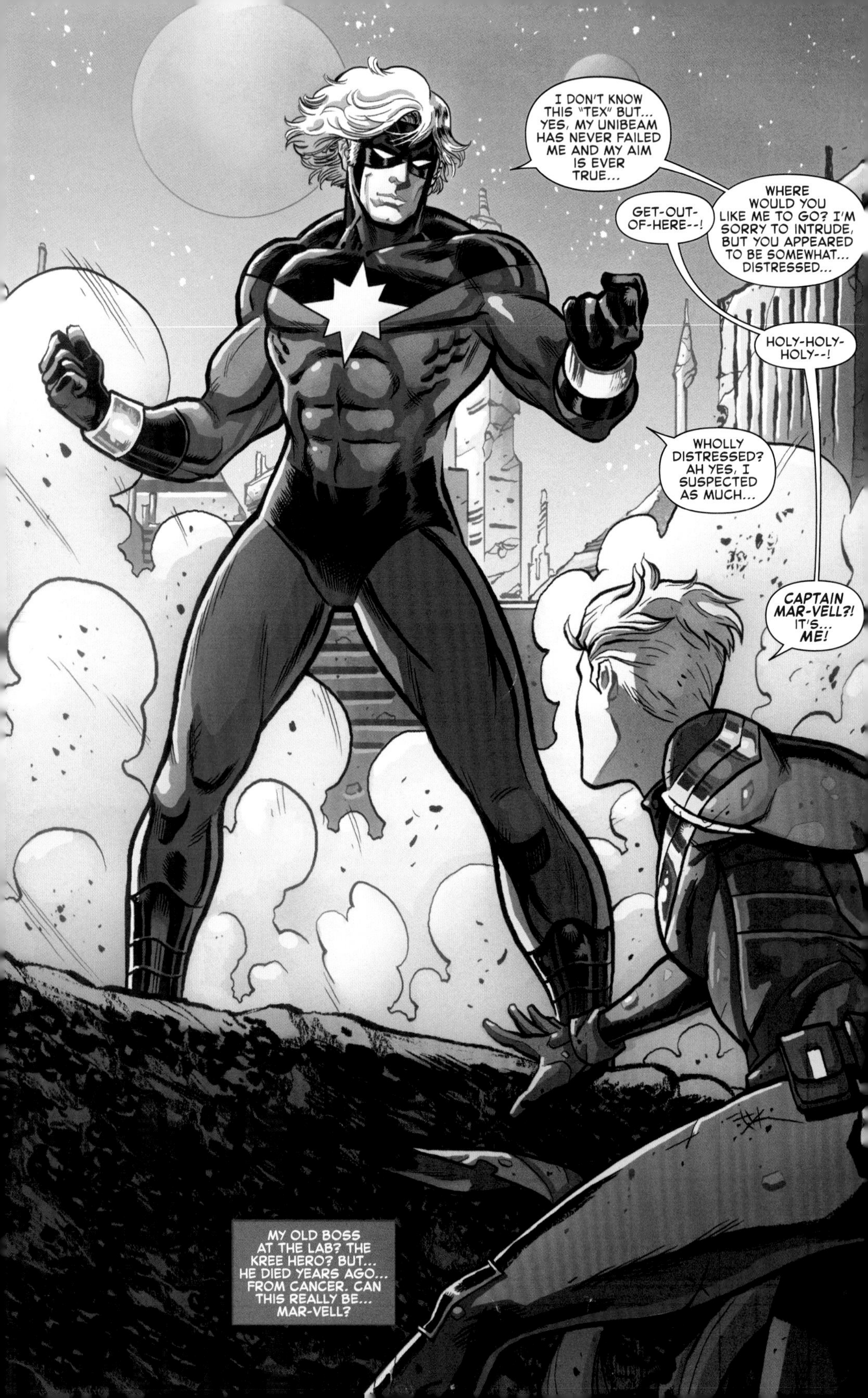
I DON'T KNOW THIS "TEX" BUT... YES, MY UNIBEAM HAS NEVER FAILED ME AND MY AIM IS EVER TRUE...
GET-OUT-OF-HERE--!
WHERE WOULD YOU LIKE ME TO GO? I'M SORRY TO INTRUDE, BUT YOU APPEARED TO BE SOMEWHAT... DISTRESSED...
HOLY-HOLY-HOLY--!
WHOLLY DISTRESSED? AH YES, I SUSPECTED AS MUCH...
CAPTAIN MAR-VELL?! IT'S... ME!
MY OLD BOSS AT THE LAB? THE KREE HERO? BUT... HE DIED YEARS AGO... FROM CANCER. CAN THIS REALLY BE... MAR-VELL?

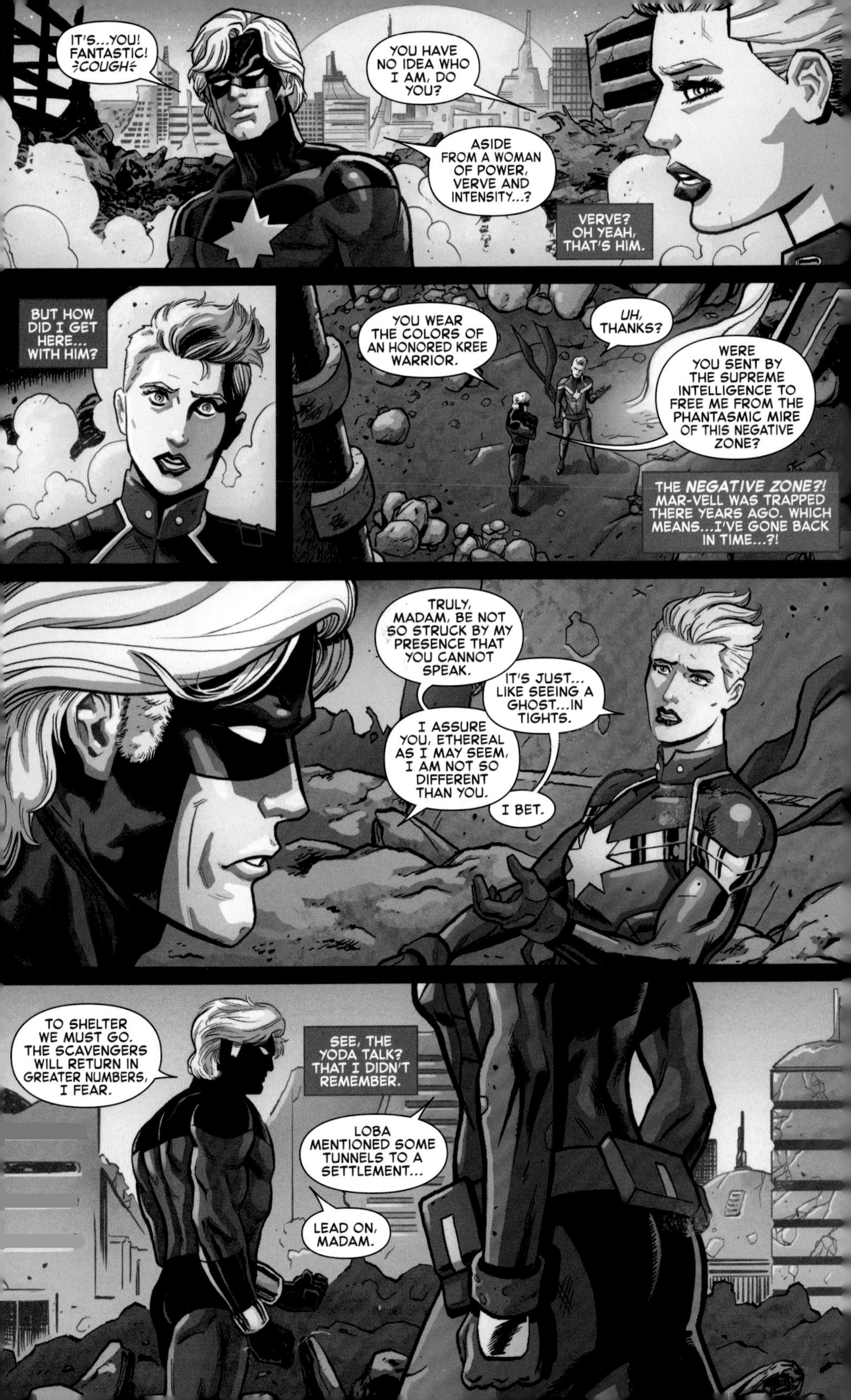
IT'S...YOU! FANTASTIC! *COUGH*
YOU HAVE NO IDEA WHO I AM, DO YOU?
ASIDE FROM A WOMAN OF POWER, VERVE AND INTENSITY...?
VERVE? OH YEAH, THAT'S HIM.
BUT HOW DID I GET HERE... WITH HIM?
YOU WEAR THE COLORS OF AN HONORED KREE WARRIOR.
UH, THANKS?
WERE YOU SENT BY THE SUPREME INTELLIGENCE TO FREE ME FROM THE PHANTASMIC MIRE OF THIS NEGATIVE ZONE?
THE NEGATIVE ZONE?! MAR-VELL WAS TRAPPED THERE YEARS AGO. WHICH MEANS...I'VE GONE BACK IN TIME...?!
TRULY, MADAM, BE NOT SO STRUCK BY MY PRESENCE THAT YOU CANNOT SPEAK.
IT'S JUST... LIKE SEEING A GHOST...IN TIGHTS.
I ASSURE YOU, ETHEREAL AS I MAY SEEM, I AM NOT SO DIFFERENT THAN YOU.
I BET.
TO SHELTER WE MUST GO. THE SCAVENGERS WILL RETURN IN GREATER NUMBERS, I FEAR.
SEE, THE YODA TALK? THAT I DIDN'T REMEMBER.
LOBA MENTIONED SOME TUNNELS TO A SETTLEMENT...
LEAD ON, MADAM.

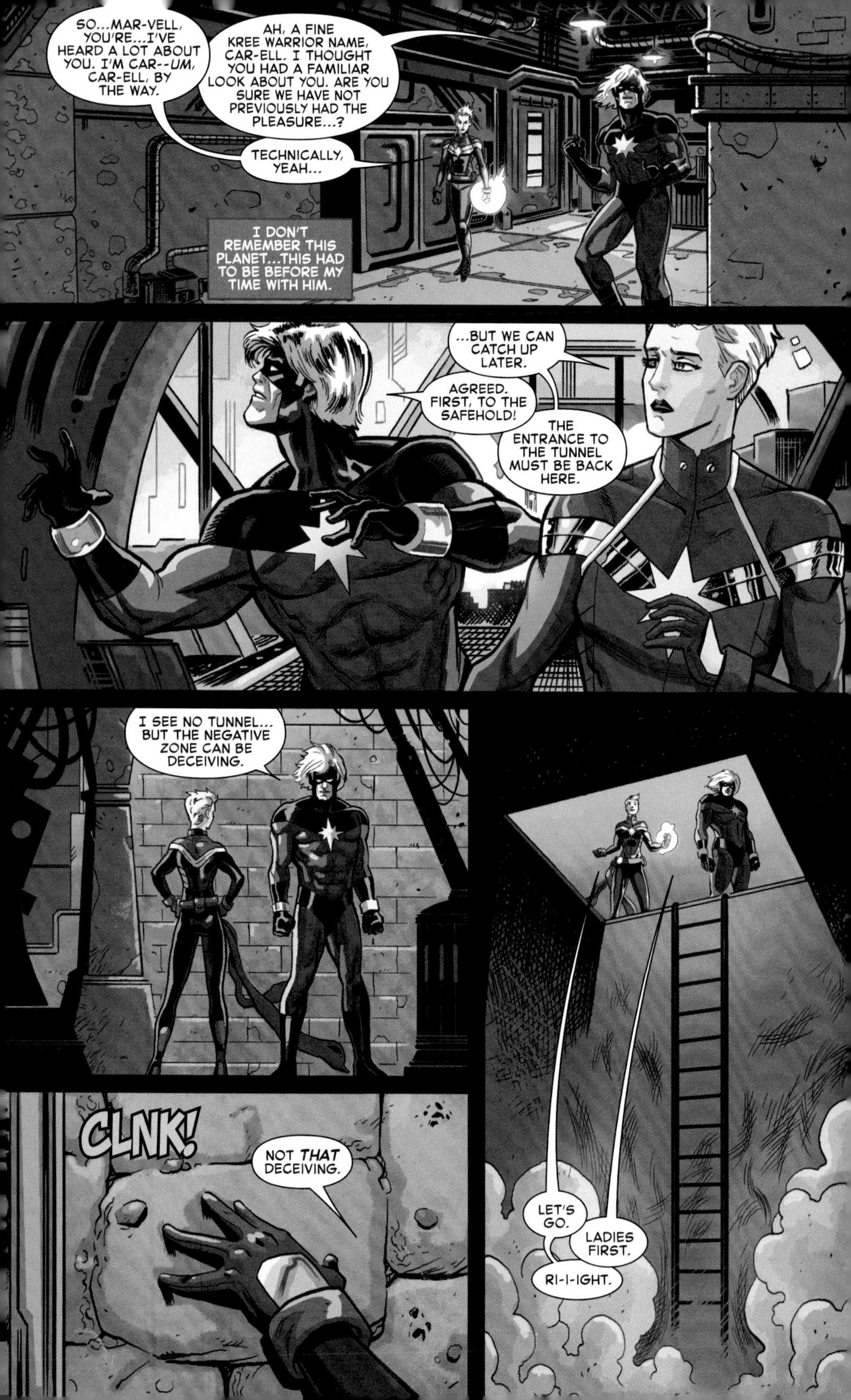
SO...MAR-VELL, YOU'RE...I'VE HEARD A LOT ABOUT YOU. I'M CAR--*UM*, CAR-ELL, BY THE WAY.
AH, A FINE KREE WARRIOR NAME, CAR-ELL. I THOUGHT YOU HAD A FAMILIAR LOOK ABOUT YOU. ARE YOU SURE WE HAVE NOT PREVIOUSLY HAD THE PLEASURE...?
TECHNICALLY, YEAH...
I DON'T REMEMBER THIS PLANET...THIS HAD TO BE BEFORE MY TIME WITH HIM.
...BUT WE CAN CATCH UP LATER.
AGREED. FIRST, TO THE SAFEHOLD!
THE ENTRANCE TO THE TUNNEL MUST BE BACK HERE.
I SEE NO TUNNEL... BUT THE NEGATIVE ZONE CAN BE DECEIVING.
CLNK!
NOT *THAT* DECEIVING.
LET'S GO.
LADIES FIRST.
RI-I-IGHT.

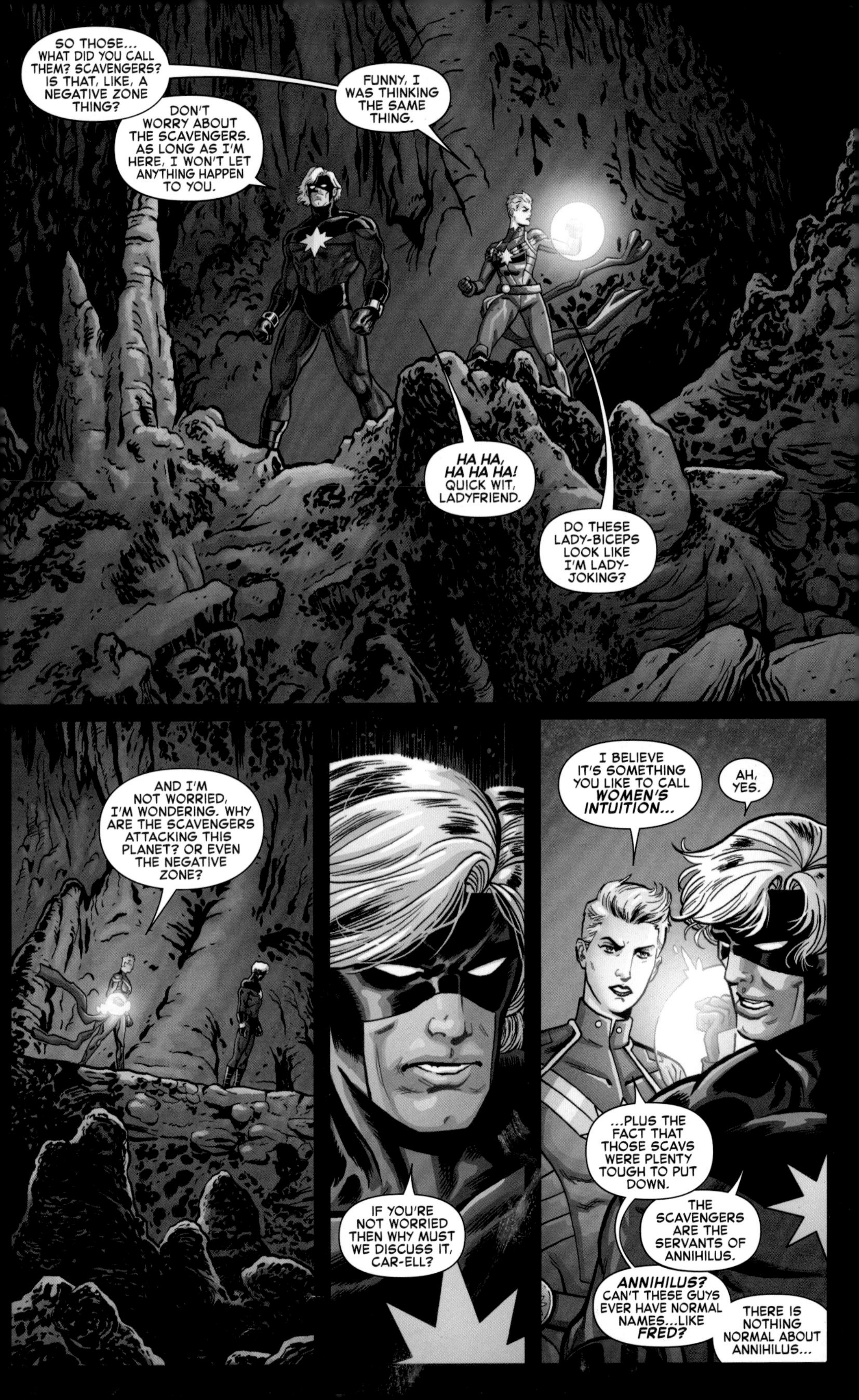
SO THOSE... WHAT DID YOU CALL THEM? SCAVENGERS? IS THAT, LIKE, A NEGATIVE ZONE THING?
FUNNY, I WAS THINKING THE SAME THING.
DON'T WORRY ABOUT THE SCAVENGERS. AS LONG AS I'M HERE, I WON'T LET ANYTHING HAPPEN TO YOU.
HA HA, HA HA HA! QUICK WIT, LADYFRIEND.
DO THESE LADY-BICEPS LOOK LIKE I'M LADY-JOKING?
AND I'M NOT WORRIED, I'M WONDERING. WHY ARE THE SCAVENGERS ATTACKING THIS PLANET? OR EVEN THE NEGATIVE ZONE?
IF YOU'RE NOT WORRIED THEN WHY MUST WE DISCUSS IT, CAR-ELL?
I BELIEVE IT'S SOMETHING YOU LIKE TO CALL WOMEN'S INTUITION...
AH, YES.
...PLUS THE FACT THAT THOSE SCAVS WERE PLENTY TOUGH TO PUT DOWN.
THE SCAVENGERS ARE THE SERVANTS OF ANNIHILUS.
ANNIHILUS? CAN'T THESE GUYS EVER HAVE NORMAL NAMES...LIKE FRED?
THERE IS NOTHING NORMAL ABOUT ANNIHILUS...

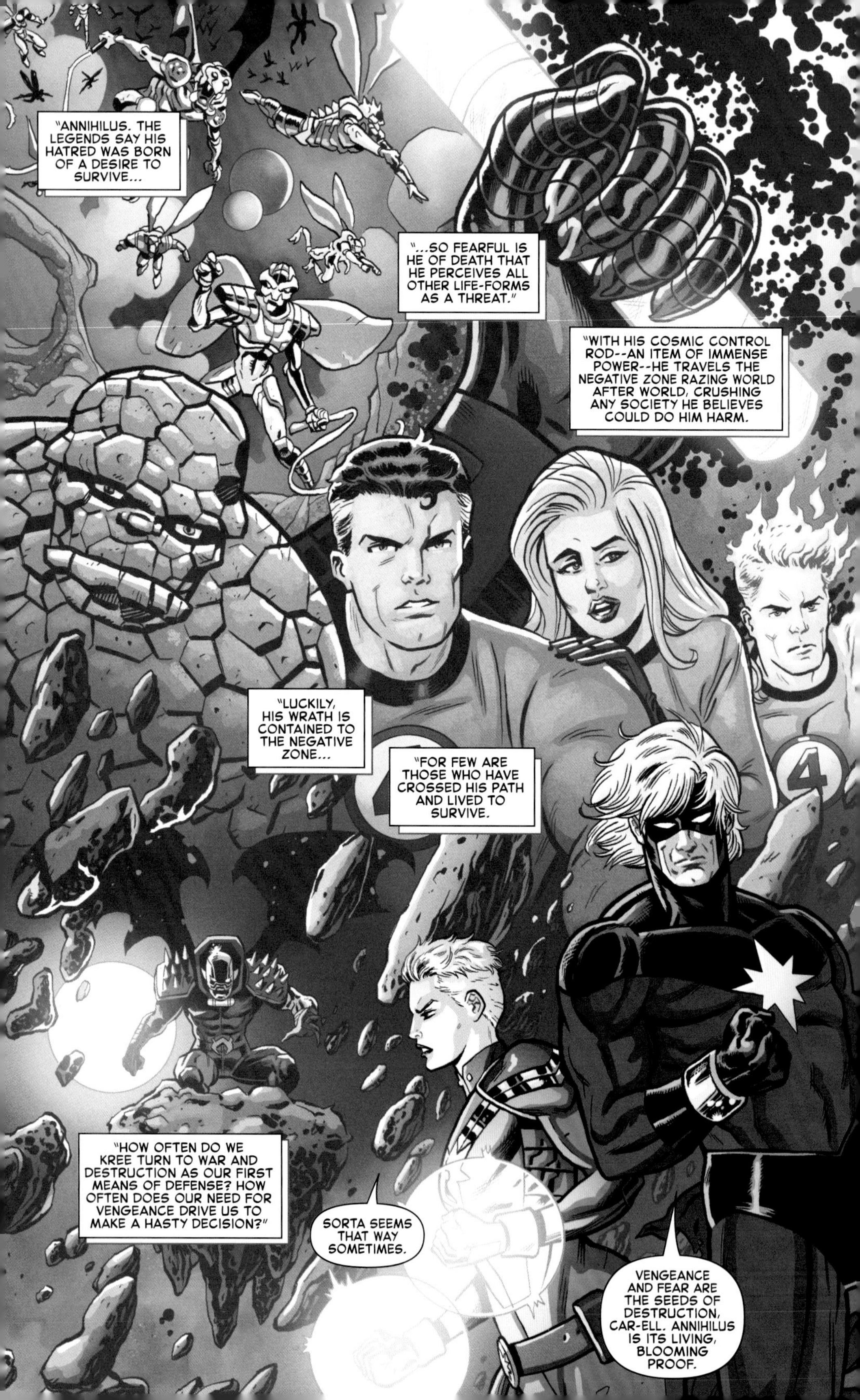
"ANNIHILUS. THE LEGENDS SAY HIS HATRED WAS BORN OF A DESIRE TO SURVIVE...
"...SO FEARFUL IS HE OF DEATH THAT HE PERCEIVES ALL OTHER LIFE-FORMS AS A THREAT."
"WITH HIS COSMIC CONTROL ROD--AN ITEM OF IMMENSE POWER--HE TRAVELS THE NEGATIVE ZONE RAZING WORLD AFTER WORLD, CRUSHING ANY SOCIETY HE BELIEVES COULD DO HIM HARM.
"LUCKILY, HIS WRATH IS CONTAINED TO THE NEGATIVE ZONE...
"FOR FEW ARE THOSE WHO HAVE CROSSED HIS PATH AND LIVED TO SURVIVE.
"HOW OFTEN DO WE KREE TURN TO WAR AND DESTRUCTION AS OUR FIRST MEANS OF DEFENSE? HOW OFTEN DOES OUR NEED FOR VENGEANCE DRIVE US TO MAKE A HASTY DECISION?"
SORTA SEEMS THAT WAY SOMETIMES.
VENGEANCE AND FEAR ARE THE SEEDS OF DESTRUCTION, CAR-ELL. ANNIHILUS IS ITS LIVING, BLOOMING PROOF.

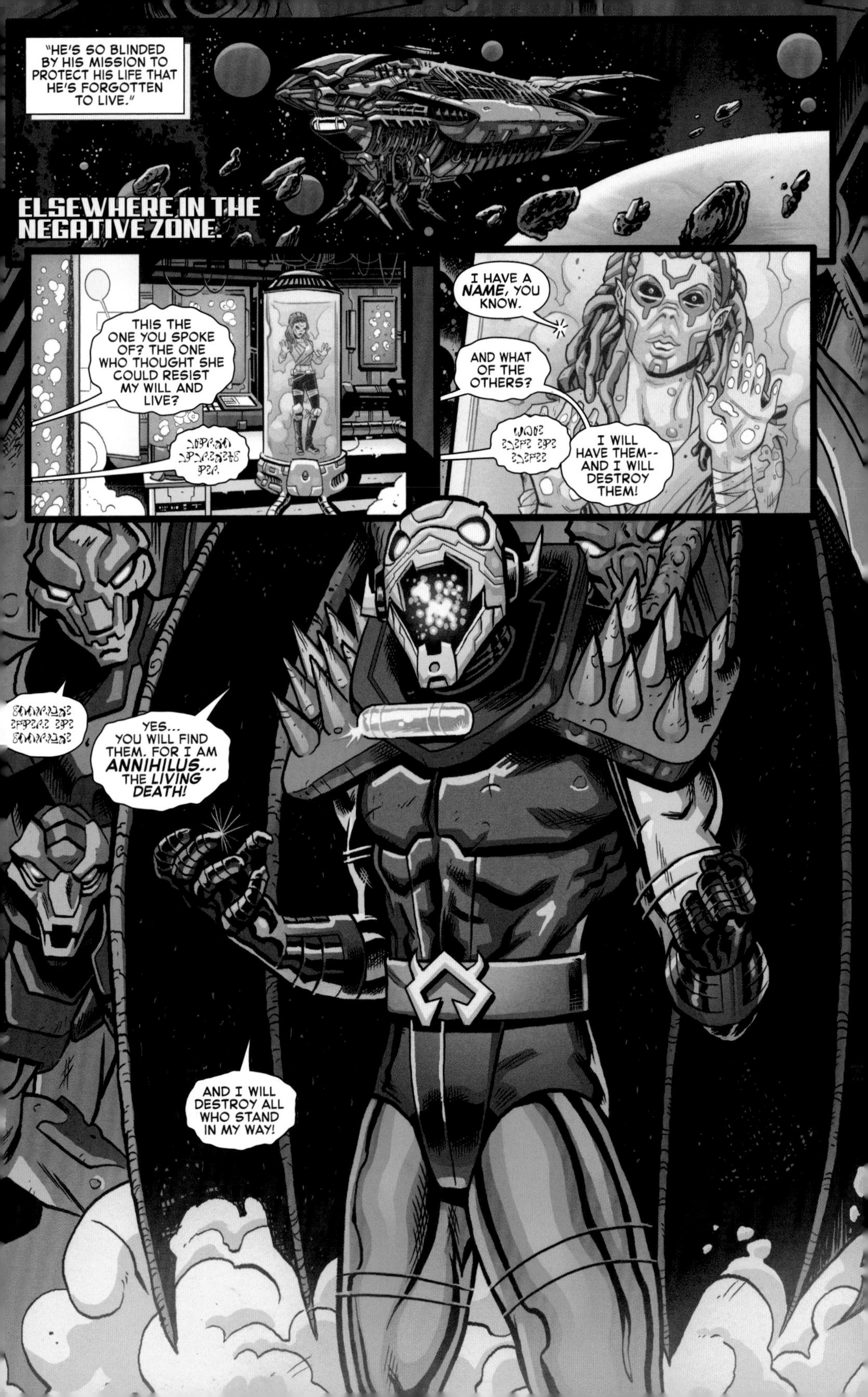
"HE'S SO BLINDED BY HIS MISSION TO PROTECT HIS LIFE THAT HE'S FORGOTTEN TO LIVE."
ELSEWHERE IN THE NEGATIVE ZONE.
THIS THE ONE YOU SPOKE OF? THE ONE WHO THOUGHT SHE COULD RESIST MY WILL AND LIVE?
I HAVE A NAME, YOU KNOW.
AND WHAT OF THE OTHERS?
I WILL HAVE THEM-- AND I WILL DESTROY THEM!
YES... YOU WILL FIND THEM. FOR I AM ANNIHILUS... THE LIVING DEATH!
AND I WILL DESTROY ALL WHO STAND IN MY WAY!

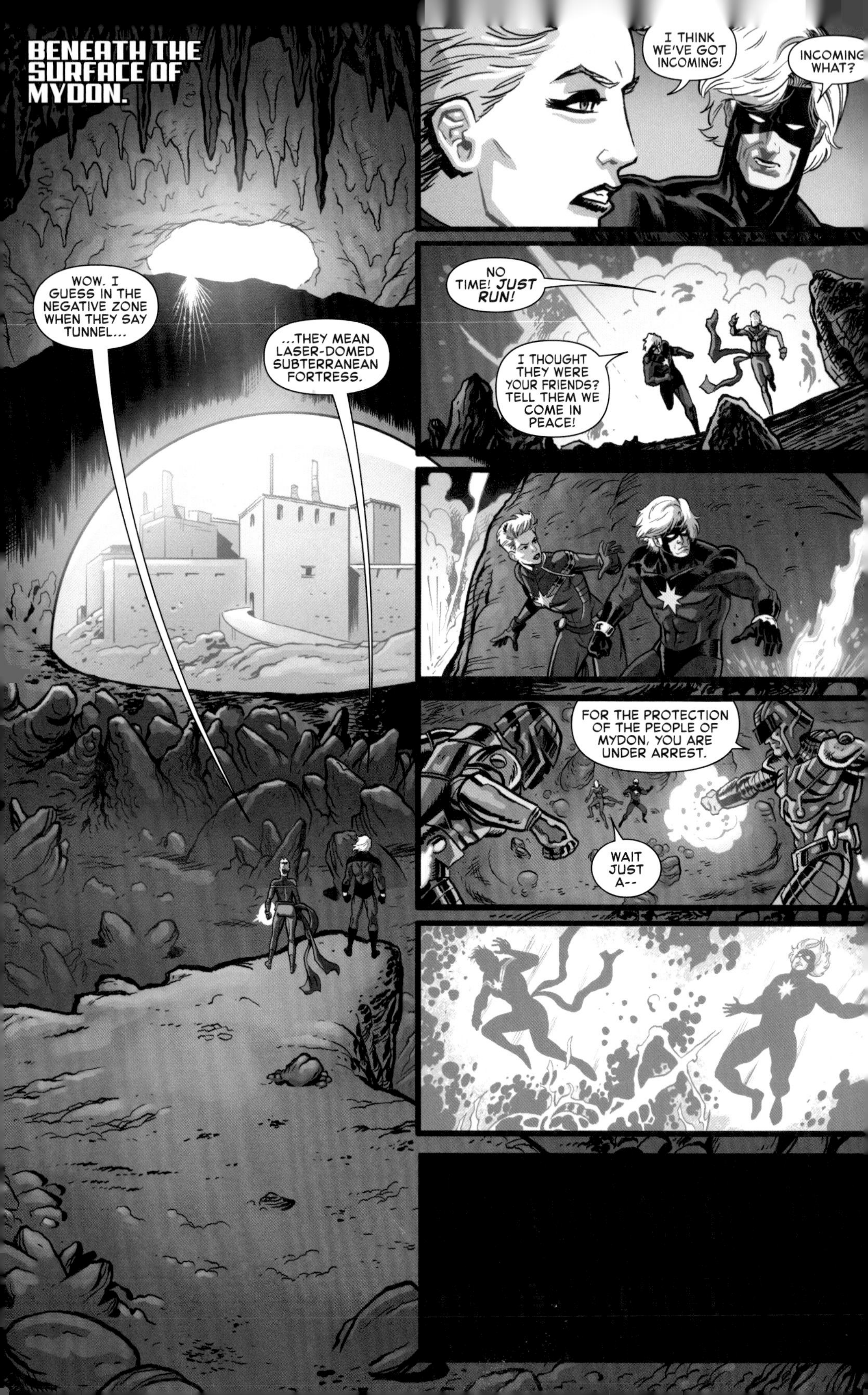
BENEATH THE SURFACE OF MYDON.
WOW. I GUESS IN THE NEGATIVE ZONE WHEN THEY SAY TUNNEL...
...THEY MEAN LASER-DOMED SUBTERRANEAN FORTRESS.
I THINK WE'VE GOT INCOMING!
INCOMING WHAT?
NO TIME! JUST RUN!
I THOUGHT THEY WERE YOUR FRIENDS? TELL THEM WE COME IN PEACE!
FOR THE PROTECTION OF THE PEOPLE OF MYDON, YOU ARE UNDER ARREST.
WAIT JUST A--

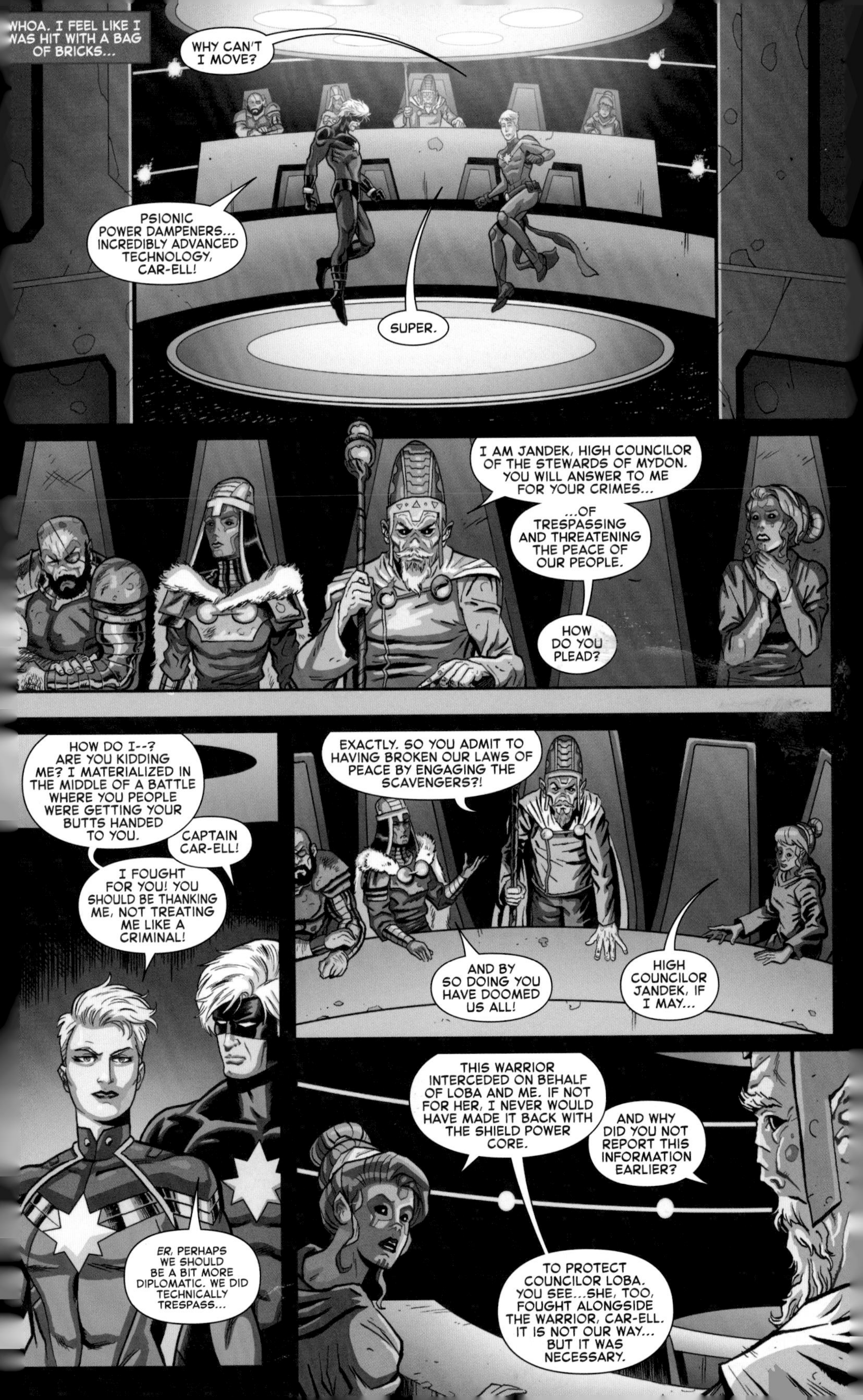

WHOA. I FEEL LIKE I WAS HIT WITH A BAG OF BRICKS...
WHY CAN'T I MOVE?
PSIONIC POWER DAMPENERS... INCREDIBLY ADVANCED TECHNOLOGY, CAR-ELL!
SUPER.
I AM JANDEK, HIGH COUNCILOR OF THE STEWARDS OF MYDON. YOU WILL ANSWER TO ME FOR YOUR CRIMES...
...OF TRESPASSING AND THREATENING THE PEACE OF OUR PEOPLE.
HOW DO YOU PLEAD?
HOW DO I--? ARE YOU KIDDING ME? I MATERIALIZED IN THE MIDDLE OF A BATTLE WHERE YOU PEOPLE WERE GETTING YOUR BUTTS HANDED TO YOU.
CAPTAIN CAR-ELL!
I FOUGHT FOR YOU! YOU SHOULD BE THANKING ME, NOT TREATING ME LIKE A CRIMINAL!
ER, PERHAPS WE SHOULD BE A BIT MORE DIPLOMATIC. WE DID TECHNICALLY TRESPASS...
EXACTLY. SO YOU ADMIT TO HAVING BROKEN OUR LAWS OF PEACE BY ENGAGING THE SCAVENGERS?!
AND BY SO DOING YOU HAVE DOOMED US ALL!
HIGH COUNCILOR JANDEK, IF I MAY...
THIS WARRIOR INTERCEDED ON BEHALF OF LOBA AND ME. IF NOT FOR HER, I NEVER WOULD HAVE MADE IT BACK WITH THE SHIELD POWER CORE.
AND WHY DID YOU NOT REPORT THIS INFORMATION EARLIER?
TO PROTECT COUNCILOR LOBA. YOU SEE...SHE, TOO, FOUGHT ALONGSIDE THE WARRIOR, CAR-ELL. IT IS NOT OUR WAY... BUT IT WAS NECESSARY.

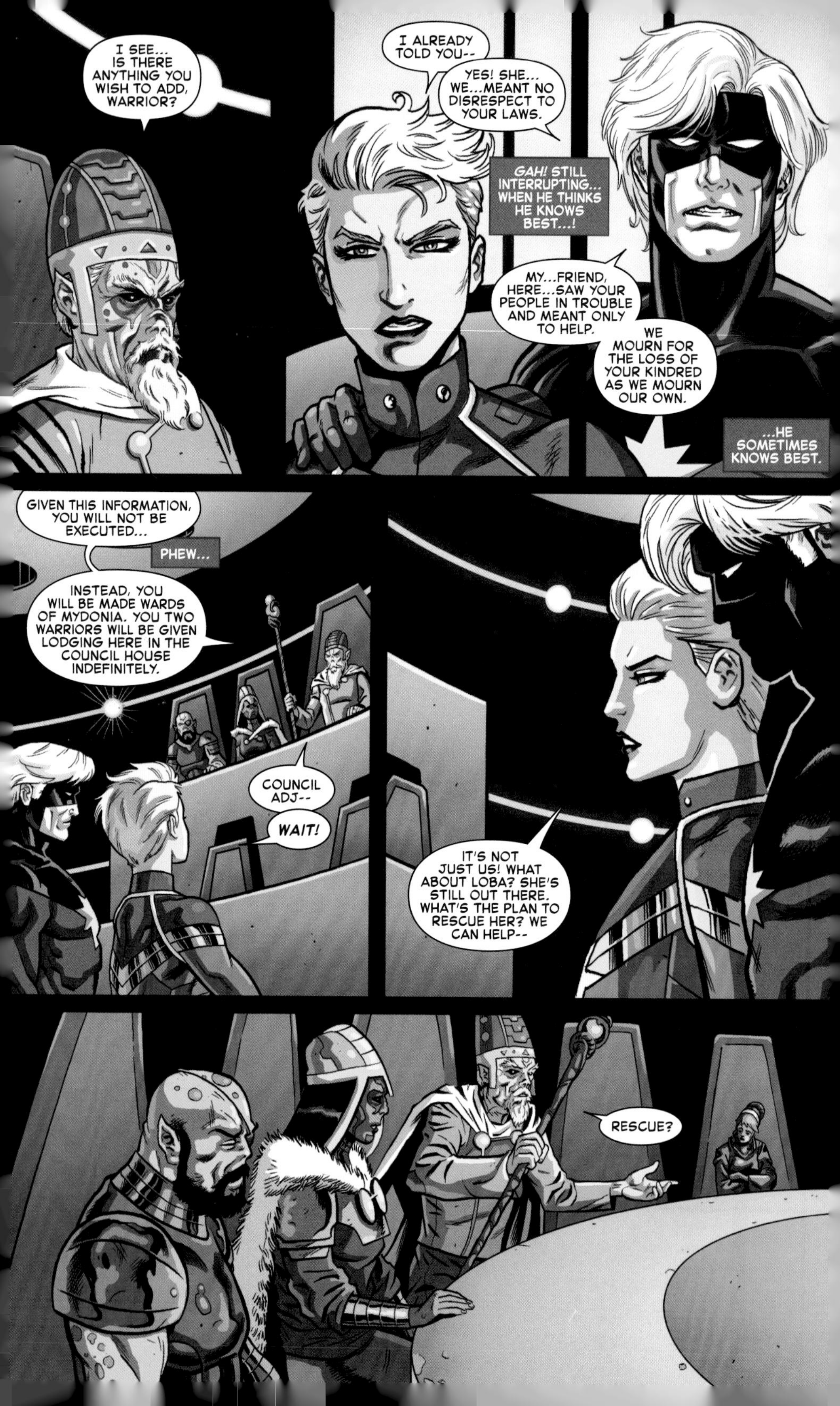
I SEE... IS THERE ANYTHING YOU WISH TO ADD, WARRIOR?
I ALREADY TOLD YOU--
YES! SHE... WE...MEANT NO DISRESPECT TO YOUR LAWS.
GAH! STILL INTERRUPTING... WHEN HE THINKS HE KNOWS BEST...!
MY...FRIEND, HERE...SAW YOUR PEOPLE IN TROUBLE AND MEANT ONLY TO HELP.
WE MOURN FOR THE LOSS OF YOUR KINDRED AS WE MOURN OUR OWN.
...HE SOMETIMES KNOWS BEST.
GIVEN THIS INFORMATION, YOU WILL NOT BE EXECUTED...
PHEW...
INSTEAD, YOU WILL BE MADE WARDS OF MYDONIA. YOU TWO WARRIORS WILL BE GIVEN LODGING HERE IN THE COUNCIL HOUSE INDEFINITELY.
COUNCIL ADJ--
WAIT!
IT'S NOT JUST US! WHAT ABOUT LOBA? SHE'S STILL OUT THERE. WHAT'S THE PLAN TO RESCUE HER? WE CAN HELP--
RESCUE?

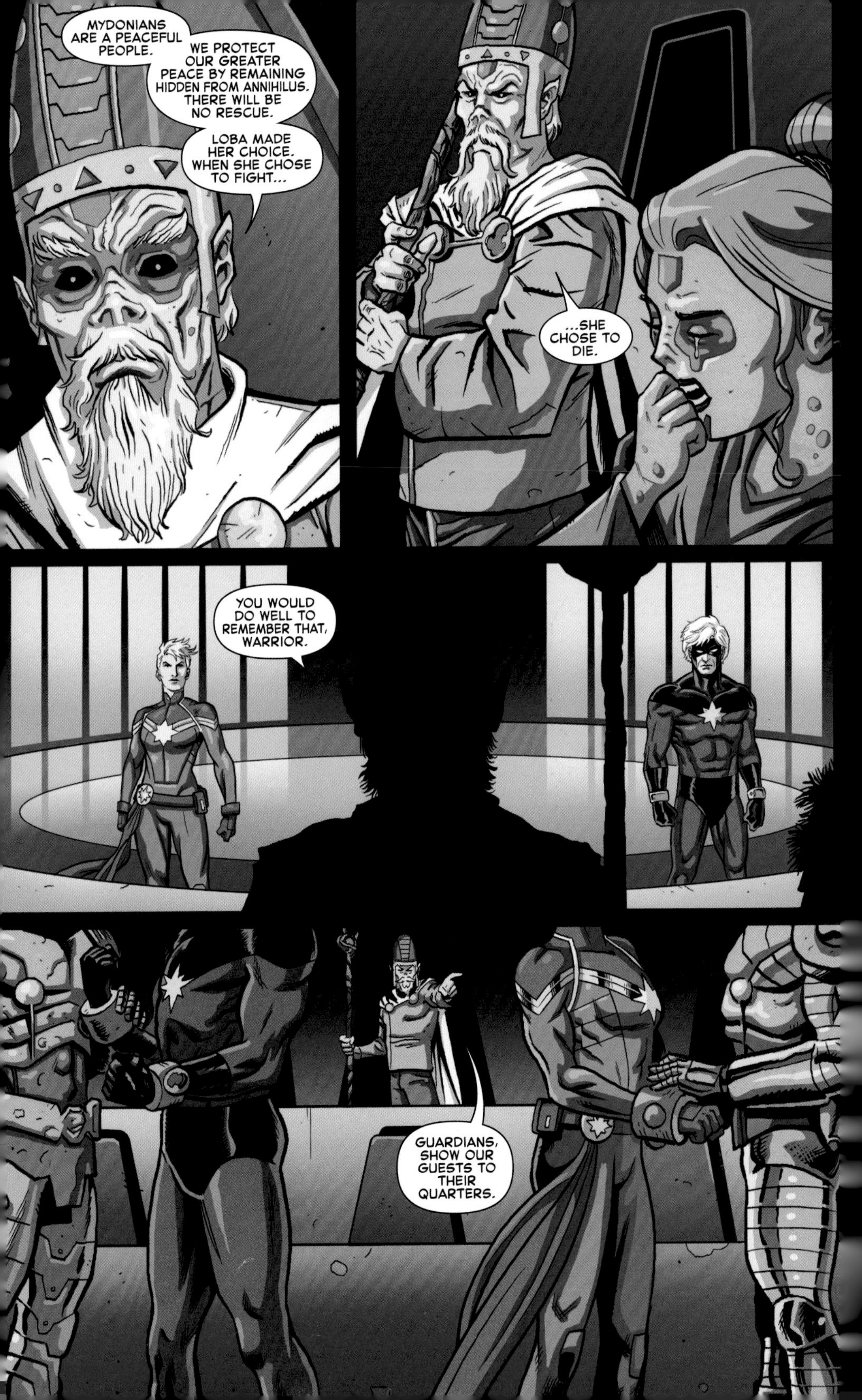
MYDONIANS ARE A PEACEFUL PEOPLE.
WE PROTECT OUR GREATER PEACE BY REMAINING HIDDEN FROM ANNIHILUS. THERE WILL BE NO RESCUE.
LOBA MADE HER CHOICE. WHEN SHE CHOSE TO FIGHT...
...SHE CHOSE TO DIE.
YOU WOULD DO WELL TO REMEMBER THAT, WARRIOR.
GUARDIANS, SHOW OUR GUESTS TO THEIR QUARTERS.

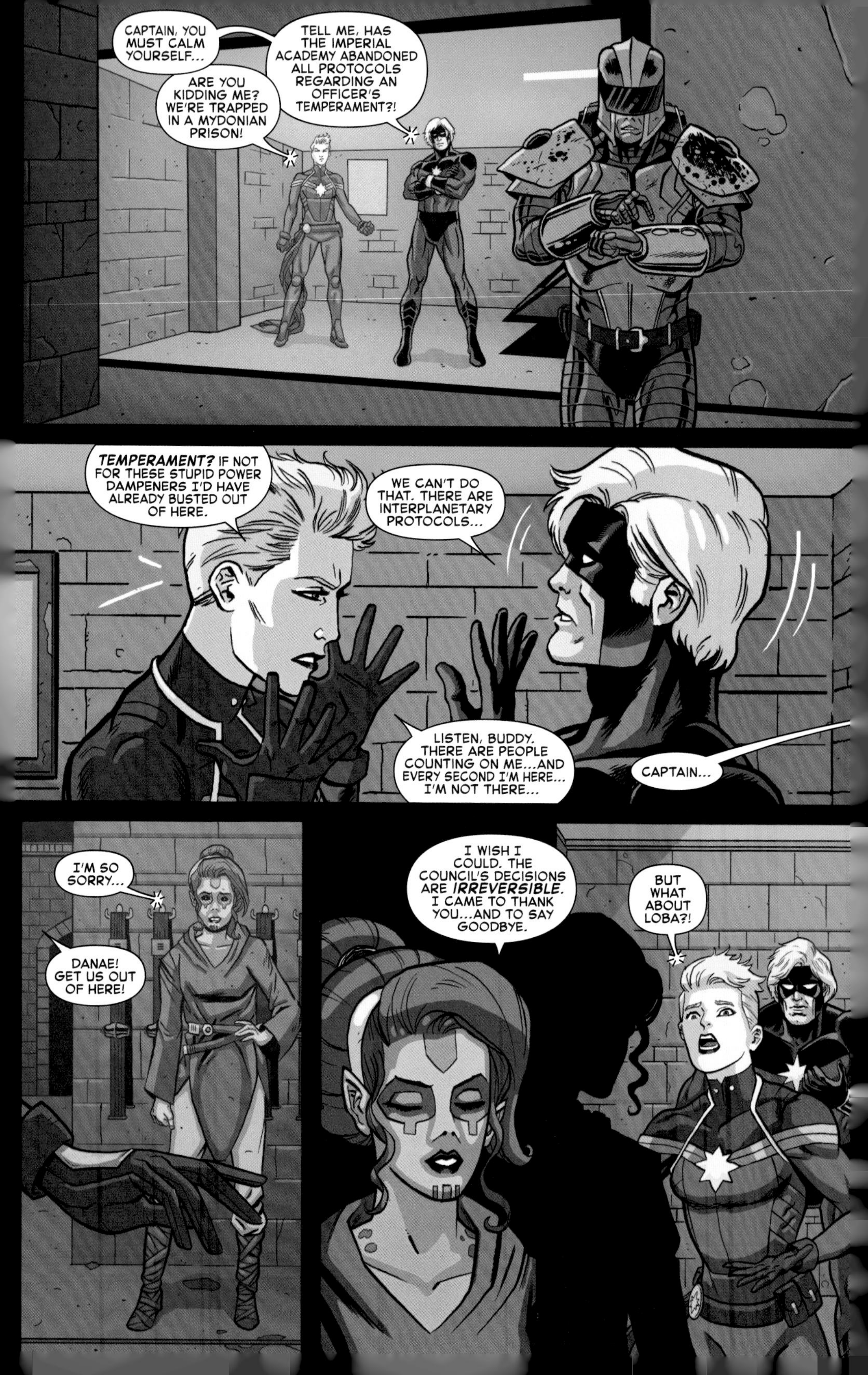

CAPTAIN, YOU MUST CALM YOURSELF...
ARE YOU KIDDING ME? WE'RE TRAPPED IN A MYDONIAN PRISON!
TELL ME, HAS THE IMPERIAL ACADEMY ABANDONED ALL PROTOCOLS REGARDING AN OFFICER'S TEMPERAMENT?!
TEMPERAMENT? IF NOT FOR THESE STUPID POWER DAMPENERS I'D HAVE ALREADY BUSTED OUT OF HERE.
WE CAN'T DO THAT. THERE ARE INTERPLANETARY PROTOCOLS...
LISTEN, BUDDY. THERE ARE PEOPLE COUNTING ON ME...AND EVERY SECOND I'M HERE... I'M NOT THERE...
CAPTAIN...
I'M SO SORRY...
DANAE! GET US OUT OF HERE!
I WISH I COULD. THE COUNCIL'S DECISIONS ARE IRREVERSIBLE. I CAME TO THANK YOU...AND TO SAY GOODBYE.
BUT WHAT ABOUT LOBA?!

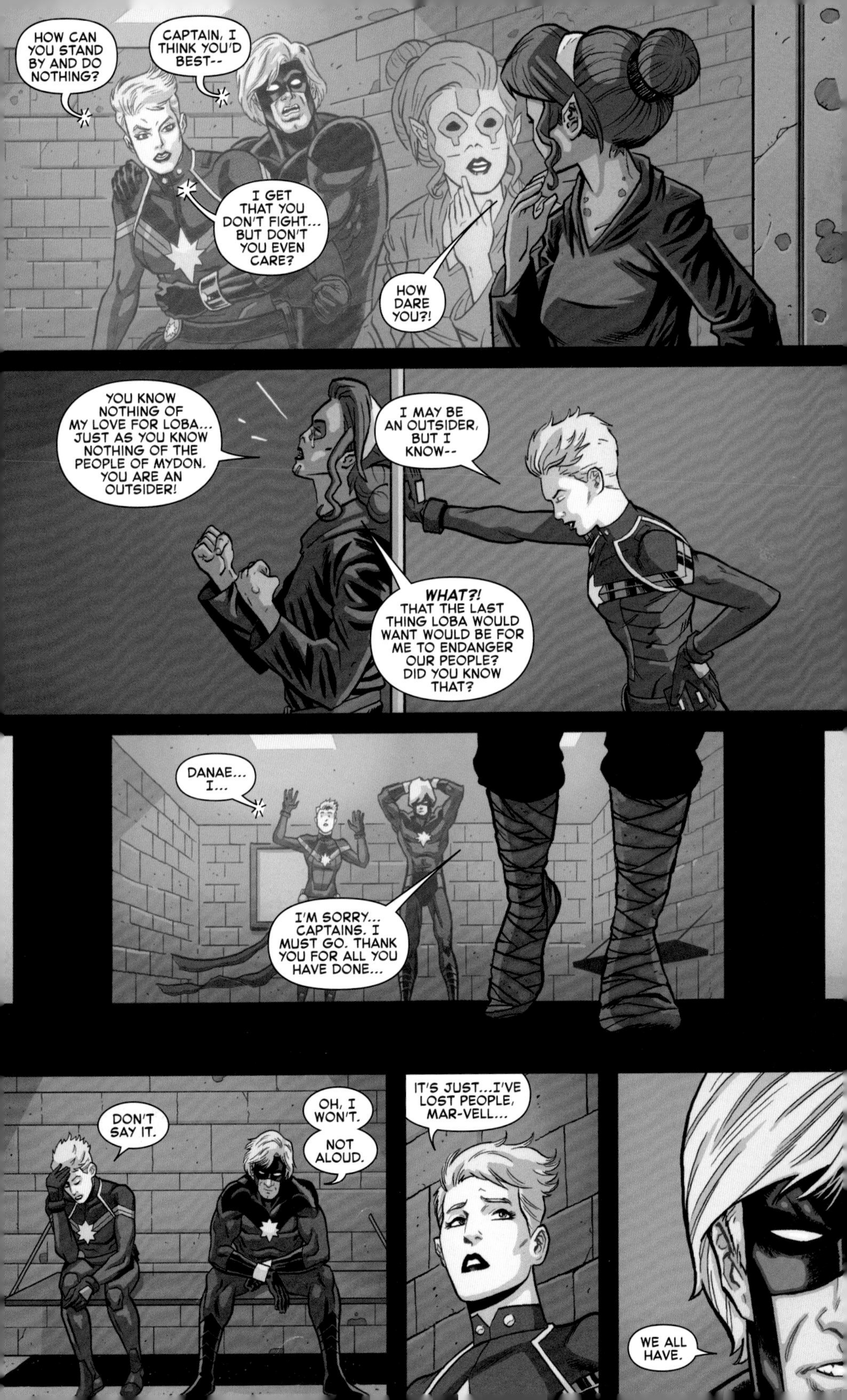
HOW CAN YOU STAND BY AND DO NOTHING?
CAPTAIN, I THINK YOU'D BEST--
I GET THAT YOU DON'T FIGHT... BUT DON'T YOU EVEN CARE?
HOW DARE YOU?!
YOU KNOW NOTHING OF MY LOVE FOR LOBA... JUST AS YOU KNOW NOTHING OF THE PEOPLE OF MYDON. YOU ARE AN OUTSIDER!
I MAY BE AN OUTSIDER, BUT I KNOW--
WHAT?! THAT THE LAST THING LOBA WOULD WANT WOULD BE FOR ME TO ENDANGER OUR PEOPLE? DID YOU KNOW THAT?
DANAE... I...
I'M SORRY... CAPTAINS. I MUST GO. THANK YOU FOR ALL YOU HAVE DONE...
DON'T SAY IT.
OH, I WON'T.
NOT ALOUD.
IT'S JUST...I'VE LOST PEOPLE, MAR-VELL...
WE ALL HAVE.

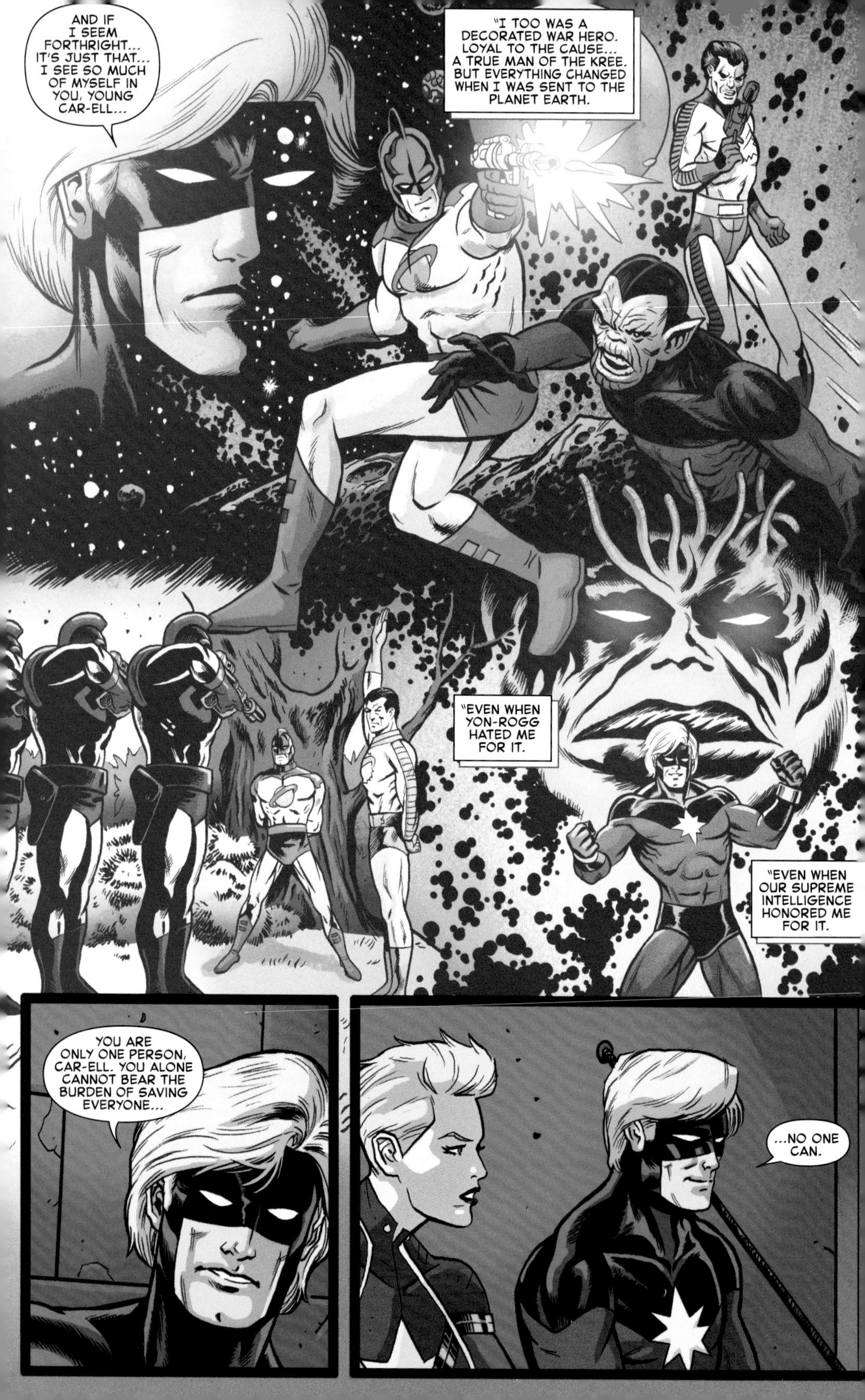
AND IF I SEEM FORTHRIGHT... IT'S JUST THAT... I SEE SO MUCH OF MYSELF IN YOU, YOUNG CAR-ELL...
"I TOO WAS A DECORATED WAR HERO. LOYAL TO THE CAUSE... A TRUE MAN OF THE KREE. BUT EVERYTHING CHANGED WHEN I WAS SENT TO THE PLANET EARTH.
"EVEN WHEN YON-ROGG HATED ME FOR IT.
"EVEN WHEN OUR SUPREME INTELLIGENCE HONORED ME FOR IT.
YOU ARE ONLY ONE PERSON, CAR-ELL. YOU ALONE CANNOT BEAR THE BURDEN OF SAVING EVERYONE...
...NO ONE CAN.

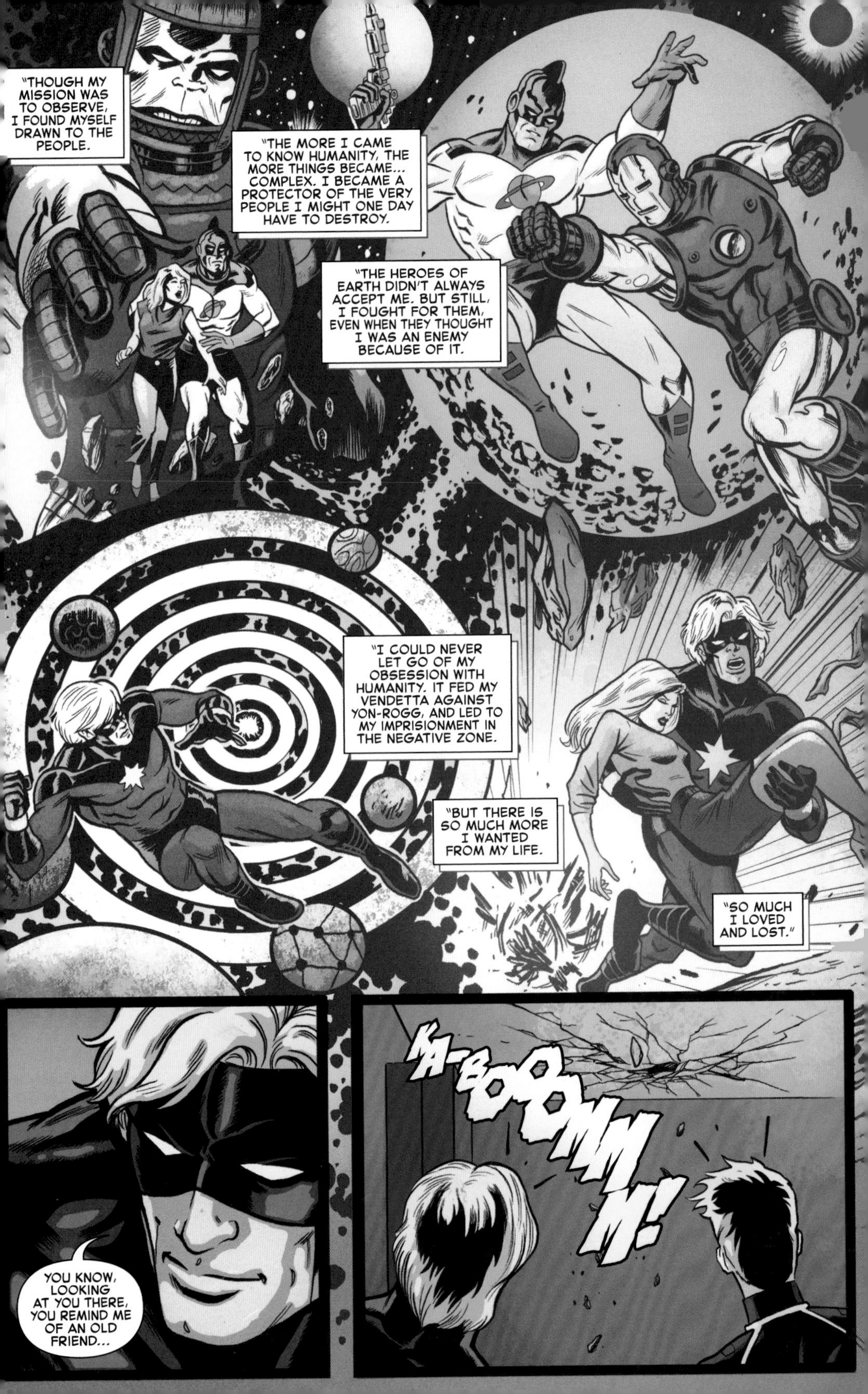

"THOUGH MY MISSION WAS TO OBSERVE, I FOUND MYSELF DRAWN TO THE PEOPLE.
"THE MORE I CAME TO KNOW HUMANITY, THE MORE THINGS BECAME... COMPLEX. I BECAME A PROTECTOR OF THE VERY PEOPLE I MIGHT ONE DAY HAVE TO DESTROY.
"THE HEROES OF EARTH DIDN'T ALWAYS ACCEPT ME. BUT STILL, I FOUGHT FOR THEM, EVEN WHEN THEY THOUGHT I WAS AN ENEMY BECAUSE OF IT.
"I COULD NEVER LET GO OF MY OBSESSION WITH HUMANITY. IT FED MY VENDETTA AGAINST YON-ROGG, AND LED TO MY IMPRISIONMENT IN THE NEGATIVE ZONE.
"BUT THERE IS SO MUCH MORE I WANTED FROM MY LIFE.
"SO MUCH I LOVED AND LOST."
YOU KNOW, LOOKING AT YOU THERE, YOU REMIND ME OF AN OLD FRIEND...
KA-BOOOMMM!

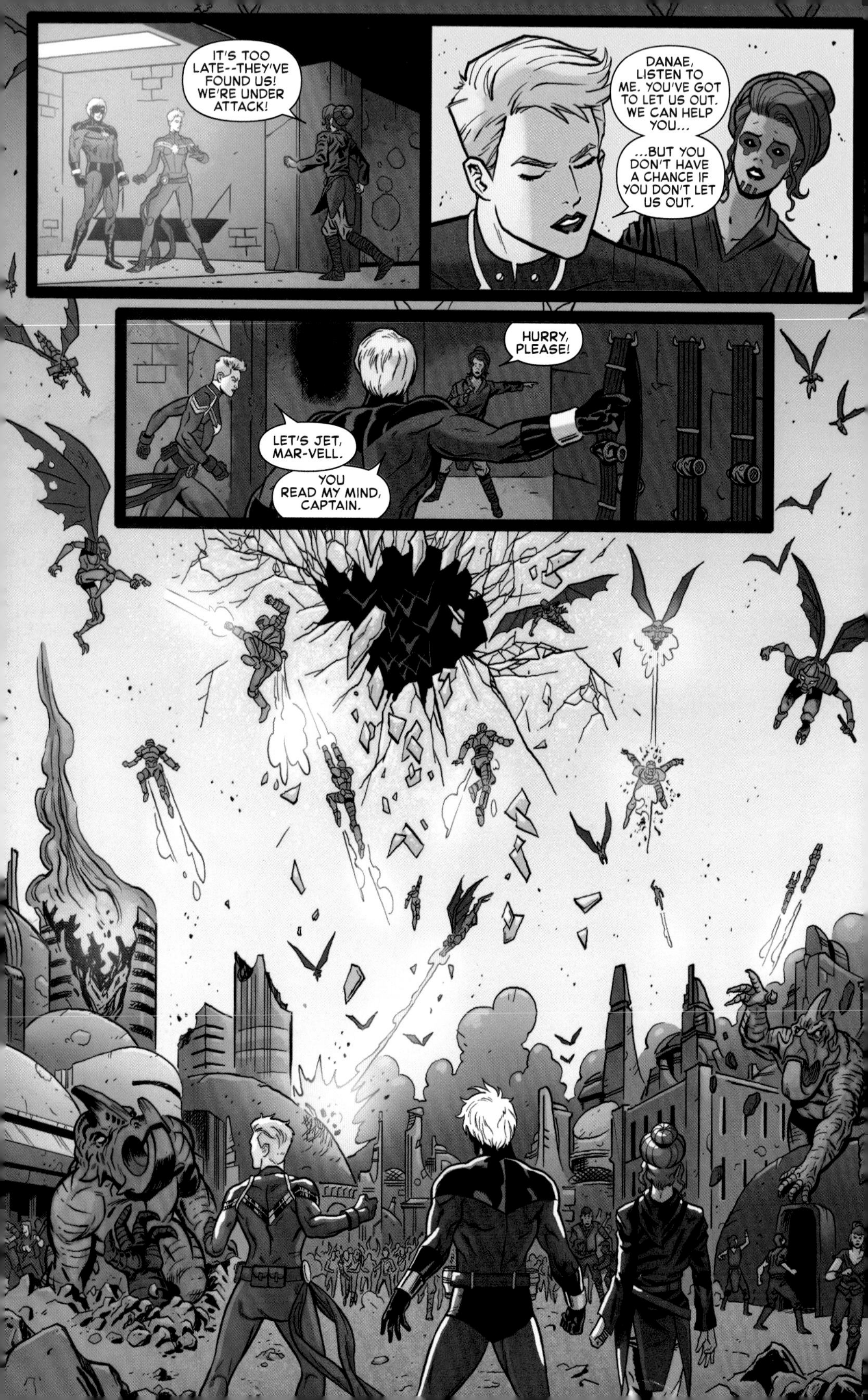
IT'S TOO LATE--THEY'VE FOUND US! WE'RE UNDER ATTACK!
DANAE, LISTEN TO ME. YOU'VE GOT TO LET US OUT. WE CAN HELP YOU...
...BUT YOU DON'T HAVE A CHANCE IF YOU DON'T LET US OUT.
HURRY, PLEASE!
LET'S JET, MAR-VELL.
YOU READ MY MIND, CAPTAIN.

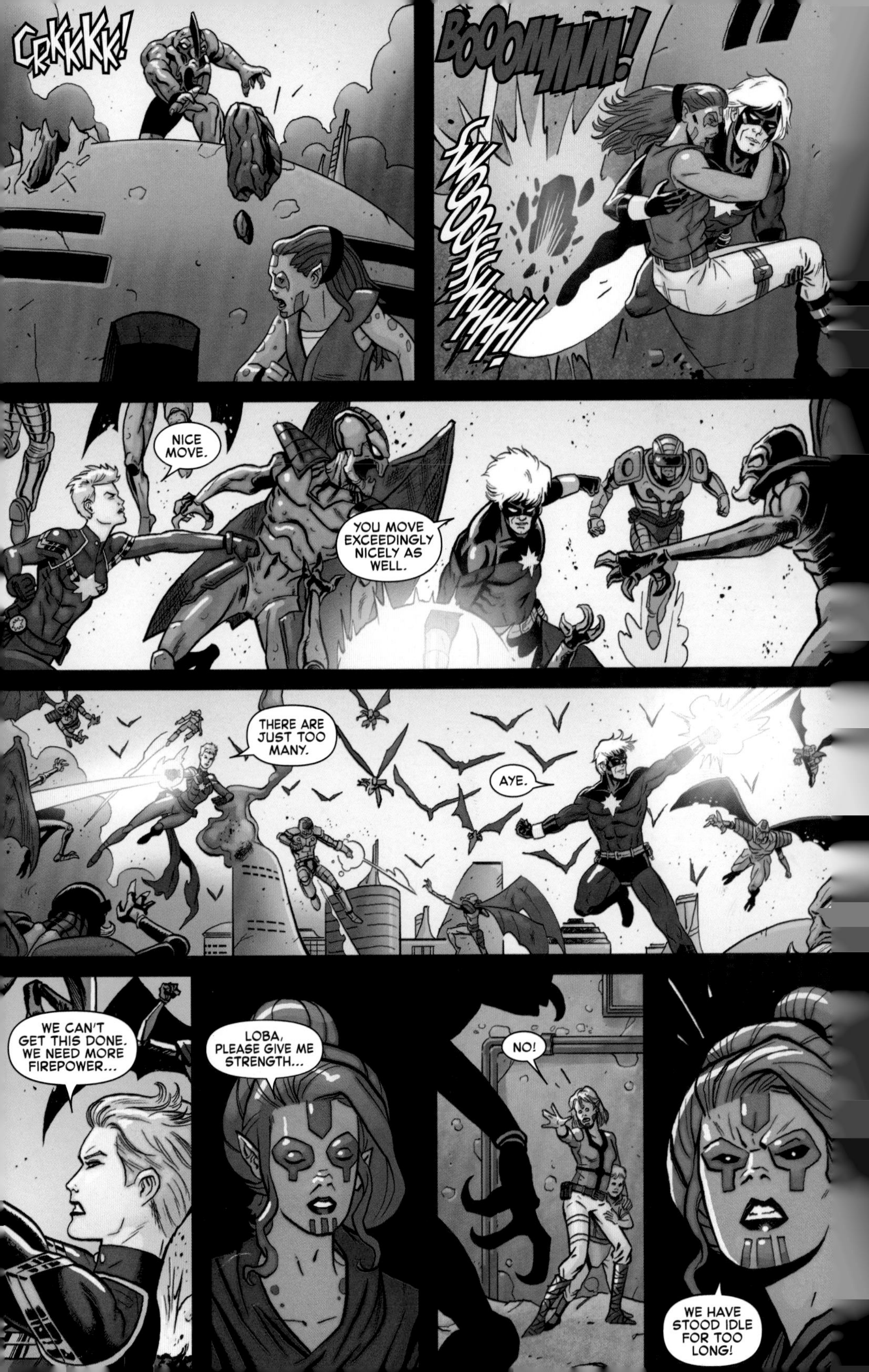
CRKKKK!
BOOOMMMM!
WOOOSHHHH!!
NICE MOVE.
YOU MOVE EXCEEDINGLY NICELY AS WELL.
THERE ARE JUST TOO MANY.
AYE.
WE CAN'T GET THIS DONE. WE NEED MORE FIREPOWER...
LOBA, PLEASE GIVE ME STRENGTH...
NO!
WE HAVE STOOD IDLE FOR TOO LONG!

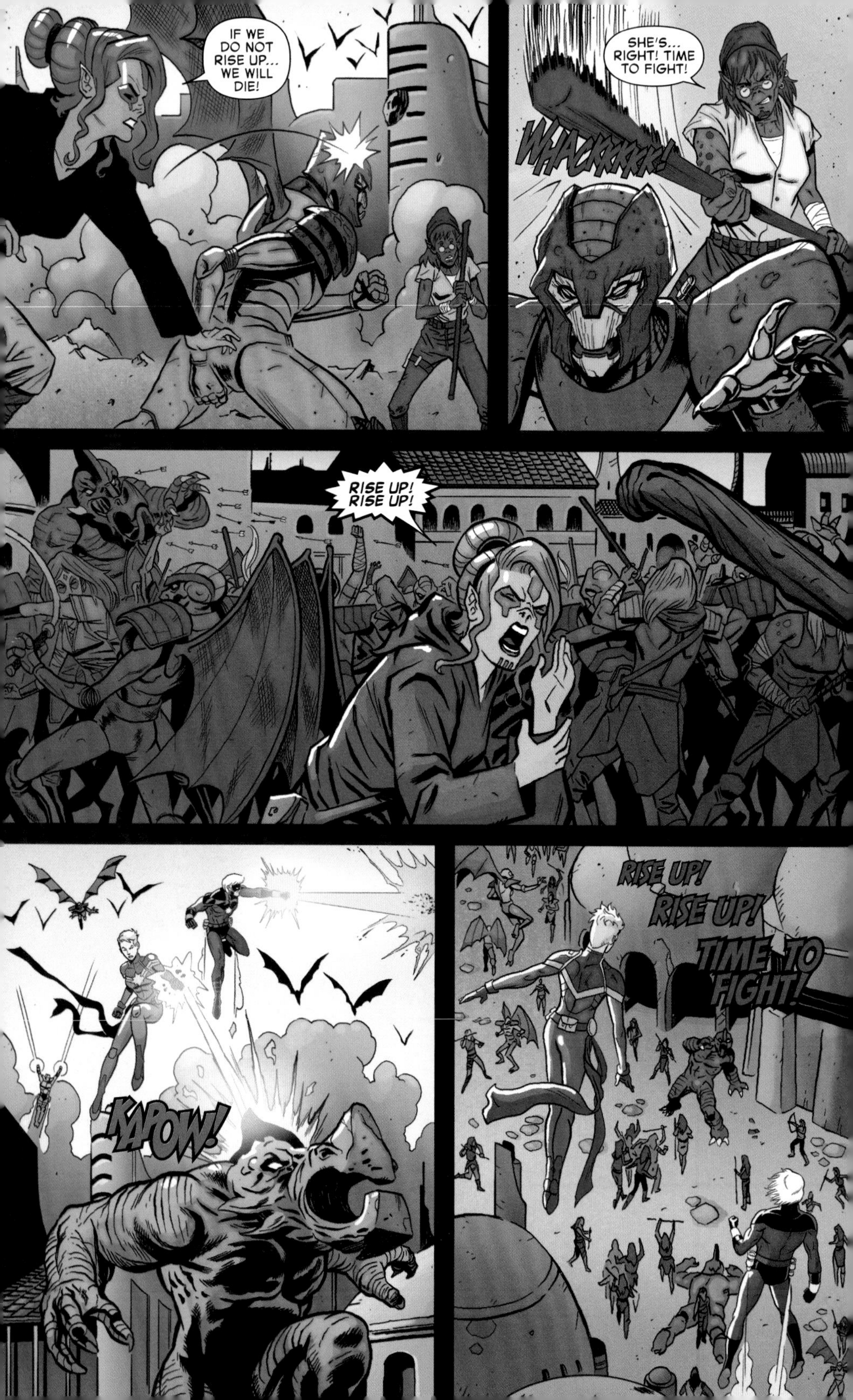
IF WE DO NOT RISE UP... WE WILL DIE!
SHE'S... RIGHT! TIME TO FIGHT!
WHACKKKKK!
RISE UP! RISE UP!
KAPOW!
RISE UP!
RISE UP!
TIME TO FIGHT!

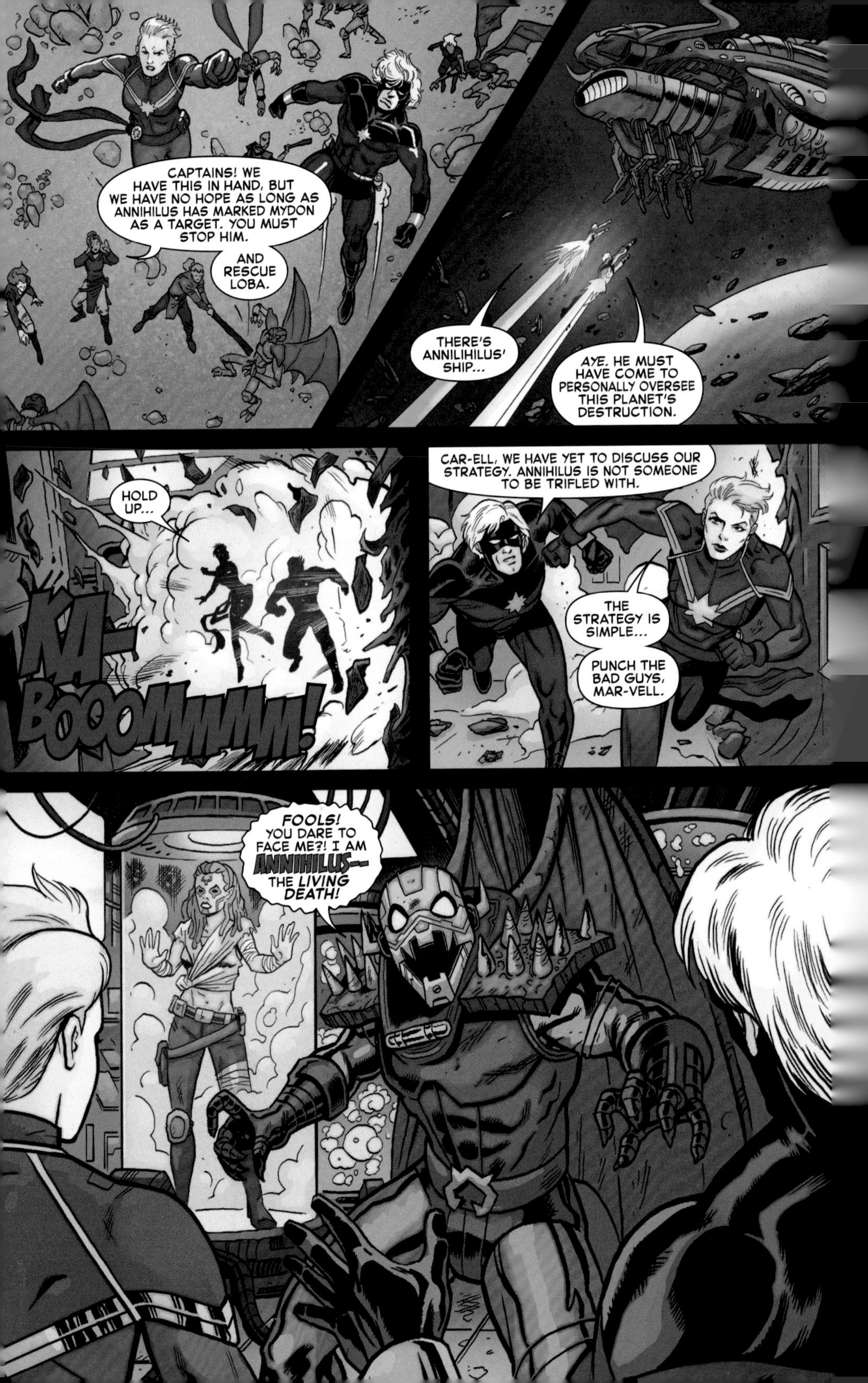
CAPTAINS! WE HAVE THIS IN HAND, BUT WE HAVE NO HOPE AS LONG AS ANNIHILUS HAS MARKED MYDON AS A TARGET. YOU MUST STOP HIM.
AND RESCUE LOBA.
THERE'S ANNILIHILUS' SHIP...
AYE. HE MUST HAVE COME TO PERSONALLY OVERSEE THIS PLANET'S DESTRUCTION.
HOLD UP...
KA-BOOOMMMMM!
CAR-ELL, WE HAVE YET TO DISCUSS OUR STRATEGY. ANNIHILUS IS NOT SOMEONE TO BE TRIFLED WITH.
THE STRATEGY IS SIMPLE...
PUNCH THE BAD GUYS, MAR-VELL.
FOOLS! YOU DARE TO FACE ME?! I AM ANNIHILUS-- THE LIVING DEATH!

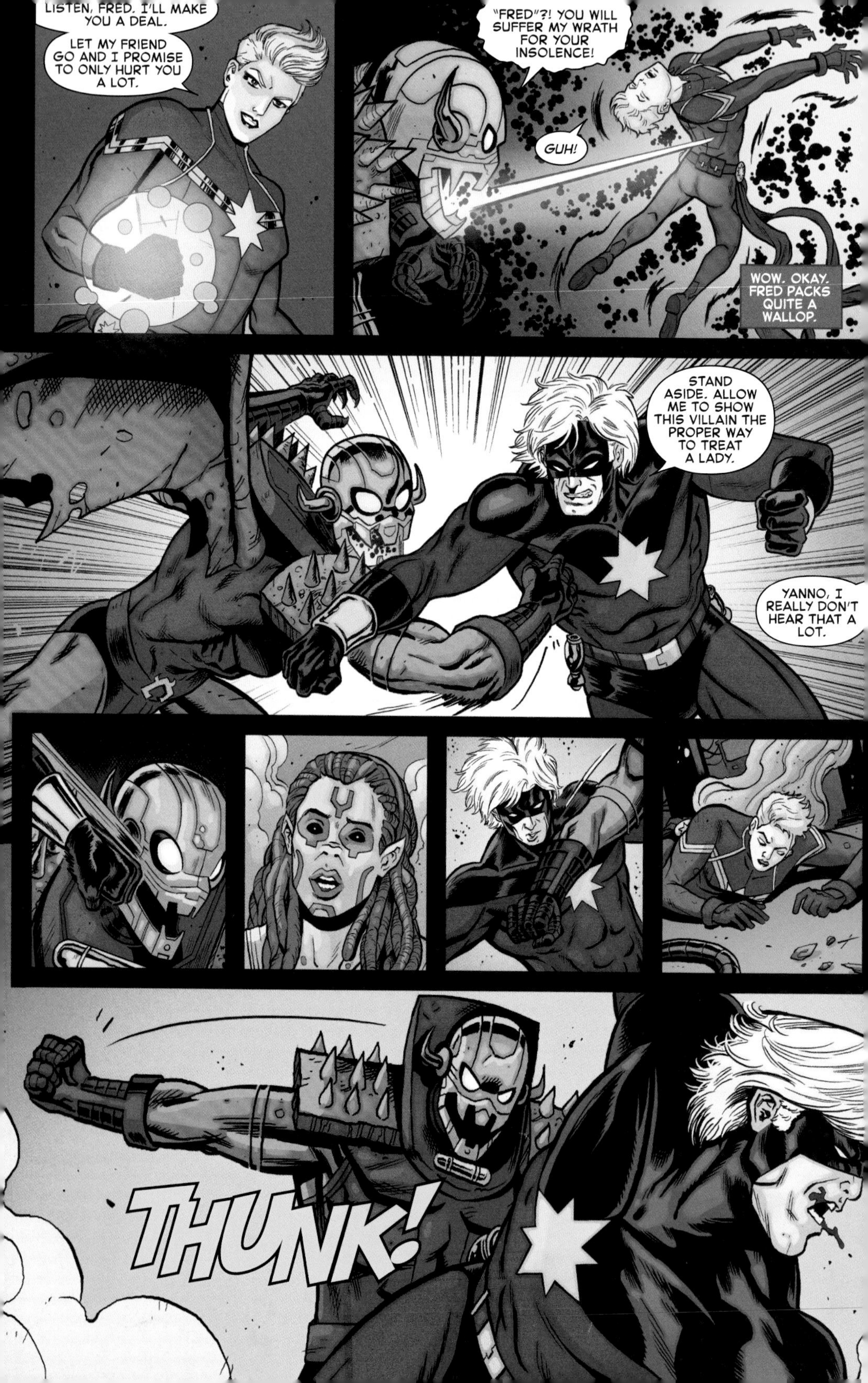
LISTEN, FRED. I'LL MAKE YOU A DEAL.
LET MY FRIEND GO AND I PROMISE TO ONLY HURT YOU A LOT.
"FRED"?! YOU WILL SUFFER MY WRATH FOR YOUR INSOLENCE!
GUH!
WOW. OKAY. FRED PACKS QUITE A WALLOP.
STAND ASIDE. ALLOW ME TO SHOW THIS VILLAIN THE PROPER WAY TO TREAT A LADY.
YANNO, I REALLY DON'T HEAR THAT A LOT.
THUNK!

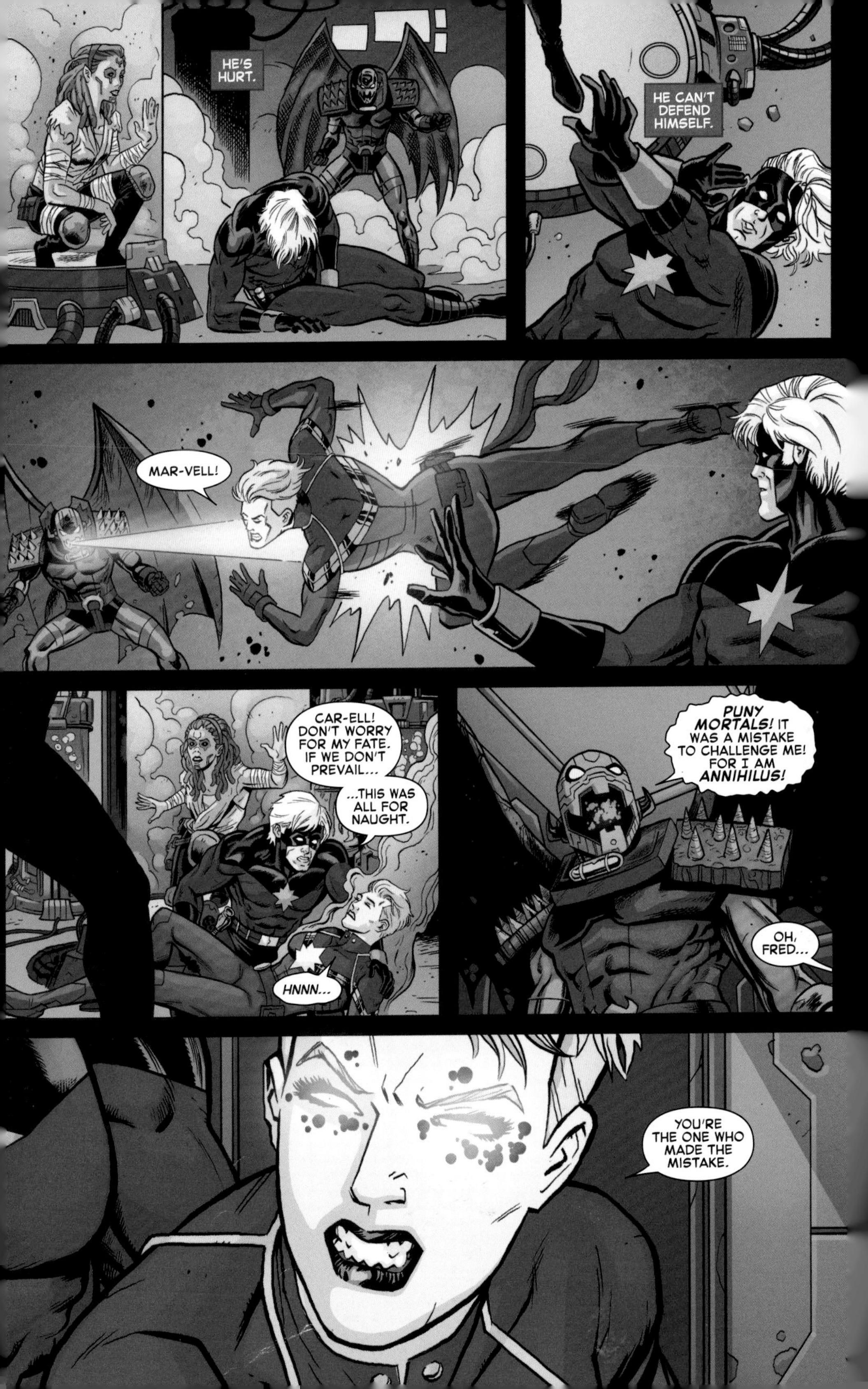
HE'S HURT.
HE CAN'T DEFEND HIMSELF.
MAR-VELL!
CAR-ELL! DON'T WORRY FOR MY FATE. IF WE DON'T PREVAIL...
...THIS WAS ALL FOR NAUGHT.
HNNN...
PUNY MORTALS! IT WAS A MISTAKE TO CHALLENGE ME! FOR I AM ANNIHILUS!
OH, FRED...
YOU'RE THE ONE WHO MADE THE MISTAKE.

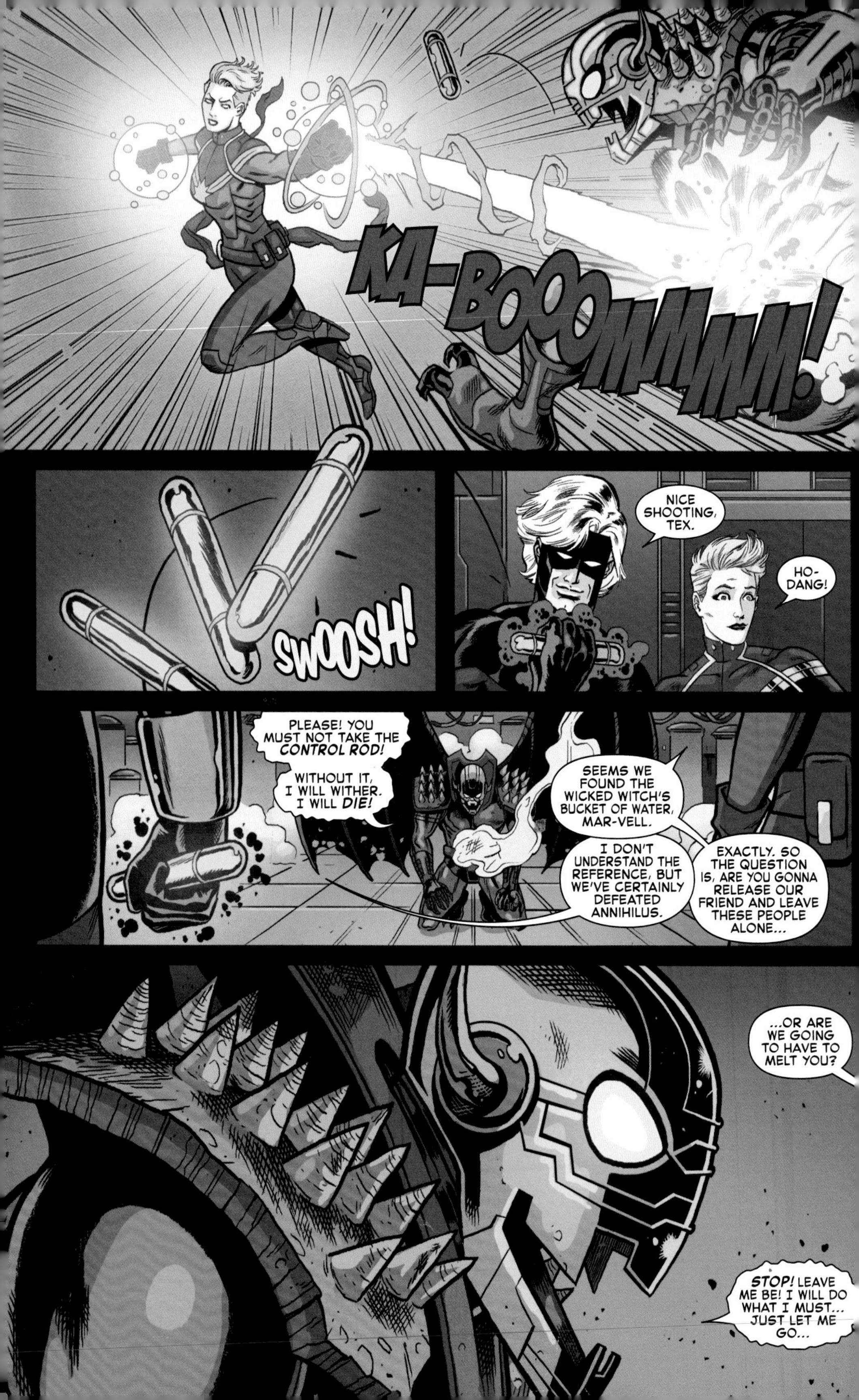
KA-BOOOMMMMM!
SWOOSH!
NICE SHOOTING, TEX.
HO-DANG!
PLEASE! YOU MUST NOT TAKE THE CONTROL ROD!
WITHOUT IT, I WILL WITHER. I WILL DIE!
SEEMS WE FOUND THE WICKED WITCH'S BUCKET OF WATER, MAR-VELL.
I DON'T UNDERSTAND THE REFERENCE, BUT WE'VE CERTAINLY DEFEATED ANNIHILUS.
EXACTLY. SO THE QUESTION IS, ARE YOU GONNA RELEASE OUR FRIEND AND LEAVE THESE PEOPLE ALONE...
...OR ARE WE GOING TO HAVE TO MELT YOU?
STOP! LEAVE ME BE! I WILL DO WHAT I MUST... JUST LET ME GO...

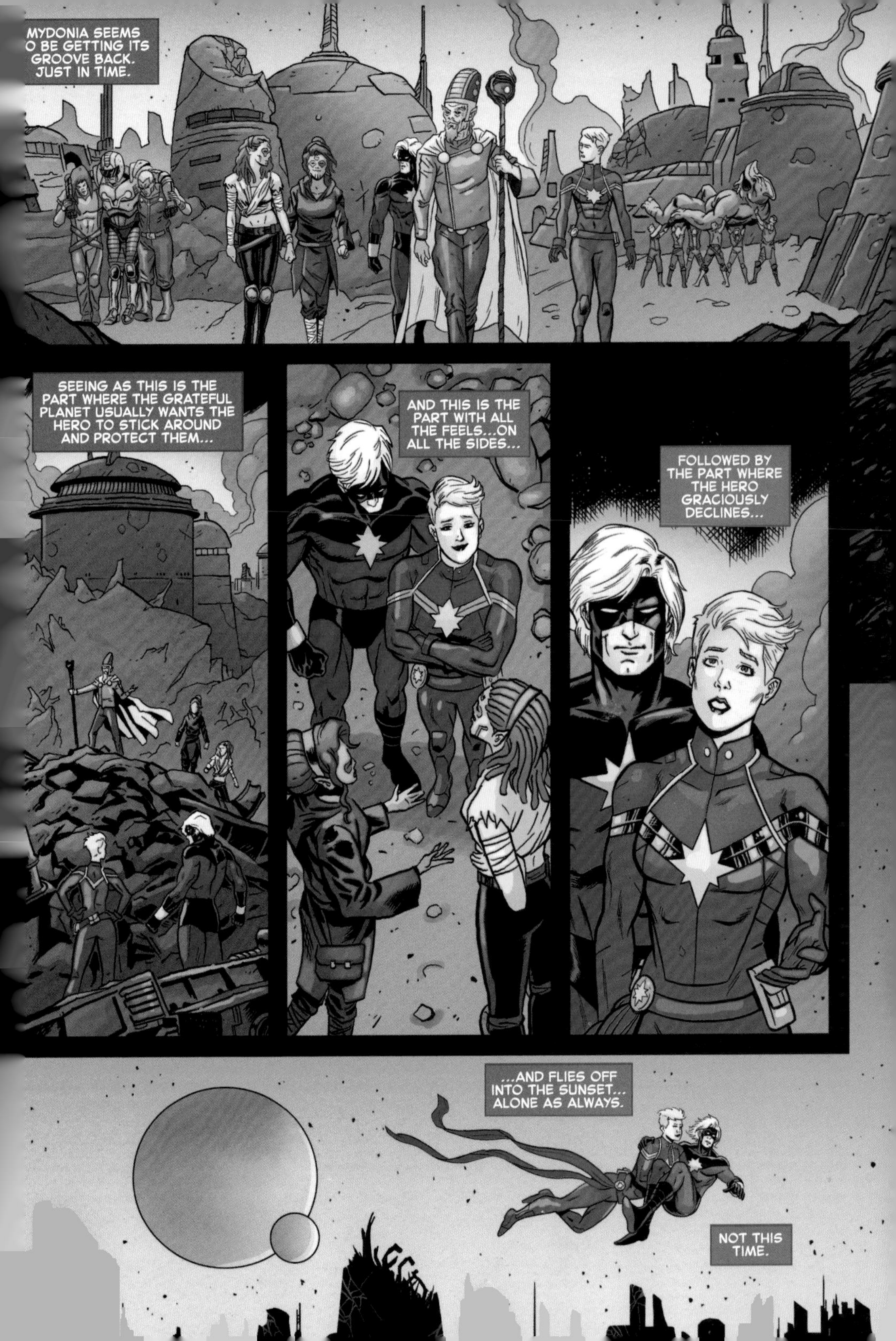
MYDONIA SEEMS TO BE GETTING ITS GROOVE BACK. JUST IN TIME.
SEEING AS THIS IS THE PART WHERE THE GRATEFUL PLANET USUALLY WANTS THE HERO TO STICK AROUND AND PROTECT THEM...
AND THIS IS THE PART WITH ALL THE FEELS...ON ALL THE SIDES...
FOLLOWED BY THE PART WHERE THE HERO GRACIOUSLY DECLINES...
...AND FLIES OFF INTO THE SUNSET... ALONE AS ALWAYS.
NOT THIS TIME.

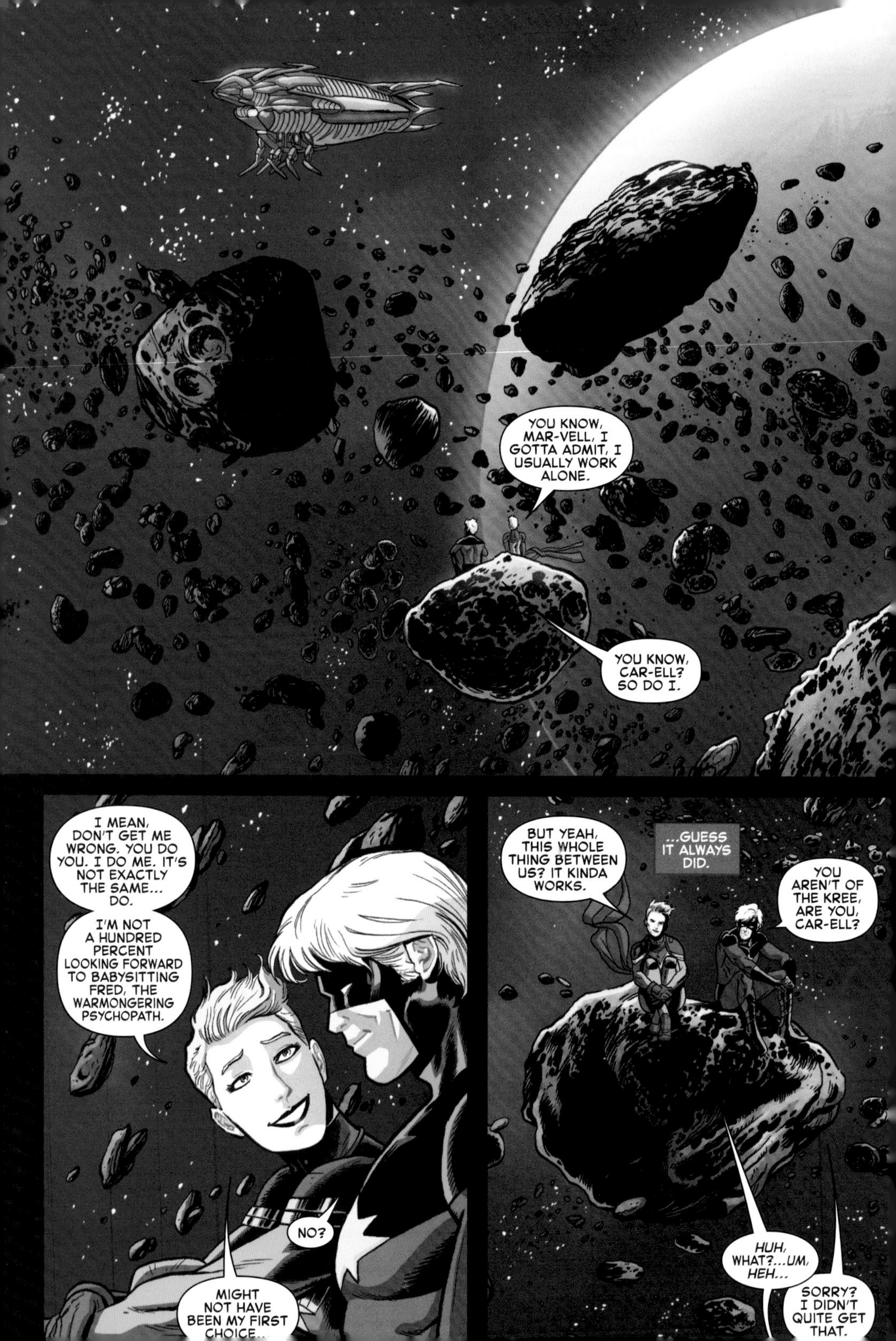
YOU KNOW, MAR-VELL, I GOTTA ADMIT, I USUALLY WORK ALONE.
YOU KNOW, CAR-ELL? SO DO I.
I MEAN, DON'T GET ME WRONG. YOU DO YOU. I DO ME. IT'S NOT EXACTLY THE SAME... DO.
I'M NOT A HUNDRED PERCENT LOOKING FORWARD TO BABYSITTING FRED, THE WARMONGERING PSYCHOPATH.
NO?
MIGHT NOT HAVE BEEN MY FIRST CHOICE...
BUT YEAH, THIS WHOLE THING BETWEEN US? IT KINDA WORKS.
...GUESS IT ALWAYS DID.
YOU AREN'T OF THE KREE, ARE YOU, CAR-ELL?
HUH, WHAT?...UM, HEH...
SORRY? I DIDN'T QUITE GET THAT.

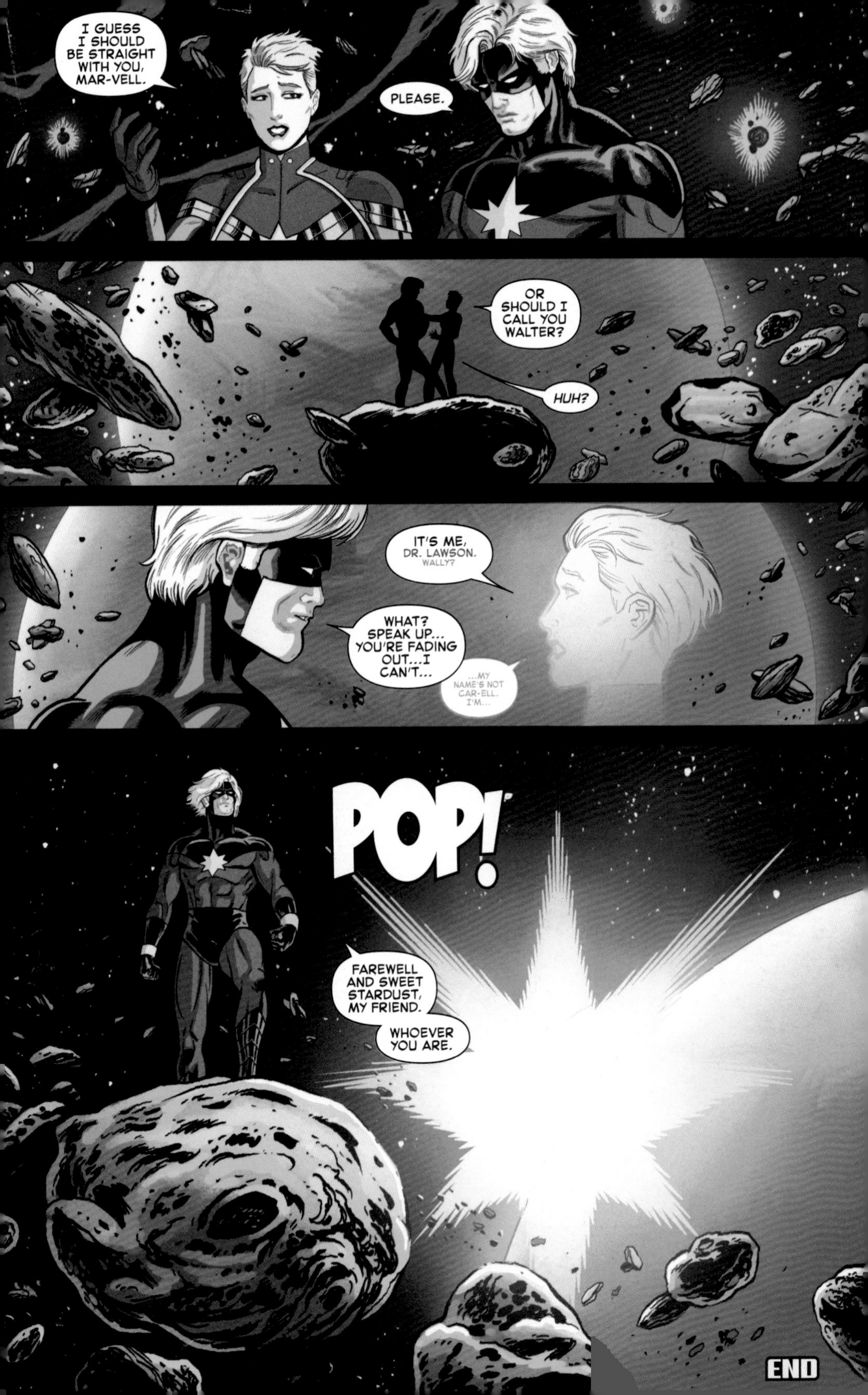
I GUESS I SHOULD BE STRAIGHT WITH YOU, MAR-VELL.
PLEASE.
OR SHOULD I CALL YOU WALTER?
HUH?
IT'S ME, DR. LAWSON. WALLY?
WHAT? SPEAK UP... YOU'RE FADING OUT...I CAN'T...
...MY NAME'S NOT CAR-ELL. I'M...
POP!
FAREWELL AND SWEET STARDUST, MY FRIEND.
WHOEVER YOU ARE.
END

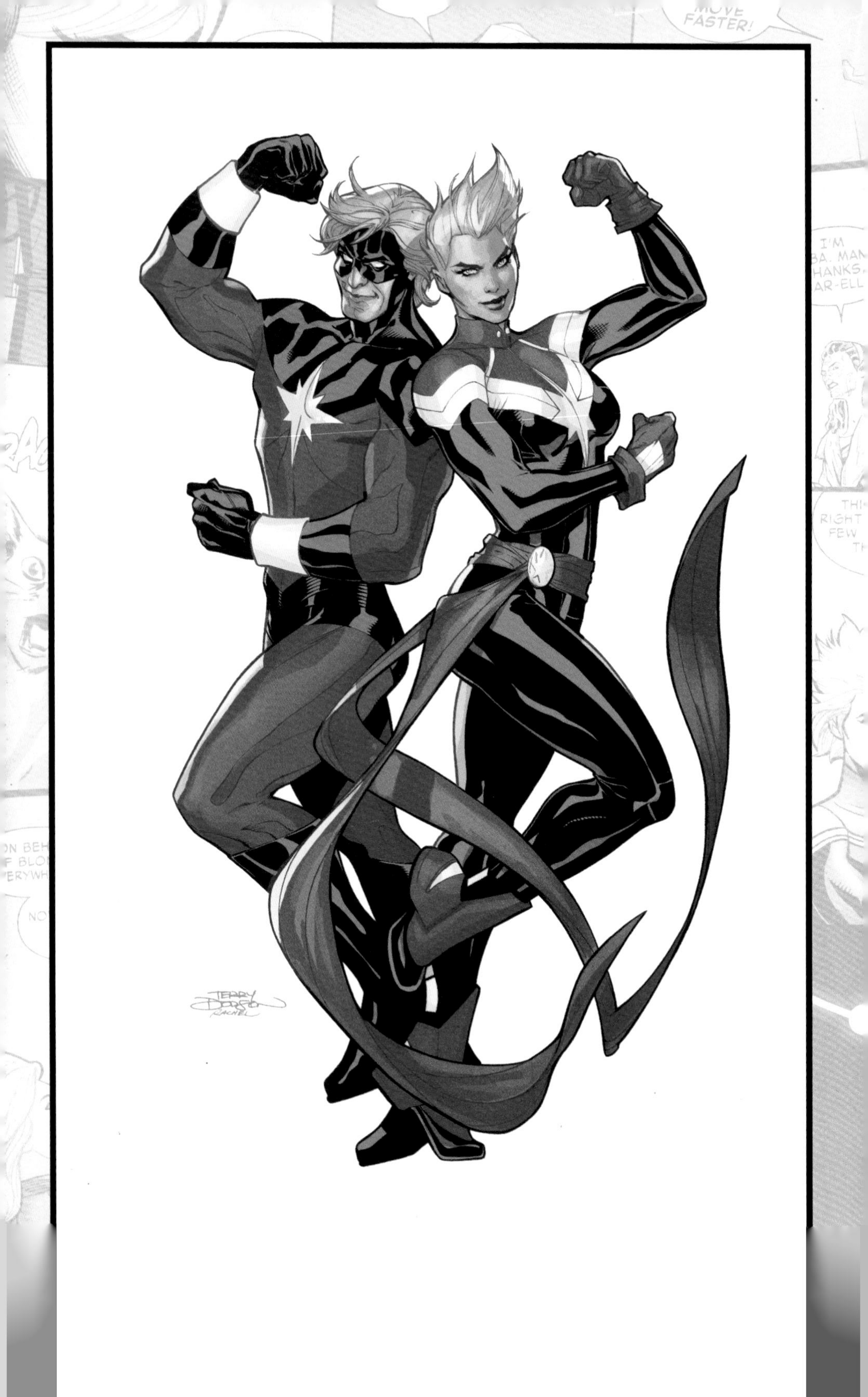
TERRY DODSON
RACHEL